best vacation ever

ALSO BY
JESSICA CUNSOLO

She's With Me
Stay With Me
Still With Me
Be With Me

best vacation ever

JESSICA CUNSOLO

wattpad books

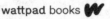

wattpad books

An imprint of Wattpad WEBTOON Book Group

Published in Canada by Wattpad WEBTOON Book Group, a division of Wattpad WEBTOON Studios, Inc.

36 Wellington Street E., Suite 200, Toronto, ON M5E 1C7 Canada

www.wattpad.com

First Wattpad Books edition: June 2023

ISBN 978-1-99025-996-8 (Trade Paper original)
ISBN 978-1-99025-997-5 (eBook edition)

Library and Archives Canada Cataloguing in Publication information is available upon request.

Printed and bound in Canada

1 3 5 7 9 10 8 6 4 2

Cover design by Mumtaz Mustafa

To my best friends

ONE

One Week to Cuba

Lori

That guy is staring at me, I'm sure of it. He follows my movements as I squat, the heavy bar resting on my shoulders. We're the only ones in this section of the gym, where the long barbells and squat racks are, and he's directly behind me. I can see him in the mirrors that cover the walls, not even trying to hide the fact that he's a creep.

Stop it! I want to yell, but my voice is caught in my throat.

His gaze roams freely over my legs and butt as I stand to set the bar back on the rack. His eyes meet mine in the mirror and hold them.

You're being a perv! is what I want to shout. My best friend Faye would, if she were here, but she hates the gym. Faye wouldn't stand rooted to the spot in horror, too timid to tell him off.

I take a sip of water, breaking eye contact first, and inwardly curse myself. Thankfully, he reracks his weights, and I exhale in relief. But as he passes me, his hand grazes my butt, so fast it's like it barely happened. I jerk my head to glare at him, but he smirks at me and continues walking to the free weights. As he lifts a dumbbell with the same hand that touched me, the large lion tattoo on his bicep flexes, taunting me.

I should say something to him. *I should say something, I should say something,* just say something, *Lori!*

Clutching my metal water bottle so tightly my knuckles turn white, I march over to him, my pulse beating louder and louder in my ears with every step I take.

"Hey!" I exclaim in a voice that doesn't sound like mine. "Quit staring at me!"

The guy faces me, his eyes dropping to check me out before a corner of his mouth lifts. "Not staring, just enjoying the view you're so generously providing."

My face burns and I sputter as I try to think of something to say. Faye would think of the comeback to end all comebacks, but I only stand there, my pulse racing with anger and embarrassment.

"If you're gonna stand there, at least make yourself useful and hand me that fifty-pounder over there." The guy gestures to the dumbbell rack, that smirk still in place. "Bend over while you do it though, you're so good at that."

My mouth opens and closes once before I spin on my heel and speed walk as far away from him as I can possibly get. His chuckle follows me like a taunt, burning in my brain even when I can't hear him anymore.

This is why I never say anything. I've just made it ten times worse than if I'd ignored him. What if he thinks it's okay to come up to me now that I spectacularly failed to stand up for myself? I wish I knew exactly what to say to put him in his place. I scrub the spot he touched with my own hand as if that can erase the memory.

Still fuming at myself and the stupid lion tattoo guy, I refill my bottle, staring at the faded, cracked Grant's Gym logo painted on the too-white wall above the water fountain. The light overhead is so bright, like a spotlight, and the air's stuffy and rank, permeated with the smell of sweat. The second my bottle is filled, I dart all the way to the front of the gym near the large windows, and as far from Pervy Guy as possible. A few regulars wave as they see me, but I keep my head down until I reach the leg machines. I know it's rude, but I'm afraid that if I talk, I might cry.

Taking a deep breath, I try to let go of what happened so I can focus on my workout. I adjust my headphones and change the playlist to a Spanish hits one before placing my water bottle on the floor. When I look up, I see Mr. Blue Eyes; his eyes are so bright they make the blue of my own seem dull in comparison. My pulse speeds up, and I force myself to stop gawking at him as he talks to some guys by the benches.

I've never had the nerve to start a conversation with him. Faye tells me I should, but I'm always lost for words when he's in my vicinity. I don't like staring at him because I don't want to act like the creepy guys that stare at me, but he's so . . . wow. He's not the model type of pretty like Faye's brother, Adam. Mr. Blue Eyes is a rugged, manly type of handsome. I like to imagine he uses his muscles for chopping wood, wrestling bears, leading his men into battle, or some other ridiculous romance novel stereotype.

I busy myself with adjusting the weights on the leg press, then peek over at the place I last saw him, in a totally nonstalkerish way. He's not there, and my heart sinks. That sucks. Maybe today would've been the day I got up the nerve to speak to him. I bend down to pick up my water bottle, and when I stand, I spot him. It's like he's moving in slow motion as he runs a hand through his thick black hair, pushing it off his forehead. He's like a walking shampoo commercial.

As I'm reminding myself not to gawk, his head shifts, and we're looking straight at each other, with eye contact and everything. There's a burning heat in my stomach when he smiles. Is he smiling at *me*? I peer behind me in case he's looking at someone else, but no one's there.

He's smiling at me.

I return the smile, and I hope he can't tell that I'm squealing inside. It must be all the encouragement he needs because he's in motion. His long legs striding. Right. Toward. Me.

Oh crap. Ohcrapohcrapohcrap. What should I do? What would Faye do? She's the master of flirting and can make guys fall to their knees begging for her to give them the time of day, and why isn't she here when I need her?

Because I spent all that time panicking about how I should act and what I should do with my arms, the result is that I stand there staring at him with my mouth open until he reaches me.

He stops right in front of me. Smiles. His lips move. He's saying something, but all I hear is Maluma singing in my ears. He looks down at the leg press and back at me, his lips moving again. He must be asking if I'm done with the machine.

I frantically rip out one earbud. "Yes," I say, flinching at my excessive volume.

His eyebrows draw together, as if confused why I'm still awkwardly standing in front of the machine he wants to use. This is the closest I've ever been to him, and I'm positively failing at my one chance to make him fall in love with me.

He opens his mouth to say something, probably to ask what my issue is, but before I can embarrass myself any further, I turn around while popping my earbud back in, and speed walk the hell away from him.

"Maybe today would've been the day I got up the nerve to speak to him," I mimic myself in my head and roll my eyes at my sheer stupidity. Yeah, because talking to him went real well, *and* I gave him my leg press machine before I even used it.

Ugh. What is *up* with me? I should quit while I'm ahead and leave now, but I've had such a shitty workout today I've totally wasted the gas it took to get here, and that's not exactly cheap, at least not cheap enough that the money I get from lifeguarding can comfortably cover it all. Maybe just one more exercise to make the drive here worth it, then I'll head out. Back extensions always make me feel strong, and that's exactly what I need after failing to stand up for myself with one guy or flirt with the other.

The equipment is on a forty-five-degree angle, so I lean on it and adjust the pads on my hips. Then I bend down over it so my head is close to the floor and my bottom is in the air and bring myself up with a straight back. Even though I'm a little sore, I decide to hold extra weights to really ramp up the intensity.

On rep six, I lift back up to peek at Mr. Blue Eyes. As if he feels my gaze, he looks in my direction. I dip back down to do another rep, and when I pull myself back up, I realize that he's not looking *at* me, he's looking at something behind me. When I go back down, I check to see what he's looking at, and even upside-down, I recognize Pervy Gym Guy with the lion tattoo behind me. Then there's a flash.

Blood rushing in my ears, I straighten and stumble off the machine. The weights slip out of my hands and land on the padded floor with a muffled thud. Pervy Gym Guy is looking at his phone, which he just used to take a picture of my butt.

My heart sinks and my vision blurs. I don't know what to do; I feel so disgusted and violated. I want to cry or slap that pervert or run away and hide. I want to yell at him until his head explodes. Destroy his phone with a barbell. Instead, I stand here helplessly, staring daggers at him, without doing any of those things, without grabbing his phone and bashing him with it.

Before I can blink, Mr. Blue Eyes is in Pervy Gym Guy's face, and Mr. Blue Eyes's arms are gesturing wildly.

I rip my headphones out so I can hear what he's saying.

"—the fuck raised you? I've never seen something so disrespectful. Who the fuck do you think you are to treat a human being like she's only here for your disgusting lonely jerk-off session later tonight?" Rage radiates off Mr. Blue Eyes, I can feel it from all the way over here.

"Whoa, chill out, dude. She's hot—"

"Chill out?!" Mr. Blue Eyes is bigger than Pervy Gym Guy, and gets even closer to him, making Pervy Gym Guy shrink into himself.

I glance around the gym, and *everyone* is looking at us. Looking at *me*.

My breathing turns shallow, and my head spins. I *hate* being the center of attention. I hate causing a scene. I hate everyone staring at me.

I don't know what happens next, because I scramble out of there and into the changing room before more people come over to judge me, to get a look at the girl too weak to speak up for herself.

Why violate someone like that while they're in the gym? This is the second time in one day I've had an issue with that guy. I should've said something harsher the first time instead of floundering the moment he talked back and embarrassed me. I should report him to management. I should tell Faye so she can rip him a new one. I should *do something*.

Throwing all my things into my bag without bothering to zip it up, I grab my car keys, faltering as I exit the changing room. People are looking at me. A group of girls in the corner are whispering and gawking. A bunch of guys close to them are doing the same, and one points at me. My breath halts. I'll tell management another time. I need to *leave*. I need to get out of here right *now*.

Racing through the gym with my head down, I'm almost at the door when a voice behind me calls out, "Hey, wait up!"

Even though everything seems hazy, I spot Mr. Blue Eyes jogging toward me in the reflection of the glass door. I should've known it was him calling out to me. Even his voice is perfect. Deep and silky.

If I was too embarrassed to talk to him before, no way do I want to face him now, after he had to start a fight with a stranger because I froze, too worried about other people staring to demand Pervy Gym Guy be brought to justice.

The cool evening air hits me as I exit the gym, the setting sun turning the sky shades of pink and purple. I inhale the summer freshness, my heartbeat already steadier. It must be around eight, and the calmness of the night helps me clear my head. I don't think anyone followed me, so I relax my pace, strolling along the side of the redbrick exterior.

"Hey! Hold on a second!"

A quick glance behind me reveals Mr. Blue Eyes jogging my way. He doesn't have any of his belongings with him; it looks like he ran out when I did.

My stomach drops. I increase my pace, lengthening the distance between us, and right before I cross the street, the end of my mortification only seconds away, I stumble and drop my bag and keys. I sense him gaining on me, and I need to get to my car before that happens, so I hastily swoop down to pick up my stuff, not looking back but knowing he's close.

Please let me stop embarrassing myself in front of him!

I straighten and step off the curb to cross the street in a rush.

A few things happen simultaneously. That deep voice yells something much louder and more urgent than before. A horn blares, and I whip my head around. Headlights blind me. A force knocks into me, taking my breath away as I'm tackled to the ground. The car I stepped in front of continues harmlessly along, the driver not even stopping to see if it hit me or not.

I take a shaky breath. I almost got hit by a car! I'm such a coward that in my haste to run away from Mr. Blue Eyes, I walked right into the path of an oncoming car!

"Are you okay? Man, you gave me a scare," comes his voice from under my shaking body.

Wait. Under me?

I finally tune in to my surroundings. I'm lying on top of Mr. Blue Eyes on the grass, my face mere inches away from his. His arms are iron bands wrapped around my waist after pulling me out of danger, and our legs are tangled together. I'm pressed so close to him that despite everything, I notice that although his eyes are blue, there's a tiny ring of hazel around his pupils.

"You *are* okay, right?" he presses again.

Oh my goodness! I'm still lying on top of him staring at him like a total creeper.

I scramble off and sit up. My voice is thick, and I physically can't bring myself to make direct eye contact with him. "Yeah, I'm fine." I clear my throat as I assess my limbs. "Are you?"

He sits up beside me and dusts off his hands. "Yeah, but geez. Way to kill a guy's ego. You'd rather jump in front of a moving car than talk to me."

That makes me look right at him. He's still gorgeous, even with the ruffled hair. "That's—that's not what happened!"

He's smiling at me, and his teeth are so white and straight I'm 90 percent sure his dentist actively practices witchcraft.

"Of course it isn't." That smile never falters. "Not to lecture you or anything, but you should probably look both ways before crossing the street."

"Yes, thank you for refreshing me on first-grade skills. I promise I don't make jumping in front of cars a habit." I pick up the things that have fallen out of my bag, and he helps. I die a little inside when he gathers a bunch of tampons and deposits them into my gym bag.

"Guess I'll have to take your word for it," he jokes, helping me up and holding my keys out.

I take them, and when our fingers brush, electricity zips all the way up my arm. "Yeah, well . . . thanks for saving my life, I guess. And for what happened in there with Pervy Gym Guy."

He lifts an eyebrow at the nickname, and I don't realize I said it out loud until it's too late.

"He deleted the pictures, and I don't think he'll be coming to Grant's anymore," he says.

Pictures? As in plural?

Something on my face must alert him because he quickly adds, "Some people are just disgusting."

I give him a small smile, genuinely grateful for his interference *twice* today, but still embarrassed, especially about jumping in front of a car. My face is so hot I'm sure it's beet red.

"Yeah, thanks for that." I back away toward my car. I need to escape so I can die of embarrassment alone, the way you're supposed to. "And thanks again for the whole car thing. I guess I'll see you around."

Before he can say another word, I whirl around and run all the way to my Honda.

There is no way in hell I can ever show my face around here again.

—

While the incident from the gym weighs heavily on my mind, I don't have time to dwell on it, because as soon as I get home, I'm summoned to dinner. While everything today *sucked*, I have bigger problems now because tonight, for the first time in seventeen years, I'm going to disobey my parents. I've had nightmares about this exact moment but here I am, sitting at the mahogany dinner table that's been in our family for generations, about to tell them I'm ending three generations of Robertson tradition. Mom watches me fidget as I tug at the collar of my shirt. The grandfather clock behind her ticks in time with each beat of my heart.

"Something wrong with your dragon roll, Lori?" she asks, placing more on one of the heirloom china plates handed down from her great-grandmother. In the center of each, there's a hand-painted bluebird in midflight. I never thought I'd be so envious of a plate.

"Nope, it's great," I say, stuffing a piece into my mouth to prove my point. It tastes like ash, and I take a sip of water to wash it down. We've had sushi three times this week because the Japanese restaurant is open late enough to cater to Mom's schedule, but that's not the issue.

"Have you gotten your summer work schedule yet?" Dad asks me, refilling my crystal glass.

"Yes. They sent it two weeks ago when school ended."

Since I turned fifteen, I've been a part-time lifeguard at the community center and occasionally teach swimming to local kids. It's not the most exciting job, but better than being forced to go to summer science camp.

"Email it to me," Dad says. "We can plan a day around it to tour the campus again. Plus, I've been eyeing some volunteer opportunities at the hospital I think you'd be great for. Nothing major, mostly in the office, but it's important for you to get some experience in a hospital setting."

This is it. The opening I've been waiting for. A bead of sweat drips down my forehead, and I wipe it away. "Actually . . . about that . . . I . . ." *Deep breaths, Lori.* "I don't think that's a good idea."

Creepily in sync, my parents' heads swing over to look at me, and I shrink into my seat.

My parents, Paul and Mary Robertson, are both heart surgeons at the top of their field, and all my life I've heard about how I'm going to follow in their footsteps and be an amazing surgeon like them. Like their parents. Like their parents' parents. We've watched educational television after dinner, had conversations about tricuspid valves and atrial fibrillations, and they've even made me practice suturing supermarket chicken. I've been told that I was going to be a surgeon since before I even knew what a surgeon *was*. So, for them, my life is going exactly as they planned, especially once they saw my early acceptance letter to Life Sciences, one of the hardest programs to get into at the University of Toronto. They even googled "surgeon family photoshoots" to get inspiration for all the cute photo Christmas cards we'd send out each year in matching scrubs, with stethoscopes dangling from our necks. The thought terrifies me.

"What were you thinking?" Mom asks, setting her chopsticks down to fix me with a stare. Her gaze is intimidating. Her eyes are the exact same shade of blue as mine, but they're surrounded with lines from years of stress.

I've rehearsed this speech many times in my head. "It's not a big deal, but before I become a doctor, I think I should have more real-world experience." I sip my water, peering at them over the edge of my glass. The fact that they're not smashing their spicy salmon rolls to bits or grounding me for eternity must mean I'm doing a good job, so I push ahead, a tiny bit more confident. "I want to defer my admission to next year, so I can take this year off to backpack through Europe."

Okay, maybe I wussed out on the whole *I don't think I want to be a surgeon* announcement, but baby steps.

The air thickens as their silence persists. All I hear is the throbbing of my pulse in my skull and the incessant ticking of the grandfather clock. Right before I crack from the overwhelming quiet, Mom and Dad glance at each other, then erupt into laughter.

"Yeah. Good one, Lori," Mom says, then sips her wine.

My voice is shaky when I say, "I'm not joking. That's what I want to do."

Mom sets her glass down, then brushes aside some nonexistent crumbs on the white tablecloth. Dad's face is unreadable. "I wouldn't be alone, obviously," I add, trying to convince them before they shut it down outright. "I've done a lot of research. There are lots of gap year programs online. Some of them even give college credit. Studies show that students who defer for a year end up being more successful at university. I've printed out some sample itineraries for you to look at. Here's the best part, I have more than enough money saved up to pay for it myself, *and* I'll earn more lifeguarding this summer."

Mom sighs as if praying for the patience to deal with me, and my breath catches in my throat. "That all sounds magical and wonderful, but you know most people who take a year off don't return to school," she says.

"That's not true—"

Dad tosses his linen napkin over his plate. "Look, Lor, getting an education is more important right now than traveling. You'll have plenty of time for that once you finish med school." He points to the picture of his mother, Lorraine Robertson, sitting on the fireplace mantel. It's in a heavy golden frame, and he touches it every time he passes by. "Your grandmother would be so proud of you. You know how hard she worked to become one of the first female surgeons in Canada, and now you're carrying on her legacy."

My stomach twists. I've always felt all this pressure to be like her. I've been hearing about how hard she worked, and how accomplished, smart, and passionate she was since I was old enough to hold her heavy picture frame in my little toddler hands. She died before I was born, but she's been a constant part of my life, always around, always haunting me, her eyes following me as I walk by, accusing me. *Why don't you want to carry on my legacy? Why are you such a disappointment?* I try to avoid this room when I can, avoid a picture that should hold no power over me but somehow controls my fate. But since we eat all our meals here, that's virtually impossible unless I snag the seat facing away from the fireplace.

"Don't you think I deserve a little break before I hop into ten or more years of schooling?" I plead, confidence draining from my voice. It's a losing battle, and the room is closing in on me.

"You have been working hard," Mom says, "but you need to do well on the MCAT or you won't be accepted into medical school after your undergrad, and all of that hard work will have been for nothing. This is not the time to slack off, Lori, not even for a single summer. This is a time for working, volunteering, and studying."

I swallow hard and weave my hands together under the table to stop them from shaking. The rest of my life looms in front of me, so I make one last-ditch attempt. "But what if I don't want to go to med school?" I blurt, shocked as the words leave my mouth before I can stop them.

"Of course you're going to medical school! It's what you're

good at. It's what the Robertsons are good at," Dad declares, his words settling on my chest like a weight, meaning my second attempt to stand up for myself today has gone just as terribly as the first one at the gym.

"Now, pass the avocado rolls," Mom says, ending the conversation about my future just like that.

TWO

Six Days to Cuba

Faye

I FaceTime Lori twice before she picks up.

"Finally!" I exclaim, even though her screen is dark and I can't see her. "I have *news* and it's *huge*! Can you come over?"

"Faye?" she groans. There's rustling on the other side of the phone, and then a light turns on. She's in bed. "It's late, I have work tomorrow. What's going on?"

"It's only like nine p.m., grandma. You need to come here. I have news!" Lori and I do everything together. We've been best friends since ninth grade, but sometimes her responsible nature gets in the way of my fun.

"Last time you said you had 'news,' it was that Jenna McAndrews got highlights that you thought 'washed her out.'"

"They totally did." That was when Jenna and Adam were dating, so Lori got to see them firsthand when she walked past the pair of them in my kitchen.

Lori rolls onto her side, her eyes half-open. "Well, I can't come, so tell me the news."

I can barely hold in my excitement. My smile takes up almost my whole portion of the screen. "Ray's appendix burst today, and they rushed him to the hospital! Isn't that great?"

Now Lori sits up in bed and rubs her eyes. Even half asleep, she's gorgeous. Her brown hair doesn't even stick up in every direction like mine does in the mornings.

"That sounds awful," she says. "Why are you acting like we've won the lottery?"

I was going to ease her into it, but I just can't hold it back anymore. "Adam is letting us come to Cuba with him next week!" I blurt.

She's silent for a moment. "Are you saying we're invited to Cuba with your hot older brother and his friends? What does that have to do with Ray's appendix?"

I huff. I wish we could just speed up this whole explanation thing and get right to the jumping-up-and-down-with-excitement part, but Lori is practical.

"Okay, first, *ew*. Adam is not hot. His friends are, but he's an ogre."

In both the literal and figurative terms of the word. He's mean, on top of being the uglier of the two of us, at least in my opinion.

He's only fourteen months older than me, so he's only a grade ahead. But if you didn't know we're related, you'd never realize it since he barely blinks at me in the halls. Even so, all through high school, girls have come up to me to say that Adam is hot and ask me to put in a good word, which is annoying and useless since Adam pretends I don't exist.

Adam and his friends just finished their first year of university and are celebrating by going away on an all-inclusive tropical vacation. I've been wanting to go on vacation forever, but my parents wouldn't let me go without them unless Adam comes too, and he would rather die than voluntarily go to Cuba with me. I'd pleaded with him to let me and Lori come, but he refused, adamant that it was a guys-only, no-little-sisters-allowed trip. Nothing's swayed him, and I haven't had high hopes because Adam's never done anything nice for me. Desperate, I was about to offer to do all his chores for the year, but thankfully I didn't go that far because it all worked out.

I prop my phone up against my pillows so she can still see me while I sort through the piles of clothes I've dumped onto my bed. The trip is in exactly six days, and I need to figure out what to wear.

To Lori, I say, "Since Ray can't go to Cuba, his brother Freddy felt guilty going and canceled. That completely screws over Adam and his friends since they were getting a group rate. It's so last-minute that no one else can come, and they already had to ask Dylan's cousin to come to cover Eli's cancelation. So now there are two free spots! Adam can either sit around with his dick in his hand or let us take their place!"

I shriek and do a little dance on the bed, and she holds the phone farther away to escape my excited sounds.

I find my laptop under the mess of clothes and wake it from sleep mode. "I'm emailing you the information now. I know how your parents are so they can totally call mine, and they'll answer all their questions. We have to buy the tickets quickly though, but *we're going to Cuba*!"

I'm so preoccupied with forwarding her all the information that I don't realize she's quiet until she clears her throat.

"Um, Faye? I don't think I can come."

"What?" I dive for my phone and hold it as close to my face as possible to see her better. "Why can't you come?"

Lori chews on her bottom lip. I know that look, and I clench the phone tighter in my hand.

"My parents just finished telling me how this summer is for studying, working, and volunteering only."

"So?" I exclaim. Lori's parents have such a tight hold on her, it makes me appreciate my mom and dad's relaxed take on parenting even more. Lori's lucky I'm around to force her to get out occasionally, or she'd be locked in a tower, wilting away studying until she's thirty. "It's a *week*, not the whole summer!"

Lori frowns and looks away from the camera. "I don't know, Faye. I really want to come . . . I'll try to talk to them."

This can't be happening. The stars have aligned to allow us to go on this trip, and I cannot allow Lori's superstrict parents to ruin it!

"I'll come over and convince them. I'll get my dad to come as well. That worked last time when we went to Niagara for the weekend. You *have* to come, Lori. At least look at the emails I sent you."

She sets her phone on her bed and gets up, and I hear her shuffle around her room. Once she's back, she props her phone on what I assume is her computer screen so I can still see her. "Before I bring it up to my parents, are you sure Adam's letting us come? Or did he just say 'maybe' and you interpreted it as 'pack your bags'?"

"Lori. We're *G-O-I-N-G*." I spell the word out for her. "He had a bunch of conditions, but I have the confirmed itinerary in my hands as we speak." I flap the stapled pages in front of the camera before pressing it to my nose and audibly inhaling. I sigh in contentment. "Smells like suntan oil and the ocean."

She laughs, her mood lightening. "You're ridiculous. What were the conditions?"

"Oh, I wasn't really paying attention. I'm sure it was the usual 'don't embarrass me, I don't want to see you the whole trip' blah blah blah." I fall back to lie on my bed. "Kellan's coming."

It's an effort to not start daydreaming about Kellan Reyes.

"Obviously Kellan's going." She hesitates. "Does he know you're going?"

Kellan is Adam's best friend, who I'm always around since Adam's friends are always over. Though I've known Dylan the longest, Kellan is my favorite. Kellan and I even hang out without Adam all the time, and it's in a totally non-datey way even when it's just the two of us. But when Adam has his friends over and if he's in a good mood—which is rare—he lets me hang out with them. I'm naturally flirty and flirt with everyone, and so does Kellan, so Adam thinks he has nothing to worry about.

Key word: *thinks.*

Because a few weeks ago, I slept with Kellan.

Twice.

Adam doesn't know, and never will, since Kellan and I swore to never tell anyone. Well, anyone except Lori obviously. She's my best friend, so when I say, *I won't tell anyone*, what I really mean is *Lori and I won't tell anyone.*

I sigh and shake my head to rid myself of images of Kellan. "I don't know. He hasn't messaged me about it. Do you think it'll be awkward?"

Lori's full lips stretch into a thin smile, and I can tell she's trying not to laugh. "Faye. It's you. It's almost impossible to embarrass you; Do you even possess the gene for that emotion?"

"You're right. I'm going to have fun either way. Get me a hot vacation fling," I say.

"Geez, Faye, we're sharing a room, right? I don't want to hear any of your sex noises!"

"That means you're coming! *Yes!*"

"I'll talk to my parents," she says, lifting her phone properly up to her face as I hear her laptop click shut.

"Good," I say. "And don't worry about the sex noises. I'll put the 'do not disturb' sign on the door." I chuckle, leaving her to decide if I'm joking or not.

"Great. Can't wait to sit on the floor in the hallway, waiting for your booty call to leave."

"You're such a team player."

Lori jumps and lowers the phone, leaving me with a perfect view of her ceiling.

"Lori, what are you doing up? I thought you said you had a headache and were going to sleep?" Her mom asks from what I'm assuming is the doorway to her room.

"I am," she replies before holding the phone up to her face. She's chewing her lip again. "I'll talk to you tomorrow, Faye."

"Okay, bye!" I say, keeping it simple in case her mom is still standing there.

As soon as I hang up, I immediately text her: *Make sure you're convincing! We need to go!*

I'm going to Cuba! With Kellan. He's going to be shirtless practically all week. We're going to be around each other on the beach, in the pool, at the club . . . All. Week.

I squeal into my pillow.

—

I don't hear any news from Lori that night or the whole next day, but the following day, when I leave my room with wet hair after my shower, a very distinct voice flows up to me. Cracking a smile, I comb my hair with my fingers and bound down the stairs. I almost miss a step when I hear the word *Jenna*.

My brother and his friend Dylan are on the couch, watching some game on television.

"What was that about Jenna?" I ask at the bottom of the

stairs. Neither boy moves his eyes from the television or bothers to acknowledge me.

My nostrils flare and I move to block their view. They shout protests right away.

"You're not getting back with Jenna, right, Adam?" I stare him down as Dylan tries to peer around me.

"What, Faye? Move," Adam says.

I don't move. "Adam!"

"Go to hell," he retorts.

"If you get back together with Jenna, I'm already there."

He exhales heavily and glares at me. "We're not getting back together. Happy?"

I grin at him, plopping down on the couch and squeezing in between him and Dylan. "Extremely."

Adam grunts in annoyance but makes room for me anyway. Dylan drops his tattoo-covered arm over my shoulders and licks my ear.

"Ew!" I shriek, pushing him off me and swiping away the saliva. He just laughs and turns back to the TV.

Besides Kellan, Dylan is Adam's other best friend, and one of my favorites. I've always been close to Dylan, probably because I've known him since I could walk, and sometimes I feel like he treats me more like a little sister than my actual brother does. Adam even once suspected me of wanting to date Dylan because of how close we are, and the mental image of me with a dude that's like my brother almost made me puke. He's never brought it up since, especially since I often announce that Dylan is my favorite "brother," even if we like to flirt because of our personalities.

"So, if you're not getting back together, why were you talking about her?" I ask Adam, not caring that he's actively trying to ignore me.

Adam had been dating Jenna for about two years, until two weeks ago, when she dumped him after we graduated. Like, literally. We had just thrown our caps in the air when my brother went to congratulate her, before he even congratulated me, and she was all, *Oh yeah. We're over.* Not that I care. She tried to make my life a living hell the whole time they were together.

Adam was cagey about the reason and never told me, not that he tells me anything normally, but according to Dylan, the only person Adam confided in, it's because she didn't want to do long-distance. She must be using the term very loosely because Adam already goes to the University of Toronto, and she's going to Western U in September, and they're only two hours apart. Unless that was a total bullshit reason that Dylan gave me to stop me from hounding him.

For some reason, my brother was like the golden child at school—everyone loved him, which totally baffles me because he didn't even do anything. He wasn't on any teams or clubs or councils; he just kind of . . . existed. Apparently when he's not too busy being a complete dick, he actually has a sense of humor. Personally, I think he's just a giant, grumpy baby.

Jenna used to *love* that her boyfriend was Adam Murray. I don't know much about their relationship, since Jenna is basically my mortal enemy, but it seemed like Jenna was dating Adam's name, not Adam. She would strut around school wearing his sweaters and be all, *Oh, this old thing? It's just my* boyfriend's. *You know. My boyfriend,* Adam Murray? *Yeah, it's his. And I'm wearing it, because he's my boyfriend.*

Adam doesn't reply, so Dylan volunteers the answer. "She's going to drop off his stuff tonight."

My eyebrows rise to my hairline. "Wow, you actually got her to bring it back. How'd you manage that?"

Adam shrugs, already bored with the entire conversation. "Told her she wasn't getting her stuff until I got mine."

"Wow, ruthless." I yawn.

"Oh, shut up, Faye. I can still be civil."

"She's a bitch and you know it. You know it was her life's mission to make me and Lori miserable, right? I'm your sister! Shouldn't you be all protective and all *no one messes with my little sister but me*?"

"You bothered her just as much as she bothered you." Adam rolls his eyes and checks his phone. "Plus, you and I both know you're completely capable of taking care of yourself. You yell at me any time I say something."

I don't know what he's talking about because he never says anything. "Well, duh, I can take care of myself. But it would be nice if my own blood wasn't sleeping with the enemy!"

"If you were ever in any real trouble, I would've stepped in, even if you'd get mad at me for it."

"Bullshit!"

He would not have. He never has. His doing nothing basically encouraged her to keep being a bitch to me and Lori.

"She's never—"

"Prom," I state, silencing him immediately, because he knows I'm right.

It was no *Carrie* moment with pig's blood or anything, but she still ruined Lori's prom, and Adam was just there all *None of my business.* A girl from school invited a bunch of the girls in our grade over to her house for a pre-prom party, with pictures and appetizers and everything. Jenna was there, and she *literally* pushed Lori into the pool. My running theory is that Jenna saw how gorgeous Lori was and got jealous. She denied it to Adam and said it was an accident, and he believed her.

"It was an accident, they bumped into each other," Adam clarifies. "And it worked out. Lori looked great at prom."

She did, but that was because there were eighteen girls committed to fixing her hair and makeup, and someone even called their mom to deliver a backup dress for Lori to wear.

I scoff. "Well, duh. Lori could wear a paper sack and still be ten times prettier than Jenna."

Adam gets up, clearly sick of getting the third degree. "Jenna will be here in five. Make yourself scarce, Faye."

I jump up beside him. "What? I haven't gotten to say anything to her since the pool incident!" And I have some *very* colorful words to share with her. The only time I saw Jenna after that was at the actual prom, where I couldn't kick her ass because of all the teachers, and then at graduation where, again, there were way too many witnesses.

"Faye, you're—" Adam starts.

"Let's go to Tim's," Dylan interrupts, rising from where he was lounging on the couch and sliding between me and Adam. "I want an Iced Capp. Keep me company, Faye?"

I know exactly what he's doing, and my narrowed eyes tell him that, but he just smiles at me in the lazy way that's all Dylan.

I debate for a moment before relenting. "Fine. But you're buying. And I want a donut."

"Deal," Dylan says, and I don't miss the appreciative nod Adam sends his way when he thinks I'm not looking. Jerk.

I follow Dylan to his car and buckle in as he reverses out the driveway and heads down my quiet street. Before he can argue, I grab his aux cord and plug in my phone to play my music as punishment for siding with Adam.

He groans when a boy band fills the speakers of his car but doesn't protest since he knows I'm not letting him get his cord back.

I look over at Dylan. He's conventionally good-looking. He's half–white Canadian, half-Jamaican, with black hair shaved in a fade and eyes just as dark, set against the light brown of his skin. His entire left arm is covered in black-and-white tattoos with the occasional pop of color, which, combined with his height, definitely gives him that badass vibe, even though he's a teddy bear. But I've never been attracted to Dylan. Every time I look at him, I remember the scrawny little kid that pushed my face into my birthday cake when I turned eight, and nine, and ten, *and* eleven. It took me longer than I'm proud to admit to realize he shouldn't be allowed anywhere near me when I blow out my candles.

We pass Jenna's BMW as we turn out of my subdivision, and I scowl.

"He *really* isn't getting back together with her, right?" I ask Dylan.

"Not that I know of," he says without taking his eyes off the road.

"Why did he date her?" I grumble, remembering all the shit she pulled on me over the years. "He knew she hated me. He knew I'd come home from school pissed off about how she started rumors about me or made Lori cry, and he just opened the door to our house and invited her into my safe space. Why would he do that, Dyl?"

"You handled her all right, all things considered," he says, signaling and pulling into the Tim Hortons parking lot. "And she's not terrible. You guys just always butt heads."

"You're supposed to be on my side! Remember when she spread that rumor that I was blowing the PE teacher and almost got him fired and me expelled?"

No one believed me when I said I wasn't, and even Adam and Dylan asked me if it was true. Kellan's the only one who undoubtedly believed me, who sat with me in the principal's office even though he wasn't supposed to be there, telling me stupid jokes to keep me from shaking.

Dylan's lips spread into a thin line. "I'll give you that one. But Adam didn't know it was her who started the rumors, *if* it even was her who started them."

I didn't talk to Adam for like three weeks after he refused to break up with or even reprimand my mortal enemy.

"Why does he hate me?" I ask quietly, more to myself than to Dylan.

Dylan opens his mouth, closes it, then replies, "He doesn't hate you, Faye." But his hesitation says it all.

I slump into my seat as he inches the car forward in the drive-thru line. "Why can't he like me? I'm his sister, but it's like he can't even tolerate being in the same room with me."

He hates hanging out with me, hates having to do anything with me at all. Even Lori's shocked anytime he shows his face when we hang out at my house.

"Is he . . . is he still mad about the Zach O'Sullivan incident?"

Dylan gives an uncomfortable laugh. "I think *incident* isn't a strong enough word for what happened, Faye."

"What happened wasn't my fault," I mumble for what seems to be the millionth time in the last year.

"I know. It takes two to make a relationship start and end. But he did *explicitly ask you* not to get involved with his friend."

"Adam has *lots* of friends! I can't be expected to not date all of them!"

Dylan snorts. "He just doesn't want you to date his *best* friends, in case it ends up like Zach . . . which it did."

I cross my arms and grumble, "Well, Zach was a self-absorbed asshole."

"Maybe," Dylan concedes, "but he was a self-absorbed asshole who was one of Adam's best friends, who now won't even look at him, never mind talk to him."

Zach and I dated for a whole three months before we started

fighting more than kissing, and it was over before I knew it. After that, Zach ran the opposite direction from Adam whenever he saw him and stopped inviting him to hang out. He didn't even ask him to come to his nineteenth birthday but invited everyone else.

"Zach still talks to you, Alessio, and Kellan."

Dylan shoots me a look as the car inches forward. "He also didn't fuck our sisters."

I huff in reluctant agreement. "Fine, I'll give you that. But I'm not dating any of his friends right now—" barring secretly sleeping with Kellan twice "—so why does he still hate me?"

"Have you talked to him about it?"

"No. You think Adam and I can have a serious heart-to-heart? You're delusional."

All I've ever wanted was for us to be closer, or at least to be *friends*. Hell, I'd even take him simply stomaching my presence for longer than an hour.

"Well, we'll be in Cuba for an entire week. There's nowhere for him to run."

He's right. We're going to be at a resort in five days. Sure, it's a big resort, but not big enough for him to ignore my existence. Maybe we can connect there. Maybe we can take a step forward in our relationship. It would be better than nothing.

Dylan pulls up to the speaker and lowers his window.

"I'll have an Iced Capp and a jelly-filled donut," I tell him, looking out my window, wondering what Adam and Jenna are talking about.

They broke up. I graduated high school. Maybe Adam and I can have a fresh beginning, and Cuba can kick-start it for us.

THREE

One Day to Cuba

Lori

I can't believe I'm walking through the airport right now, my carry-on backpack over my shoulder, boarding pass safely tucked away in the front pocket. I thought my mom would make a big deal over my leaving for a week instead of focusing on my MCAT prep, but I've been mopey since my parents shot down my gap year idea. I think they believe that this trip will satisfy my urge to travel the world and find myself, so they let me go to Cuba, on the condition that I focus on the MCAT earnestly when I get back. It physically pained me to agree to that, but I knew I'd have to study for the MCAT anyway, so I might as well get a trip to Cuba with my best friend out of it.

Faye was ecstatic when I told her. Today she even showed up at my house hours earlier than she needed to with all her luggage until it was time to go to the airport. She hasn't stopped talking since, even while we were checking in and dropping off our bags.

"I am so excited!" Faye exclaims as we walk to our gate. The number of times she's said that today alone is in the hundreds.

"Me too, Faye," I say. We sidestep groups of people as they rush about the busy airport, only just managing to stay side by side instead of single file.

"I can't wait, I really need this vacation," she says, tightening the straps of her backpack. "This last year of high school has fucked me harder than any guy ever has."

I burst out laughing. "TMI, Faye."

"It's true! I just barely graduated. At least now we can relax on the beach, meet some boys, get your mind off your Sexy Gym Guy . . ."

"Oh my gosh, Faye," I mumble, remembering how she reacted when I told her about my run-in with Mr. Blue Eyes. She's given him his own nickname. "If you were there, you would've murdered me." We turn a corner to get to our gate, and I scan the area for Faye's brother.

"I probably would've," she admits. "You need to stop being so damn shy! Oh, there's Adam, he's waving us over."

And that's when I see *him*, standing with the group of guys talking to Adam.

Instead of brushing it off and playing it cool like a normal person, or even stopping dead in my tracks like a normal-but-slightly-more-awkward person, I grab Faye's forearm and pull her through the nearest door. I'm one hundred percent sure our transition was neither graceful nor unnoticed.

"What is your issue, Lor?" Faye asks once the door safely separates us from the group of probably now confused boys.

"That was him!" I exclaim, my heart beating erratically as if it can't decide whether to be excited or terrified.

"What are you talking about?" Faye asks, eyebrows drawing together and bottom lip pouting out.

"I'm *talking* about how the incredibly good-looking guy

from the gym who saved my ass last week is the very same extremely good-looking guy talking to your brother!"

Her warm brown eyes widen in recognition. "No shit!"

She pushes open the door to look, but I yank her back in.

"Don't go out there!" I order.

Please tell me he's not coming on this trip with us. Or maybe tell me he is? I'm not sure which I'd prefer. I'm already worried about making a fool of myself in front of Faye's hot brother, so I don't need another hot guy to make me worry about my every move.

Faye rolls her eyes at me. "Yes, Lori. Let's stay in here all week. Who needs to go to Cuba when we can spend all our time enjoying the scenery of this beautiful ro—"

She cuts herself off as she peers around the room for the first time, which gets my attention, because Faye is never speechless.

I follow her gaze and . . . yup . . . of course.

That's a row of urinals.

And that's a bunch of confused men staring back at us.

My face heats, probably making me look more like a tomato than a teenage girl.

Faye recovers a lot faster than I do.

"Yes." She looks around the room and up at the ceiling as if examining it. "Everything seems in order here. We'll report this back to our supervisor." She grabs my arm and pushes me out the door. "Carry on."

"Supervisor? Carry on? Really, Faye?" I don't know how she comes up with these things.

"What?" she defends, not even a bit fazed. "It was better than standing around gawking at a bunch of men with their pants practically around their ankles."

I groan. "Do you think your brother and his friends saw that?"

A sly smile spreads across Faye's face as she looks in their direction. She doesn't bother answering me. I follow her gaze. Her brother is ruining his perfect face with a frown aimed at us, and the other guys are staring at us.

"You're right," Faye says without taking her eyes off the group. "Sexy Gym Guy *definitely* earned his nickname."

"Faye!" I exclaim, not because I disagree or need to point out *she* gave him that nickname, but because we're almost at the group and they can probably hear us.

"Oh, don't get your panties in a twist." She grins at me, making zero effort to lower her voice. "I know you have first dibs."

Before I can say I don't want "dibs" on a human being, Adam stops us.

"What were you two doing in the men's washroom?" he asks, impatient.

"Supervising," Faye answers without hesitation, and I reflexively slap her with the back of my hand.

He rolls his eyes. "Whatever. Can you at least *try* not to embarrass me in front of my friends this week?" His voice is low, and I glance at the four other guys a few feet behind him.

Faye pouts. "But I wanted to have some fun this week too."

"We'll be on our best behavior," I add before Faye can piss him off. "Thanks again for letting us come."

His captivating hazel eyes give me a once-over as if trying to decide whether I'm lying.

"Come on," he grumbles. "I'll introduce you."

We follow him over to the group, and I pray my face isn't bright red.

"For those of you who don't already know, this loser is my sister, Faye, and that's her friend Lori." Adam gestures to us noncommittally.

"Hey, Lor," Dylan and Kellan greet. I'm familiar enough with them, even though I'm always quiet when they're around.

"Fayanna." Kellan winks at her suggestively.

Faye flirts right back. "Kellan." She shoots him that smile that can make any boy melt.

He's the only person Faye's ever let call her by her full name more than once and live to tell the tale. Probably because if you could draw Faye's dream guy, it would be an illustration of Kellan Reyes.

He's shorter than the rest of the boys but still over a head taller than Faye, standing at five foot eleven, which I only know because Faye loves teasing him about it. He has tousled black hair, deep-brown eyes, full lips, and a tan that lasts all year round, which he attributes to his Filipino genes. He's not the most built or muscular person, which is obvious when he's standing next to Mr. Blue Eyes, but he's got broad shoulders and a lean, athletic build from the sports he plays. Throw in his perfectly straight teeth and his penchant for mischief, and you've got walking, talking Fayanna Murray catnip.

Faye says that she and Kellan haven't really talked to each other since the last time they slept together, but it seems like nothing's changed. At least Adam's still in the dark about it.

Adam ignores the obvious flirting. "Lori, I'm not sure if you've met Alessio, and this is Dylan's cousin Dean." He gestures at the guys as he says their names, ending with Mr. Blue Eyes—Dean. "Faye, try not to bother us this week."

I've only met Alessio a few times when he was coming or going from Faye's house, but I do know he's dating Jenna's cousin. I wave at the boys and smile, trying to channel my inner Faye and be cool for once.

"Lori, huh?" Dean says to me as everyone carries on their

own conversations. "You ran off so fast the other day I didn't get the chance to ask your name."

Adam glares at us, probably hoping I don't say something embarrassing to his friend. I chew my lip as my face heats. "Yeah. I'm not the greatest in awkward situations."

He bites back a smile. "Jumping in front of a car to avoid me isn't *that* awkward."

"That's not what happened!" I defend myself but end up laughing.

"If you're that desperate to get away from me, I wonder what's going to happen when we're stuck on a trip with each other for a week," he teases, and I'm drawn in by the playfulness in his eyes.

I'm wondering the same thing, Dean.

FOUR

Day One of Cuba

Faye

Our flight was delayed for a couple hours, so by the time we arrive in Cuba it's around midnight.

Although it's dark and I'm exhausted, the beauty of the country is obvious. The people on the shuttle bus from the airport to the resort would probably have kicked me off if I'd exclaimed *That's so pretty!* one more time.

The resort is huge. There are a bunch of small, three-story hotels scattered on the property instead of one superlarge one with fifty floors. There are also three pools, two beaches on either side of the resort, and among other things, a large common area/lobby with couches and bars where people can hang out.

The seven of us are staying on the top floor of the same building. The room Lori and I are sharing has a perfect view of the beach in the distance. The five guys are across the hall from us, with three rooms shared between them. When I asked Adam who's getting the third room to themselves, he told me it depended on who would have "company" that night and needed the most privacy.

I almost vomited all over him.

I know Alessio, Dylan, and Kellan but have never met Dean, even though he's the same age as Adam and has apparently hung out with them before; he took Eli's ticket when he couldn't come. He's Dylan's cousin, and I can sort of see the resemblance between him and Dylan. Dean's definitely sexy, I'll give Lori that, but I'd never have thought he was her type. She's always had a crush on my brother, and he looks nothing like Dean.

My brother is all light with blond hair and hazel eyes, lean and tall, and honestly, he's kind of mean. Dean, however, has got that dark hair going for him. He's tall and muscular, and superfriendly and approachable. I'd wonder how they were even friends, except that Kellan is Adam's exact opposite as well, and they're best friends.

Maybe friendly people are attracted to mean people to balance out? I don't know. But if Adam had a group of friends all moody and bitchy like him at the house all the time, I'd jump out the window, so I can't complain. This has all worked out for the best, since I don't like Eli anyway, and now I can scheme to get Lori to at least kiss Dean by the end of this week.

We go to bed once we're all checked in, so we don't get to explore, but I set an alarm for 6:30 a.m. At 6:31, I'm jumping on Lori's bed, yelling at her to wake up so we can leave the room.

She throws the remote control at me, but I'm persistent, and we get breakfast about half an hour later.

The resort is huge, and the warm morning sun kisses my face as we wander around. Everyone is friendly, both the workers and the other guests, waving hello to us as we pass by. Beautiful palm trees, which are starkly different to the full pine trees I'm used to back home in Toronto, are growing all over.

We don't see the guys for most of the day, either because

they're avoiding us or they're still sleeping, but no way am I missing precious time in the sun.

Eventually, we plant our butts on beach chairs on beautiful white sand, with a perfect view of the crystal clear ocean, and that's where we stay for most of the day. I'm working on my tan, eyes closed and headphones in, and Lori's beside me reading a book and being boring.

Freezing cold water hits my body, jerking me out of my tranquil state. *"Ahh!"*

I rip out my headphones and glare at the source of my discomfort, which is, of course, Kellan. He has an empty water bottle in his hand and an annoying smile plastered on his face.

"What?" I ask flatly, wiping the water off my stomach.

He grows visibly delighted at my annoyed tone. If he wasn't so damn hot, I'd push him into the sand.

"They say you get a better tan in the water. I was helping you out." He moves my stuff from the chair beside me and makes himself comfortable.

His hair is messy and curled like he's been swimming in the salty ocean all day. He's shirtless, which I've seen countless times, but damn, it never gets old.

"You're such a pain in the ass, you know that?" I pick up my bag, which he dumped onto the sand, and move it somewhere else.

He closes his eyes and lies back in the chair, intertwining his fingers behind his head. "Not as much as you are. I wasted all morning running around for you."

I sit up and study him, keeping my eyes trained on his face instead of where they want to roam. "What are you talking about? I've been here since like eight a.m."

"There's a foam party in the red-wristbands-only pool tonight." He completely ignores my question.

"That's nice. If you haven't noticed, Lori and I have blue wristbands." I wave my arm in front of his face as proof, but his eyes remain closed.

"Because you don't turn eighteen until later this year. Unlike me and the guys, who are all nineteen."

I feel a headache coming on. "Did you come here to bother me and state the obvious?"

His eyes stay closed, and one hand remains behind his head as he reaches into the pocket of his swim shorts, pulling out two new red wristbands.

"Don't say I never do anything for you." He opens his eyes to gauge my reaction, an arrogant smile playing on his full lips.

My eyes light up as if he just pulled out a million dollars. I was bummed Lori and I wouldn't have easy access to the fun parties or the booze, but not anymore.

"Where did you get these?" I reach for them, but he holds them out of my grasp.

"Remember how I said I was running around all morning? I was trying to find someone to get me these."

With red wristbands, Lori and I will no longer be stuck in the PG-13 sections of the resort. We can get drinks and go to all the X-rated parties.

"You're the greatest!" I try to reach for the wristbands again, but he's not done being a pain in the ass, keeping them beyond my reach.

"I want a kiss for them," he whispers, but Lori, who's on my other side, hears anyway.

She sets her book down and takes off her hat. "I'm gonna go jump in the ocean. Thanks for the wristbands, Kellan."

Then it's just the two of us. Just me and Kellan and his stupid, flirty smile.

"She heard that, you know," I inform him.

"I know you wanted to keep everything between the two of us, but you really expect me to believe you didn't tell her?" he asks, gesturing at Lori's receding form. "You FaceTimed her the second after it happened, didn't you?"

I smile innocently at him. "At least I waited until you left to call her."

He grabs my wrist and secures the new red wristband on it, then rips off the blue one while I pretend that I don't feel sparks wherever his skin touches mine. He slips the extra band in my bag to give to Lori later, not bothering to close it again.

"Does my brother know?" I ask him, gesturing to my wrist.

Kellan nods. "He wouldn't admit it to you if you asked, but he told me it was a good idea, since you'd find a way into the red events anyway. At least you won't get yourself in trouble this way."

Damn straight a piece of paper isn't keeping me out of the cool parties. At least now Lori won't be nagging me the whole time because she doesn't want to get caught.

"Plus," Kellan adds, raking a hand through his hair, "he said this way he can watch out for you. Don't tell him I told you, though, because he'd deny it."

If I was drinking, I would've done a spit-take. My brother said that? Adam "I ignore my girlfriend tormenting my sister" Murray? The last time he "watched out" for me was a week ago when he stole my brownie midbite to "make sure it didn't have nuts."

I'm not allergic to nuts.

I snort. "Adam's a buzzkill. I'm not planning on sticking around him at the red events."

"Either way, you wouldn't be getting into those events without yours truly." He puckers his lips and gestures to them, a playful gleam in his eyes as he waits for his thank-you kiss.

No one tells me what to do. Especially not a pain-in-the-ass, stupidly good-looking boy.

I smile, but he misses the mischievous intent behind it. "Fine, I'll give you what you deserve."

Satisfied that he's getting his way, he closes his eyes and leans toward me.

I lean in and swiftly grab the water bottle in my open bag, and in one motion, whip off the lid and empty the cold liquid all over him.

His eyes pop open in shock, his mouth wide, disbelief written all over his beautiful face.

I bite my lip and try not to laugh. "Don't say I didn't warn you."

A challenge ignites in his dark eyes and a smirk molds his lips. "And this is your warning . . ."

I yelp as he stands up, but I'm faster. I run away from him in the general direction of the ocean, laughing and screaming as Kellan chases me, not even caring that I break a flip-flop. His carefree laugh is music to my ears as we splash into the infinite blue water.

—

Lori and I eat dinner together. I haven't seen Adam or any of his friends for most of the day, and I don't mind. I'll see them at the foam party, so I put on my cutest bikini and force Lori to do the same. I may not be tall, toned, and have legs for days like her, but I know for a fact that my curves look sensational in bikinis.

I'm wearing a hot-pink halter bikini set that's always a crowd-pleaser and has never failed to get all eyes on me, and Lori's in a light-blue string bikini that she totally rocks.

We hear the music and laughter before we even reach the resort's red-wristbands-only pool.

"Do you think Dean will be here?" Lori asks nervously as we flash our wristbands at a worker to get access to the pool.

"That's a dumb question," I answer as I take in the scene in front of us.

Even though it's pitch-black outside, the pool and surrounding area are bright with purple and blue and red lights. There's foam covering the pool, and half-drunk late teens and early twentysomethings with wrists covered in glowstick bracelets are splashing around, throwing foam at each other.

"You're right. Obviously he's here." Lori scans the sizable area, trying to spot Dean in the crowd.

I grab us a couple of glowstick bracelets and drag Lori over to the packed bar where I'm sure we'll bump into Kellan. He's probably over there, flashing his perfect smile at some unsuspecting girl while she falls for his stupid charm.

Not that I'm jealous or anything.

As I'm scoping out the yummy boys from all around the world, Lori gets my attention by frantically slapping me with the back of her hand.

"Ow! What?"

"That's Dean! Oh my goodness, he's so hot."

I follow her gaze and can confirm that he is so hot.

He's in the shallow end of the pool, the top half of his body visible, water dripping down the crevices of his sculpted chest and abs. It's been less than twenty-four hours but he already seems like he's got a nice solid tan.

Lori's staring at him with wide eyes. I'm guessing that even after all that time at the gym, she's never seen him shirtless.

"Lor, stop drooling," I tease, and she looks away with a blush.

"Sorry. I can't help it." She sneaks another glance at him.

Her eyes move from Dean and land on the two girls he's talking to, both devastatingly pretty.

She sighs, her mood souring. "I could never compete with them, Faye."

My nostrils flare in frustration. Lori is so insecure that she never realizes exactly how gorgeous she is.

"Yes you can, Lor! Go flirt with him! He won't even notice those girls once you pay attention to him."

She frowns. "They look like Bollywood princesses."

"And you look like a pretty, pretty princess! I used *two* 'pretties' in there, Lor, and you know I don't go throwing those around all willy-nilly." I totally do and she knows it, but she still cracks a smile.

We shove our way through the bar, which to my relief, or maybe disappointment, is Kellan-free. The bartender notices Lori and abruptly abandons everyone else who is waiting to take her order immediately.

I elbow her as if to say, *See! You're so hot you just got service before everyone else!* but she shrugs it off, her mind already elsewhere.

I order two drinks and hand one to Lori, who will probably nurse it all night, and we sit on some foam-free pool chairs.

Lori stirs her drink with her straw. "I barely even know how to flirt, and it's even worse around Dean. I turn into a bumbling idiot around him."

"I can't deny that." She glares at me, and I laugh. "But it's not too late to change."

"I'm not like you, Faye. I can't turn a guy into mush with just a look."

Pride swells within me, but I push it down. This is not about reveling in my many skills; it's about helping Lori. I lean forward, ready to drop some knowledge on her ass. "It's not hard. I'll give you some easy, never-fail, beginner tips that basically always work with the right confidence."

She nods eagerly, giving me her full attention like she does in class.

"Okay, first and foremost, you need to laugh."

Lori laughs, loud and obviously fake.

"No, not now!" She stops. "I mean when he talks to you and says something funny or tells a stupid joke, you need to laugh. And not like that. Make it sound realistic, not like a dying robot on crack."

She nods. "Laugh like a nondying robot minus the crack. Got it."

I roll my eyes but know she gets the point. "Okay. Other than the laughing, obviously you need to smile. Body language is important, too, so lean in when he's talking, but not like, uncomfortably close. Bat your eyes at him or bite your lip to draw attention to them. Make excuses to touch him too. One of the easiest and very basic no-fail examples is exclaiming 'you're so funny!' then play-shoving his arm. And of course, *be confident*!"

Lori's eyes are wide, and I can tell she's trying to memorize anything I can give her. Flirting often comes easily and naturally to people, so I'm sure once she gets going she'll be fine.

She continues to stir her drink. "Laugh, smile, lean in, bite my lip, bat my eyes, touch him, tell him he's funny, be confident. Got it."

I stand up, signaling the end of our conversation. "That's it! Now go get 'em, tiger!"

Lori scrambles to stand with me, her wide blue eyes giving her a deer-in-the-headlights look. "What? Like, right now?"

"No time like the present," I reply cheerfully. "And look, he's getting out of the pool, go get him while he's alone!"

Both of us watch in fascination as Dean walks up the steps of the pool, looking like he's in a movie and there's a slow-motion camera panning down his perfect body.

I turn back to her and give her some tough love. "If you don't go talk to him right now, I swear I will leave a pack of condoms on his nightstand with a note signed by you, explaining in great detail how much you dream about his thick, hard, huge c—"

"Okay, okay!" She cuts me off with a scowl, setting her drink down. "Geez, Faye, you play dirty."

I beam at her, satisfied. "Not as dirty as he'll want to play with you once he reads the note I leave him."

"Oh my gosh!" She throws her hands up to stop me from talking and quickly turns away from me, hurrying off toward Dean.

Satisfied Lori's on her way to getting Dean naked, I head to the second bar at the other side of the enormous pool, giving me a chance to check out the boys I've got to work with.

As I'm walking, a guy in the pool catches my attention. Even covered in foam and with a girl basically attached to him, I know it's him. I'd know Kellan anywhere.

My heart is ten times heavier as I try to process all the different emotions battling within me from seeing him standing there in the pool. His hands are on the waist of a half-naked girl for support as he lifts her into one of the tubes floating in the pool. She laughs as she settles in, touching his shoulder in the way I just instructed Lori to do, then wraps her arms around him in a hug.

I know we're not exclusive or anything but seeing him with another girl is making me feel things a single girl shouldn't be feeling. I've never actually *seen* him with someone else before, and I don't like the way my stomach lurches and heart squeezes, or the way my throat feels tight.

I tear my eyes away and continue toward the bar with a new purpose. I need lots of vodka inside me. Like right now.

I spot a tall, handsome guy at the bar as I get closer, and eye him with interest.

And maybe him too.

FIVE

Night One of Cuba

Lori

As I make my way over to Dean, I replay Faye's advice in my head.

Smile, laugh, lean in, bite my lip, bat my eyes, touch him, tell him he's funny, and be confident.

Confidence.

I take a deep breath and try to channel my inner Fayanna.

"Hey, Dean!" I call out, immediately cringing. I hope he doesn't think I sounded as annoyingly enthusiastic as I think I did.

"Hey," he answers, his face lighting up as I approach him. "Haven't seen you all day. How are you enjoying Cuba so far?"

Okay, good start. Remember Faye's advice.

He runs his hand through his hair to get the water out, and suddenly I've never felt more nervous. He's so handsome, even with the sunburn on his chest and shoulders. He'll never give *me* the time of day. How did I think this was a good idea?

I force what I hope is a confident smile. "It's been fun. We stayed at the beach and swam all day. I love swimming; I've been a lifeguard for years. I even almost finished a book I brought. I love reading. How about you?"

I'm babbling. *Get it together, Lori! Use one of Faye's techniques.*

I bite my lip like Faye said and do what I think is batting my eyelashes. Two birds with one stone, right? Pairing one technique with the other should make me even more irresistible.

He tilts his head as he studies my face. "Yeah . . . it was good. We got a late lunch and . . ." He cuts himself off as his eyebrows draw together with concern. "Hey, do you have an eyelash in your eye or something? It must be painful if you're biting your lip like that."

I immediately stop batting my eyes and release my lip as I stare up at him with alarm.

Quick! Move on to the next one, Lori!

I laugh loudly, hoping I don't sound like what Faye called a dying robot on crack. "You're so funny!" I exclaim a bit too theatrically and move to play-shove his arm like I was instructed.

Somehow, I screw that up too and end up missing, making my hand slap his chest . . . hard. He winces, since I'm sure that didn't feel good on his sunburn, but he doesn't complain. I'm so shocked I don't even move my hand away; I just leave it resting on his chest. It's like every nerve in my body died of embarrassment, leaving me unable to function.

Now he's looking down at me and I'm looking up at him. We're staring at each other and all the while my stupid hand is crossing all kinds of personal-space boundaries by remaining on his hard chest.

"How drunk are you?" he asks with a hint of amusement.

Great. I'm so terrible at flirting that the only explanation for my awkwardness is that I'm drunk. I've literally only had two sips of my vodka cran!

"Oh, no. I'm not drunk at all. Not a big drinker," I answer

quickly, feeling like I'm drowning and desperate to not embarrass myself even more. "Bet you can't even smell the alcohol on my breath, see?"

And then I blow on him.

I mother-flipping *blow on him.*

I'm going to die. Right here on this spot. The ground could open and swallow me whole, and I'd still prefer it to being here.

He blinks twice, unsure of exactly what's happening.

That's it. Abort mission. *Abort. Mission.*

"Okay, cool." I finally pull my hand from his chest and hitch my thumb over my shoulder. "I'm just gonna go over there and die now. See you."

I pivot and hurry away before I can somehow make it worse.

As if I could make it worse. He's so out of my league, standing there all ruggedly handsome and genuinely nice, he makes me flustered. I should've just told him I was drunk—at least that way I could've blamed my awkwardness on the booze. He'll never want to get near me again.

I've never been more embarrassed in my life, and Jenna McAndrews, though she denied it, once cut a hole in the back of my pants without my realizing, and I walked around all day with my underwear exposed until someone eventually told me.

I spot a girl in a purple bikini talking to a bunch of people poolside. Her long black braids sway as she laughs; her deep-brown skin is covered in dripping foam as one guy splashes her from the pool. She's talking and smiling and flirting with ease—she even play-slaps one of their arms.

I scowl. *That's* what that's supposed to look like. Not whatever sorry excuse I just pulled.

"Hey! Lori, wait!" a deep voice calls out.

The shivers down my spine tell me exactly whose voice that

is, but I'm not sticking around to claim the "most awkward conversationalist" title.

When I don't stop walking, he runs around me and stops, forcing me to face him.

I can see the girl with the purple bikini over his shoulder. She flips her hair and leans into one boy, laughing as they talk.

"You've gotta stop running away from me," he says, drawing my attention back to him.

He flashes me his perfectly white smile and my heart hammers in my chest.

"Sorry. Old habits, I guess." I wrap my arms around my body, suddenly aware that I'm half-naked in front of a man who looks like he's chiseled out of marble.

Plus, I just *blew in his face* like a total weirdo.

Purple Bikini Girl taps the chest of one guy she's with, and he jumps into the water. The guy comes up for air through the foam, laughing and gesturing for her to jump in too.

"Well, I promise you I don't bite, so no need to keep doing that," Dean jokes.

Why is he still talking to me? Why is he trying to make me feel better about being a total embarrassment? I'm not like Purple Bikini Girl, who was just pushed into the water by one of the other guys, yelling the whole way down.

"Yeah," I tell Dean, still plotting my escape. "I'll have to remember that."

"Good. Actually, the hotel offers this snorkeling excursion, and I think it would be fun. Do you want to do it with me tomorrow? Since you love swimming and . . ."

I've stopped listening. Where's Purple Bikini Girl? Has she come up yet? It's hard to see with all the lights and foam. The guys she was talking to are chugging beers, completely unaware that she is missing.

Dean's talking to me, but I don't hear a sound. Without a word, I hastily move around him and stop at the edge of the pool where she was pushed in.

My heart's beating in my chest, my breathing loud in my ears. *Where is she?*

"Lori?" Dean's beside me. He touches my shoulder to get my attention, but I'm focused on the water.

There. A flash of bright purple underwater when the foam and people shifted.

I kick off my flip-flops and jump into the water, diving toward her as quickly and efficiently as I can. When I reach her, I wrap my arms around her, pulling her up with me. We break the surface and I turn so that her back is resting on my chest, her head and shoulders above the water. She's unconscious.

"Get a lifeguard!" I yell over the music as I swim with her to the ledge.

Once I get there, a pair of masculine hands reaches down to grab her.

"Those guys went to get a lifeguard. Let me help!" Dean has already pulled her off me and gently sets her on the ground.

I hop out easily and follow, kneeling beside her, and let my training kick in.

I tilt her head back and listen for breathing. After five seconds of nothing, I pinch her nose and give her two breaths. Then I start compressions.

I'm distantly aware that there's a crowd huddled around me, people watching and worrying about the girl, but they're not my focus right now. It's like everything is muted—colors, sounds, voices—and all I see is the unconscious girl who needs my help.

I tilt her head back again, pinch her nose, and give her two more breaths. I start compressions again, praying that she'll be okay.

I hear a gurgle and stop compressions. The girl turns her head over and coughs out water.

I can barely comprehend what I'm seeing. It's like I was holding my breath as long as she was, and now that she's breathing, I can too. Everyone's cheering and high-fiving, and I'm staring at the girl like I can't believe what's happening.

Two officially sanctioned lifeguards rush in and take over, and I rise and move out of the way to let them do their job.

"Lori! Lori, that was amazing!" Strong arms wrap around me and pull me against a well-defined chest, not caring that I'm soaking wet and covered in foam.

Dean pulls back and looks at me. "You just saved her life."

His eyes are peering right into my soul, reaching past the hazy fog that I've slipped into and effectively pulling me out.

"I'm just glad she's okay," I reply.

He puts a hand under my jaw and tilts my head up to look at him. "No, really," he breathes, his expression awed. "That was the greatest thing I've ever seen. No one else even noticed that she was there."

People are walking by me, congratulating me and telling me I did a good job.

Oh my goodness. How many people were watching me? I stiffen.

Dean scans my face as he notices the change in me. "Are you okay?"

I force myself to keep my eyes trained on his. "Yeah. I just, um . . . I'm not used to all this attention."

And then I realize it. My bikini-clad body is pressed right up against his naked chest; his arm is securely around me. This is heaven and hell and everything I never could've imagined all wrapped in one.

Understanding fills his eyes as if all my actions since meeting him finally make sense. "Okay, why don't we go for a walk down by the beach? No people there."

I bite my lip. Dean and me alone? I already made a fool of myself alone with him once tonight.

Another guy walks by and claps me on the shoulder, telling me how glad he is that there's a hot lifeguard around to give him mouth-to-mouth whenever he might need it, and suddenly there's nowhere I'd rather be than alone with Dean on a private beach, even if that means I might make a fool of myself.

I nod at Dean, and he releases me. I retrieve my flip-flops and slip them on, following him past the stares and out of the foam party, into the quiet serenity of the beach.

SIX

Night One of Cuba

Faye

Mr. Tall-and-Handsome's name is Darius. He's twenty-two with smooth black skin and is from the UK, so he has the *hottest* accent, and I can't stop listening to it.

We sit beside each other at the bar, and by our second drink I practically have him eating out of the palm of my hand. All it'll take is one suggestion to show me his room, and I'm getting laid tonight.

Kellan's not the only one who can move on to the next hottest thing available.

I have to stop the scowl threatening to arise at the thought of him.

Don't think about him.

"And that's why I always need a room with an ocean view," I catch Darius saying once I tune in.

He's setting it up—waiting for me to be all *Oh, really? An ocean view? Why don't you show me?* and then it's a sealed deal.

Before I can decide what to say, a fun-sucking presence

appears beside me. I can practically feel the air around me shift.

"Do you have to be here?" my brother asks.

I turn in my seat to face Adam, who's apparently the resort's resident grumpy baby, along with his friends Alessio and Dylan.

"It's a large party, Adam. You didn't have to come to this bar if you knew I was here." My irritation is written all over my face, and I hope my cranky brother doesn't scare Darius off.

"We were just coming over to say hi," Dylan answers, eyeing Darius.

"Well, thanks for stopping by. See you later." I smile tightly at him and gesture back to Darius with my eyes, hoping they get the hint and realize they're being major cockblocks right now.

"Hey, can you ask the bartender for a rum and Coke?" Alessio asks Darius, taking a seat on my other side.

What is happening right now? Why is this happening to me?

Darius gives him an uncertain look but orders anyway.

"These guys'll be on their way shortly," I apologize to Darius as I sense a new presence behind me.

"Really, Faye? This guy? You're going to lock Lori out of her room tonight for this?"

I take a calming breath and turn to face Kellan. Why is he looking at me like he's . . . what? Disappointed? Jealous? I didn't see him caring about me when he was all over that girl two minutes ago.

I narrow my eyes at him, but before I can say anything, Darius stands and backs away. "Yeah, I'm going to go. Catch you later, Faith."

"It's *Faye*," I call after him, but he's already gone. I try not to let my annoyance that he got my name wrong show on my face, especially not in front of Kellan.

He sits down in Darius's empty seat with a satisfied smirk. "Wow. You sure know how to pick 'em."

"You would know," I shoot back, and he shuts up.

Good.

"Where's Lori?" my brother asks as if he gives a damn.

Scanning the pool area, I spot her not too far off, talking to Dean. *Good for her.*

I point out her and Dean, and turn back to my drink, simmering in anger. I don't see my brother *all day* and the one time I *don't* want to see him, he cockblocks me. I hope he doesn't go and cockblock Lori too. That's totally something he'd do.

"Where?" Dylan asks. "I see a smoking-hot babe talking to Dean."

"That *is* Lori," Adam snaps, crossing his arms over his chest.

What's his problem?

Dylan's and Alessio's eyes widen in recognition. *"Whoa."*

Alessio tilts his head. "I knew she was hot, but damn, she's even better without clothes on."

My nostrils flare, and I try to swallow the rising jealousy. At least Kellan's not staring at her like he's never seen her before.

"You have a *girlfriend*, Alessio," I remind him in a tone that's harsher than necessary. "You remember Olivia, right? You've been with her for five years." Olivia is Jenna's much nicer, much quieter cousin. She's my age but so smart she skipped a grade and ended up in Adam's class. I'm not sure how smart she really is if she's dating Alessio, but to each their own.

"*Yes*, I remember Olivia. Doesn't mean I don't have eyes," he quips, downing the rest of his drink.

"Did she just slap his chest?" Kellan wonders aloud, and I turn around with alarm.

What? What is she doing? Why is her hand sitting on his chest like that?

"Hey, there you guys are!" It's the Bollywood princesses that Dean was talking to before, plus another who happens to be the girl who was all over Kellan earlier.

They're even prettier up close than they were from afar, and now my annoyance level is more than I can take.

I chug the rest of my drink and stand up.

"You guys are cramping my style. I'm going to go somewhere you're not."

I storm off to another, more secluded section of the large, irregularly shaped pool, a section that's not visible from the bar.

Who am I to stand in the way of Kellan scoring tonight? If he wants to bang some girl, then I'm not stopping him.

But you want him to choose you.

I shove that thought deep, deep down in my mind. Kellan would never choose me; I'm his best friend's kid sister. Nothing more than a quick, convenient fling.

"Running off to find that guy who didn't even remember your name?"

I want to punch Kellan's self-righteous smirk off his handsome face.

"What are you doing here? Why aren't you continuing where you left off with that girl wrapped all around you?"

I sound jealous. Why did I say that? I didn't even see them kiss, though that was definitely the direction it was going. But I know we're not exclusive, and I know he has every right to hook up with whoever he wants, even though the thought makes bile rise in my throat.

His stupid smile widens, and there's an amused gleam in his eyes. "You're jealous."

"Am not."

"Are so," he taunts.

I take a step closer to him, ignoring the tension in the air.

"Am. Not."

He takes a step even closer to me, causing my heart rate to pick up and goose bumps to rise along my arms. "Are. So."

I close the rest of the distance between us. We're toe to toe now, and I tilt my head all the way back to look at him.

"I. Am. Not."

Kellan's smile should warn me he's up to something mischievous, but I'm more focused on calming my heart rate.

"You're so jealous I can feel it rolling off you in waves. Why don't we cool off?"

"Wait—wha—"

Before I can process anything, Kellan wraps his arms around me and leaps into the pool, the two of us splashing through the foam together and swimming up to the top.

"Kellan!" I splash him, wiping the foam from my eyes. "What the hell?!"

He just laughs, carefree as always. "What?" He swims toward me. "Doesn't that feel better? You came to a pool party and haven't even been in the pool yet."

"I would've preferred to go in on my *own* terms, not get thrown in by some douchebag."

My insult only spurs him on, and he moves closer to me the way a lion hunts its prey. "Oh, douchebag, huh? I don't seem to recall you ever referring to me as a douchebag. The only other name you've called me is 'God,' as in *oh God! Oh Go—*"

I splash him again to cut him off, my face heating but controlled by the chill of the pool. "Something is seriously wrong with you!"

He laughs as he reaches me. "The only thing wrong with me is how much I love teasing you."

And then he kisses me, and I melt into him, feeling like everything is how it should be. I don't care about the other girl he was just with. I don't care that my brother is somewhere at this party, and we're supposed to be hiding this from him. I don't care about the roar of people cheering for something in the background. I don't even care that I'm covered in foam. All I care about is the way he feels pressed up against me, and the way his mouth moves perfectly in sync with mine.

I wrap my arms around his shoulders and sink into him, kissing him with all I've got, surrounded by people and foam and the night's fresh air.

SEVEN

Night One of Cuba

Lori

Before we leave the party, Dean grabs a hotel towel and wraps it around my shoulders. It's a beautiful night, but I'm glad to have it. I would feel really silly talking to him all covered in foam. Plus, even though it's darker out here, having a towel wrapped around my half-naked body makes me feel a lot less vulnerable in front of him.

We walk along the shoreline, our shoes in our hands and our feet in the sand as the tide gently brushes over them. The night is calm, the opposite of my heart every time I look over at Dean and catch him already looking at me.

"So," Dean starts, breaking the comfortable silence. "You graduated high school last week, right? What's the plan for next year?"

"Life Sciences at the University of Toronto."

Even in the dark I can tell the corners of his lips pull up as he says, "Try not to sound *too* excited about it."

"No, no, I am. It's just . . ." I trail off. What's the point of telling him what I really want when my own parents won't even listen?

"Just what?" he encourages.

I wrap my arms around myself. "Nothing, it's stupid."

He gently knocks his shoulder against mine as we walk, forcing me to meet his eyes as we come to a stop.

"It's not stupid," he says. "Tell me."

It must be something in the tone of his voice or the seriousness in his eyes because I open my mouth and blush as I say, "I want to take a year off and backpack through Europe. I want to see the world—figure out who I am and what I want to do with myself, you know?"

"That's not stupid," he reassures me. "Why aren't you doing that instead of going to U of T?"

We start walking again, and he falls in place beside me. Now that he's not intensely gazing into my eyes, I feel less flustered and start talking freely.

"I brought it up to my parents, and they shut it down immediately. They want me to get my degree right away and then go to med school. They're *very* excited about med school."

He looks thoughtful. "That sucks. I guess traveling can get pretty expensive, though."

"Oh, no. I would pay for it. They just don't like the idea."

"Well, how hard did you fight for it?"

Not hard at all. "Umm . . ."

He laughs, assuming my answer from my hesitancy.

"If you really want something, fight for it. Life's too short to let other people make your decisions for you."

That's a good philosophy in theory, but Dean doesn't know my parents.

"It's not that easy . . ."

"But it *is* that easy. Figure out what you want in life, and don't let anyone take it from you."

I frown and study my feet as we walk.

Dean's silent for a second, then says so quietly I almost miss it, "I had a twin brother, you know."

My head snaps over to look at him.

Had?

He's not looking at me; instead he's gazing out at the ocean. I can imagine a sadness in his eyes. "Dustin. He died when we were fourteen; he had a heart defect."

I don't know what to say. What could you possibly say to something like that?

"I'm so sorry," is what I come up with.

He looks over at me briefly with a small smile. "It's been just over five years, but it still hurts. Sometimes I think about all the things he didn't get to do but that I still can."

Again, I don't know what to say, so this time I say nothing.

"The point is," he continues, "it made me realize that life's too short and to go after what you want while you still can." The sadness leaves his face. "And for you, that means standing up for yourself and making your own decisions."

I'd like to think I already do those things, but I know Dean's right.

"And what did that mean for you?" I ask. "Have *you* gone after what you wanted?"

"I've tried to. I quit soccer, even though I've been playing my whole life and my parents were pushing me to go pro, because even though everyone said I had a decent chance, I just didn't care about it."

I play with the end of the towel that's still wrapped around me. "Weren't you scared?" Maybe his parents are different than mine. Maybe they haven't spent every waking moment talking about soccer, but something tells me that isn't the case.

He pauses for a minute, his expression contemplative. "I was always a scrawny, shy kid, at least until I hit my growth spurt in tenth grade and started playing sports other than soccer to bulk up a bit."

I stare at him, trying and failing to picture Dean, this large man who owns his presence and fills any room he enters with it, as a shy, scrawny teenager. My mind remains blank.

"Anyway, before I hit my growth spurt, this older kid always bothered me and Dustin because of our stutter. We hadn't stuttered in years, but by that point he picked on us regardless. A month after Dustin passed, that older kid was saying some really horrible stuff about us. Even though he was bigger than me, and even though I'd never been in a fight before, something in me went 'fuck it.' I went over and punched him right in the face."

My eyes are wide. "You won the fight?"

A laugh escapes him. "No, I got my ass handed to me. But I got some good hits in, and I didn't regret it."

I press my lips together to hold back a confused smile. "So, the moral of the story is to go around hitting people if that's what I want?"

He laughs again, and it's less constrained this time. "No. I'm not promoting violence, and I don't make getting into fights a habit. I don't think I've been in one since like, tenth grade, which feels like forever ago now." He shakes his head with a shy grin. "But I'm saying sometimes it's better to face your problems head-on instead of skirting around them, even if you're scared. As I said, life's too short not to go after what you want, and to answer your question, sure I was scared about disappointing my parents, but it's *my* life, not theirs, and I should spend it how I want. So, if deep down you know you'll regret not fighting to travel, then that's all the reason you need to not just lie down and accept your fate."

From the way he's talking, it's like he knows I don't even want to go to med school, but all I've told him is I want to take the year off. His words resonate with me, though. Life really *is* too short to let my parents dictate how I live it, and maybe it's best if I face them head-on and tell them I'm not going to med school. But that's easier said than done now that there's an ocean between us, and I'm not staring right into their expectant eyes.

"Other than quitting soccer and beating up bullies, are you still going after what you want?" I ask him, and my joke makes him smile.

"I think so," he says, and the playfulness in his eyes makes me blush and stare at the sand. He clears his throat. "I'm getting my BA in linguistics, and then hopefully I'll be accepted to get my master's in speech-language pathology. I'd really like to help kids the way my speech pathologist helped me and Dustin. I'm currently volunteering at the clinic I used to go to, and I love it. I'm already learning so much and I'm mostly only watching and assisting."

"It sounds like you're pretty passionate about what you do." That's what my parents sound like when they talk about their work. On the other hand, I sound like I'm being tortured when I talk about my future. "Did you always know that was what you were going to do?"

"Not really, but we're kind of forced to pick early on, aren't we?" His gives an awkward laugh. "I'm just lucky to really love what I do."

We *are* forced early on, some, like me, more than others. "I wish I could feel like that about my future."

He playfully bumps his shoulder into mine. "Well, hopefully that year off to travel will help you with that."

That was the plan. Too bad my parents shot that dream down faster than I could even bring it up.

—

Dean and I walk and talk for what feels like hours, and before we realize it, it's two a.m.

Back at the hotel, he stops in front of the door to my room. "So um, about that snorkeling excursion . . ." Dean trails off.

"Snorkeling excursion?"

He displays his perfect smile, although it's a little hesitant. "Before you became a hero tonight, I asked you if you wanted to go on a snorkeling excursion that the resort runs tomorrow."

Dean wants to go do a fun activity with me? *Me?* The girl who blew on his face and slapped him right in the sunburnt chest? Is this a trick question?

"Um, yeah, sure! I love swimming," I say before he realizes *who* he asked to spend time with.

"Yeah, you mentioned that before," he laughs, and I turn to face my door so I can pull the key card out of my bikini top.

"Then you know I really mean it." I cringe and swipe my key card, opening the door. "See you tomorrow! Good night!" I say before he has time to change his mind.

He says good night, and I close the door behind me, a giddy and excited feeling coursing through my veins.

The room is dark, and I leave it that way, but something seems off.

From where I stand in the little entry hall, there's a door to the bathroom to my right, and straight ahead is the sliding door to the balcony, but I can't see into the main part of the room where the beds are located.

I pause for a second and tilt my head, listening.

Oh.

My.

Gosh.

I sprint out of that room as fast as humanly possible and frantically shake my head to get the mental image out of it.

Those were sex sounds.

And those were definitely Kellan's flip-flops and swim trunks I noticed in my rush out.

Gross.

Outside the room, I lean against the wall beside my door and slide down to sit on the floor, setting the towel underneath me so it's more cushioned. With a sigh, I knock my head back on the wall; I'm going to be stuck here for a while.

Instead of dwelling on what I've just walked in on, I reflect on what happened to me tonight.

I actually had a normal, real conversation with Dean. Granted, I royally embarrassed myself in front of him first, but after that we talked for hours, and I *wasn't* awkward.

Life's too short to let other people make your decisions for you.

He's right. I should be more assertive about what I want, more like Faye.

I glance at the door to my room, which she's effectively kicked me out of.

Okay, maybe I'd be a bit more considerate, but still confident like her. She always knows what she wants and *always* gets it once her mind is set. If she wanted to travel and not go to med school, she'd do everything in her power to make it happen.

"Lori?"

There's a pair of legs standing in front of me. I follow them up to red swim trunks, a lean, naked torso, and my eyes finally land on Adam's handsome face. He looks like he just got back from the pool party, his blond hair still sporting some water droplets and a towel draped over his shoulders.

No matter how many times I'm around him, I'm always struck by how good-looking he is. "H-hey."

He looks around the empty corridor before his gaze lands back on me, his eyebrows drawn together.

"What are you doing out in the hallway?"

Crap. What's an appropriate reason to be sitting on the floor out here alone at two in the morning? *Waiting for your best friend and your sister to finish banging* doesn't seem like the best option.

"Oh. I—uh. I'm—uh . . . I forgot my key card! Yeah. I'm locked out. And I'm sitting on the floor because I'm—uh, waiting for Faye! You know her, off socializing."

Anyone else would clearly notice that I'm lying; I mean, that wasn't the smoothest of deliveries. But, luckily for me, I'm always this awkward around Adam, so he'll just think I'm a total weirdo, as per usual.

He raises an eyebrow. "You know you can get another one from the front desk, right?"

My eyes go wide. Of course I know that. Why couldn't he have accepted that answer and gone to his room?

"Yeah . . . but you have to change all the cards and prove it's your room, and it's a whole process. I'll wait."

I smile to reassure him and resist the urge to glance at the room door. *Come on, Adam. Stop interrogating me and go to bed.*

He studies me, as if considering something. He looks around the hall again and then sighs, decision made. To my complete surprise and horror, he slides down the wall to sit beside me.

I can only imagine what facial expression I'm making, because he says, "What? I'll wait with you until she comes."

He *can't* wait with me until she comes. She's not coming.

I glance at the door. Well, *actually* . . . never mind.

But the only way I can get into my room is if Kellan walks out of it, and Adam *cannot* be here to see that.

"Oh, no! You don't have to do that! Honestly!" I try to sound as confident as I can to make him go away, but for some reason he wants to be all chivalrous.

He rests his arms on his knees and leans his head back on

the wall. "It's two a.m. I can't leave you out here for who knows how long. It would be on my conscience if something happened to you."

My mouth opens and closes uselessly, unable to form words. Clearly, he's not going to leave me alone, but we cannot be here singing kumbaya and having a campout when Kellan walks out of that door.

Think, Lori!

I scramble to stand up and grab my towel, holding it self-consciously in front of me.

"Actually, I—uh—I have to pee! Mind if I wait in your room?"

Before he can say anything, I stride to the other end of the hall where his group of rooms are, praying he'll follow without more questions.

To my utter relief, he does, moving to stand in front of me to swipe his key card. I try to stop glancing at my room door so I don't give Faye away, and once he opens the door, I all but shove him through and slam it behind us.

Once we're in the safety of the room, I relax a bit. Their room looks exactly like ours, but with a different color scheme. There are clothes thrown all over the dresser and their suitcases are wide open on the floor.

"The bathroom's right there." Adam gestures.

I know where the bathroom is. Why is he telling me?

When I stand there looking confused, he continues. "I thought you had to pee?"

Oh yeah!

"Yes! I totally do." I scramble into the bathroom and close the door behind me. I don't have to go, so I run the water for some noise and wait a couple seconds, then flush the toilet and wash my hands.

Once I'm done, I open the door and stand in the room,

awkwardly shifting from foot to foot. Adam's sitting on one bed and flipping through television channels.

It hits me that I'm alone in a room—a bedroom—with Adam Murray, the boy I've had a crush on for the longest time. I've never actually been alone with him; Faye or one of his friends are always there too. But now we're alone, together.

And we're both half-naked.

I sit down on the other bed, wrapping my towel tighter around myself and shivering.

"Are you cold?" Adam asks, and without waiting for an answer, he gets up and grabs a sweatshirt from his suitcase, holding it out to me expectantly.

I stare at the hoodie like it's covered in slime. How many times have I daydreamed about wearing Adam Murray's hoodie? How many times have I daydreamed about being alone with him in a bedroom?

I take the hoodie, which somehow seems familiar to me, and shrug it on with a mumbled thanks. It smells like him, and I try not to let my inner fangirl embarrass me even more than it already has.

He sits back down on the other bed, facing me. There's a random show playing in the background, but it's not in English. I try not to squirm under his gaze.

"So," he starts, "that was cool what you did back there, saving that girl."

I didn't even see him at the party. I wonder where he was when he saw that.

I shift uncomfortably. "Thanks. It was kind of automatic, I guess."

"I almost forgot that you're a lifeguard. You were amazing."

I wrap my arms around myself and snuggle into the hoodie, then I notice why it's so familiar; it's one that Jenna always wore.

The realization slaps me right in the face. About two weeks ago he was literally sleeping with the girl responsible for making high school hell for me.

"Yeah," I start. "It's been a while since I've been in a pool. Oh, wait, your girlfriend pushed me into one at prom."

Oh my goodness. Oh my goodness. Did I *actually* say that? I've never said anything like that to him about Jenna before. Why did my mouth decide to do that now?

To his credit, he has the decency to look sheepish.

"She swore up and down that was an accident." He rubs the back of his neck with his hand, accentuating the lean muscles in his torso. "But I'm sorry it happened."

I'm taken aback for a second. He's never apologized or said anything about Jenna's behavior before. Not even when I went up to him at our eleventh-grade semiformal to say hi, and she "accidentally" spilled the entire punch bowl on me.

"Yeah, well, it was only one of many times she ruined high school for me."

Who is talking right now? Why am I suddenly brazen enough to badmouth Adam's ex-girlfriend to *Adam*?

He shifts, looking just as uncomfortable as I was earlier at the pool when everyone was staring at me.

"Maybe I should've said something more to her, but Jenna was jealous anytime I was even around you, never mind mentioned your name. It didn't help that you're always at the house. Plus . . ." His eyes roam my face, and I sit there, stunned as he moves closer to me, our knees basically touching in the space between the two beds. "You've always been the most gorgeous girl in the room, Lor, and Jenna knew that. I've always known that."

My heart leaps into my throat and impairs my breathing. Did I fall asleep in the hallway and I'm actually dreaming this right now?

Adam Murray told me I'm gorgeous.

I've had countless fantasies about him saying something like that to me.

"I know you probably don't believe me when I say that, but it's true."

Is he moving closer to me?

Before either of us can decide what to say or do next, the door swings open, and Kellan saunters in.

I jump off the bed like I've been caught doing something wrong and move away from Adam.

"Hey, Lor, what are you doing here?" he asks me, apparently completely oblivious that I walked in on him and Faye earlier.

My eyes dart nervously at Adam before I answer. "Oh, I was waiting for Faye to get back since I forgot the room key. Did you see her on your way up?"

I subtly nod my head, waiting for him to catch on.

His eyes widen for a fraction of a second before he realizes that I know where he was and what I want him to say.

"Yes. Yeah. I passed right by her when I was walking to the room."

I back toward the door, eager to get out of here before Adam asks any questions.

"Great, I'll be going then. Have a good night!"

I scramble out the door and down the hall to my room, checking behind me to make sure the coast is clear before I scan my key card.

The bathroom light is on and there's a cool breeze filling the room from the open balcony sliding door.

"Really, Faye?" I call out.

"What?" She opens the bathroom door in her pajamas, hair wet from her shower. The room fills with the scent of her pineapple shampoo.

"Couldn't you have put a sign on the door so I wouldn't get a surprise when I walked in?"

I plop down on my bed, which is still neatly made from this morning, so I know Faye kept her business on her own bed.

"Oh shit," she laughs. "I thought I heard the door open and close." She throws me my moisturizer that she was using and sits on her bed.

I catch it and set it down on the nightstand. "Seriously. Can we agree to put up the 'do not disturb' sign so I don't get a surprise show every night?"

She runs her fingers through her hair to brush it. "Okay, okay. Sorry, that was inconsiderate of me. But Lor—wow—it was so good. Better than last time, even. We rushed over here so fast I forgot my flip-flops down at the party. I've only got one pair left now! Wait, why are you in Adam's hoodie?"

I look down at the hoodie I've completely forgotten about, surprised I'm still in it.

I tell her about what happened with Adam, and she listens with rapt attention, and when I'm done, she jumps on my bed and tackles me with a hug.

"You are the best friend *ever*!" she exclaims, squeezing the life out of me.

"Yeah, yeah." I laugh. "Just remember the sign! And if you're trying to not get caught, be more discreet next time."

She sits up and salutes me. "You got it."

EIGHT

Day Two of Cuba

Faye

"What are you doing here, Faye?" My brother's irritated voice greets me as I stroll past him into his room, leaving him to close the door behind me.

"It's ten thirty, and none of you have come down for breakfast yet. I'm bored." I sit on a person-shaped lump on the bed and bounce up and down.

"Ow, Faye!" comes a muffled voice from beneath the covers. "Okay! Okay! I'm up! Get off me."

Victorious smile on my face, I shift off Kellan and stroll to the sliding door.

"We've only got thirty more minutes until the breakfast buffet closes. Let's go!" I rip open the curtains to let the sunlight in only to be met with two irritated groans, and a pillow thrown at me, courtesy of Kellan.

Adam drops onto his bed, his body language and facial expression screaming his boredom. "Remember how you promised not to bother us this week? It's day two, and we're not off to a good start."

"Yeah, why aren't you off annoying Lori?" Kellan stands to stretch, and I try not to ogle his shirtless body.

I wave my hand noncommittally. "She and Dean went snorkeling. He said he asked if you guys wanted to join."

That gets my brother's attention, and he sits up straight. "He went with Lori?"

Geez, what's his deal?

"Yeah, remember, bro?" Kellan grabs the first shirt his hand touches in the messy suitcase on the floor and slips it on. "We all said no so we wouldn't cockblock him."

I struggle not to smile proudly at that. With us working together, those two will be all over each other by day five.

"At least they're not wasting an entire day sleeping like you peop—"

I don't even get to finish my statement before my brother strides past me and into the bathroom. The door slams shut behind him.

I turn to Kellan. "You'd think he'd be less of a rude, grumpy child in Cuba, right?"

Kellan laughs, searching through his suitcase for his swim trunks, then comes up behind me and plants a sweet kiss on my neck.

I only enjoy it for a second before reminding myself that he's not my boyfriend, and my oblivious brother is a measly few feet away.

I shove him away from me and turn to face him.

Adam is right there! I mouth to him.

He puts his hands back on my waist and pulls me closer toward him.

I don't care, he mouths back, leaning in and giving me a proper kiss that spins my whole world upside down.

Somehow, even though I'm lost in all things Kellan, I hear the bathroom door handle turning. I automatically shove Kellan's chest with both hands and step away from him.

He's still wearing that stupid grin when my brother walks out of the bathroom, and I feel like hitting him and kissing him all at the same time.

My brother looks back and forth between the two of us with that harsh expression, making my heart beat faster than it already was. Did he see anything? Does he know?

Adam releases a long-suffering exhale. "Are you guys going to stand there all day or get ready so we can go?"

Kellan and I share a confused glance, but he recovers first. "Well, you took forever in there."

Kellan shoves him playfully as he walks past and locks himself in the bathroom.

I prop my hand on my hip. "Are you going to be in a foul mood this whole trip?"

My brother ignores me and walks to the door.

I'll take that as a big fat *yes*.

"Where are you going?"

He doesn't even turn to look at me. "Wake up Alessio and Dylan."

I huff and sit on his bed. I'd say Adam's not a morning person, but really, he's not a morning, afternoon, or night person. At least not when I'm around.

I hear him open the door, but it closes quickly, as if he changed his mind. Suddenly he's standing right in front of me.

"If you're going to sleep with guys, at least go to their rooms. You locked Lori out, and she was waiting in the hall for you to finish for who knows how long."

Lori told me about running into Adam, but she thought he believed her when she told him she forgot her key.

"There was no guy." I try to act indignant. "Lor told you what happened."

He rolls his eyes. "Yeah, because Lori's a fantastic liar. Even Kellan, like usual, tried covering for you by saying he saw you come up the stairs, but obviously he saw the guy leave your room. I'm not stupid. Try thinking about others sometimes, Fayanna."

Did Kellan say that? Or is that what Adam assumed happened? The angry and disappointed look my brother saves only for me sears into my brain, and my chest tightens. He turns around then pauses, looking at me before saying, "And on that note, stop flirting with Kellan. It's weird and gross, and it makes everyone uncomfortable."

My heart speeds up. "I flirt with all your friends."

"Yeah, but Dylan's like your brother, and Alessio has a girlfriend. Kellan's the only one who'd actually take you seriously, and the thought of you and my best friend together makes me want to stab myself in the eye with a rusty fork. *Especially* after what happened with Zach. So quit it."

His words are a kick in the stomach, but still, I force myself to ask, "Why would it be so bad if Kellan and I got together?"

His eyebrows draw together and his head rears back like I've just asked him the most ridiculous question with the most obvious answer. "Faye, you go through guys like most people go through socks—" he holds up a hand when I open my mouth to argue with him "—not judging, I literally don't care, I'm just stating facts." He drops his hand when I relax my defensive stance. "The point is, he's my best friend, not a fling, and when shit goes sideways, I don't want to have to be in the middle. He'll always be at the house; you'll always be around each other. That shit is awkward, and I don't like it. Plus, last time you dated one of my best friends, you made him hate my guts to the point where he crosses the road to avoid walking past me. He still won't return my calls. So don't go there and ruin my friendship with Kellan, got it?"

And without waiting for a response, he leaves me completely speechless as the door slams closed behind him.

Well, that answers that question. I wonder what Adam would do if he found out I've already gotten with Kellan. He's pissed just *thinking* about it. How pissed would he be if he learned the truth? But it's different with Kellan. It's not like it was with Zach, but I don't think Adam would believe me if I told him that. I don't want to drive this wedge deeper between us, and that's exactly what will happen if he finds out about me and Kellan, I'm sure of it. At least for now he doesn't suspect Kellan, or we'd both be screwed.

—

By the time everyone is up and ready to go, we've missed the breakfast buffet so we get lunch instead.

Even though there are two different beaches on either side of the resort, my brother *insists* on going to the one that's the farthest from our rooms.

We're lying in a row on beach chairs. Dylan's beside me, then Kellan, then Alessio. At the very end and farthest from me, where he can pretend that I'm not here, is Adam.

Kellan's waving to someone in the distance, and I follow his line of sight to spot the three girls everyone was hanging out with at the foam party. My eyes narrow, following their path as they walk up to us like we've all been best friends forever. An image of the tall girl in the middle with her toned arms wrapped around Kellan flashes through my mind, and I try to push it away.

I'm the one he went back with last night, and that fills me with a stupid sense of pride, especially as I watch the ridiculously pretty girl hug Kellan and press up against him.

My nostrils flare in annoyance at Kellan, at her, and especially at myself.

Kellan is not your boyfriend. Kellan is not your boyfriend.

Then why do I feel like ripping Kellan's hand off as he places it on her bare hip when they're pulling out of the hug?

Her friends are talking to Dylan, Alessio, and Adam, and the boys are lapping up the attention. The other two girls are just as pretty and have a similar beautiful shade of warm brown skin as the one talking to Kellan.

I try very hard not to shoot daggers at them with my eyes.

The one Kellan was flirting with yesterday is in a bright-yellow bikini. It's doing a great job catching Kellan's attention, and suddenly I wish I had one.

"Hey, Faye!" Dylan gets my attention. "Come say hi to these girls we met yesterday!"

I trudge through the sand over to them and school my expression into one of mild disinterest.

"This is Priyasha, Anaya, and Kiara," he tells me, and I smile and introduce myself, trying to be as friendly as possible.

Priyasha has full lips that seem to always be curved in a smile. Her brown hair has caramel highlights, and her presence is one I instinctively know fills a room. She laughs at something Alessio says, and even I feel the positive energy radiating from her.

Anaya is quieter and shorter than her friend, with curly black hair that ends before her shoulders, and a body even curvier than mine. She listens as the guys talk, but her eyes keep flitting around the beach as if looking for someone.

Kiara is the one in the yellow bikini being all friendly with Kellan, and I try not to glare at her. Her black hair is long and shiny, and her warm brown eyes seem to be inviting. Even though

I want to hate her based on appearance alone, she actually seems pretty nice. It's not her fault Kellan won't be exclusive with me.

Wait, *what*?

Why did I just think that?

Kellan and I have never talked about exclusivity before. Do I really want that with him or am I just jealous he's not paying attention to me? An icy shiver snakes down my spine. Is that what this is? Am I jealous? Over *Kellan*?

"Where's Dean?" Anaya asks, twirling a piece of hair around her finger.

Is Anaya into Dean or is she just curious? Is she into one of the other guys?

I glance at the four boys. Kiara is all over Kellan. My brother is ew. Dylan is good-looking and has the whole badass-tattoo-sleeve thing going for him, but he's annoying. And Alessio is cute if you're into pretty boys with baby faces, but he has a girlfriend.

"He went on a date with my best friend Lori," I answer before anyone else can, not so subtly signaling to her that Dean is off-limits.

"It wasn't a date," my brother cuts in.

I press my molars together. Adam is such a cynic. It is *so* a date and there's no need to tell Anaya otherwise.

We talk to the other girls for a while, and I realize that they're really nice, which is annoying. Now I don't have a justifiable reason to hate them other than the fact they're flirting with the boys that Lori and I are flirting with.

They're all nineteen and from Ontario too, but they live about eight hours away from us. They're in Cuba with some other friends who went to the other beach today. When I ask why the girls didn't go with their friends, Priyasha tells me it's because they wanted to go tubing, and all the resort's activities start from this beach.

"Tubing sounds fun, we should all go." Kellan sends Kiara his award-winning smile, and I have this overwhelming urge to punch all his teeth in.

"Yes, that would be so fun! Should we wait for Dean to get back?" Anaya asks, eyeing the open ocean for the boats used to bring people back from snorkeling.

"Yeah, we should wait for him." Kiara lifts a shoulder like she's indifferent, but there's a sly expression on her face. "But they only take seven people at a time, so it would have to be me, Kellan, Dean, Dylan, Adam, Anaya, and Priyasha." She shrugs at me and Alessio. "Sorry, you two."

Alessio and I glance at each other. She doesn't sound the least bit sorry.

Smart. Leave out the girl and the dude with the girlfriend. Maybe she's not that nice after all.

Kellan says something to Kiara, and she giggles.

"No!" I announce before I can think it through. "Why wait? Let's all go now. I'm sure they'll make an exception for eight people. No need to wait for Dean."

"But—" Anaya starts, but I interrupt her, hooking my arm through hers like we're fifth graders skipping to recess.

"No time like the present!" I tell her, leading her toward the tent where the activity sign-ups are.

I glance back to see everyone following, with Kellan and Kiara walking side by side and laughing at some stupid thing Kellan probably said.

My hands tighten into fists.

—

As I predicted, they make an exception for eight people. It wasn't even a big deal.

We're on a little boat that's towing the tube out to sea. It's basically a big yellow tube that looks like a banana, and you sit on it one behind another and hold on to the strap on the tube in front of you so you don't fly off once the boat moves.

We're far out when the boat comes to a stop. We put on our life jackets and one at a time climb onto the banana tube. Somehow, I end up near the end, with Kellan in front of me and Dylan behind me. Kiara, of course, ends up right in front of Kellan, and I swear, if I hear her giggle at another one of his pointless jokes, I'm kicking them both off this banana.

I'm too busy scowling to notice that the boat is moving, dragging the banana behind it, and the momentum causes me to half land on Dylan.

"If you wanted to get closer to me, all you had to do was ask, Faye," he jokes, flicking my nose, and I elbow him in his life jacket–covered chest before scooting back up into position.

Soon I lose track of time and let myself give in to how much fun I'm having. The bouncing of the tube makes me squeal and grab on tighter, while the ocean spray soaks me from head to toe.

But then we take a sharp turn and I notice Kellan place a steadying hand on Kiara's waist, and I see red.

I don't take a second to think. When the boat turns again, the banana follows suit, and I hook my hands in the straps of Kellan's life jacket and lean the opposite way from the turn. Together, we fly off the tube and land in the water.

I pop up for air and roll my neck. Hitting the water hurt a lot more than I thought it would.

Somehow, the entire banana didn't flip over with us, and the boat goes farther away before looping back around to get us.

"What the hell, Fayanna?" Kellan wipes the water from his eyes and splashes water at me.

I splash water right back at him. "What?"

"Why did you throw us off?"

He's so . . . *ugh*.

"I was trying to throw myself off to escape your pathetic flirting with Kiara, but I guess the universe decided you needed to go for a swim too."

I send him my best scowl, but Kellan just shoots me that stupid smile he has when he thinks he knows something.

"You're jealous."

I roll my eyes at him. "Am not."

I *so* am.

"Why can't you just admit you're jealous and that you *like me*?" Kellan's knowing grin widens even more, as if that was possible.

"Because I don't *like you*," I say, burying the part of me that knows I'm lying. "Why would I like an asshole like you who flirts with anything that moves?"

Kellan swims closer to me. His hair is messy and curled in an undeniably sexy way, his dark eyes twinkling with mischief. "Because I make you laugh, I'm great in bed, and I'm ridiculously good-looking."

I focus on treading water, willing myself not to give in to him. "More like ridiculous-looking."

"Just admit you like me."

"And if I did?" I challenge, my heart beating faster, secretly hoping he'll give me an answer I want.

He's serious for a second, but then his full lips twist into a victorious grin. "Then I'm right, like always."

I splash him with water, ignoring the feeling of my heart deflating, as the boat pulls up beside us.

He is such a jerk. I have no idea why I like him.

There's no escaping it, though. Jealousy has laid it all out for me. I actually *like* Kellan and want to be more than his readily available secret booty call. But there's no way he feels the same way. He basically said as much a few minutes ago, and he's already back at it with Kiara, making a joke about how he fell off the tube.

Dylan helps me back onto the banana, and I vow to ignore Kellan for the rest of this dumb activity, and hopefully the rest of this trip.

Otherwise, I'll do something stupid, like tell him I want to be with him, and not only ruin this trip, but also my life.

NINE

Day Two of Cuba

Lori

Something's changed since last night. I'm letting my guard down a bit, so I don't feel quite as awkward around Dean now.

I mean, I dumped a carton of yogurt on him at breakfast this morning, but that was an accident! Plus, he was a good sport about it and laughed it off, so I don't think my face turned *as* red as it might have.

We hang out and talk in the shade until it's our turn to go snorkeling. The boat they use is a tiny, special kind of boat that mostly uses wind power instead of an engine, and the part we sit on is an elevated mesh net, so we can feel the water underneath us. Our combined weight makes the mesh dip a little in the middle, pulling us toward each other until we're touching almost everywhere. I attempt to focus on the cool splashes of water instead of the heat from everywhere Dean's body touches mine, but it's *very* hard. He catches me staring at the part of his thigh that's pressed up against mine, and I quickly glance away, praying my face isn't bright red.

We make small talk until the boat comes to a stop. The resort is nothing but a tiny speck in the distance, and the water is a more vibrant aquamarine than it was near the shore. There are a bunch of similar boats all spread out in the same area, and a lot of people are already in the water.

On my hands and knees, I lean over the edge of the boat, which is almost flush with the water's surface, and peer into the ocean. Through the crystal clear water, I see millions of fish swimming around.

Our tour guide and boat driver, Matias, tells us that fish love bread, which is news to me, and he pulls out a bag. He breaks off a piece and throws it into the water near me, and instantly, a *swarm* of fish attacks the piece of bread.

Startled, I yelp and leap back, conveniently falling right onto Dean's lap.

From what I can see, these aren't the cute little bright tropical fish you see in pictures. Some of them are, but most are gray and huge.

I've never seen anything like it in my life.

"Having second thoughts?" Dean teases me, his hands burning me where they're resting on my thighs.

I'm still sitting on him like a total freak.

"Uh, no. No way." I scramble off his lap and out of his personal space, even though he didn't seem to mind.

"They won't bite," Matias reassures me, throwing some more bread in the water, and I watch, fascinated, as swarms come up to the surface.

"Let's go then." Dean's smile is wide as he puts on the goggles, snorkel, and flippers that Matias gave us earlier.

He sits on the edge of the boat, his feet dangling in the water as he peers back at me, his eyes twinkling with excitement.

"Are you coming?"

I've never been this close to enormous fish before. Some are bigger than my arm.

"Um, yeah. In a second."

Dean slips into the water and bobs beside me. "What are you waiting for?"

I have no idea. Maybe for there to be fewer fish in this general area?

I sit on the side of the boat like Dean had earlier and let my feet dangle in the water.

"I'm waiting to . . . acclimate."

Dean raises an amused eyebrow, his hands on either side of me grabbing the boat, his arms caging me in as we bob with the ocean current.

"Acclimate? Is that your way of saying you're scared?"

This is ridiculous. It's just fish. Why am I being such a baby about it?

Matias throws more bread into the water beside Dean, and he's swarmed by dozens of large gray fish.

I react and flinch away from the water, my legs automatically kicking Dean right in his broad chest, pushing him out into the water.

Oh my goodness. *Get it together, Lori!*

I almost snap at Matias that he's not helping, but I don't want to seem like even more of a total scaredy-cat, especially not in front of Dean.

"I—I'm so sorry," I sputter as Dean laughs and swims back to me, placing his hands on either side of me again.

"If you don't want to come in, you don't have to. I mean, you jump in front of a moving car to get away from me, you kick me in the chest to get out of snorkeling with me; geez, you'd think I'd take a hint, right?"

I know he's teasing me, but shame burns through me, and

my face heats despite the coolness of the water lapping at my feet.

"That's not true!"

The current of the ocean pushes him closer to me, and I can feel the heat radiating off his body.

"Lor, it's okay. Really."

There's sincerity in his voice and authenticity in his gaze. It hits me that he's letting me choose. He came all this way and still doesn't care if I don't do it. If Faye were here, she'd push me in.

I can hear the laughter and excitement of the other snorkelers surround us. Why am I making this a big deal? There are tons of people doing this.

Filled with resolve, I grab the snorkeling equipment Matias gave me. "I want to."

Matias throws more bread right beside us, and it takes all I have not to kick Dean again. I put on the flippers, snorkel, and goggles, take a steadying breath, and slide into the ocean beside Dean. Before I can change my mind, I stick my head in the water to look around and—

Oh, wow.

It's beautiful.

There are fish of all colors and sizes, but still mostly gray ones, and they're all swimming around me, with me, under me. It's amazing.

I pop out of the water and take the snorkel out of my mouth, looking for Dean. He's where I left him, his goggles pushed up on top of his head, already looking at me with a wide smile.

"Have you seen this?!" I ask him, pointing down toward the water.

He shakes his head, then slips his goggles and snorkel into place and sticks his face right in the water as he flips onto his stomach.

I do the same, and again I'm taken aback by the sheer surrealness of it all. If they're touching me, I can't tell, but there must be hundreds just within twenty feet of me. Someone grabs my hand, and I find Dean floating right beside me, looking around with wonder like I am.

We hold hands and slowly swim around, occasionally pointing out different fish to each other. Even though Dean and I are only an arm's width apart, plenty of fish swim between us.

I don't know how much time passes, but eventually Dean tugs my hand, and we pop out of the water to hear Matias calling us to come back. I'm reluctant as we swim to the boat; I wish I hadn't wasted all that time being a chicken earlier.

Dean helps me onto the boat and lifts himself up after me with ease. Taking off our equipment, we tell Matias we had fun as he steers us toward the resort.

I try not to stare at Dean's profile as he lazily tilts his head back to soak up the sun. His cheeks are already getting a little red. I'm glad we did this—I'm glad I did this, but I'm even happier it was with him.

"Thanks for making me do this," I blurt.

Dean raises a lazy eyebrow. "I didn't make you do anything. You did it because you wanted to."

I contemplate his words and realize he's right. The smile on my face grows wider.

—

We thank and tip Matias as we hop off the boat and head over to the beach chairs where we left all our stuff. Dean runs to the bar to grab us some water since it's superhot out in the sun, and I sit on my beach chair to reapply sunscreen.

When I check my phone, I find a text from Mom.

I emailed you some links to MCAT prep courses. Pick one you want to take this summer.

A huff escapes me. Typical. My parents can't even go a day without getting all giddy about med school. Why couldn't this wait until I got home?

I try to keep my breathing calm and press my luck as I type back my response. *Med school isn't for another 4 years. Don't you think it's a little too early to take an entrance test course??*

Her response is quick. *It's never too early for prep courses.*

I was having a good—no—a *great* day with Dean, and my parents can't even wait a week to cram med school down my throat. And they're completely ignoring the fact that I don't even *want* to go to med school. Sure, they dismissed my declaration about wanting to take a year off, but deep down under their own belief of what's best for me, they know it's what I really want.

I text her, *I'll think about it and let you know.*

But I won't. I'll get home, and she'll inform me she's already enrolled me in a course she likes, and I'll take it without complaining because that's what's expected of me.

"I leave you for two minutes and you're pouting. It's illegal to be upset on vacation, you know," Dean says, handing me a cool water bottle.

I slip my phone back into my bag. "Even here you can't escape overbearing parents pushing you to be a perfectionist like them."

He sits beside me with a thoughtful frown and pushes his sunglasses onto his head. "The med school thing again?"

Even though I told him last night, I'm still surprised he remembers.

"She's signing me up for an MCAT course. No one cares that I don't want to be a doctor." The words come out on their own, and it registers somewhere in the back of my mind how easy it is to talk to Dean.

He frowns, and I realize that's the first time I've told someone I don't want to go to med school. "Well, what do you want to be?"

I'm taken aback. What do I want to be? I want to travel, but then what?

"I don't think anyone's ever asked me that question, not even Faye. Everyone just assumes I'll go to med school and be a doctor like my parents."

Dean gives me a sad smile, like I'm missing out on something. "Do you always do what you're told?"

Yes.

"No."

He raises an eyebrow.

"I don't!" I defend myself, knowing I'm lying but suddenly wishing I wasn't.

His sad smile transforms into a mischievous smirk.

"Prove it."

Prove it? How can I? I always do what I'm told; I hate letting people down.

But looking into Dean's hypnotizing eyes, bluer than the ocean behind him, suddenly all I can think about is proving it to him, and more importantly, to myself.

TEN

Day Two of Cuba

Faye

By the time we get back to the beach after tubing, we're all tired from the sun and head to our respective rooms to shower and get ready for dinner.

My shower is quick, and I'm left in an empty room with nothing but my thoughts and some soft Spanish music playing from the television. Lori's taking forever to come back from her date with Dean, and I need someone to talk to about my stupid crush on Kellan. I actually *like* Kellan. *Kellan Reyes*. The annoying boy who pulls my ponytail when he sits behind me and knows just the right buttons to push to get under my skin. The easygoing boy who's never been in a fistfight in his life, except for the time he punched Connor Davis when I was in eleventh grade because he shoved me and called me a whore, and Kellan witnessed it. Kellan got suspended for that, but we never spoke about it again, and Connor gave me a wide berth afterward.

A knock on my door breaks through my thoughts, and I open it to see Dylan standing there in a loose T-shirt and shorts.

"Everyone's sleeping and I'm bored. I figured you would be too." He shrugs as a way of explanation, and I let him pass me into the room.

"You were right; I am bored. I have no idea when Lori's getting back." I close the door and sit on Lori's bed as he lounges on mine.

Dylan uses the remote to flip through the television channels before giving up and putting it back on the music video channel.

"So . . ." he starts, setting the remote down. "What had your panties in a twist today? And why did you throw Kellan off the banana tube?"

I sputter. "Wh—You—I have no idea what you're talking about."

Dylan quirks an eyebrow. "I was sitting right behind you, Faye. I saw you throw him off."

My mouth snaps shut. He's right. He would've seen that. *Shit.* What do I even say to that?

"I get that Kellan usually pisses you off, but you were extra uptight today." Dylan continues, stretching on the bed and settling in. "What gives?"

My heart pounds in my chest for a few moments, and a heavy silence fills the room, causing Dylan to sit up.

"Out with it," he prompts, but I hesitate.

Should I tell him? I need someone to talk to or I'm going to explode, and Lori's not here right now.

I narrow my eyes at Dylan as I consider it. I trust him; that's never been an issue. He's always had my back like a brother even when my actual brother didn't. He's the one I called in tenth grade when I was drunk off my ass and needed a ride home from a party without my parents finding out. After the third time, he'd asked why I never called Adam for help, since according to him that's a brother's job. When I shot him a raised eyebrow, I think he pieced it together himself, because he pressed his lips together and helped me into the car. I stopped calling him after that, but he's never ratted on me or told Adam, so I'm confident he'll keep quiet about this if I tell him.

I pick my words carefully. "What would you say if I told you I, theoretically, liked Kellan? Like, *like-liked* him."

He tilts his head at me. "Theoretically?"

"Yes."

"Then I would say that you're stupid. Theoretically."

Not helpful.

"Okay, and what if I told you I—again, theoretically—slept with him a few times? Theoretically."

His eyes widen. "Fucking *shit*. Really, Faye?"

That's not encouraging. "Theoretically," I remind him.

"Do you even understand the word 'theoretically'?"

"What would you say?"

"I would say you're *really* stupid."

A long-suffering sigh escapes me. "Dylan, I need advice here. What do I do?"

He bites back a stupid, knowing smirk. "Oh, so it's *not* really theoretical?"

"Stop being a smart-ass," I groan. "I don't know why I thought coming to you for advice would be a good idea. You barely have two brain cells to rub together."

"Hey, these two brain cells got me into the University of Toronto. It's quality over quantity."

Huffing in frustration, I flop onto my back on the bed.

"Seriously, Dylan. I'm screwed here. I need some male perspective."

"Well, my male perspective is also saying that you're screwed. Does Adam know?"

"If you're not going to help, I'm kicking you out—"

"Okay, okay." The laughter in his voice dies. "Don't kick me out, I'm sorry. It's just easier joking about it than facing the reality that Adam is going to lose his shit if—when—he finds out."

"I know." My voice comes out small, and I can't meet his eyes. "We already have a shitty relationship, and he won't be happy about me and Kellan."

"Well, if you're worried about Adam, then what do you need advice on? How to stay away from Kellan? How to hide it better?"

I think about it. Do I want to stay away from him? Do I want to get over it? Do I want to figure out how to compartmentalize my feelings for him and keep it strictly about sex? Cut it off completely?

The revelation hits me at once. "I want advice on how to make Kellan like me."

"Faye . . ." He groans, and I don't need to hear him tell me it's a terrible idea that probably won't end well.

"I know, I know. I'm stupid. Just tell me what I should do."

"Right, right, right." He pauses, hopefully coming up with a perfect solution. "What have you been doing so far?"

Being crazy and jealous. "Oh, you know, just playing it cool."

He snorts. "As evidenced by your actions today."

I chuck a pillow at him, and it hits the side of his head before falling harmlessly to the floor.

"Real mature, Faye." He picks the pillow up and throws it back at me, so I clutch it to my chest as he says, "Have you tried just telling him how you feel? Simple but effective."

"What? No! I can't do that!"

"Why not?"

Because it's obvious he doesn't feel the same way about me.

"I can't just tell him that! And after all that with Kiara today?

It's obvious he doesn't see me the same way. I'll look like an idiot if I admit I like him while he doesn't feel the same . . ."

I toss the pillow I was clutching behind me as thoughts form quickly in my mind.

"Oh no," Dylan says, "I know that face. You're about to have a terrible idea."

I ignore him and sit up straighter. "I realized my feelings when I saw him with Kiara, and I was jealous. I have to make him see me the same way I see him. I have to *make* him realize what he's missing."

"Don't say it—" Dylan says at the same time I exclaim, "I have to make him jealous!"

Dylan frowns. "Faye. If you're planning on going through with this, and ignoring everything that happened last time with Zach, then just tell Kellan how you feel."

Kellan's words from earlier come back to me. *Just admit you like me.*

And if I did?

Then I'm right, like always.

I shake the memory from my mind. No. I can't tell him I like him, because it'll only end in smugness from Kellan for being "right," and humiliation for me. Plus, if I tell him I like him and he doesn't feel the same, it's going to change *everything* between the two of us. No more late-night talks or surprise donuts, and definitely no more kissing and touching. I'm not making the first move, not unless I'm confident he feels the same way.

"If he sees me with other guys, he'll realize what he's missing."

I didn't recognize that I really liked Kellan until I started getting jealous. If he sees me with other guys and realizes that I'm not sitting around pining for him, then he'll get jealous and realize he wants me too, right? It always works in the movies.

"You can't tell anyone, Dyl. Promise me."

Dylan stares at me for a few beats before he sighs, the fight seeping out of his tense shoulders. "If you're going to commit to this and I can't stop you, then fine. I have your back, you know that."

Squealing, I launch myself off the bed, tackling him in a hug.

"You're the best, Dyl!"

He laughs and shoves me off him. "Yeah, yeah. But if you're going through with this, you need to figure out what you're going to tell Adam. I'm not telling him, but he's going to find out eventually."

"I know, I know." I frown, straightening my clothes, which have gotten all twisted. "I don't want to think about Adam right now. Let's figure out one thing at a time, since there's no point in telling Adam anything if Kellan doesn't even like me."

Dylan purses his lips but doesn't say anything. He can't be happy about the situation I put him in, where he has to keep things from Adam and Kellan, but I can count on him to keep this secret.

—

Eventually Dylan goes back to his own room, and Lori returns from her date with Dean. All it takes is a knowing smirk from me and her entire face lights up in a blush.

"Nothing happened!" she exclaims.

My smile widens. "I didn't say anything."

"It's written all over your face." She dumps her beach bag on her bed. "I had a lot of fun. We swam with fish, and they were huge."

I sit up and lower the volume on the television. "And how was the kiss?"

She stumbles, looking back at me with wide eyes. "There was no kiss! It wasn't a date."

Deflated, I lean back against my headboard. "Boo, it totally was. Are you sure he didn't make a move to kiss you and you ruined it with your awkwardness?"

"No, I didn't—" She pauses, her lips pursed as she thinks. "No, I'm positive I didn't misread the situation. There was no maybe-kiss that I ruined."

"Perfect, you have five more days to get it done."

I can't see her face since her back is to me, but I'm sure she's rolling her eyes. She zips her luggage back up and turns to face me, shower supplies in hand.

"Yeah, yeah. What's going on with Kellan?"

I school my face into disinterest. "Nothing's going on with Kellan. I'm just taking it a day at a time."

She raises an eyebrow. "Really? Because we ran into Dylan in the lobby, and he told me you threw Kellan off the banana tube in a jealous rage."

Dammit, Dylan. "I did no such thing."

"Mm-hmm," she replies, totally not believing me, heading into the bathroom, and closing the door behind her.

I'm not going to tell Lori about liking Kellan and my plan to make him jealous. She's my best friend and we usually tell each other everything, but she won't approve. It's one thing to just sleep with my brother's best friend a few times, but to make it a regular occurrence? To make it official? There are too many things I haven't thought through, and Lori's always so practical and is going to point them out, the first being how and when I should tell Adam. She's always so perfect—always so considerate. She's going to make me second-guess the genius of my plan, and I'm not ready for that. One thing at a time. Get Kellan to realize how insanely amazing I am and that he should lock it down, and then I'll worry about the rest.

—

Walking into the pink party at the red-wristbands-only pool is like being transported into a cotton candy wonderland. The music is loud and upbeat, with people crowding around talking, dancing, and laughing. The pool water is a crystal blue, and I have no idea how they cleaned up the foam from last night so perfectly, but there are no traces of it anywhere. Almost the entire surface of the pool is covered in little pink floating balls the size of golf balls, and there are pink blow-up floats strewn about. All the lights are different colors of pink, and everyone is in a pink swimsuit.

Lori's in a pink-and-white tie-dye bikini top with jean shorts over her bottoms, and I'm in a baby-pink string bikini.

My eyes automatically scan the area for Kellan, and I find him in the middle of the pool on a hot-pink flamingo floaty with Kiara on the one next to him. My face heats as they laugh and flirt, splashing each other and throwing the little pink balls at each other.

"There's Dean!" Lori waves when he spots us.

"Hey," Dean says when he reaches us, his cheeks newly sunburnt.

"Hey," Lori and I greet in sync.

"Where is everyone?" I ask, not seeing my brother anywhere.

Dean scans the pool. "Alessio's over there talking to Priyasha and Anaya. Dylan and your brother were at the bar when I last saw them, and Kellan's trying to get lucky with Kiara over there in the pool."

He says it innocently, but his words are like a punch in the gut.

I try not to let it bother me, but it's obvious that I'm not paying attention to whatever Dean and Lori are talking about. Why am I even trying to make him like me if he's into Kiara? His stupid grin pops into my mind and my heart softens.

A familiar face at the other end of the pool comes into view. Darius. I'm not interested in him, especially since he got my name wrong, but he's near the bar in plain sight of Kellan and Kiara, and he's easy to flirt with.

"I'm going to the bar. See you later," I announce, interrupting whatever Lori was saying, and don't wait for a response before confidently sashaying over to Darius. He notices me immediately.

"Hey, Faith," he greets, his eyes appraising my body.

"It's *Faye*," I correct, and he smiles, clearly not remembering how last night played out.

"Of course, *Faye*. Can I get you a drink?"

Not exactly a big gesture since it's an open bar, but I put on my best flirty demeanor and nod as I sit beside him.

He orders me a fruity drink that's a little too sugary for my taste, but I still pretend to be enjoying myself, laughing at the appropriate time and giving him all the right cues. But the whole time, I'm subtly looking back at Kellan in the pool to see if he's noticed me so obviously flirting with Darius.

He hasn't.

Maybe we're too far out for Kellan to notice us. We need to get closer.

There's a chicken fight starting in the pool, where someone sits on someone else's shoulders and faces another pair, and they try to knock each other off into the pool. A plan forms in my mind.

"Hey, why don't we enter the chicken fight contest?" I say, pointing to where other people are already playing.

Darius follows my line of sight and sends me a confident smile. "If it means getting your legs wrapped around me, I'm in."

Forcing myself not to roll my eyes, I grab his hand and lead him toward the pool. We *coincidentally* pass right by Kellan and Kiara.

"Faye!" Kellan calls out, and I pause, pretending to look around like I don't know *exactly* where the voice is coming from. "Faye!" he calls again, and this time my eyes find his.

"Oh, hey guys," I say like I only just noticed them and haven't been staring at Kellan for the last twenty minutes.

Kiara looks less than thrilled that Kellan's stopped his flirting to talk to me, but she does nothing more than stand in the pool pouting with her arms crossed over her chest.

"Where are you off to?" Kellan asks.

"We're going to go win the chicken fight. Aren't we, Darius?" I put my hand on Darius's muscled arm, pressing myself closer to him and fighting the urge to glance at Kellan.

"You know it." Darius smiles confidently, dropping the hand that was holding mine to put his arm around me.

"Hey, why don't you guys enter too?" I exclaim like the thought has *just* crossed my mind. "It'll be fun!"

My eyes find Kiara's, as if issuing a challenge, and her brown eyes narrow.

Kellan starts, "Oh, I don't kn—"

"Let's do it," Kiara interrupts, never taking her gaze from mine. *Challenge accepted.*

"Great!" I say, my tone light. "See you there."

"May the best couple win," Kiara shoots back cheerfully.

As soon as we turn around, I let the fake smile slip from my face like Darius's arm.

"So, who was that girl?" Darius asks, glancing back as we walk toward the other end of the pool. "She's hot."

I glare at him, and he raises his hands, palms open, in an innocent gesture. "But, you know, you're hotter."

My eyebrows furrow. "Right."

The pool is large and irregularly shaped, and we're at the round end. There's a worker with a mic standing on the side of the pool, announcing the chicken fight currently taking place. The DJ is set up not too far from where we are, but it's not much louder since the speakers are spread out over the pool area.

After telling the announcer that Darius and I want to participate, we watch as the two couples in the pool try to knock the top person off the bottom person's shoulders and into the water.

"I'm going to grab another drink. Want one?" Darius offers, and I shake my head no.

Not even five seconds after he leaves, a dark presence appears beside me, and I stiffen.

"What are you doing?" Adam asks.

I glance at my brother, who's scowling at me. "Having fun. One of us might as well."

"Have you seen Kellan?" He slurs a little, and I eye him.

"Are you drunk?" I don't think I've *ever* seen my brother drunk. He rarely drinks.

"No," he says a bit too defensively.

Whatever. Scanning the pool, I find Kellan talking with Kiara, Alessio, and Priyasha, and point them out to Adam.

"How come Olivia didn't come?" I ask Adam, referring to Alessio's girlfriend of five years. Maybe he didn't invite her because he didn't want to see Jenna's cousin while actively trying to forget about Jenna. But surely Alessio would want her here.

"What? It's a guys' trip."

"Yeah, but then Ray and Freddy canceled. How come you didn't invite Olivia in their place? You've known her longer than Alessio has. You guys went to elementary school together."

He squints as if trying to focus. "What? Faye, you're asking too many questions. Don't do anything stupid." And with that he leaves me, heading toward Kellan and Alessio.

Clearly my brother drunk is even more useless than my brother sober.

"So, what's going on with you and Kellan?" Kiara's standing beside me in a metallic-pink bikini, looking out at the pool like she didn't say anything.

"I have no idea what you're talking about."

She faces me, one perfect eyebrow raised. "Right."

Is this where I'm supposed to tell her I like him and to back off? I'm not going to do that. I can't control who Kellan's with any more than he can control who I'm with. I want him to *choose* me. I want him to *want* to be with me, and telling Kiara to stay away from him won't do anything except tip my brother off to what's going on. I may not like that she's flirting with Kellan, but who am I to tell her to stop?

I'm spared from having to reply when Darius and Kellan appear at our sides, Darius holding a half-empty beer bottle.

They make small talk, but Kiara just stares at me like she has more to say and isn't happy.

"Hey, shorty!" says a loud voice on the microphone, the announcer looking right at me. "You're up!"

I pat Darius's arm. "Let's show 'em who's boss, Dar."

He doesn't seem to mind that I've just branded him with a new nickname as he smiles and sets his beer down somewhere. We stand beside the announcer, a guy in his early thirties with a shaved head who's wearing white pressed pants and a pink T-shirt with a name tag that reads "Omar."

"And who wants to face these two?" Omar asks into the microphone.

I brush my hair over my shoulder as there are some whistles and catcalls, and then Kiara yells, "We'll do it!"

She steps forward with Kellan a few feet behind her.

"You're usually my chicken fight partner at parties, Fayanna.

You sure you want to go up against the champ?" Kellan jokes, his tone light and flirty.

Despite being a little put off that he's not exhibiting any jealousy, I smile confidently at him. "You're about to find out what it feels like to lose. Come on, Dar."

As Darius and I jump into the pool, the large crowd cheers. Darius slips under the water, and when he stands, I'm lifted into the air. Seated on his shoulders, his hands on my thighs for support, we wait as Kiara and Kellan get into position as well.

"Best of three!" Omar announces. "Go!"

Kellan and Darius walk closer to each other, and Kiara and I grab onto each other's forearms. It's hard to keep balance sitting on Darius's shoulders while trying not to let Kiara, who has a height advantage on me, knock me into the pool. She digs her nails into my forearms with a force that tells me it has nothing to do with the game, and my competitive fire flares. The cheers from the crowd fade from my ears as I focus on trying to knock her smug face into the water. She shoves me, and I almost lose balance, but Darius rights me before I fall. Then, as we round on them, I grab Kiara's forearms and pull, and she falls sideways into the water.

The drunken crowd cheers, and Darius gives me a congratulatory high five. I glance over at Kellan, but he doesn't seem to mind me blatantly flirting with Darius. Kiara gets back on Kellan's shoulders, and before I know what's happening, I have an arm in my face and then I'm in the water.

I pop back up for air and Kiara's laughing with Kellan. Okay, she's *seriously* pissing me off. Darius helps me back onto his shoulders, and Kiara and I square off. We eye each other and there's an intense animosity in her eyes. She pulls my hair not even a second after we start, which is *so* against the unspoken rules. I push her off me, and our attacks become less and less like a friendly game, and more and more personal.

"Can you just lose already?" Kiara exclaims.

She pulls my hair again, and I've had it. We push and pull each other, and soon I lose my balance.

"Ahh!" Kiara and I both go airborne, landing in the water with our arms wrapped around each other.

"I can't believe you pulled my hair!" I say when we pop up for air.

Kiara doesn't react. She just covers her mouth with her hand.

"What?" I ask, looking around.

The crowd is silent for a moment, then there's cheering and whistling and more catcalls, and a drunk guy yells, "Take the rest off!"

Darius's eyes are trained directly on my chest, and I follow his gaze. I'm standing completely topless in the middle of the pool for all to see.

Great.

"What? You've never seen boobs before? Grow up!" I yell to no one in particular.

Somehow, I notice Kiara, who looks a bit too smug and satisfied. *She did this on purpose.* I was in a string bikini; it wouldn't be hard to pull off.

"Faye!" I turn as Kellan, who's now standing on the side of the pool with a concerned but amused grin, throws a towel at me.

I snatch it but don't make a move to cover up. Somehow, I feel like that would admit defeat to Kiara, and I'm nothing if not prideful. I walk out of the pool with as much confidence as I can muster, and only once I'm completely out do I wrap the towel around myself.

Everyone's still staring at me, so with a flourish of my arms, I announce, "Hope you enjoyed the show!" I'm met with more cheers and whistles, which just makes me laugh.

Kiara's glowering in the pool, and my smile widens even

more. *Ha!* Did she expect me to run off with my tail tucked between my legs? Clearly, she doesn't know who she's messing with. Fayanna Murray doesn't know the definition of shame.

"If you wanted to get naked, all you had to do was tell me, and we could've gone back to my room." Darius winks, and this time I actually roll my eyes.

"Don't get ahead of yourself," I tell him, fixing the towel so I don't need to hold it up.

"Are you okay, Faye?" Kellan asks as he approaches us.

I glance around at all the guys checking me out and realize this is a great opportunity to make him jealous.

"Never been better," I tell him, watching as a tall, tan guy comes up to me.

"Why haven't I been lucky enough to cross paths with you yet?" New Guy asks with a charming smile, and I turn to give him all my attention.

"Well, it looks like today is your lucky day," I shoot back, mentally reminding myself not to look at Kellan.

Fortunately, or unfortunately, depending on how you see it, I don't have to, because Kellan clears his throat over whatever New Guy is saying. "Okay, have fun, Faye," he says before turning to leave with Kiara.

I scowl. He's not jealous. Not in the slightest. He wasn't bothered by my flirting with Darius, and he doesn't care that all these guys are falling over themselves to talk to me. Obviously I know *why* they suddenly want to talk to me, but so should he. Doesn't he care about me? Even a little?

Suddenly, I don't want to talk to any of these guys. I don't even want to be at this party, surrounded by all these people having fun and laughing and flirting. The last thing I want to do is watch Kellan and Kiara swap spit and hear Kiara's stupid gloating in my mind.

When I tune in, New Guy is saying something about going to the bar, Darius is saying that we made a great team, and about four other guys are saying something to me that I don't care to remember.

"Maybe another time," I announce to them all before leaving to find Lori.

She's easy to spot, since she's with Dylan and Dean. The cousins make an eye-catching pair, both tall and broad-shouldered.

"Hey, Faye," she greets when she sees me, then pauses. "Are you not wearing clothes under that?"

I glance down at the towel. "Bottoms, yes. Top, no. Long story. But I forgot my key card, can I use yours?"

Lori glances around, presumably wondering if I'm heading back with Kellan since it's still early.

"Just me tonight," I tell her before she can ask. "I'm not really in the party mood. I'll let you in when you knock."

She frowns. "Is everything okay? Want me to come back with you?"

I eye Dean and Dylan, who are each taking a shot a few feet away from us. "Everything's fine. You stay, have fun. I just want some alone time."

I can tell from her face that she doesn't believe me, but I do just want to be alone. She reaches into the pocket of her jean shorts and pulls out her key card.

"If you change your mind, let me know."

I take the card from her and step backward. "I'm good. Thanks. Have fun. Do something I'd do." She laughs and shakes her head at my suggestive hand gestures before turning back to the cousins.

As soon as I'm in the room, I flop onto my bed and stare up at the ceiling. I was *so sure* my plan would work. It was simple. Make him jealous, and he'll realize that he's head over heels for me. Why isn't it working? He can't possibly like *Kiara* as more than a vacation hookup, right?

A loud knock at my door interrupts my thoughts. I can't believe Lori's already checking up on me.

"I told you," I proclaim as I open the door, "to go suck some di—"

It's not Lori. It's Kellan. Standing in front of my door with his sexy tousled pool hair and amused grin.

"Don't let me stop you from finishing that sentence."

Tucking the towel covering my chest more securely under my arms, I meet his deep-brown eyes and try to ignore the fluttering in my heart. "I was going to say, 'go suck some disgustingly fruity drink with a paper or reusable straw.' They're better for the environment, you know."

He arches an eyebrow. "Uh-huh. That was definitely what you were going to say." He pauses, studying me. "You look upset."

I do? "Oh. No, I'm just pissed because I left my last pair of flip-flops at the party." It's true, I did. That's three brand-new pairs of flip-flops gone before day three. "What are you doing here?" I can't stop the butterflies from spreading through my stomach. *He's here for me! Making him jealous worked!*

He rubs the back of his neck with his hand. "I saw you leave. I just wanted to make sure you're okay."

The flirty demeanor slips over me in an instant as I run my hand down his arm and step closer. "Me? I'm always okay. I'm sure you can help me feel bett—"

"Are you done yet, Kellan?" The voice makes me freeze.

Kiara appears from the stairwell, and I instantly step back from Kellan, clutching the towel closer like it can stop the hopeful swell in my heart from deflating. Did he bring her up to his room? And he made her wait in the stairwell like I wouldn't find out?

Kiara reaches us and stands beside Kellan as if they're some united front. "You said you'd only be a second," she continues, her whiney voice scraping against the inside of my skull. "I want to go back to the party."

The only thing stopping me from snapping that no one's holding a gun to her head and forcing her to be here is my interest in hearing Kellan's response.

He spares me a quick glance before telling Kiara, "Yeah, I'll be right there."

Apparently satisfied, Kiara gives me a once-over before turning and heading back down the stairs.

"Are you sure everything's okay?" he asks, a bit more solemnly than last time.

With my hope deflated, I put my hand on the door. "Yup. Don't let me stop you from having fun."

Before he can see my heart shatter, I step back into the room and close the door.

ELEVEN

Night Two of Cuba

Lori

We're only at the party for a few minutes when Faye marches off, and I'm left staring up at Dean and praying I'm not blushing.

"Is she okay?" Dean asks, looking confused but also concerned.

It was obvious she tuned out after Dean made that comment about Kellan trying to get lucky with Kiara in the pool. Her jealousy was practically radiating off her in waves, but I can't tell him she's jealous, so I say, "Yeah, she's fine."

Before I can think of something else to say, a group of guys run past us. They crash into me as they go by, and I lose my balance. Before I land on my face, Dean catches me, and his arms wrap around me like they belong there.

I'm out of breath, and I'm sure that being hyperaware of everywhere my half-naked body is pressed up against his isn't helping. Craning my head back to meet his eyes, I'm struck by the color. They're a hypnotizing blue, and from this close I can see the little rings of hazel I remember from last time. For a second, neither one of us moves. His eyes flit across my face and

I wonder if he's having trouble remembering to breathe also. He clears his throat and rights me before stepping back.

"Are you okay?"

The heat rushes over my face instantly. "Yeah, thanks. At some point you're going to have to stop coming to my rescue."

He laughs, and an easy smile brightens his features. "Nothing's wrong with needing rescuing every once in a while."

"Hey! You spilled my fucking beer!" A loud, angry voice rings out to us from near the bar, and we turn to see a wide-eyed Dylan looking up at a guy twice his size.

Dean looks over at his cousin, then back at me. "Like Dylan, for example, probably needs some rescuing."

I follow him over to where Adam, Dylan, and the other guy whose beer he apparently spilled are standing. The guy's rounding on Dylan, whose hands are raised like he can ward him off.

To call the guy large is an understatement—he's a mountain of solid muscle. Adam is tall and lean, and Dylan and Dean are both tall and have muscle, Dean more than Dylan, but none of them have a thing on Angry Dude. He looks like he could grab a cousin in each hand and take a bite out of their heads without breaking a sweat.

"I wasn't done drinking that beer!" Angry Dude is saying to Dylan, who's backed himself up against the bar.

"Relax, man, it was an accident," Adam says, looking from Angry Dude to his friend behind him.

Dylan continues, "The beers are free. I'll order you another one."

"But I wanted *that one*." The veins in Angry Dude's neck bulge, and my heart beats faster.

"Hey, why don't we all calm down?" Dean says to Angry Dude, somehow getting between him and Dylan and Adam.

Angry Dude looks Dean over as if sizing him up. "Why

don't *you* mind your own fucking business? This is between me, Tattoos, and Blondie over there."

"Terry, man, it's no big deal," Terry's friend says.

He isn't as large or intimidating as Terry, and is shorter than Dean, Dylan, and Adam, but he shows no fear as he places his hand on Terry's arm and tries to pull him back.

Terry shrugs him off easily, and his eyes remain laser focused on Dean. "No, I want to hit someone, and these two assholes are running around picking a fight with me. If they want a fight, they got one. I break my punching bag on the daily. Let's go."

I'm frozen in place. Should I do something? No one else is doing anything, but then again, half the people are drunk, want entertainment, or oblivious.

"There's no need for a fight," Dean says, his posture and tone calm. "We're all on vacation, why don't we have fun?"

I want to be closer to my friends, so I step over and put a hand on Dean's sculpted back to let him know I'm here with them. He acknowledges me with a glance, but unfortunately, so does Terry, and I basically shrink under his glare.

"This your girl? I'll beat her up too."

Protests sound from both Dylan and Adam, but Dean's voice is the deadliest.

"Hey!" Dean warns, his cool demeanor instantly vanishing as he steps forward while simultaneously pulling me behind him. "This whole thing is a misunderstanding. There's no need to act like a giant douchebag who's obviously overcompensating for something."

Terry's gaze turns fiery. "You saying I have a tiny dick?"

Dean returns his glare, confidence and anger radiating off him. "If the tiny shoe fits."

Terry grabs the beer bottle closest to him on the bar and whips it at the floor, sending pieces of glass flying everywhere.

I squeal as glass torpedoes around us, but I'm not hit, because as I jump, Dean does as well, pushing me back and holding me to his side as he does.

Adam and Dylan jump the opposite way so they're now facing us, and I meet Adam's wide eyes.

"I think *you* should leave," the bartender tells Terry, noticing his hostile behavior for the first time.

"I think you should leave!" Terry fires back at the innocent bartender.

Dylan snorts. "Quick comeback, my guy."

"I've had enough of you—"

Security is on us now, cutting Terry off and showing up right before it looks like he was going to take a swing. They're about to remove all of us, when the bartender says something in Spanish and security rounds on Terry, pulling him out of the pool party and leaving the rest of us alone.

Terry's friend is left behind. "Sorry, guys. He's not usually that bad. He's drunk and fighting with his girlfriend. Not making excuses, but yeah. Sorry about that." He rubs his neck awkwardly before turning to follow his friend.

Dean, Dylan, Adam, and I are all staring at each other, trying to process what just happened.

Dylan's the first to speak. "Dude was *definitely* overcompensating."

And with that, the tension evaporates, and we all start laughing. I realize belatedly that I'm clinging to Dean's side, his muscled arm wrapped around me, pulling me close, and heat spreads through my face and down my neck in a bright blush.

I step back from him and angle some hair in front of my face to conceal the redness. Dean looks at me and smiles reassuringly.

"Is everyone okay?" Adam asks, since we're a bunch of half-naked people around broken glass.

We all take inventory of our various body parts and determine that we're unhurt. We offer to help the staff clean up the glass, but they shoo us away. It's a good thing there are multiple bars at this party or there would've been more people around to witness Terry's wrath.

"Well, I don't know about you guys, but I need to get drunk ASAP after that fiasco," Dylan says once all the glass is cleaned up. He leans over to the bartender. "Four shots of tequila, please."

Tequila?! I've never had tequila. It's basically Faye's drink of choice when she goes to a party, but I'm not really a drinker. Those four shots better be all for Dylan.

"Hey, what happened with that guy, anyway?" Dean asks as Dylan tips the bartender more than necessary, probably for having his back.

"Literally nothing," Adam says, eyeing the little shot Dylan offers before reluctantly picking it up. "Dylan and I were talking, waiting for our turn to order, and he backed up into *Terry* by accident."

"Yeah, the whole dropping-his-beer thing was an overreaction," Dylan adds, holding a shot out to Dean, who takes it, and then turns to offer one to me.

I stare at the drink but don't make a move to take it from him. It smells like rubbing alcohol. Everyone's looking at me, waiting expectantly for me to accept the shot, but I hesitate.

"I'll take it for you," Dean says with a gentle smile, reaching for what would be his second shot, and it hits me: no one's forcing me.

Faye's not here ordering me to have fun, and my parents aren't here demanding I be responsible, and the guys aren't peer-pressuring me into doing something I don't want to.

I take the drink from Dylan's outstretched hand before Dean does because I *want* to.

"It's okay," I tell Dean, holding the sticky glass between my pointer finger and thumb.

"Hell yeah!" Dylan exclaims, holding out his own shot. "To Terry!"

We laugh and echo his statement, clinking our glasses together before downing our drinks in one gulp. I almost choke on it, and it stings the whole way down, but I still force a swallow. Dylan laughs and hands me a lime, which I gladly accept and greedily suck on to get rid of that awful lingering taste.

"Four more tequilas, please!" Dylan immediately orders, then turns to face us with a mischievous gleam in his eyes. "Tonight's gonna be fun."

—

After those first two tequila shots, I have another two, and now I'm done with tequila, maybe forever. I just can't get over that aftertaste. And the burning on the way down. And the smell. I could gag just thinking about it.

I switch to some fruity drink and nurse it for a while as the guys do some more shots. Adam leaves after his fifth shot in a row to "find Kellan," and reappears a bit later.

I'm having a lot of fun with the guys. I'm a little tipsy—we all are—but that's not the only reason. The guys are *funny*. We're sitting around a small table, and we're laughing and trading stories and enjoying ourselves. It's also the first time I've hung out with Adam and Dylan not as Faye's friend, but as Lori. It's a cool feeling.

Eventually, Faye finds me at the bar and asks me for the room key. She seems upset but says she's okay. I don't fully believe her, but I think she can tell I don't really want to leave yet and tells me to stay and have fun. I wonder what she was up to all night. It must've been something good if she was missing her bikini top.

"Four more tequilas for my four amigos!" Dylan says as he comes up to our table with a little plate of four shot glasses filled with that burning liquor, limes resting flat on top of each. I'm surprised he could carry them over here without spilling any; he's a little tipsy.

"There's three of your amigos here. You don't normally count as your own amigo," I laugh as he sets the plate down.

"Huh? There's four of us here." He points at each of us, ending with himself. "One, two, three, four. Four of my amigos!"

"But that's not—"

Dean leans in closer to me, laughter on his lips. "You can't beat him with logic. I'd just let it go."

I giggle until Dylan removes the shots from the plate and sets one down in front of each of us. The smell wakes up my gag reflex instantly.

"None for me, thanks." I push the shot back into the middle of the table.

Dean follows my lead and gestures at his beer. "I'm okay for now too."

"Looks like it's just you and me!" Dylan slaps Adam on the back. Adam looks like he's going to puke on the spot.

"Man, I don't think that's a good idea," Adam says, his words slurred.

Dylan ignores him as he puts two in front of Adam and the other two in front of himself. "We're on vacation!" he exclaims. "Plus, you just got dumped by your girlfriend. So, if anyone needs these, it's you."

Adam sighs, probably thinking about Jenna, his total witch of an ex. I can't stand her. When Faye told me they broke up, I basically jumped for joy, and not just because I've always pined after Adam.

"All right." Adam picks up a shot in each hand, and Dylan lets out a drunk "Whoop!"

I lean over to Dean as the other boys clink their glasses together and take the shots, one after another. "Do you think we should cut them off at some point?"

Dean shrugs. "They're big boys, they can make their own decisions."

My gaze goes from him to something over his shoulder, and I gasp like it's the most spectacular thing ever.

"What?" Dean asks, turning around to check out what I'm so happy about.

"They have face painting!" Emboldened by the alcohol, I grab his hand before he can react and pull him from his chair, forcing him to follow me.

Obviously I'm not strong enough to pull Dean, so he allows me to drag him over to the face-painting station. There are workers supervising the paints, but you can paint your friends yourself. One station opens up almost immediately after we get there, so I pull Dean to it and force him down in the seat.

"You're painting my face?" Dean chuckles, looking at the paints laid out on the table.

"Yup. Then you're painting mine," I state, picking up a brush. "What do you want?"

"Surprise me."

Since it's a pink party, most of the paints are pinks, but there are some other colors too. I pick up a palette and focus on making sure my painting actually resembles what I want it to.

"What are you turning me into?" he asks, his eyes closed.

"You said to surprise you."

He opens an eye to peek at me. "Is it manly?"

"Oh yes. Very," I giggle.

Dean bites back a smile, seeing right through me. "Excellent."

Since his eyes are closed, I take a second to shamelessly examine his handsome face. His jaw is sharp and defined, with some sexy stubble that I forbid myself to touch with my hand like a total creep. Should I ditch the brush and use my fingers to discreetly feel up his face, or would that be superweird? Maybe I'll stick to the brush, just in case tipsy-Lori does something sober-Lori will die of embarrassment from in the morning.

Once I declare him done, we switch spots so he can paint my face.

"After I'm done, we can both look in the mirror together," I tell him as he paints.

His brows are drawn together in concentration, and his nose scrunches in the cutest way as he examines his work.

"I'm done," he proclaims, adding a few extra lines on my face for good measure.

"Let's see!" I hop up and grab a mirror that's sitting on the table.

We press our heads together to see ourselves in the glass, and my heartbeat ramps up. I'm so preoccupied with our closeness that I don't pay attention to my reflection, but Dean laughs at his.

"You said I was manly!" He turns to face me, his eyes playful rather than accusatory.

I smile innocently and nod.

"I'm a pink bunny!" he laughs, not even pretending to be mad.

I giggle at his face, especially the two buck teeth I painted. "I mean, you're a very manly bunny. Do you like it?"

Dean doesn't even check the mirror again when he says, "Of course. I love it!"

I've been giggling a lot tonight. Maybe it's because of Dean, or maybe it's the booze. Either way, I don't really care, I'm having too much fun. I can't stop myself from giggling again. He's always so sure of himself. He doesn't care that people walking by are looking at him funny, not like I would. He doesn't even care that he's more sunburnt than he was yesterday.

"Do you like yours?" he asks, and I realize I still have no idea what he's painted on my face.

I look in the mirror again and see a beautiful pink butterfly on the side of my face.

"It's so pretty!" I exclaim honestly, putting the mirror down as other people move into the painting station.

His wide smile makes my pulse jump. "Good, I'm glad."

"Let's show Dylan and Adam!" I tell him, looking around for the boys who are no longer at the table where we left them.

I really bonded with them today. Adam and Dylan may be incredibly drunk, but I felt less like a little sister tagging along and more like one of their friends.

Dean taps my arm. "Hey, do you remember what color swim trunks Dylan and Adam were wearing?"

I give him a weird look. "Is that a trick question? It's a pink party, everyone's in pink."

"Yeah, I just mean . . . well, look." He places his hands on my shoulders and turns me around before pointing to something. Once I see what he's pointing at, I get why he asked.

There are two guys, the top halves of their bodies submerged in the bushes as they bend over on the outskirts of the party. All that's visible in the dark is their brightly colored swim shorts and legs.

"Is that . . . ?"

I don't even have to finish my question before Dean and I are heading over to the two pink shorts. When we get there, the stench of vomit hits my nose almost immediately.

"Dylan? Adam?"

Two groans answer Dean, then more retching sounds. Great.

Dean looks at me. What are we supposed to do?

It's redundant, but I ask, "You guys . . . okay?"

More groans from the bushes.

Guess that answers that. Now what? I've never dealt with puking drunk guys before! Faye's only puked once after drinking. It was at a New Year's Eve party, and by the time she puked, Kellan had already driven us back to her house and she passed out almost immediately after.

Dylan plops himself down on the ground beside the bush with his eyes closed and his chest dirty; he obviously missed the bush at some point.

"Lor, why don't you see if you can find Kellan or Alessio to help me get them back to our room?" Dean suggests, helping Dylan lean against the fence beside the bushes. "I'm going to get them water and a towel to clean them up. Unless you want to switch?"

I eye the puke on Dylan's chest, and the smell hits me again. It's a no-brainer. "Nope! I'll be back with Alessio or Kellan!"

Before Dean can change his mind, I escape like the coward I am, glad he's taken control of the situation.

Even though it's around two a.m., the party is still in full effect. There are people having fun everywhere, but there's no sign of Alessio or Kellan. Eventually, I find Kiara and Anaya, who I was introduced to earlier by Dean.

"Hey, have you seen Kellan or Alessio?" I ask them.

Kiara crosses her arms across her chest and huffs. "Kellan went to bed. Something about not being in the party mood."

Is he with Faye? Best to not walk in on that again.

"How about Alessio?"

"We haven't seen Alessio since, like, the beginning of the party," Anaya tells me with an apologetic shrug.

I thank them and head back to Dean. Looks like we're going to have to do this on our own.

By the time I get back, both Dylan and Adam are sitting with their backs against the fence, their eyes closed and a nauseated expression on their faces. From what I can tell, Dean's done a good job of cleaning them up.

"Any luck?" Dean asks me, and I shake my head.

Dean eyes the two boys and then me. "Well, Lor, looks like it's up to us to help these idiots to their room."

The two idiots protest at Dean's use of the word, but it's only a groan.

"Well, I haven't been to the gym since I got here, so I guess it'll be my workout," I joke, eyeing Adam, whose lean body should be lighter than Dylan's, though he's still bigger than me.

Dean laughs. "That's the spirit."

He helps Adam to stand and so do I, putting Adam's arm around my shoulder so I'm supporting his weight. He sways a bit but stands with little work on my side.

"I can manage on my own," he protests, but his eyes are closed, and the weight I'm supporting says otherwise.

"It's okay, I'll help," I tell him as Dean pulls Dylan up and mimics my position with Adam. Dylan looks like he's in a much worse state.

"I'm okay . . . really. I don't need help," Adam protests and tries to push off me, but he instantly sways. I catch him before his face becomes acquainted with the cement floor.

"It's okay," I tell Adam, wrapping my arm around his waist as his arm slips over my shoulder again. If it wasn't a superinappropriate time, I would've totally squealed about how I have my arms around *Adam Murray*.

"Dude," Dean tells his cousin, "if you puke on me, I'll kill you."

I cast a sidelong glance at Adam. "Ditto."

Dylan just groans and Adam slurs out, "I make no promises."

Slowly, we guide them out of the party and toward our little three-story hotel. It feels like forever by the time we get there, especially since we had to stop twice to let Dylan puke. I feel bad for Dean, having to practically carry Dylan all the way, but if I let go of Adam, he'll face-plant into the asphalt, even though he keeps insisting he doesn't need my help.

Since there's only three floors, our building doesn't have an elevator, so we're forced to help the boys up the stairs. By the second landing, Dean and I are both sweating, and not from the heat.

"Guess we should've cut them off. For some stupid reason I didn't think their drinking would become our problem," Dean says as he catches his breath. "You'd think I would've learned my lesson by now."

"At least they'll be too hungover to drink tomorrow, right?" Or I hope so.

Dylan makes that sound he made before he puked on our walk over, and Dean instantly goes on high alert.

"Come on, let's get Tweedle-drunk and Tweedle-drunker upstairs before they puke again."

Although I could get projectile-vomited all over at any minute now, I laugh.

We get up to our floor and I lean Adam against the wall in front of his room while Dean helps Dylan to their shared room.

"Are you sure you don't want me to help you with him?" Dean asks again, like he did on the way over.

Before I can turn him down again, Dylan leans over and empties his stomach contents all over Dean's shoulder.

"Ugh! You are dead tomorrow," Dean tells him as he swipes the key card, and Dylan manages a laugh.

"I'm okay," I tell Dean with a chuckle. "You've clearly got it worse than I do. See you tomorrow."

He's cut off when Dylan, again, vomits and aims right for Dean, and frankly I'm surprised he still has stuff to puke up.

"Oh come on!" Dean exclaims as they enter the room, and the door swings shut behind them.

I can't help but giggle since it's actually pretty funny, especially since Dean's face is still painted like a pink bunny. I'm sure by the morning, or maybe next week, Dean will think it's funny too.

"Where's your key?" I ask Adam, who's much more coherent than Dylan.

He reaches into his pocket and hands it to me, but when I swipe it, nothing happens.

"Isn't this your room?" I ask, swiping the key repeatedly.

"I get the spare room tonight. Kellan and Alessio are sharing," he manages to say, and I sigh.

With my help, we walk a few doors over and the key works on the first try. Not even a second after we're inside and the door shuts behind us, Adam rushes to the bathroom and hunches over the toilet, resuming his pukefest.

I flinch at the sound of his retching. At least he held it in until we reached a toilet.

As I stand there awkwardly, I'm suddenly hit with nerves. What do I do now? We're alone in the room and will continue to be alone since he has the extra room tonight. I guess it's up to me to make sure he's okay? I could leave him here, but he's so helpless, his arm on the toilet seat and his head resting against it.

"Remind me to kill Dylan in the morning," Adam says as he closes his eyes, still leaning against the toilet.

After grabbing a water bottle from the mini-fridge, I sit on the edge of the bathtub near him.

"You might have to beat Dean to it," I joke, handing him the bottle. He takes it but makes no move to open it, just setting it down on the floor beside him.

He groans and lifts his head from the toilet seat, leaning back on the tub beside me. "This is why I don't drink. I just wanted *one night* where I didn't think about Jenna."

My breath hitches. Is he still in love with her?

"I always make the wrong decisions," he continues as his eyes close and his head rests on the edge of the tub. "Not like you. You always do the right thing."

The statement takes me by surprise. I do? I slide off the edge of the tub and sit beside him on the floor, leaning back with my knees pulled up. "You don't make wrong decisions."

He doesn't move his head from where it's resting. "I do. I ruined high school for you. Or rather, I didn't say anything to Jenna."

Someone plunged their hand into my throat and is squeezing my trachea, at least that's what it feels like. My voice comes out small. "High school wasn't terrible for me."

His head lolls over to look at me. "But it could've been better. I could've made it better."

Words stick in my throat. This is not where I thought the night was going. Hell, this isn't where I thought my *week* was going. Just this morning I was scuba diving with Dean, and now I'm on the bathroom floor with Adam *freaking* Murray, and he's spilling his guts—literally and metaphorically.

Shrugging, I avoid his gaze. "You didn't owe me anything."

I sense rather than see him put his head back on the tub edge. Relief spreads through me now that his intense gaze is off me. "You're Faye's best friend, and Jenna was my girlfriend. I should've stood up for you, told her to back off with the jealous shit. Should've reassured her."

Maybe it's the buzz I'm still feeling, or maybe it's the image of Faye's "I'm trying really hard to stay strong and not break down" face after a bad incident with Jenna that pops into my head, but something makes me open my mouth and say, "You should've stood up for your *sister*."

Adam's intense eyes find my face again, and I wish I could grab my words and shove them back into my mouth where they belong. He studies me for a few seconds, then looks away. "Faye didn't need my help. She's strong, not like you."

He might as well have slapped me for the hurt that goes through me. What does that mean? Does he think I'm weak? *Am* I weak? I can squat almost twice my weight, so I know he doesn't mean physically, and that's what kills me the most.

"What does that mean?" It comes out as a whisper, almost like I don't want to know.

His eyes widen like he just realized how that statement sounded. "No, I didn't mean that, I just meant . . ." His eyes close, and he presses the cold water bottle to his forehead. "This would be easier if the room wasn't spinning."

I can jump in and save him from explaining himself, but drunk-Lori tells nice-Lori to stay quiet, because both Loris want to hear what he has to say.

"You're sweet," he continues, "dependable. Predictable. I always know you'll do the right thing, because, you know, I always know what to expect when it comes to you. You choose the safe option. Faye's not like that. Faye can take what's thrown at her and give it back ten times worse. You're just . . . not like that."

Sweet. Dependable. Predictable. I don't think I've ever hated those words more in my life. He's saying I'm simple; not a firecracker who lights up the room like Faye. Not someone that people want to know; not someone worth anyone's time. So not only am I weak, but apparently I'm boring. Does everyone think this? How has no one said something before?

My silence prompts him to keep talking. "It's not a bad thing. Seriously, Lor, you're gorgeous and perfect and everyone knows it. I've always thought—" He cuts himself off by promptly sitting up and emptying the rest of his stomach contents all over my lap.

"Crap! Seriously, Adam?" Cringing, I jump up, causing the vomit to slide down and thoroughly coat the rest of my legs. "I thought you were done."

"Yeah," he says, wiping his mouth with the back of his hand. "Me too. Sorry."

Glancing down at the mess on the floor, both Adam and the vomit, I wonder what sweet, predictable Lori would do.

I sigh. "Let's get you cleaned up and in bed."

He answers me by throwing up on my bare feet. Fantastic.

"Wanted to make sure you got the spot you missed?" I ask dryly, but my attempt at humor is lost on him.

"I swear I didn't aim," he mumbles, then leans back against the tub with his eyes closed.

"Oh, no," I tell him, "you are *not* falling asleep before getting in bed because I can't carry you."

He mumbles something that sounds like an agreement, and I help him stand up, careful to keep the vomit that's apparently only on me from touching him. We walk over to the bed where he plops down and tries to take off his shirt.

My breathing hitches and my hands pause midreach. I'm about to take Adam's shirt off. I'm about to *strip Adam Murray*! How many times have I daydreamed about this?

Keep it together, Lori. You're helping a drunk friend.

Quickly, I help him pull off the tank top, ensuring I don't touch him and getting it off without lingering or looking at him.

I throw the shirt on the floor and pull the bedsheet over him before he tries to take his swimsuit bottoms off, but he looks like he's already asleep. Rolling him into recovery position, I wonder if I should stay and make sure he's okay or leave him alone.

I should go back. It's incredibly late and Faye's probably waiting to let me in. I've got the door halfway open before I pause and remember that Kellan's probably with Faye. In my room. Doing things that I don't want to witness.

Sighing, I glance at the extra bed. It's untouched since this room has two single beds, and Adam's got the room all to himself tonight. The squishing sound under my feet draws my attention to the mess I'm covered in, and I make my decision. Closing the door, I head into the bathroom and take a shower.

Once I'm standing in the room freshly showered, covered in just a towel and without any clean clothes, I realize this probably wasn't the best idea. One glance at Adam's sleeping form in bed stops me from asking to borrow clothes. I have no choice. Plus, it's Adam's fault I need new clothes anyway, so he won't mind. I rifle through his luggage and put on an oversized T-shirt, ignoring the little girl in me who's giddy at the thought of wearing his clothes against my bare skin. I use the wet towel to clean up the puke trail on the floor and throw the gross towel into the tub. As my head hits the pillow on the bed parallel to Adam's, all I can think about is that I hate the word *predictable*.

TWELVE

Day Three of Cuba

Faye

An incessant knocking on the door wakes me up from what would've been the only full hour of sleep I've had all night. A quick glance at the bedside clock tells me it's seven a.m. Wow, now I know how Lori feels when I wake her up with calls every morning.

"I'm coming!" I grumble at the person who hasn't stopped knocking. Kicking off the covers with more animosity than necessary, I stomp over to the door and throw it open. "What?"

"You're unusually cranky this morning," Kellan says, the mischievous twinkle in his eyes defusing my anger. "Usually, you're up and ready to go by now."

Self-conscious, I run a hand through my hair to smooth it out. "Yeah, I didn't sleep well."

After Kellan left with Kiara, I couldn't stop thinking about us, and why he doesn't see me as anything more than a hookup. I thought about what he was doing with Kiara, about what I can do to make him like me back, and about all things Kellan. Apparently, all that thinking isn't good for sleep because I tossed and turned all night.

"Yeah, me too," he says, shifting his weight to lean on the doorframe. "I wish I had the spare room last night because Alessio woke me up when he came in."

My ears perk up. That means he *wasn't* in Kiara's room last night, and she wasn't in his. "You got in before him?"

He glances away quickly. "I left the party not long after you did. I wasn't feeling it."

Hope blooms in my heart. Maybe he *does* feel the same way about me?

"So, what brings you to my doorway this fine morning?" I ask, gesturing him to follow me in and closing the door behind him.

"I remembered you saying . . . hey, where's Lori?"

I glance around the small room like it's all new to me. Hey, where *is* Lori?

"You didn't notice she wasn't here?" He raises a disapproving eyebrow, a frown ruining his pretty face. "Did she come back last night?"

I guess I was too caught up in my own business to remember that I'm sharing a room. "I borrowed her key card last night and told her I'd let her in when she came up. Maybe I didn't hear her?" I gasp, cutting myself off. "I left her with Dean last night! Maybe she stayed the night with him?" A girl can hope.

He shakes his head. "Dean shared the room with Dylan last night. We should—" A knock at the door interrupts Kellan, and I open it.

Standing there, in nothing but flip-flops and a men's

T-shirt that just barely covers her ass, is Lori, who shifts her feet uncomfortably as she looks between me and Kellan with red cheeks.

My smirk says it all, so she quickly rushes out, "It's not what it looks like!"

I bite my lip to keep from laughing. "Uh-huh. Get in here before you cause a *scandal*." Now a laugh slips out and her blush deepens. Lori's had my back countless times from my various walks of shame, so she knows I'm just having some fun.

"I swear it wasn't like that. Hey, Kellan." She drops the clothes she was holding in her hand on the floor and unzips her luggage.

"Then whose shirt is that? Whose room did you stay in last night?" Kellan asks with a teasing smirk, crossing his arms and leaning against the wall.

She straightens up with new clothes in her hands. "Adam's."

The words hit me like a slap across the face. "But—my—that—what?" I've never had a problem with words before, but I can't even process what that means. Lori and *my brother*?!

Her eyes widen as she struggles to speak. "No! Not like—that's not what—it's not that. I swear!"

"Then why are you in Adam's clothes? Why were you with him last night?" I try to tame the accusation in my tone, but we all hear it. It was fun when I thought Lori slept with some other guy, but now that it's my brother, I feel like hitting something, preferably Adam.

"Nothing happened!" She hugs the clean clothes to her chest as her blush spreads. "He and Dylan got really drunk last night, and I helped Adam to his room while Dean helped Dylan. Adam puked on me, so I took a shower there when he passed out, and I slept in the spare bed. That's all."

The rising anger in my chest diminishes as I process her words. "Oh." I knew Adam was drinking last night, and I can totally see him puking on her; he's not very considerate. "Why didn't you come back here?"

"Because." Her eyes bounce back and forth between me and Kellan, who's still leaning against the wall. "You know."

Kellan and I register her words at the same time as he straightens up, and we both rush to explain.

"Oh, no—"

"That's not—"

We stop and look at each other. I take a deep breath. "I came up alone last night. Kellan stopped by right before you did."

Disbelief crosses her face before she masks it. "Uh-huh. I'm going to take a shower with my own shampoo. See you later, Kellan."

She disappears into the bathroom, and then the rush of running water from the shower is the only sound in the room. Kellan and I stare at each other almost awkwardly.

"So, uh," I start, uncharacteristically hesitant. "How come you stopped by?"

"Oh, yeah." He shakes his head, then reaches into his back pocket and pulls out something that was sticking out. "I remembered you said you have no more flip-flops. I don't think the resort sells any, so I brought you my extra pair."

He holds out the flip-flops and I stare at them like I've never seen shoes before. I told him I lost all my flip-flops? *I* don't even remember saying that, but *he* does?

"Are you gonna take them or stare at me all day?" he teases.

I spring back to life and accept the flip-flops, placing them on the floor to slip into them.

"They're like nine sizes too big."

The boyish smile he shoots me melts my heart. "Well, they

are men's size eleven. I figured they're better than nothing, at least for the beach and stuff."

I was planning on stealing Lori's flip-flops, but now I want to wear these, even if they are huge on me. "Thanks."

"Yeah," he replies.

The hesitancy and shyness that surrounds us is foreign to me, and while I don't like it, I kind of do too. It feels like it's a fresh start.

He hitches a thumb over his shoulder toward the door. "Anyway, sounds like Dylan and Adam had a fun night. Better go mess with them a bit now that they're nice and hungover. See you at breakfast."

Biting my lip, I watch him leave and lean against the door, my heart fluttering against my chest as I stare at Kellan's flip-flops on my feet. He may not know it yet, but I'm going to make him realize his feelings for me, and I'm going to make it happen before we go home.

—

"Have I ever told you how much I love you?" Dylan asks me as I sit beside him.

We're at the beach, stretched out on chairs next to each other. I'm in the sun, but Dylan and my brother are both too hungover to do anything other than sit in the shade and nap. When I complained that Dylan was being boring, he promised he'd be back to normal if I let him sleep it off for a bit, and he wasn't wrong. It's midafternoon, and he's almost back to his annoying self.

I laugh, nodding to the plate of chicken nuggets from the beachside snack bar I just handed him. "Yes, but only when I bring you food."

"Doesn't make it any less true," he says around a full mouth, and I roll my eyes at him as I lie back in the chair.

Adam sits up from Dylan's other side and looks at me. "Where's mine?"

"When I said I was going to get snacks and asked who wants something, you stayed quiet." I pop a french fry into my mouth. "Plus, I like him better."

"I was sleeping," Adam grumbles, but I ignore him and instead focus on Dean, Lori, Alessio, and Kellan, who are playing two-on-two beach volleyball.

Lori's partnered with Dean, and she's had this goofy grin on her face the entire time. From what I can tell, they're beating Alessio and Kellan, which isn't a surprise because Lori's always been really athletic, at least way more than I am.

Dylan follows my gaze, folding his tattooed arm behind his head. "You know, when you're not around, Lori's actually really cool."

I raise an eyebrow at him. "What does that mean? She's not cool when I'm around?"

He shakes his head. "No. I'm saying that I've only ever hung out with her when you're around, and she's always really quiet. When you're around, you usually do all the talking for the both of you, but she's cool by herself."

Pouting, I think back on all the times Lori has been at my house when Adam had his friends over. I didn't realize I do all the talking, but that's natural for us. I'm the loud, outgoing one; Lori's the shy, quiet one. It works.

My brother sits up to butt into our conversation. "He's saying that it's cool to see who she really is when you're not around to walk all over her."

I'm taken aback. "I do not walk all over Lori."

Adam snorts.

"I don't!"

"Uh-huh." He stands. "I'm going to get myself some food since *someone* didn't bother thinking about anyone other than herself, as usual."

As I watch his retreating form, it's like there's smoke coming out of my ears—I'm fuming. He's literally the *worst* brother. He's mad about me not bringing him food when I *offered*, but the last time he offered to bring me anything was *never*.

Sitting up, I place my feet in the sand and face Dylan. "Seriously, why are you friends with him?"

He sits up to face me as well. "You guys are—watch out!" Before I can turn to see what I should watch out for, Dylan grabs my arm and yanks me off my seat and toward him, and a heavy object whizzes by my head before there's a loud smack.

"Sorry!" Alessio calls out, and I realize the volleyball would have taken my head off at full force if Dylan hadn't pulled me out of the way.

Dylan—who I'm lying on top of half-naked—laughs at Alessio.

"You guys okay?"

I crane my neck and see Kellan, who's holding the offending volleyball. His eyes dart from me, to Dylan, then back to me, and I belatedly realize I'm still lying on Dylan like a rag doll.

"You need help, Faye?" Kellan asks, his lips set in a straight line as he gestures for me to get off Dylan.

Is that . . . ? Oh wow.

He's jealous.

As I bite my lip to stop my smile, I hop off Dylan with a mumbled apology.

"It's all good," Dylan says, rolling his neck.

Kellan glances between us again, and I swear I almost squeal with delight at the realization. It's so obvious I'm disappointed in myself for not getting it sooner. He's not jealous of me being with random people who he knows I'll never see again; it could never develop into anything more than a fling. But he sure as shit would be jealous if I was with someone like Dylan, someone who lives near me since it totally *could* develop into something when we get back home.

Holy shit. I'm a genius. I want to grab Dylan's hands and jump around in circles. I have so much energy coursing through my veins now.

Kellan nods toward the volleyball net. "You guys wanna play?"

Dylan stands and stretches. "You know what? I'm feeling a lot better. I'm game. Just give me a few."

"Me too," I say.

Kellan nods once, then turns and rejoins the game, throwing us a glance over his shoulder as he goes.

I jump from my seat and stand in front of Dylan, my back to our friends. "Dylan! Dylan, did you see that?" I bite my lip to keep from squealing and bouncing up and down.

"See what? The ball flying toward you? Yeah. Why do you think I pulled you out of the way?"

"Not that!" I shove his shoulder and he frowns. "Kellan was jealous! Of us! We made him jealous! He cares, Dyl!"

"He was jealous?" Dylan's dark eyebrows draw together as he looks over my head to scan Kellan, but I don't dare turn around to follow his gaze.

Stupid boy. Of course he's oblivious to stuff like that. "Yesterday I tried making him jealous with other guys, but he didn't care. At all. But with *you*, he got jealous."

Dylan's jaw snaps shut as the wheels in his head spin; his focus is on my excited face. I know the moment realization slams into him because he inhales sharply. "Don't say it—"

"We have to make him jealous!"

He closes his eyes and groans.

"Come on, Dyl!"

"Fayeee . . ." His eyes pop open and he runs his hand through his hair. "You're my friend, and I told you I'd have your back with this stupid 'make him jealous' plan, but that was before it included me. He's my best friend, and it's not right to play games with him like that."

He's right. I know he's right. But even now I can feel Kellan's heated gaze on Dylan and me as we talk, and I've never gotten that kind of reaction from him before. He's starting to realize how he feels for me. Because of *Dylan*.

"But we wouldn't be playing games with him. We're just . . . giving him a light shove in the right direction."

Dylan glances over my head again. "He's staring at us and doesn't look happy."

The giddiness in my chest bubbles through me, and it takes everything in me to keep my feet firmly planted in the sand. "I know. I told you! We're going to help him realize he likes me."

This is stupid. I'm being stupid. But Kellan's staring at us. He'll think about what it means to lose me. He'll realize he can lose me, that I'm worth more than a secret fling.

"Please, Dyl?" I shoot him my best pleading eyes and pout. "I just . . . I really, really like him. And watching him flirt with Kiara made me realize just how much. If I realize he really is jealous, then I'll talk to him. I'll tell him how I feel."

I *will* tell him how I feel *if* he really is jealous of me and Dylan. He'd have to confront his feelings then, and I wouldn't get laughed at for spilling my guts if he's realized he feels the same way.

Dylan studies me for what feels like an eternity, before releasing a long-suffering sigh. "Fine."

This time I do let my excitement show, jumping up and down and throwing my arms around him. "Thank you, thank you!"

He grabs my shoulders and peels me away from him. "But we're not going out of our way to make him jealous. No blatant flirting or anything, because you're *you*, and that would be gross."

I'm not offended by his statement because I know exactly what he means and feel the same about him.

"But," he continues, "if you want to stand near me around him and laugh louder or whatever so he reads the situation however he wants to read it, then fine. But I'm not changing the way I act around you to make it seem like we're something we're not just to make him jealous. I realize you would've done those things without me even knowing you were making him jealous, so at least now I'll know why you'll randomly start laughing at me when Kellan walks in the room."

"You know me so well."

"I do." He shoots me a crooked grin. "It's annoying."

Dylan really is my best friend after Lori and, ironically, Kellan.

"But," Dylan adds, "the second you realize he's jealous, you're telling him how you feel."

I nod my head vigorously. I've already come to that conclusion. I don't *want* to play these stupid games, but it's a matter of protecting myself. I can't have Kellan stomp on my heart then hand it back to me in pieces, because a rejection from him would hurt more than it would from anyone else. I know it deep in my core. It would break me, so I need to be certain before doing anything.

"Promise," I say. "Let's go join the game."

Our friends have stopped playing and are standing around talking, and when they see us, Lori runs over to me. Dylan ruffles her hair because he's Dylan and he's annoying, then continues to the guys, who chat some distance over.

Lori's voice is excited but lowered so the guys can't hear us. "Oh my gosh, Faye! I'm having so much fun."

I grin. "I can tell. You've been ogling Mr. Tan-Buff-Sweaty-and-Shirtless over there all day."

She follows my gesture to Dean and snaps back to look at me, her face heating. "I am not!" She pauses and adds even lower, "It's not obvious, is it?"

"Not nearly as much as it would be if I were the one doing the ogling."

As she glances at him, a small smile forms on her face. "I think I . . . like . . . Dean."

I raise a teasing eyebrow. "I thought you liked my brother?"

Her face reddens completely as she bites her lip. "Adam is . . . hot. Dean is too, but Dean . . . I think he gets me. You know?"

Hell, anyone with eyes can tell that Dean's gorgeous. My brother *definitely* isn't but thank goodness Lori doesn't have a real crush on Adam. I was always fine knowing she thought he was hot, which was *barf*, but this morning when I thought something had actually *happened* between them, I didn't like it. Not one bit.

But I'm glad Lori's connecting with Dean. I should tell her how I feel about Kellan—how I *really* feel about him. I start to tell her, but the words get stuck in my throat. What if she thinks my plan is juvenile? What if she tells me that it's not right to keep this from Adam? What if she tells me she doesn't think Kellan could ever see me as anything more than a fling?

"What's wrong?" she asks.

"Nothing," I blurt before I'm tempted to spill my guts. "Let's head over to the game."

I eye the boys in front of me with a newfound interest because of my new knowledge. This plan is easier now that it makes sense. If Kellan's jealous, that means he cares about me. He just needs a push in the right direction, and now I have a game plan.

THIRTEEN

Night Three of Cuba

Lori

Tonight is a perfect night to leave the resort and go to a local club, La Cueva. At least, that's according to Faye, who has experience with these kinds of things, thanks to her fake ID.

It's only a little humid out, so I leave my hair down instead of braiding it since it won't frizz too badly. We're walking on the sidewalk beside the road because the club is only five minutes away. The night is calm, and a few cars drive by. As they do, I stare at their beauty; they all seem perfectly preserved from the fifties.

We walk a few feet behind Kiara, Anaya, and Priyasha, with the guys following along behind us.

"I can't believe Alessio invited them," Faye huffs, glaring at the girls ahead of us.

"Don't be mean," I reply, nudging her with my shoulder. "You just don't want Kellan to flirt with Kiara." Plus, they're nice, but I'm sure Faye doesn't want to hear that right now.

The three girls ran into us as we were leaving the beach after our volleyball game. They overheard us talking about heading to a club off the resort this evening, so we invited them. I think it's fine, the more the merrier, but Faye's a little salty about Kiara and Kellan, even if she refuses to tell me.

"I don't own him," she mutters sourly, adjusting her shirt as we walk.

She borrowed my white crop top to wear tonight, but she fills it out much better than I ever could. She's shorter and curvier than I am, so I try not to feel like a twelve-year-old standing beside her in my blue halter top and shorts.

Faye glances back, probably to check out Kellan, and I follow her movement, but when Adam stares back at her, she swings her gaze back to me.

"Would it really be so bad," I say, treading carefully, "if Adam found out about you and Kellan?"

For a full five seconds, she stares at me like I've grown a second head before saying, "Are you serious? Adam would kill me. Plus, there is no 'me and Kellan.'"

There is *so* a her and Kellan, but she doesn't want to admit to herself how much she likes him. "I don't think Adam would mind if you got with Kellan."

Her mouth drops open. "Did you say something to him?"

"What? No! Of course not! I didn't say anything!" When she breathes out in relief, I continue, "All I'm saying is you wouldn't be so stressed trying to hide everything if you came clean."

"I'm not saying anything to Adam because there is no me and Kellan. Plus, Adam already hates me, even more after what happened with Zach, and I don't want to give him another reason to do so." She straightens her spine to stand taller before I can argue with her. "So, screw Kellan. I'm going to find another guy to take my mind off him tonight, if you know what I mean."

I know exactly what that means. I resist the urge to groan. "Can you at least put the 'do not disturb' sign up, so I don't walk into anything?" I wonder how long I'll have to sit out in the hall tonight. Maybe I can hang out with Dean and Dylan again like last night.

"Yes, I promise. Are you excited for your first time in a club?" she asks. She's been going to clubs back home since someone made her a fake ID, but I was too chicken to get one with her. My parents would've grounded me for eternity.

"Yes," I answer. "Plus Dylan promised he wouldn't drink as much as last night."

"Dylan lied."

"I certainly hope not. I don't know how we'll carry him back to the resort from here."

"That's what *Dean* is for." She waggles her eyebrows as she glances back at him, and I grab her arm to pull her front-facing again. She's so obvious!

"Stop that!"

"What? Don't you think he looks *hot* tonight? We should tell him you think so." She takes a deep breath and turns around, shouting, "Hey, Dean! Lori thinks—"

I cut her off by shoving her and pulling her to face forward. She erupts into laughter as my own face heats.

"What is wrong with you?" I whisper as Dean's fast footsteps approach us.

Her wide smile tells me it could've been way worse. "Just helping things along. Hey Dean."

"Hey," he says as he falls in step beside us. "What were you yelling about?"

"Lori will tell you," Faye says, then turns to wait for the other guys while Dean and I walk on alone.

Faye was right before; he looks as handsome as ever, even

with a new faint sunburn on his forearms. His white T-shirt stretches across his broad shoulders and does nothing to hide the muscles underneath. His black hair is disheveled in a way that some people would spend hours trying to duplicate, but I know he just hopped out of the shower and ran his hand through it since we were running late. He sends me his perfect smile, and I realize I've been staring at him stupidly instead of answering his question.

"Oh, um." His spicy-woodsy scent is divine and distracting. "Ignore her. She started drinking when we were waiting for you guys in the lobby."

"She is quite a character. I don't think I've ever seen anyone nearly take a volleyball right to the face before and immediately make an inappropriate joke about balls."

When we turn the corner toward the loud music, I forget whatever I was going to say; the sight is astonishing.

It's a nightclub, but it's inside a *literal* cave.

No one was exaggerating when they were talking about it, because the entrance is *actually* carved into the side of a mountain. People are standing around in groups chatting, and a small line has formed at the entrance. Even outside lights flash in time to the music, and bouncers stand next to the front door. My nose wrinkles as the cigarette smoke gets heavier the closer we get to the entrance.

"Wow," Faye says as she catches up with us. "How cool is this?!"

"Supercool," Anaya says as she joins us, followed by everyone else. "Our friends are gonna be so pissed that they didn't want to leave the resort tonight. What are we waiting for? Let's get in there!"

The small line moves quickly. No one asks for ID, which is

good because we didn't bring any, and we pay the entrance fee.

"Oh, wow." I repeat Faye's earlier statement because it's all that comes to mind.

The club's owners didn't disguise the fact that we're in a cave, and I'm grateful for that. I wish I could reach up and touch the stalactites hanging from the ceiling. The walls are the cave's natural sides, no perfectly straight walls anywhere, but the floor is level with concrete. There are two bars on either side, and a dance floor occupies the rest of the space with a DJ at the end. Multicolored strobe lights flash in time with the catchy music. It's not a large club, but not tiny either, and even though we're in a cave, it doesn't feel stuffy in here.

"Let's do shots! First round's on me!" Alessio yells over the music, slinging an arm around Kiara and Priyasha, steering them toward one bar.

"Hell yeah! Come on, Lor," Dylan tells me, pulling me after them.

"You promised you wouldn't drink as much as last night," I tease, leaning in close to be heard over the music.

"I can drink without getting that drunk." He pauses then adds, "Probably."

I eye him skeptically as Alessio passes around shots of a gold liquid, and my eyes burn as I make a rookie mistake and sniff it. Tequila. Yay.

Adam's right beside me, so close his body heat gives me goose bumps. He shakes his head as I hand one to him, passing it on to Anaya beside him instead. Unlike Dylan, he doesn't seem too eager to jump back into tequila tonight. But despite last night, he looks just as hot as he normally does, with his hair lightly gelled away from his eyes and a green shirt that makes his hazel eyes even more blazing.

Kellan raises his glass once everyone except Adam has one. "To new friends," he announces, and Dylan suggestively knocks his shoulder with mine, making me blush.

"To new friends!" we cheer back, clinking glasses together before drinking.

The alcohol burns the entire way down and now I'm officially done with tequila, unlike Faye, who orders another round for everyone.

"None for me," I tell her, moving aside so the people who are drinking can be closer to the bar.

I scan the crowd. Everyone in here looks around our age, maybe older. Most people are wearing wristbands, which tells me they're tourists from other resorts. At the side of the dance floor against the wall is a small raised platform, where club-goers are dancing like they're onstage.

Not too far from us, a girl is dancing with a guy, moving around with a grace and confidence rivaled by no one else. Her dark braids sway behind her as she spins, and that's when I recognize her; it's the girl I saved in the pool Friday night. Her purple bikini has been replaced by a tight black dress, and the guy she's with seems familiar.

Her gaze meets mine, and she tilts her head to the side as we stare at each other. The guy she's dancing with notices, then says something to her while pointing at me. Her eyes widen a fraction, then she waves at me.

My legs move on their own accord. It's been almost two days, and I had wondered how she was. I'm almost halfway to her when a strong hand wraps around my bicep and pulls me to a stop. As soon as I turn around, the hand disappears, and I'm looking up into Adam's angry eyes.

"Where are you going?" he demands, getting close to me to hear over the music.

"Over there to talk to—"

"You shouldn't be wandering off by yourself. Not here, and not at any nightclub ever."

"I didn't think it was a big deal . . ." It was only a few feet away.

"Come on," he grumbles, pulling me back to the group as if I'm a child, even though I neither asked nor expected him to babysit me.

I try to shrug him off. "It's fine, I'll be right over . . ." but when I look back, the moving crowd swallows up the girl, so I drop it.

When we reach the group, I stand off to the side while everyone talks over the music to each other and dances and drinks.

"What's wrong?" Faye asks, sidling up beside me and scanning the crowd.

"What? Nothing?"

She sways a little on her feet. "Are you sure? I want you to have fun!"

I don't want Faye to worry about me, so instead I paste on a smile and wiggle my hips to the music. "I am having fun! Just taking a breather. But don't worry about me, go talk to Kellan." Taking a page from her book, I grab her shoulders, spin her around, and push her toward Kellan who's talking with Alessio. She stumbles but catches herself, then struts over to join the boys.

As I continue my search for the girl from Friday, Anaya grabs my hand. She leans in so close I can smell her flowery perfume over the alcohol and sweat in the air. Her brown eyes bore into mine. "You are *so* pretty. You need to stop shrinking back in corners!"

I shrink back in corners? "Um, thanks?"

"Let's dance!" she exclaims, chugging the rest of her mixed drink before setting it down on the bar.

Before I can answer, she pulls me by the hand onto the dance floor, bringing Kiara and Priyasha with us. I call out for Faye, but she waves at me and laughs at something Dylan says.

The music is so loud it vibrates through my bones, and we get swallowed up by the crowd as we make our way to the middle of the floor. Anaya releases my hand and before I know what's going on, we're all dancing and laughing and having a great time. The music is a mix of Spanish and English songs that are popular back home, so we get to sing along.

Kiara spins me around, then I spin her around, but we lose our balance and slam into someone behind us. The guy turns around, ready to yell at us, but he pauses when he eyes me and Kiara. He says something to Kiara and gestures to the two of us with a suggestive wink, but she just laughs at him, grabs my hand, and pulls me back into our little group of girls. We're laughing and sweating and singing at the top of our lungs, and after snorkeling, it's the most fun I've had on this trip.

Is this what I was missing throughout high school? Is this how much fun Faye was having at all those parties I didn't go to, because I was scared that I wouldn't know anyone there?

As we dance, a few guys try to grab me, but Priyasha throws her arms around me, and we dance together instead. Her brown, caramel-highlighted hair is splayed out over my shoulders, mixing with my sweat, but she doesn't care. She points at the small stage where some people are dancing. "We're going to dance up there. Right now."

Dancing with all these people around is nerve-racking enough. But dancing on stage? In front of a crowd? Where I'd feel all those eyes on me? Yeah, that'll be a big fat "heck no."

"Um . . . I'm okay," I tell her, planting my feet.

"Nope, I'm not taking that answer!" she replies, pulling me with her to the stage.

Kiara, Anaya, and Priyasha get up on stage right as the other people get off. It's tiny; there's only room for four or five people to dance around. They gesture for me to come up with them, but I shake my head. People are already staring at them, singing along with them, *looking* at them.

Glancing around, I make eye contact with Adam, who's at one bar with Alessio and Dean. Adam looks from the girls on stage to me standing right in front of it, and his eyebrows draw together in disbelief, as if the thought of me getting up on stage is absolutely absurd. He shakes his head subtly with a straight face, his eyes staring into mine meaningfully.

Suddenly, the word *boring* flashes through my mind. Predictable.

My eyes shift over to Dean. He sees me and waves.

Do you always do what you're told?

When Kiara reaches her hand down to help me up, I accept. She pulls me onto the stage, cheering along with Anaya and Priyasha.

I'm frozen. All these eyes are on me.

"Come on, Lor! Have some fun!" Anaya shouts. She grabs my hand and starts dancing, and I force myself to move along with her, even if it's robotically.

I gasp as the song fades into a Maluma song. "I love this song!" I exclaim to no one in particular, and Anaya's red lips part in a wide smile.

"Prove it, sister!" She releases my hand and bumps her hip into mine.

I want to dance, but not if everyone's looking at me. But scanning the crowd, it's clear no one's really paying attention to me. Everyone's busy having their own fun, and the people that are looking at us are dancing along with us. No one's staring. No one's making fun of me. No one's making me uncomfortable.

Priyasha grabs my hand, turning me so that I'm facing her instead of the crowd. "Follow my lead!"

She moves her hips and I follow suit, too busy trying to copy her to worry about people watching.

"Yes Lori!" Kiara throws her dark hair over her shoulder and copies our moves, and so does Anaya. In no time we've somehow choreographed a simple dance and are all moving in sync. We're singing aloud and dancing like everyone in a crowded club isn't watching us, because really, they aren't. And even if they are, I'm having so much fun that I've totally forgotten I'm up on stage, anyway.

"Room for two more?" Alessio yells up at us, and even though there's definitely not, we encourage him and Dean to jump up onto the stage.

Now I'm between Dean and Anaya, and Alessio's between Kiara and Priyasha, and the two boys copy our dance moves while sending us goofy grins.

"You look ridiculous," I tell Dean over the music, which makes his smile grow wider and his moves more exaggerated.

The stage is so small that we're practically standing on top of each other. Alessio's unbuttoned his shirt to just before his belly button, and it looks like he has no intentions of stopping. With a laugh, I jump off the stage before this turns into a full-on strip show.

"Come back, Lor!" Priyasha calls out, but I point to the bar and yell, "I'm going to get a drink."

The small crowd at the bar lets me make my way through them to order a cranberry juice.

"Hey, baby. Let me buy you a drink?" a voice directly behind me says in my ear. His sweaty hands are on either side of my waist, slipping under the hem of my shirt to slide up my bare skin. Suddenly I'm reminded of Pervy Gym Guy, about how I froze when I should've done something, should've stood up for myself when he purposely touched me, when he took a picture of me bent over.

Shifting quickly, I push the stranger away, but he holds on, his grip on my waist suffocating. I crane my neck to look up at him, grimacing as the sweat-and-beer odor combination envelops me. His smile is innocent but cocky, and a quick glance at his wrist indicates he's from a different hotel than I am.

"No thanks," I reply loudly so he can hear me.

Now he's in front of me, but his hands are still on my waist, on my bare skin. My throat closes as he tugs me closer. "Then let's dance."

A feminine hand wraps around my bicep and yanks me out of his grip. It's the girl from the resort.

"She's with me." She wraps her arm around my shoulders and looks up defiantly at the guy.

His smirk grows and a challenge ignites in his eyes. "I've got two arms, one for both of you. And my bed's big enough for later."

"Kick rocks," she sneers, and before I know what's happening, she grabs the drink the bartender is holding out to me, passes it to me, places bills on the bar, and then pulls me away.

"I love clubs, but I also hate 'em, you know?" she continues, tugging me along. "Like it would be awesome if I could dance without being touched for once."

I'm so overwhelmed by her larger-than-life presence that all I can do is gawk at her. In a way she reminds me of Faye, which must be why I warm to her instantly.

"It's so . . . hey, you okay?" She stops pulling me along once we reach a hallway that leads to the washrooms. We don't have to yell over the music here.

Shaking my head to snap out of it, I smile at her even

though I'm embarrassed. "Yeah. Thanks for back there. You didn't need to pay for my drink." I'm grateful for her help, but I wish I didn't freeze up like that; I wish I had been able to get rid of that guy by myself. If she hadn't appeared, would I have pried his sweaty hands off me? Put the much-needed distance between us? Stood up for myself the way I so desperately want to?

She waves me off. "It's nothing. But *I* should thank *you*. Thomas told me you're the one who pulled me out of the pool on Friday. So yeah, thanks."

This time I wave her off. "I'm just glad you're okay. I haven't seen you since then. How are you?"

She shrugs and leans against the wall beside me to let other people by. "I'm all right. Shit happens. I'm Naomi, by the way."

"Nice to meet you. I'm Lori."

"Well, I'm *really* glad to have met you. You're the only person who noticed I was at the bottom of that pool. I can't swim. I shouldn't have been playing around with the guys near the deep end, but then again, they shouldn't have pushed me in."

"I'm sorry," I tell her, for lack of anything else to say.

"Thomas felt terrible after," she continues. "I was pissed, and he begged for my forgiveness. Like on his knees, begging. My other friends too. I keep thinking that *no one* noticed I didn't come back up. How can you push someone into a pool and not notice they didn't come back up? Yeah, yeah, the foam was in the way, but still."

I don't want to say "I'm sorry" again, but I do. I can't imagine what she must be going through.

"But *you* noticed," she continues, scanning my face. "I don't even remember seeing you anywhere near me. How *did* you notice?"

I'm sure my cheeks are already flushed from the heat in the club; otherwise they would've lit right up from embarrassment.

"I'm a lifeguard," I sputter, trying not to think of the real reason. "I mean, not at that moment. But I was already watching you, so I noticed. But like, not creepily!"

Great, Lori. The fastest way to admit something's creepy is to tell someone you weren't being creepy.

An amused smile spreads across her face. "You were watching me? Why?"

"Not creepily!" I add again for some stupid reason and feel like face-palming. Now I have to tell her the reason, so she doesn't think I'm some stalker, which is even more embarrassing. "This is going to sound really dumb, but I had just embarrassed myself in front of this guy I really like, and I noticed you being all confident. I was wishing I was more like you when I saw them push you in."

She raises an eyebrow. "You're not confident? You were dancing on stage like you owned it a few minutes ago."

Now I know for a fact my face is fully red if it wasn't already. "That was . . . I don't know. Not me."

She tilts her head to the side and analyzes me. "Sure looked like you. Looked like you were having fun too."

How can I explain it to someone who's already so sure of herself? But no matter what I say, she's right. I was having fun. I didn't care that people were watching me.

Instead I ask, "How are you so confident?"

If she thinks it's a strange question, she doesn't show it. She purses her lips as she thinks. "Honestly? It's a combination of things. But I guess mainly it's because I know who I am and what I want, and I don't give a fuck about what other people think about me. If people don't like you, fuck 'em. If you're having fun and they don't like it, fuck 'em. As long as you're true to yourself and you're not hurting anyone, then who cares? Be who you wanna be and don't apologize for it."

Nodding, I think about her words. Faye has said some combination of them to me over the years, swear words included. Is that the secret to confidence?

Be who I want and don't apologize for it. Who *do* I want to be? The cell phone with unread messages from my mom burns a hole in my back pocket. I don't want to be a doctor, that's for sure.

"Now, tell me about this guy you have a crush on," Naomi says, and I take a sip of my drink to hide my stupid grin.

Adam's face pops into my head, but then an image of Dean replaces it and stays there. The butterflies in my stomach start up. "His name is Dean. He's handsome and manly, but he's so sweet and caring. He never forces me to do something I don't want, but he also encourages me to come out of my shell. I think he gets me. And no matter how many times I embarrass myself in front of him, he still hangs out with me."

Naomi laughs. "Sounds like he likes you. My advice? Keep being yourself; clearly it's working. But don't worry about embarrassing yourself. Be who you are and be confident in it. Is Dean, by chance, the guy who was dancing beside you on stage?"

"What? Yes! How did you know?"

She shakes her head at me like I'm missing something that she's seeing, then looks over my shoulder toward the bar. "He's right over there. You need to go talk to him."

I follow her gaze and there he is, talking with Kellan, Anaya, and Kiara. He's so easy to find because my eyes are drawn to him.

"Right now?" I ask her hesitantly, but she grins and spins me around to face my friends.

"Yes, now! I'll find you later. Maybe we can hang out at the beach tomorrow. Now go get 'em, tiger!"

With a little shove from Naomi, my feet pull me toward

Dean. Be myself. I *have* been myself, and all that gets me is embarrassed.

As I approach the group, Dean spots me. His smile is welcoming and distracting. So distracting that when I'm only a few steps away from him, my feet stumble over nothing and I lose my balance. I watch, horrified, as my cranberry juice goes flying. The bright-red liquid lands all over his pristine white shirt, soaking it right through.

I threw my juice at him!

Kellan's loud laughter knocks me out of my horrified stupor as I cross the rest of the way to Dean.

"Oh my gosh! I am so sorry! I didn't mean to do that. Oh crap!" I need to make this right, fast. I'm not supposed to be embarrassing myself anymore and here I am. I assaulted his poor shirt! And he's soaking wet now.

I'm too shocked to process what's happening. I swap my empty glass for a single small napkin, which is literally the only one on the bar. I yank his shirt up and use the little napkin to wipe the juice off his skin. It's soaked and useless in an instant.

"I'm *so* sorry. You've been nothing but nice, and here I am throwing drinks at you. When we get home I'll get you a new shirt, I promise." The little napkin has basically disintegrated, so now I'm hastily swiping at his skin with my hand as if I can wipe the liquid off with nothing more than willpower and sheer desperation.

Dean's gone completely still, and I feel his heated gaze boring into me. Only then do I look up at him and freeze when I realize what I've done—I've lifted his shirt and started groping him.

And I'm still doing it.

I stare at my hands, which are resting against his perfect abs, then back up at his face. His amused smile hits me right in the stomach.

"It's okay, Lori. Really."

Why can't the ground open and swallow me whole? Why am I not wearing thick enough foundation to hide the blush lighting up my entire face? I probably look like a tomato. A clumsy tomato. A clumsy tomato who's *still groping him.*

Dropping my hands from him like he burned them, I take a step back with wide eyes. "Sorry."

"Stop apologizing." There's a look in his eyes. He's amused, yes, but there's something more, something deeper and heated, and I like how it makes the butterflies in my stomach erupt.

"I—I didn't mean to—" Yank up his shirt and go to town feeling him up.

He laughs, unbothered. "You know, this is like the third time you've felt me up in the three days we've been here," he teases, smirking. "You must like my chest or something."

My mouth moves before my brain can catch up. "Actually, it's technically only the second time since the first time we were back home in front of Grant's Gym, meaning the *new* first time was oh my gosh I'm going to stop talking now."

I am *so cringey*. I don't even need him to talk to know what he's thinking: that I'm a weirdo who keeps count of how many times we've touched.

Get out before you make it worse!

"Yeah . . . so, um . . . bye."

With my chin tucked, I turn and scurry away before I can make anything worse, but I only go a few steps before a hand comes down on my shoulder.

"Hey, wait!" Dean says with a laugh, releasing my shoulder and coming around to stand in front of me. "I thought you were done running from me?"

I wouldn't have to run from him if I weren't such a total, embarrassing loser.

"Yeah . . . yes. Right. Not running. Just . . . going to stand over there." I point in a random direction that Dean doesn't bother looking toward.

"Dance with me?" It's a question, but his demeanor is all confidence.

He wants to dance with me? After all of that? "Okay. Let me clean myself up, and I'll be right back."

Before he can protest, I spin around and run for the restroom. My hands are soaking wet and sticky from the juice, so I can't even imagine how he must be feeling. Naomi's disappeared, so at least she didn't witness my epic failure at an attempt to flirt, unlike Kellan, who I swear I can *still* hear laughing.

After using the washroom and tipping the attendant, I search for my friends. They've shifted so they're closer to the dance floor, and Faye has joined them. Great. Kellan's going to tell Faye about the scene I made, and she's going to *love* poking fun at me about it for the rest of the night. It's only when I've gotten closer that I freeze. Something's different about this scene. Faye and Dean are separate from the group, and she's standing closer to him than she normally would. Maybe she can't hear him over the music?

No. She's biting her lip and nodding along to something he's saying, looking up at him through her lashes. She throws her head back and laughs, and it's like I can see her lips move and say, *That's so funny!* Then she shoves his shoulder playfully.

Oh. My. Goodness.

The room spins as I process what I'm seeing. That's what she told me to do when I asked her how to flirt. She's pulling her moves on *Dean*. She's *flirting* with Dean, only a few hours after I told her I had a crush on him. The music is drowned out by the rushing in my ears, and I put a hand on the wall to steady myself. Faye's my best friend. Why would she do this? She can get anyone she wants, and she chooses the one person she knew would affect me.

She steps even closer to him and now I've seen enough. I can't stay here—I *won't* stay here and watch this. Tearing my eyes away from the scene in front of me, I run for the exit. The air is suddenly too thick to breathe, and I need to get out before the spinning of the room gets worse.

As soon as I'm out of the club and into the fresh air, I can breathe more easily, but there's no way I can go back in, so I keep walking.

Alessio's outside with Priyasha and some other people having a cigar, and I pause for a second. "I'm going back to the resort. Let everyone know if they're looking for me."

"Want us to come with you?" Alessio asks, but I shake my head quickly. I want to be alone, and I don't want to cut his fun short.

"No. See you tomorrow," I say through the thickness in my throat.

I continue my journey past the club and around the corner until the music fades into the distance, and only then does the knot in my stomach release the tiniest bit.

Faye can talk to whoever she wants, and so can Dean—I don't own them. But Faye *knows* how I feel about Dean and she's still flirting with him. She's—she's selfish! She's supposed to be my best friend, and I always thought she's had my back. Apparently, I don't know anything, but one thing's for certain, I'm not vacating the room for her to have fun with Dean tonight. I want a shower and my pillow and I'm not leaving my bed for anyone.

The bitter laugh escapes before I can stop it as I stomp

toward the resort. She told me she'd find another guy to take her mind off Kellan, and it looks like she did.

I'm almost at the security gates of the resort when a large hand takes me by surprise and wraps around my bicep, yanking me to a stop.

"Ahh!" I shriek, spinning around and striking out quickly into the guy's throat, just like Sensei Dan taught during that one week of self-defense in gym class.

"Grurg—" The guy makes a noise and gasps for breath.

He releases me and grabs his neck, bending over a bit, but his light hair catches my attention just before I sprint away.

"Adam?" The adrenaline coursing through me still hasn't worn off as my heart pumps erratically. "What the heck are you doing sneaking up on me like that? You almost gave me a heart attack!"

He peers up at me and straightens, still rubbing his neck. He clears his throat, but his voice comes out a little raspy. "Sneaking up on you? I've been calling your name for the last two blocks." He clears his throat again. "Fuck, I think you knocked my Adam's apple into my stomach."

"I'm so sorry!" I'm glad it's dark so he can't see how embarrassed I am. "Reflexes."

"Your reflex is going right for the jugular?"

I shrug. "I guess."

He shakes his head and rolls his neck. "Why didn't you stop when I called you? You can't wander off! It's almost three in the morning, and you're by yourself in a foreign country."

His tone sounds patronizing, and with the mood I'm already in, I have no patience to deal with it. Something darker replaces the earlier guilt I was feeling. "I didn't hear you. And I told Alessio where I was going."

"Telling Alessio where you're going doesn't mean shit. Plus, he's drunk! You're lucky I saw you leaving; you shouldn't be out here by yourself."

My hands clench as my shoulders stiffen. I can't decide my future, and I can't talk to Dean without embarrassing myself, and I can't stand up to pervs groping me, and I can't trust my best friend to have my back, and I can't take a damn walk without supervision. I'm tired of *can't*.

I snarl through my teeth, "It's a two-minute straight walk from the club to here. I'm fine."

"You still can't just leave. This isn't like you. And what was that on stage? The Lori I know would never dance on stage."

The Lori he knows. He means the Lori he thinks is *boring*.

"It wasn't like I was naked," I defend myself, even though I don't owe Adam or anyone else an explanation. "And even if I was, it wouldn't matter because I was having fun."

"You don't need to change who you are."

His words are sweet, but he says it in a way that causes my blood to boil. I've had enough of his condescending tone. He's not my dad, and he's not in charge of me. I'm not changing anything. I was having fun.

"I'm fine," I say through clenched teeth. "I'm going inside now. Go back to the club."

Before he can say anything, I turn around and walk the last few feet toward the entrance of the resort. I can feel Adam's eyes burning into the back of my head until I flash the security guard my wristband and enter the resort.

I don't care what he says, I wasn't doing anything I didn't want to do. Yes, the girls were insistent, but I could have walked away any time. I'm glad I didn't. There's nothing wrong with experiencing new things—things I never would've done by myself. I laughed and had fun and right until the last few minutes, it was the most fun I've had in a long time.

After letting myself into my room and washing my minimal makeup off in the shower, I slip into my pj's. The moisturizer Faye keeps taking from my luggage is sitting on her nightstand, so I march over and grab it. I also take back my charcoal nose strips and hairbrush and throw everything back into my luggage before zipping it up. Usually I don't mind, but right now the thought of her taking my stuff really pisses me off. I slip into bed and close my eyes, hoping that I can get to sleep before my sense of betrayal grows any bigger and won't let me rest.

FOURTEEN

Night Three of Cuba

Faye

La Cueva was everything I imagined it to be and more. The crowd is young, and the music is amazing. It's not as big as the clubs I've snuck into back home in Toronto, but it's even better. It's a literal *cave*, and it's times like these I wish I didn't always forget my phone at home, or in this case, back at the hotel. The pictures would've been so cool.

The lights flash in time with the music as I wave Lori off when she asks me to dance, so she gets pulled into the crowd by Kiara, Priyasha, and Anaya. My plan tonight is in full effect: make Kellan realize he wants me as more than a fling by flirting with his friends and making him jealous. So far, I think it's working. I've been over here laughing with Dylan while pretending I don't notice Kellan glaring at us from the other side of the bar, instead of listening to whatever my brother's droning on about.

Kellan looks so good tonight. It feels like it's been forever since I've kissed his pouty lips instead of only two days. His button-up navy shirt is unbuttoned enough to hint at his bronzed skin, and under this light, his dark eyes are smoldering. Even the sharp cut of his jaw seems more noticeable tonight. He looks so perfect and yummy and lickable and maybe I should slow down on the tequila shots.

"Want another shot?" Dylan shouts over the music. "It's my turn to buy a round."

"Later," I shout back as the current song flows into a Maluma song, one that Lori and I always blast in the car and sing along to at the top of our lungs. "I love this song! We should dance!"

Not giving him a second to think about it, I drag Dylan onto the dance floor, letting the music and alcohol flow through me as I move my hips with the beat. He keeps a respectable distance and doesn't touch me, but dances and sings along with me. I'm having so much fun I don't even care that he's butchering the song with the wrong lyrics. Barely a few verses go by before he ditches me for a pretty girl in a red dress, but I don't care. I'm having too much fun dancing by myself.

"I was wondering what was taking you so long to get on the dance floor," says a deep, teasing voice from behind me, almost right in my ear. "You always jump at the chance."

Kellan's there, a mischievous smile lighting up his face, and looking as sexy as ever. He's moving in time with the beat, and I'm almost mesmerized. Kellan isn't a bad dancer, and he knows it.

"I was waiting for the right song," I say, ignoring my racing heart as he steps closer to me, still moving with the music.

"Have I told you how good you look tonight? I've been trying to give you space, but damn, I just can't resist," he says. His eyes send shivers down my spine as they skim over me.

The white crop top I borrowed from Lori is slightly too tight for me, which was a strategic move as well as a hit to my self-confidence. I keep tugging on it because I feel like a sausage stuffed into a tube sock, but my boobs look undeniably great.

"You've been trying to give me space?" I repeat, my mind racing back through all our interactions over the last few days. "Why?"

A flush creeps across his cheeks and neck, probably from the heat. "That's what you wanted. Right?"

My chest tightens, and I stop dancing altogether. "I did?"

He shakes his head, then steps closer to me and places his hands on my hips, making my breath hitch.

The song changes to another, and I glance around for help. "Hey, is that Lori dancing on the stage?"

It *is* Lori. She's holding hands with Anaya between Kiara and Priyasha and moving like she owns the place. Her long brown hair sways around her and her skin glistens with sweat, and she looks confident and so hypnotically beautiful. I want to cheer for her. Dancing on stage is something *I'd* do while begging Lori to join in, but this strange reversal makes me happy. It's about damn time she let loose.

"Yeah. She looks like she's having fun," he says, then turns back to me, not caring that Lori looks like a goddess on stage. "Dance with me?" He tugs me closer until we're touching practically everywhere.

The temperature rises a million degrees, but I manage to take a miniscule step back, even though that's the absolute last thing I want to do.

"Adam is *right there*." I gesture to my brother, who's within viewing distance at the bar with Alessio and Dean.

His eyebrows draw together. "So?"

I push through the lump in my throat. "He's not supposed to know about anything between us."

Kellan frowns, but I know he'd never betray my trust. We promised we'd never tell anyone, especially Adam.

"It's just a dance, Fayanna."

Risking a glance at my brother, I see he's now alone at the bar, and his eyes zero in on Kellan's hands on my hips. *Shit.* I quickly step back to force his hands to fall to his sides, ignoring the punch to the gut I feel at Kellan's deepening frown. "Later, okay?"

He nods slowly, taking a few steps back. "I can take a hint. See you around."

A wave of nausea hits me as I watch him walk away. What am I doing? I've been making a fool of myself basically all vacation to get Kellan's attention, and when I finally get it, I push him away? If I wasn't wearing perfectly applied makeup, I'd grind the heel of my hand into my eyes for clarity. Why do I keep screwing this up? What is wrong with me? Come to think of it, what's the big deal if I dance with Kellan and Adam sees? I flirt with his friends in front of him all the time! It doesn't mean anything!

My mind made up, I push through the crowd to follow Kellan and take him up on that dance. It would be nice to feel like the old us for a minute, not like the crazy version of myself I've become ever since recognizing my feelings for Kellan.

I come to a clearing in the crowd, and my confidence deflates as Kellan joins my friends dancing on stage. Lori's retreating form moves through the crowd, so she must have just jumped off, but she doesn't see me. Dean jumps off as well, and so do Alessio and Priyasha, but that doesn't stop Kiara and Anaya from pulling Kellan onto the stage and pressing up against him like they're making a fucking Kellan sandwich. My blood boils as Kellan laughs in his carefree way and turns on the charm that comes so naturally to him, which I'm sure pleases Kiara to no end. The gold dress she's wearing makes her brown skin look that much more flawless, and her heels make her legs look that much longer. I might as well be in a potato sack standing next to her. Anaya looks just as gorgeous, and I can't stand around and watch this.

Marching through the crowd, I find Dylan talking to a pretty Asian girl with dark hair. She's tracing the tattoo on his forearm with her finger, and Dylan is lapping up the attention. Dammit. I needed to talk to him, but I don't want to cockblock anyone.

I should find Lori. It's been a few hours since we got here, and I barely saw her this whole time, except to witness her dancing on stage like she owned it. But I think she's with Dean, and like with Dylan, I don't want to interrupt anything.

I must have been standing in this same spot stupidly staring at Dylan for longer than I thought, because he notices me and waves me over. I have no other option than to join them.

"Hey Faye! This is . . ." He gestures to the girl beside him, but clearly forgot her name already. He quickly fills in, "My new friend!"

She rolls her eyes but doesn't seem upset in the slightest. "I'm May. My *new friend* said it's his turn to buy a round. You in?"

I need a shot of tequila more than I need to breathe right now, but a quick glance at the closest bar reveals Dean, Kellan, Kiara, and Anaya are there now. The latter three must have left the stage when I turned around.

"Yes. But let's go to that bar over there!"

Before she can protest that it makes no sense to go to the other bar, I grab Dylan and start pulling him toward it. May follows along beside us, and I promise myself I'll leave them to get back to their flirting after one round. Then I'll find Lori, and maybe she'll snap me out of my mood and give me a pep talk to go up to Kellan and act normal.

This bar is more crowded than the other one, but neither

Dylan nor May says anything about it. The music is still loud over here, but less so since we're in the farthest corner from the DJ.

Dylan orders us a round of tequila and it doesn't burn going down as much as it did at the beginning of the night. As Dylan turns to the bartender to order a second round of drinks, May turns her sultry gaze on me.

"So, are you guys like, together?" She gestures between me and Dylan, whose back is to us.

My eyes bulge. "Me and Dylan? Ew, no."

"Perfect. So you don't mind if I . . ." She trails off, leaving me to pick up what she's insinuating.

"He's all yours."

She flashes me a satisfied smile. "Perfect. What resort are you guys at anyway?"

I tell her the name, and she pouts. "Boo," she says. "I'm at the resort next door. Guess that'll complicate things with McHottie over there." She hitches her thumb over her shoulder to point at Dylan, who's still waiting for the drinks.

I shrug for lack of anything else to say. Security would make it hard for either of them to walk into the resort they aren't staying at.

"So," she says, even though the music makes it hard to talk. "What's up with the two of you? You're really just friends with him? He's, like, totally hot."

"Yup, just friends. Dylan's just . . . Dylan." He's good-looking, I know that because I have eyes, but he's never given me massive butterflies. He's never made my heart pound out of my chest or sucked all the air from my lungs when he walked into a room. Not like Kellan does.

I must have developed a stupid, dreamy look on my face because May clues in immediately. "Ah. There's another guy."

I force myself not to glance in Kellan's direction. "Even if there wasn't, Dylan would still be all yours."

She leans against the bar, close to where Dylan is now paying for our drinks, and scans the crowd. "So where's the dreamboat you're all hung up on?"

Like magic, and against my will, my eyes zip right to Kellan. I can see him clearly even from here. Dean's white shirt is now stained bright red, but that's not the most important thing at this minute. All I care about is that Kellan and Kiara are all over each other. She dips her head in low and close to his, and I swear she plants a kiss on his neck.

The room is spinning, whether from alcohol or jealousy I'm not sure, but the pounding in my chest is ten times louder than the music. I have no claim on Kellan, but the way Kiara's hand rests on his chest as he leans in closer to hear whatever she's saying and the way her chest presses up against him makes my vision blur. I need him to pay attention to *me*, but I can't just march over there and cause a scene, especially after I'm the one who stupidly turned down a dance with him when he was so obviously flirting. He looks up, and from across the room we make eye contact. We stare at each other for one beat, two, then he looks away and laughs at something Kiara says.

He wants to flirt in front of me? Fine. Two can play at that game, and I can play it better, especially since I know flirting with his friends makes him jealous.

Where's Dylan? Once I find him, Kellan will realize I'm not sitting around pining after him, even though that's *exactly* what I'm doing. I spin around, planning to drag Dylan over to my friends and openly flirt with him, but he and May are now all over each other just like Kiara and Kellan.

Fuck. Fuck fuck fuck. Fuck it all straight to hell. The frustration clawing at my chest isn't letting me think straight, and

I'm sure the tequila isn't helping. But I don't feel drunk—I just feel *angry*. And hurt. And like curling up into a ball and crying. And like slapping him and shouting, *Why am I not good enough?!*

You can't be angry at him for a game you started, says a small voice in the back of my mind, but I push it all the way down and stuff it in a box labeled "future Faye's problems" and kick it into the recesses of my head. Yes, I started flirting with his friends first, and yes, this is me getting a taste of my own medicine. But if he thought of me as more than a fun, discreet sidepiece, we wouldn't be in this mess. We would be . . . together? I don't know, but it doesn't matter because we *are* playing games and I'm *not* more than his secret fuck buddy.

Fayanna Murray is no one's dirty little secret, and I'll be damned if I let Kellan use me then toss me aside for the next girl when he's done, not while I have real feelings for him. Not ever.

The bartender finally places three shot glasses in front of Dylan, and before I can think about it, I grab two of them and throw them both back in quick succession. Then I reach for the third and swallow it down immediately after the first two, ignoring the bewildered looks on Dylan and May's faces. The sting of the tequila is dulled by the hollow pit in my stomach, but I grab a lime slice anyway and suck on it.

"What the hell, Faye?" Dylan exclaims, but my gaze zeroes in on Dean, who's still wiping what's probably cranberry juice off his shirt with little bar napkins. Dylan's preoccupied with May, so his cousin will have to be the next best thing.

Without taking my eyes off the prize, I say, "I'll get the next round."

Straightening my spine and plastering on a smile I definitely don't feel, I stride over to Dean with the confidence that comes so naturally to me in times of distress. He's close to Kellan, but still far enough away so that our conversation won't be overheard.

"Hey, Dean," I say cheerily over the music as I sidle up to him, closer than I'd normally be, close enough to not be misinterpreted.

"Hey, Faye. Haven't seen you all night." He plops the soaked ball of napkins on the bar.

"Yeah, I've been around. Here and there, you know?" I spare a glance at Kellan, but he's not paying attention to me.

I bite my lip in a way I know looks sexy and nod at Dean while he speaks, even though I'm not listening to a single word.

"Yeah, I get it. Hey, Lori went to the restroom to clean up, have you seen her?"

Kellan's looking at me now. *Make it more obvious, Faye!*

"Ha ha ha! Oh wow! That's so funny!" My laugh is convincing even though all I feel is darkness and hurt inside, and I shove his shoulder playfully.

He's confused, it's obvious in the pursing of his lips and the way his eyebrows draw together, but I keep laying it on. Kellan's watching. I step closer to him and lay my hand on his bicep, fully aware of the fact that Kellan's giving us all of his attention now.

"What . . . are you all right?"

"Yeah, totally fine." But I'm not fine, since now there are two Deans and I can't decide which one to look at.

"Are you sure? Whoa!" Both Deans are gripping my elbow and I realize he's the only thing keeping me from falling over. "Let's get you some water."

My brother appears out of nowhere, but there are two of him too, just like Dean. Fuck. One Adam is already bad enough, but *two*? How will I ever survive?

"Have you seen Lori? Was that her I just saw leaving the club—fuck, Faye. Seriously? Are you drunk right now?" The Adams sound angry, but why are they angry? I'm the one who fucked up with Kellan! I should be the angry one.

"I'm not drunk, I just want to sit down."

The Adams shake their heads at me, disappointment written all over their faces. "Get your shit together, Faye. I'm going to find Lori. You got her, Dean?"

"Yeah, we're fine." The strong hands on my elbows pull me up again, and I didn't even realize I was falling over.

The Adams turn around, but not before shooting me one last stern look, then they disappear. Finally. Adam's always angry, but he looked *super*angry right now. Both of him did.

"Why don't we get you some water then get out of here? Let's find Kellan and the others," the Deans say, and I decide to focus on the one on the left. He's less blurry.

"No! We don't need Kellan! I'm—"

Before I can finish the statement, bile rises up my throat.

Kellan's standing in front of me now, and that's the absolute last thing I need. "Faye? Are you o—"

He doesn't finish. I slap my hand over my mouth and shove past him, nearly knocking myself over, but I make it all the way to the toilet before I remove my hand and let loose all the tequila and tacos I had into the bowl. By the time I'm done retching, my chest hurts, and I'm sure my mascara is running down my cheeks. The pit of self-despair that was sitting in my stomach earlier grows tenfold. It's a fucking canyon now.

Puking in the club bathroom? So classy, Fayanna. I'm really setting the bar high here.

I wipe my mouth with the back of my hand and lean against the dirty stall. I don't want to think about why the floor is wet, and my head hurts too much to care anyway. This is an all-time low, and I feel sick for reasons other than the alcohol.

I'm making such a mess of things. Clearly flirting with other guys in front of Kellan isn't doing anything except making a fool out of me. Does Kellan *really* want to be with a messy, unreliable girl who flirts with other guys and pukes her guts out at the club? I certainly don't want to *be* her, but here I am.

Since when have I ever let a guy affect me like this? I've never made a fool of myself for any guy, I've *always* been the one holding the cards, so why am I acting so stupid over Kellan?

Because you love him, you idiot.

Memories flash in my mind: of Kellan bringing over jelly-filled donuts even though no one else likes them, because he knows they're my favorite; of Kellan cracking jokes during scary movies, even though it annoys everyone else, because he knows I hate scary movies but I still want to hang out with Adam and his friends; of Kellan knocking on the door of my class when he was still in high school, to deliver my favorite drink from Starbucks; of Kellan's lips on mine, his hard body pressed against me . . .

Well, fuck me. It's been there all along. I thought I'd be cool with casual sex—I've been fine with it before—but with Kellan I developed feelings. I want more than casual sex, and apparently, I wanted it all along. I'm in love with Kellan, and I blew my shot. I've been screwing it up this whole trip, ever since stupidly deciding to make him jealous yesterday. Ever since I did that, I've spent less time with him. Can one day really screw everything up that badly? Apparently. I must have a special talent for screwing things up in the shortest amount of time possible.

"Faye? You in here?" Kiara calls out, but I'm too busy wallowing in self-pity to tell her *Duh, there's only three stalls in here, where else would I be?*

She pushes the stall door open and looks down her nose at me, her lips in a straight line. I can only imagine what she's thinking.

She breaks the silence first. "The bathroom attendant told me we're kicked out. No puking policy. We need to leave the club."

"Fantastic. Give me a few minutes." So the room can stop spinning.

She doesn't move for a moment, then she sighs. "You can't pass out here. Come on, get up."

She grabs some toilet paper and wipes my face even though I pull away from her. The last thing I need is the girl Kellan's going to end up with making me feel even more stupid.

"I'm fine. Why are you in here? To gloat?"

Her shoulders stiffen and her jaw clenches. "I'm not here to gloat. Kellan asked me to come check on you."

That's cute. Sending his soon-to-be girlfriend to witness for herself what a mess I am. It doesn't help that she's standing there looking every bit as gorgeous as when she left the resort, and I'm sitting on the piss-covered floor puking my guts out.

"I'm sure you can't wait to go back to Kellan and tell him what a disaster I am," I say, my voice laced with venom.

She shakes her head, annoyance written plainly all over her face. "Kellan doesn't care; he just wants to make sure you're safe. Come on, before security comes in here."

A humorless laugh bubbles up from my throat as she tries to help me stand. "Yeah, right. You don't need to pretend to be nice to me, you've already won Kellan. Get him those little blueberry muffins, those are his favorite."

I don't know why I'm babbling to Kiara like this when she's clearly only here to escort me out of the club. Maybe it's because she's seeing me at the lowest I've ever been, even lower than the aftermath of any stunt Jenna ever pulled. Maybe it's because I'm drunk and realized I'll never be with the guy I love. Or maybe it's because I'm throwing a pity party, and it makes sense my competition gets a front-row seat.

She finally succeeds in pulling me up and turns me to face her. With her hands on my shoulders, she gives me a little shake.

"Snap out of it. I've only known you for three days, and even I know this isn't like you."

She releases me, and I'm able to stand on my own two feet. "I didn't *win* Kellan," she continues, crossing her arms over her chest. "He only has eyes for you. Everyone can see that."

I must be really drunk. Did I hear that correctly? "But you guys were flirting all night."

She exhales sharply and looks away from me. "We weren't flirting. *I* was flirting with *him*. He was just being nice. I tried to kiss him last night and he set me straight, saying he's not into me like that. I'm obviously friend-zoned."

"But—I—" Friend-zoned? This gorgeous woman in front of me is saying *she's been friend-zoned by Kellan*? They've never done anything? He turned down a kiss? Oh wow. I'm an even bigger fool than I originally thought.

Kiara shifts and gestures to the door. "Can we go now? I'm pretty sure security has been called. Do you need help walking?"

Still reeling from all of tonight's revelations, I shake my head. "I can walk."

With her right behind me, I wash my hands and apologize to the bathroom attendant, who looks less than pleased with me, but I fish out a wad of bills from my purse and place them in her tip basket. That won't make up for the mess I made, but it's the best I can do.

The restroom door opens, revealing Kellan arguing with a security guard. He sees Kiara and I emerge and raises his hands in an innocent gesture, then wraps his arm around my shoulder and leads me toward the front door.

"You okay?" he asks, looking at me like he's genuinely concerned and not even remotely disgusted like he should be.

All I can do is nod and let him guide me out of the club and into the cool night air.

Since I'm putting all my effort into taking calming breaths and stepping one foot in front of the other, I barely say a word to anyone as we meet up with our friends. Lori's missing, and so are Anaya, Priyasha, and Alessio, but everyone else is here to witness my messy exit. Even May is here. She's watching me with sympathetic eyes, making my chest tighten more. Dylan's studying me with pursed lips. He steps toward me, but then notices Kellan's arm around my shoulders and pauses. He winks at me and turns around to talk with May again.

"Should we call a cab?" Kellan asks, his warm arm still secure around me.

"For a five-minute walk? I can handle it." I straighten my spine so I'm not leaning all my weight on him anymore as if that'll prove my point, but he doesn't release me.

He must see the determination in my eyes because his jaw clenches, and he doesn't protest, even though I know he wants to.

"All right then, let's go," he says, and we all start walking back the way we came, Kellan and I taking up the rear pitifully slowly, but he doesn't complain, not even once. He doesn't even make fun of me.

Adam, however, comes over to us, his nostrils flared, and his lips pressed together. The puking must have sobered me up a bit because there's only one of him now. "I know you're irresponsible but come on, Faye. This is bad even for you."

My cheeks burn with indignation, and we stop walking, the rest of our friends continuing without us.

"Lay off, Adam," Kellan says, but I don't need him to get into a fight with my brother on my behalf. I can do that myself.

"Don't be such a hypocrite. You were worse literally *last* night. At least *I* didn't puke on anyone." Not like he did with Lori.

If possible, his expression hardens even more. "I'm not the one who got us kicked out of a club. Plus, you're lucky we were here to watch after you. You should never get that drunk at a club."

Why am I being lectured? By *Adam* of all people? I already feel like shit, and I don't need Adam pretending to care.

"I'm lucky you were here?" I push Kellan's arm off and march closer to Adam, my hands clenched into fists. "You left! I didn't see you all night and when you saw I was drunk, you left! I can take care of myself, but if I'm supposed to be lucky that someone was here, it would be because of Kellan. Or Dean. Hell, even *Kiara*. But not you. Don't pull the concerned big brother card right now, not when you've never cared about me before. You only care about yourself and getting in trouble with Mom and Dad if something had happened to me in the club. You don't care about *me*. You never have."

I didn't realize that my voice was growing higher and higher as my rant went on, but by the end I'm practically screaming. Our friends, who are now much farther down the street than us, have turned around to stare at us.

Adam is standing ramrod straight and his muscles are stiff. But he doesn't yell back at me. In a low voice, he calmly asks, "Who's missing here, Faye?"

The sudden change of topic takes me aback. "Um, Priyasha, Anaya, Alessio, and Lori?"

"Lori," he repeats. "Your best friend. You just left the club without her; didn't even stop to ask where she was. Everyone else did. When I left, it was to go make sure she was safe. So if anyone only cares about themselves, it's you."

His statement makes all the blood drain from my face, and I'm frozen to the spot. I knew Lori wasn't here, but I didn't stop to wonder where she was. The pounding in my head gets worse.

I glance over at Kellan, but he averts his gaze. In my defense, I was a little occupied with the whole too-much-tequila thing, but I still feel like a shitty friend.

"Where is she?"

"Back at the resort," he says. "She left before you started puking."

Come to think of it, I haven't seen much of her all night. I was too busy with the stupid jealousy plan. So not only did the plan ruin stuff with Kellan, but it also made me ignore my best friend. A sharp pain runs through my head, and I wince.

"Let's get back to the hotel," Kellan pipes up, putting his arm around me again. "It's late, and we're all drunk and tired. Just drop it, Adam."

Adam opens his mouth to say something, then closes it, turns, and walks away. I don't regret what I said to Adam; I meant every word, and he didn't even bother denying it. My whole life I just wanted to be *friends* with him, but he's always done everything he could to pretend I don't exist. But he's right. I haven't been acting like myself. I had already realized that while my head was hanging over the toilet bowl.

Kellan says nothing else as we walk back, and I don't want him to. Today is a complete shit-show, and it made me realize just how much I've been fucking up.

When we finally get back to the hotel, everyone says good night, and we all go our separate ways. Adam storms into his room without a second glance, but Kellan walks me to my room. The lights are all off and the room is shrouded in darkness, but the moonlight coming in from the sliding door is enough light for us to navigate. Lori is fast asleep under the covers of her own bed, so Kellan guides me inside as quietly as possible and deposits me on the bed. The room is spinning, and my muscles are exhausted. I just want to crawl into bed and sleep until next week.

Kellan must sense it, because without my asking, he bends down and slips my shoes off, placing them gently on the floor, then peels back the covers and holds them up for me to slide under.

"I'll grab your makeup wipes. I know you hate sleeping with makeup on," he says, heading into the bathroom where my toiletry bag is sitting. I do hate that; it makes me break out.

My eyelids are already drooping as I peel off my shirt and skirt. I can't wait to hit the pillow, but I remember sitting on the disgusting bathroom floor, and even drunk, I know I don't want to dirty up my precious sheets.

Rolling off the bed, I land on the floor with a loud thud in nothing but my bra and thong, but the lump of blankets on Lori's bed doesn't move.

"Are you okay?" Kellan whispers as he rushes out of the bathroom and helps me up. "What are you doing?"

"I want a shower," I whisper, but my voice still sounds too loud.

"Do you need help?" he asks, his cheeks flushed. "Not in the shower or anything. I won't look. I just meant . . . I don't know. Not in a creepy way or anything," he stutters, which is so unlike Kellan's usual confidence it makes me stare up at him in wonder.

I don't need him to help me anymore. I'm perfectly capable of handling a shower. He's already helped me more than I ever expected him to, especially after the way I've been acting. My heart jumps to my throat as I gaze into his warm eyes. He isn't even looking at me with pity or anger or disgust.

"I'll be okay," I tell him, walking toward the door with him right behind me. "Thanks for your help, Kell. I really appreciate it."

He nods as I hold the door open for him. "Make sure you take some Advil in the morning if you have a headache."

I bite my lip, nervous. "Okay. Thanks Kellan."

He shoots me one last look before leaving my room and heading down the hall to his own.

My shower is quick and I'm more refreshed, but I'm still exhausted as I slip into bed with wet hair. Kellan cares about me. I know he does. I've been playing this all wrong. All I need is a good night's rest, water, and some time for the shame to fade, then I can approach this situation with a whole new perspective. Maybe Kellan's not lost to me. Maybe I have time to fix everything I've been fucking up. When I wake up tomorrow, it'll be day four of this trip, and day one of Operation: Stop-Looking-and-Acting-Like-a-Jackass.

FIFTEEN

Day Four of Cuba

Faye

I expect to be at least slightly hungover when I crack open my eyes in the morning, but I'm perfectly fine, almost like nothing ever happened.

If only that were the case.

Lori's not in the room, and a quick glance at my phone reveals it's nine a.m. She must have gone for breakfast and not wanted to wake me. I wonder if everyone's telling her what a sloppy mess I was.

Not today, Faye. Today's the day we turn everything around.

I'm almost glad I hit rock bottom last night. It allowed me to realize what I'm doing wrong and how to fix it, and I *am* going to fix it.

I take another shower, this time doing a better job than I probably did last night. When I emerge in a towel, Lori is walking into the room.

"Hey! Where's your moisturizer? The coconut one I like.

I swear it was right here yesterday," I ask her, pointing to the nightstand. I hope I didn't throw it somewhere last night.

She freezes for a second, then her shoulders slump and she unzips her luggage, pulling out the container and tossing it to me.

"Thanks. How was breakfast?"

"Fine," she says curtly with her back to me, pulling a swimsuit out of her luggage. "Kiara told me you had a fun time last night."

I scoff. *I'm sure Kiara told her* lots *of things about me.* "About as fun as having your teeth pulled. Where did you go?"

"Left early." She enters the bathroom and all but slams the door closed.

My hands pause their motion of rubbing moisturizer into my legs as I stare after her. I may not be the Lori whisperer, but even I recognize when she's pissed. She'll never tell me unless I ask, and it'll eat her up until she explodes. Throwing on my own swimsuit, a purple bandeau with matching cheeky bottoms, I sit on my bed and wait for her to leave the bathroom. She barely looks at me when she exits in her own black bikini, so now I'm positive my theory was right.

"Okay, spill. Why are you mad? I didn't puke on any of your things, I swear."

She pulls her beach bag from the closet. "Wow. I'm surprised you stopped thinking about yourself for a second to realize I'm upset."

I'm taken aback by the obvious shade she's throwing at me. Why would she be mad at me? I rack my brain to figure out what I could've done.

"I'm sorry I didn't stop and ask where you were before we left the club last night. That was shitty of me, I should've had your back. But in my defense, I was seeing double and could barely walk straight."

She spares me a glance, but her eyebrows are drawn together like she has no idea what I'm talking about. Okay. If not that, then what have I done?

Standing up, I ask, "What did Kiara say to you? Is she turning you against me?"

She faces me properly for the first time since entering the room, and her mouth is set in a hard line. "Kiara didn't say anything. I'm mad at you because you don't think about anyone but yourself."

Her words hit me like an imaginary blow, and I take a physical step back from the impact of them. Adam said the same thing yesterday. "What are you talking about?"

She draws her shoulders back, standing to her full height. "I don't own Dean. I know that. And I'm aware that I haven't really known him that long, but you *knew* how I feel about him, and you *still* hit on him. You can get *any* guy you want, and you had to choose the one guy you knew I liked. You haven't even said one word to him all week! Why flirt with him now?!"

I'm stunned to silence. Did I flirt with Dean last night? Technically, not really. I said about three sentences to him before running off to puke. But I *wanted* it to look like I was flirting with him, and that's what's important. Lori must have seen me right at the beginning and drawn her own conclusions, which, in her defense, is the exact conclusion I wanted everyone to draw.

"Okay, I know it looked bad, but I wasn't really flirting with Dean."

She crosses her arms over her chest but doesn't say anything, which prompts me to continue. My stomach tightens, but I push through it.

"I'm sorry I wasn't thinking of you when I did that. I'm a terrible friend, and I haven't been acting like myself during this trip. But I don't have any interest in Dean because I'm in love with Kellan." The words tumble out of my mouth before I'm able to catch my breath. "I'm in love with him, and I want to be more than his secret fling, and I hate that he only wants me as a booty call, so I came up with a stupid plan. I wanted to make him jealous, so he'd realize he had actual feelings for me instead of just lust, and I understand it's stupid now and I realize I've been fucking up all week. He was being all buddy-buddy with Kiara and I was already drunk, not that it's an excuse, but Dean was *right there*, and I just wanted Kellan to want me."

"Whoa, whoa, whoa—wait. What?" The cold exterior Lori's been wearing since walking into the room has melted, and now she's regarding me with shock and curiosity. "You're in love with Kellan? Does he know?" She pulls me to sit beside her on her bed.

"No! Are you crazy? I can't tell Kellan I'm in love with him! He'll probably laugh in my face."

"He would not laugh in your face, Faye," she says. "It seems like he really cares about you. How many guys do you know who would take your makeup off for you since they remember that you don't like sleeping with it on?"

"But—you were sleeping. How did you know about that?"

She rolls her big blue eyes. "Seriously? Do you know how loud you are? I was pretending to sleep because I was mad and didn't want to talk to you."

"Was? So, you're not mad anymore?" I ask, hope creeping into my voice. "I swear nothing frisky went on. If it makes you feel better, he was confused the whole time and after a few words I puked my guts out. Plus, I think he asked about you."

She perks up at that. "He did?" She shakes her head as if trying to focus on the topic at hand. "I'm not mad at you anymore. I get that you're going through this whole revelation and acting stupid because of it. But making Kellan jealous isn't the right way to play this. You should be honest with him instead of playing these mind games. Tell him how you feel, even if you leave out the *L* word for now."

I knew she'd say that, which is why I didn't tell her in the first place. She's always the voice of reason, and I'm the spontaneous one—it's why we work.

"I know, I know. I realized that on the disgusting bathroom floor of the club. I'm not sure what I'll do, but I'm done with the games, I promise. I'm sorry for hurting you. That must have looked really bad, but you know I'd never do anything like that to you."

She chews on her bottom lip for a moment, then says, "Even though I was pissed, I just kept thinking about Alex Castillo."

"Alex Castillo?"

"Yeah. Do you remember last year when I told you about my massive crush on him?"

It's an odd question, but I nod anyway. She continues, "I refused to talk to him at school, so you threw a party. You invited a bunch of guys that had been mean to you all through high school because Alex was friends with them, because if they came, he would too."

Oh geez. Lou, Connor, Pat, and Chris were only a few of the group of assholes always spreading rumors about me and who had labeled me the school slut, even though I had never slept with any of *them*. I think they were upset that I wouldn't touch them with a ten-foot pole. But Alex wasn't all bad, and he wouldn't show up to a party alone. Lou, Connor, Pat, and Chris wouldn't come to a party if they knew I threw it, since it was a pride thing, so I had to get another girl, Cassey, who at least two of them had a thing for, to tell them it was her party.

Lori continues, "You even managed to get kegs. Everyone said it was the party of the year, even *Jenna* was upset she wasn't invited when she heard everyone talking about it at school. But you spent the entire time hyping me up to talk to Alex, and when I chickened out, you somehow got me and Alex alone in the backyard."

I chuckle at the memories of that night. By "somehow," she means I ordered pizza, told everyone who was outside to go in and grab a slice, asked Alex to wait because Lori wanted to talk to him about something, threw Lori outside, closed the sliding door on them, then stood guard in the kitchen and didn't let anyone else outside. I knew they would hit it off, and Lori always needs a little push, or else she'd never talk to the guy she liked or do the things she totally can but thinks she can't.

Lori bites her lip. "I got my first kiss that night. It's one of my favorite memories, and it's because of you."

I shake my head. "It's because of *you*. I got you guys alone, but you did all the talking."

"But it never would've happened if you didn't orchestrate that whole thing. I still can't believe your parents were cool with you throwing a party while they were out of town."

"Ha ha. Yeah, me too." My parents had no idea, and Adam was out that night. My house ended up getting destroyed and I was grounded for like, ever, but I told Lori I was grounded for a different reason because I didn't want her to feel bad. "What does this have to do with our current situation?"

The corners of her lips curl up. "It means I know the hoops you'll jump through for me. I know, in your heart, you're a good person and a great friend, but sometimes you lose sight of things. I know you'd never try to get with Dean if you knew I liked him, but in the moment, it didn't look good. This thing with Kellan is driving you crazy; you should really talk to him."

"I know, I know. Dylan said the same thing when I told him about my stupid plan. I'm going to sort everything out today. And to make up what a terrible friend I've been to you, I'm going to pull an Alex Castillo on you and Dean."

She laughs and playfully shoves me. "You do not need to orchestrate an entire night to get me to kiss Dean."

The weight on my chest lifts. I'm so grateful to have Lori. She's the yin to my yang, the bread to my butter, the chocolate to my strawberry; one would be incomplete without the other.

"Are you sure?" I ask. "Because I'm already envisioning a scenario that includes a boat, a roasted pig, a wrench, and maybe a tame lion."

"Stop it." She giggles at my teasing. "You focus on fixing things with Kellan. But . . ." She pauses and bites her lip, and I know she's trying to figure out how to say something I won't like.

"Just spit it out."

"You should apologize to Kiara too. You've been really mean to her, and she's been nothing but nice."

My mouth drops open. "I will not! Did you forget she pulled my bikini top off for everyone to see at the pool party two nights ago?"

"She did what?!"

Oh, I guess I never told her about that. "It doesn't matter. Kiara and I will never get along, and that's fine with me." But she *was* kind of helpful last night. *And* she told me Kellan friend-zoned her. *And* I don't have definitive proof it was her who pulled my bikini top off, but still. We can stay out of each other's way and that'll be that.

"Fine. But I told her we'd meet her and her friends at the pool today, so you're going to have to get over it."

I groan and fall back on the bed. The last thing I want to do is spend time with Kiara, but I kind of owe Lori, and I guess Priyasha and Anaya aren't *terrible*.

"All right. Let me get my stuff, and we can go down."

I wonder if I'll run into Kellan today. What would I even say to him? Thanks for not laughing at my drunk ass? Sorry I'm such a fuck-up? Yeah, I don't think so.

—

Turns out, I didn't have to worry about what I'd say to Kellan, since I didn't see him or any of the guys all day. They must have been on one of the beaches, whereas Lori and I, plus Kiara, Priyasha, and Anaya, stayed at the calmest pool of the three, not the party one or the red-wristbands-only pool. Apparently Priyasha is fighting with one of the guys they came with, so they wanted to avoid the beach where he went.

With my headphones popped in and eyes closed as I lounge on a pool chair, it's almost like Kiara isn't there. Everyone asked me how I was feeling when we first came down, but other than that, no one made any comments about last night, which I'm grateful for. I'm sure if Dylan hadn't been even worse than me the night before, he'd be *itching* to make fun of me.

The day goes by quickly, and before we know it, we're grabbing dinner and heading back to the room. Lori and I take turns showering and decide to take a quick nap before the night's activities. By the time it's almost dark out, Lori and I are changed and ready to go to the event at the red-wristbands-only pool. We head down to the pool dressed in bikini tops and short shorts. I ditch the flip-flops and walk barefoot since I'm down to only Kellan's pair, and I really don't want to lose those.

Like every night, we hear the loud music before we reach the pool. There are inflatable floats shaped like pineapples and ducks everywhere with people splashing around them. Lights are flashing in time with the song, and everyone is wearing identical white T-shirts.

Tonight is a Seven Tasks event, and when we flash our wristbands at the pool entrance, the worker hands us each a white cotton T-shirt in our size and tells us there are markers on all the tables to use. Printed on the back of the shirt is a list of seven tasks beside a checkbox, and our job is to do all the tasks throughout the night and check them off. Kind of like a scavenger hunt for drunk adults, but without having to search for anything.

We venture deeper into the party, and I scan the pretty doable list of tasks. They are: do a dare, a body shot, and a piggyback ride, take a shot with no hands, swap a piece of clothing, kiss someone, and take part in a dance-off.

Slipping my shirt on, I catch Lori eyeing the tasks warily. "You don't have to do them all, you know," I tell her.

She lowers her hands and frowns. "Do you think I'm boring?"

"What?"

"Do you think I'm boring?" she asks again, emphasizing each word.

"No, I don't think you're boring," I reply, scanning the crowd.

"But you think I'm predictable?"

"Where is this coming from?" I ask.

"Just answer the question," she demands, watching me carefully.

Pausing, I think about what she wants me to say versus the truth, but as her best friend, she deserves the unfiltered truth.

"I don't think you're boring or predictable. You're just you;

you're comfortable not being the center of attention, and that's okay."

She frowns like I said the worst possible thing. "Do you think I should—I don't know—do more to stand out?"

She's not aware of it, but she already stands out in a crowd because she's so drop-dead gorgeous, at least when she's not actively trying to fade into the background.

"Why are you asking this all of a sudden?"

She shrugs and pouts at the ground.

Obviously something is up, but I won't push it. "I love you for who you are, and *you* should love you for who you are too. Do I wish you'd be more confident and show the world the Lori I know and love? Fuck yeah. But if you don't want to, then don't. All I'm saying is you prefer the background, and if that makes you happy then screw everyone else." I pause as she purses her lips in thought. "But put yourself out there a little more, you're missing all the fun."

"How do I do that? Put myself out there more?"

I gesture at the task shirt she's clutching in her hand. "Doing those tasks would be a start. They all encourage you to actually *talk* to people, to have fun with them. Maybe you'll make new friends. Who knows! But if you're having fun, who cares?"

"Yeah, I guess." She doesn't seem convinced, but she slips the T-shirt over her head and adjusts it.

"Good," I say, looking around for Kellan and our friends before spotting them talking to some other guys. "I don't care which tasks you do, as long as you check off the 'kiss someone' box with Dean."

"I—kiss—what?! You said I don't have to do anything I don't want to!"

Tilting my head, I give her my best *really?* look. "So you *don't* want to kiss Dean?"

She swallows, her words coming out choppy. "Well, I mean, I do, if he does . . ."

"Exactly. Nothing's wrong with a little push. There he is now!"

She spins in the direction I pointed, and Dean, in all his gorgeous, ruffle-haired glory, is sauntering over to us. He cleaned up the stubble that was getting a bit long, and the closer shave just makes his jawline appear that much sharper. I swear he's gotten a bit more sunburnt, but it does nothing to detract from his handsomeness. Lori squeaks and looks at me as if for help. She really needs a push—if it were up to her, she'd never make a move on him—so I give her a push, literally, right in Dean's direction.

I must have used too much force because Lori covers more ground than I anticipated, her arms flailing as she tries to keep her balance. "Ahh!"

Dean grabs her waist and releases her once she's steady. "We really need to stop meeting like this," he says, giving me a curious glance.

I wave innocently at him and leave them to their flirting, feeling triumphant that at least one of us is making progress with their crush. I barely get a few feet before Dylan practically runs me over.

"Hey, there you are!" He turns around and squats. "Hop on."

"What?"

He hitches his thumb over his shoulder to point at his shirt, where over half the boxes are checked off, then he turns to face me. "Alessio, Kellan, and I are competing to see who can get them all ticked off first. I'm still missing *piggyback ride*, *kiss someone*, and *body shot*. You're helping me with one of them, so take your pick."

Letting Dylan do a body shot off me, kiss him, or be carried around? It's a no-brainer.

"Get lower."

He complies quickly and I hop on his back, my arms wrapping securely around his broad shoulders. He wastes no time charging toward where Alessio and Kellan are standing near some pool lounge chairs.

"Ha! Piggyback!" Dylan exclaims, letting me down. "Check it off!" He hands me a marker and I check it off for him, then turn around so he can check mine off too.

Alessio rushes over. There's urgency in his voice. "Faye! Drop your pants!"

"What? Why?"

"We need to switch pants. I'm only missing switching an article of clothing and body shot, then I win!" He gets his shorts down a few inches before I grab his arm to stop him.

"Whoa! I'm not switching my pants with you; you'll stretch them out."

He frowns. "If you don't take your pants off right now, I'm going to lose. Do you want to be responsible for me losing? Can you live with yourself if I lose, Faye?"

Every time he says the word *lose* he gets a little more intense, and I take a step back while stifling my giggles. "I think I'll be able to sleep at night, yeah."

"Leave her alone, Alessio," Kellan says, wrapping his arm around me and pulling me closer. The butterflies that make an appearance every time I'm near him start up in my stomach and my breath hitches. *His arm is over my shoulders. His side is pressed up against mine.*

"You just want her for yourself to check off the body shot!" Alessio says before spotting Anaya walking by with some other people. "Hey, Anaya! Take off your pants!" he yells, rushing to her.

"He's going to end up getting slapped." Adam appears,

looking grumpier than usual, sitting down on one of the lounge chairs with his beer. He doesn't acknowledge me, and I don't acknowledge him, and that's fine with me. I'm still upset with him about last night, and he probably feels the same way, so if he wants to ignore me then so be it.

"What do you still have left?" I ask Kellan, and he turns around for me to see that all tasks are checked off except body shot and kiss someone.

"Dylan and I are tied right now, both needing the same things," he says, walking backward to the bar. "But I'm about to win."

He turns and makes his way through the crowd, leaving us all staring after him. The white shirt stands out against his smooth, tan skin, and his dark hair is all purposefully ruffled. He's the hottest guy here by a long shot and judging by the way my heart pounds in my chest, it knows it too.

"What? How did he check off swapping a piece of clothing?" Dylan asks Adam. "Literally no one is wearing clothing here!"

Adam shrugs. "We swapped flip-flops."

"That's not an article of clothing!"

"It definitely is," I tell Dylan.

"Well shit," he says, grimacing. "I could've done that instead of swapping shorts with that random guy."

"Ew!" I exclaim. "You put on a random person's shorts?" I eye the blue shorts that seem a bit too large for him with a newfound disgust.

"It's not like we traded boxer briefs," he says flatly, then claps his hands together. "Now lay down and let me pour tequila in your belly button."

I step back from him. "Okay, you and Alessio need to calm down. Adam's right, your competitiveness is going to get you punched in the face."

He pouts. "Come on, Faye. Take one for the team."

"If she's on any team," Kellan says, reappearing with a tray of shots, "it's mine."

"What? Why your team?" Dylan asks.

Kellan sets the tray of shots down on the little table between the lounge chairs. "Because I know her better." He tugs on my ponytail, and I swat his hand away.

"No. I've known her longer, therefore better," Dylan defends himself, and Kellan and I immediately lock eyes as I bite my lip. Images flash through my mind: Kellan and me naked, tangled between the sheets, his hands everywhere . . .

No, Dylan, you most certainly do not.

"Either way," Kellan says, recovering quicker than me, "she's Team Kellan, right Faye?"

When he flashes that white smile at me, I melt. All I can do is nod.

"Yes!" he exclaims, taking my hand. "You're the best, Fayanna. Shot?"

The smell of tequila hits me, and my stomach hurts. "No thanks." Why are they always drinking tequila or beer? There are so many drinks that are equally good, and they always go straight for the gross beer or the powerful tequila. After last night, I'm staying away from the drinks, for a few hours at least.

"So, are you going to help me win?" Kellan says to me, quieter this time, and again, all I can do is nod. When he's looking at me like that, with a spark in his eyes and the corners of his lips turned up, gazing at me like he can see *me*, it's almost impossible to form words.

"Perfect! I need *body shot.* You wanna do it off me or the other way around?"

Now that I realize what I agreed to, I'm sure I'm giving off a deer-in-the-headlights vibe. I'd be fine with this any day of the week, but not while my brother is two feet away, his glare drilling holes in my head.

"Kellan . . ." I start, but then drift off. Yesterday I turned Kellan down for a stupid *dance* because I was scared of Adam and look how that turned out. Plus, why am I so concerned about what Adam thinks? He obviously doesn't care about me and never will. I shouldn't have to stop my fun because I'm worried about Adam, who is more of an annoyed babysitter than a big brother anyway.

"Fuck it," I say, lying down on the lounge chair and lifting my shirt to just below my bikini top.

"Yes!" Kellan pumps his fist in the air, picking up a shot from the tray beside me.

"Are you serious?" Adam asks, sitting up straighter in his chair on the other side of the table.

"Faye! Don't do this to me!" Dylan whines. "I'll be out two hundred bucks, and that's American dollars, so it'll be even more in Canadian!" But under the put-out facade his eyes are wide. He shoots me a look, his eyes flicking from Adam to me with purpose, like he's asking if I'm sure I want to do this right in front of Adam.

I'm done ruining my could-be relationship with Kellan because I'm so concerned about what my brother thinks. Besides, it's an innocent body shot at a party; it's not like we're dry-humping all over the place. He can't be that mad at something so little and for fun.

Without getting up, I pluck the lime from the tray beside me. "Shouldn't have made the bet then," I tell Dylan to let him know it's all good, then smile at Kellan. "Ready."

Holding the lime wedge by its peel between my lips, I give him a thumbs-up and settle into the lounge chair. Kellan laughs, his fun-loving energy contagious, and the butterflies escape my stomach and erupt all over my body. He pours the shot onto my stomach over my belly button, then leans over and sucks it up, his tongue tickling but feeling heavenly at the same time as he licks up to my sternum. I giggle, willing my cheeks not to heat. Kellan slowly moves up toward my face, his body hovering above mine, and all the laughter drains from my body as my heart speeds up. Using his teeth only, he plucks the lime from my mouth, his lips coming so close to my own but still so far. As I lick lime juice from my lips, we lock eyes. His are swirling with emotions that I can't exactly place, but they're so intense I can't look away. He's not really touching me, but I still feel him everywhere, still feel the heat his body is emitting. He's so close he must be able to sense my heart beating out of my chest. *Does he feel the same way I do? Does he know how much he affects me?*

"Damn it! I can't believe Kellan's going to win four hundred American bucks," Dylan groans, breaking the spell Kellan and I are under.

Kellan shakes his head and I blink a couple of times, trying to come back to reality. He stands stiffly, pulling the lime out of his mouth and holding out a hand to help me up; if he hadn't, I'm sure my knees would've buckled. I catch Dylan's eye and mouth, *Thank you.* I have no idea what we must have looked like, gazing into each other's eyes, our faces inches from each other . . . Dylan winks.

"Thanks, Faye." Kellan's voice comes out low and thick, so he clears his throat, but his eyes are still heavy with emotion, his body still too close to mine.

"Shit! Did Kellan win?" Alessio runs over to us in pink bikini bottoms that barely hold in all the important stuff. "Did I beg Priyasha to switch swimsuits with me for no reason?"

"He has one more task left. Also, did you know you could've

just switched flip-flops with someone? That's what Kellan and Adam did," Dylan says, flinching at Alessio's pale exposed thighs.

The blood drains from Alessio's face. *"Seriously?"*

Kellan shrugs, and Adam refuses to look at us from his spot on the lounge chair. I haven't looked at him since the body shot.

"Now I only have *kiss someone* left, and the money is mine!" Kellan exclaims, turning his heated gaze back to me, and I shiver.

It's one thing to do a body shot in front of Adam, even a very sexy one, but can I actually *kiss* Kellan in front of him?

"Don't do it, Faye!" Alessio calls, "I'll give you a hundred bucks from my winnings if you don't!"

Kellan laughs. "You don't have to bribe her; I'm not going to kiss her."

"You're not?" Alessio, Dylan, and I all ask at the same time. If not me, who's he going to kiss?

Kiara's nearby and my stomach twists, but Kellan surprises us by grabbing Dylan's face, turning his head, and planting a loud, exaggerated kiss on his cheek. Dylan groans and pushes him away. "Fuck, you just won."

Kellan's face lights up. "Yes, I did. I'll collect my winnings later, though."

Alessio and Dylan huff and puff about hating losing, but they still congratulate Kellan. The boys babble on while my mind spins with thoughts of Kellan. Apparently, he's content with pretending nothing happened last night, but the gnawing in my stomach hasn't stopped since then. I used to talk to Kellan about everything, and that shouldn't change because I caught feelings. After Lori, and sometimes Dylan, Kellan's my best friend, the person I'm closest to, the person I can talk to, the one who can make my problems feel like nothing.

So why aren't you talking to him now?

The voice in my head is right. This is a problem, and it can be solved by talking to Kellan about it like I should've done in the first place.

I reach out and touch the smooth skin of his arm, just a graze to get his attention, then pull my hand back.

"Hey, Kell, you got a sec?" It comes out timidly, and I want to curse myself. I've never been shy and intimidated by Kellan before, but what I'm about to do scares me shitless.

"Yeah, sure." He says something to Alessio and pats him on the back before stepping away from them to stand with me. "What's up?"

Alessio, Dylan, and Adam are all way too close for comfort. Not that any of them are paying attention to us; Dylan's got them all engaged in some story he's telling, his arms flailing about as he talks.

I grab Kellan's forearm and tug him along with me, trying to get some distance between us and Adam. What I'm about to do requires one hundred percent of my resolve, and I don't want to falter because I can feel my brother's disapproving glare burning through my skull.

I'm going to do it. Rip off the Band-Aid. Lori, Dylan, and even *Kiara* told me I'm not acting like myself because I'm going crazy over Kellan and to tell him how I feel, so that's what I'm going to do. I'm going to muster up all the courage I have and apologize for being an ass yesterday and tell him what's going on in my head.

Now that we've put some distance between us and my brother, I stop beside a table littered with discarded beer bottles and empty drink glasses, and release Kellan's arm. He doesn't say anything, only looking at me expectantly with an encouraging smile, waiting for me to explain why I dragged him away from his friends. I stare into his warm brown eyes and open my mouth, but nothing comes out. My throat squeezes and my stomach tightens with a feeling I've never experienced before: fear of rejection.

This is weird. I've never cared enough to be afraid before. I'm about to tell him I'm in love with him and hope he doesn't laugh in my face. But this is *Kellan*. He's the boy who takes me on three-in-the-morning drives to get Iced Capps from Tim's, and we'd sit on the hood in the warmer weather and stare at the stars and talk about everything and anything. He'd tell me about the pressure he feels over student debt and needing to find another job and anything else that came to mind, and I'd tell him about how my deteriorating relationship with my brother breaks my heart and how sometimes I feel so small next to Lori's greatness. Under the canopy of the tranquil night and stars, we'd be open and real with each other, and it always felt like there was no one else in the universe except for us. He knows practically everything about me . . . everything except how I feel.

My heart hammers in my chest as I clear my throat.

"You okay?" he asks, then his eyes grow wide. "Is it about back there? Shit, I'm sorry, Faye. I wouldn't have done that in front of Adam if you weren't okay with it, and I thought—"

"No, it's not that."

A breath of relief escapes him. "Okay, then what's up?"

Do it, Faye. Stop being such a coward

"I . . ." *Like a Band-Aid. Rip it off!* "I hate this. These last few days I've been acting so stupid. But I saw you with Kiara that first night, and I got jealous."

Kellan's jaw tightens and his eyebrows draw together. It must be the most serious he's appeared this whole trip, so at odds to his normal laid-back attitude. "You were jealous? Of me?"

Resisting the urge to grind my teeth together, I nod. I really didn't want to spell it out for him, but not opening up or getting vulnerable would be the easy way out.

"What? Why?"

He's not asking to be cruel; he seems genuinely perplexed.

"Isn't it obvious, Kell?" My heartbeat is so loud, I'm grateful for the speakers blasting music, or else he'd for sure hear it. I take a breath to tell him my feelings, then hesitate as the words he spoke after I threw him off the tube come back to me.

Just admit you like me.

And if I did?

Then I'm right, like always.

What if he laughs at me? What if all spilling my guts does is give him gloating rights?

"Faye?"

There's something in his eyes, some lightness, almost like hopefulness, written in his features that causes me to open my big mouth and blurt, "I like you."

"Um. I like you too? Is that what you pulled me over here to say?"

I feel like grinding the palm of my hands into my eyes. He's so frustrating!

"No, Kellan. I mean . . . urgh!" I throw my hands up in defeat. I've *never* been in this position before. I've never had to be *vulnerable* before, and I absolutely hate it. Maybe I need some alcohol in me; I'm totally sober and rejection would be easier to handle if I had some liquid courage.

I turn to leave, but Kellan grabs my wrist and forces me to face him again. His dark eyes are intense and peering straight into mine, the seriousness of his demeanor taking me off guard.

"Don't leave. Tell me what you want to tell me."

The heat from his hand sears my wrist, and now all I can think about is how close to me he is, how long his lashes are, how strong his jaw is.

My throat is dry, and I force myself to swallow. *Rip the*

Band-Aid! Now or never. "I like you, Kellan. Like as more than friends. I've been acting stupid because I don't want only casual sex from you, I want *you*."

His grip on my wrist tightens but it's not painful. "What . . . ? What are you saying, Faye?"

All I can do is blink up at his intense stare; his eyes boring into mine makes the air around us turn up a thousand degrees. "Are you saying," he continues, his body moving closer to mine, "that you want us to be official? Me and you? Kellan and Fayanna?"

His tone isn't teasing like I feared it would be. Instead, it's heated, sultry. His words should terrify me. Admitting it out loud and being vulnerable should terrify me. But *Kellan and Fayanna* is exactly what I want. I want to be with Kellan; I've probably *always* wanted to be with Kellan and was too stubborn to see what was right in front of me.

Too overwhelmed to speak, I nod, never once taking my eyes from his, which darken at my words. The way he's looking at me is almost too intense for me to comprehend, for my mind to merge this severe version of Kellan with his usual easygoing breeziness.

"Because I've been waiting for you to say that for years, Fayanna."

My stomach tightens as I process his words. *He's been waiting for years.* He tugs me right up against him, and I suddenly hate the white shirt theme at the party for being a barrier between us.

His nose skims the length of my jaw, goose bumps rising in his path. His voice is deep in my ear. "You're the only one I want, Faye. Just you. Always you."

My breath hitches. He's not teasing me or joking. It's hard to miss the sincerity in his voice, the weight of his words. Is it really possible he feels the same way I do? That this was always something more than a fun fling for him? Can he love me back?

He pulls away slightly and any doubts I'm having vanish under his gaze. My words are still lodged in my throat, but that doesn't deter Kellan.

"I never wanted to push anything on you," he continues, "and you were so dead set on nothing ever being serious between us, between you and anyone else. I've been happy being whatever you needed me to be, as long as I could be near you, be the one to hold you when you cry, be the one to make you laugh, be the one to make you moan . . ." I shiver at his words, heart racing faster as his fingers tighten on my hips. "But fuck, Faye, it's been killing me to give you the space you needed, not when all I want to do anytime you're near is pull you close, claim you as mine."

His words are a dream. I never imagined it would be like this, that it would be this easy. I only hoped Kellan would feel the same way I did, and now his words are confirming it, his actions only backing it up. I want to be with Kellan, and for some reason, he wants to be with me. I'm so happy I don't even know what to do with myself. I'm floating on clouds; I'm dancing in the rain; I'm living in a universe where Kellan wants *me*.

I crash my mouth against his, and the revelation between us makes the sensation of his lips against mine brand-new, but at the same time not. Familiar but also like a first kiss all in one, like our lips know exactly what to do, but we're discovering each other for the first time. His tongue traces my lip, his hands crush me against him, and I'm filled with the overwhelming urge for *more*. I need more of this, more of his touch, more of *Kellan*.

Reluctantly, I pull away and lean my forehead against his. His breathing is as uneven as mine. We stand there for a few moments, catching our breath, letting our words and their meaning sink in. The sounds around us filter through my Kellan bubble, and I realize that I'm standing in the middle of a party wrapped up in Kellan's arms, where my brother could stumble upon us. If he did, there wouldn't be any misunderstanding about the situation, no chance we could joke it away.

Even though it's the last thing I want, I step away, forcing Kellan's arms to drop. He stares at me in confusion, but before he can say anything, I take his hand. I don't want Adam to ruin this right now. I'm still burning with the need for more of Kellan. I need it like I need oxygen in my lungs.

"Let's go back to my room," I say, my words dripping with meaning.

His hand tightens in mine. "Faye . . ." he starts, a muscle in his jaw jumping. "I didn't say all that to get you in bed. We don't have to do anything."

His words mean more to me than he knows, smothering all my insecurities about him only wanting me as a hookup the second they leave his perfect lips. I know he doesn't want me only as a hookup, but now I need his touch, need *him*, and I know he needs me too.

"I know," I tell him, walking backward from him until we're standing apart, our hands still attached, suspended in the air between us. "I *want* to go upstairs. Meet me there in ten?"

The worried look he's sporting melts into a mischievous smirk, which is right at home on his face. *This* is my Kellan. This playful, fun-loving man who never fails to make me laugh, who's always up for a challenge, who can't keep his hands off me when we're alone.

"Okay," he concedes, and I take another step from him, our hands forced apart by the distance. "Ten minutes," he repeats, and I turn to wade through the crowd before I give in to my urge to throw myself at him again.

Walking away, I can't keep the goofy smile off my face. Kellan *wants* me. He wants me! Sure, I didn't ask him about Kiara, and we didn't really talk about what that means for us, and I didn't tell him I love him, but for the time being, it's enough. We can worry about all that stuff later. Right now his words are enough for me. The intensity in his gaze tells me all I need to know.

I find Lori at a table near one of the bars talking to a pretty girl with long black braids trailing down her back. I have no idea who she is, but Lori's laughing, and my smile widens seeing her let her walls down and open up with other people. I cross behind Lori and notice that most of the tasks are checked off, and now I really can't contain my excitement. *Body shot* is crossed off, and I can't wait to grill her for more information on that later.

"Having fun?" I ask, plopping down in the chair beside her.

She turns to me, her eyes bright. "Oh my goodness, yes, I've been having so much fun! Where have you been?"

I send her a sly smile, remembering what just happened, the revelations I experienced. "With Kellan." I turn to the other girl. "Hey, I'm Faye."

The girl's lips curl into a knowing smirk as she assesses me. "Naomi." She shakes her empty glass. "I'm getting a refill. Lori?"

"No thanks," Lori replies, pointing to her still-full drink of what's probably vodka cranberry. With a wave, Naomi ventures through the crowd and Lori turns her full attention to me.

"You're practically glowing. What happened with Kellan?"

"I told him how I feel."

Her mouth drops open and her eyes practically bulge out of her head. "You told Kellan you *love him*?"

My hand clamps over her mouth. "Shh! Don't announce that to everyone!" I drop my hand, and she passes me her drink. "I didn't tell him I love him, but I told him I didn't want to be just fuck buddies and wanted to be with him."

She throws her arms around me, almost knocking over her

drink in the process. "I'm so happy for you, Faye! Are you guys, like, official now? Did he ask you to be his girlfriend? Are you telling Adam?"

"Whoa, slow down."

Lori bites her lip, clearly trying to keep the other million questions she has from spilling out. I take a sip of her drink—it *is* vodka cranberry—and try to remember what she asked. "I don't know if we're official or not, he didn't ask me to be his girlfriend, and there's no way in *hell* we're telling Adam, so don't say anything."

Her eyebrows draw together. "So, what happened?"

You're the only one I want, Faye. Just you. Always you.

I shiver at the memory of his words, smiling behind the straw. "I don't really know if I'm being honest. But it doesn't matter." I set the now half-empty drink back on the table so I can stare into her eyes, letting her recognize how serious I am. "Something's changed, Lor, I know it. Kellan and I are going to be different from now on—better." And even though I don't know the specifics of *how*, I don't care. We can figure that all out later, together.

She doesn't point out the obvious flaws with my statement or tell me that Kellan and I need to have an actual *real* conversation about what's going on between us; instead she squeezes my hand. "I'm happy for you, Faye."

On that note . . . "I'm meeting him in the room in like five minutes so . . . don't come up for a bit."

She bites her lip and nods. "Keep off my bed."

I laugh, pulling my hand from hers and finishing the rest of the vodka cranberry. "I promise. You just worry about kissing Dean. I see that box still isn't checked off." I gesture to her shirt as I stand, and her cheeks redden. "Have fun, Lor, I'll see you later."

"*You* have fun! But not on my bed!" she calls after me as I make my way through the crowd and head toward the pool's exit, to the hotel where Kellan will be waiting for me.

It feels like forever since I've been with Kellan, since I've been in his arms, felt his muscles flex under my fingers, felt his skin under mine, but we were together only four days ago.

I'm still wearing a dreamy expression on my face when someone steps in front of me, blocking my path. Adam's staring down at me, a scowl on his face, and my mood sours. I thought he was content to ignore me all night, especially since our last encounter, but apparently, he sought me out.

"Where are you going?" he asks.

The impatience in his tone makes me pause. Did he see me and Kellan? Does he know something? No, he can't. This is his normal "talking to my sister" tone.

"To my room," I say. "Why?"

His looks like he doesn't believe me, and now there's a pit in my stomach from doubting how ignorant he is about me and Kellan.

"It's still early, and I've never known you to leave a party early."

No. If he knew, he wouldn't be this calm and detached. He'd be freaking out.

"I don't feel good," I lie, then can't resist throwing a dig at him. "Not that you care."

I shoulder past him, and he doesn't stop me as I march out of the party and down the lit path to the hotel.

Who does he think he is, coming in all *you never leave a party early blah blah blah*? What does he know? He doesn't talk to me. He doesn't pick me up from a party unless Mom yells at him to, so how is he suddenly an expert Faye timekeeper? And why is he pretending to care where I'm going? He made it abundantly clear before we got on the plane that he wanted to pretend I didn't exist on this trip, and now he's asking where I'm going as if he cares, especially after yelling at me last night?

I scowl the entire trek back to my hotel and up the stairs, at least until I round the corner and spot Kellan. He's leaning across the hall from my door with his patent smirk, the one that has my aggression instantly melting away.

You're the only one I want, Faye. Just you. Always you.

His words fill me with butterflies, and all thoughts of my annoying brother vanish. There's just me and Kellan and the way he's looking at me like he wants to devour me.

I cross the space between us and then I'm wrapped in his arms, his lips on mine, my hands tangled in his hair. My heart is so full it might explode. All I've wanted is to be held by Kellan like this, like I matter, like I'm something to him.

He walks us until the door's at my back, and without taking my lips from his, I fish my key card out of my pocket. My hand bumps frantically at the door as I try to find the key card insert, and then Kellan's lips leave mine and trail down my jaw, over my neck, and my brain can't process anything past the sensation of his lips on me, on the trail of sparks they leave in their wake.

Without warning, his hands grip the backs of my thighs and push them up to wrap around his hips. With the door against my back and my legs around Kellan, I feel every single contour of his body pressed against my front; I feel exactly how much he wants me. I might even moan out loud, but I can't be sure because I'm too lost in Kellan, in the things he's making me feel.

The key card disappears from my hand and a beep sounds, and suddenly Kellan's lips find mine and he's carrying me into the room. The door slams shut behind him, and we don't bother stopping to turn on any lights or turn on the TV for some music.

I let out a little squeal when he throws me onto the mattress. He stands at the end of the bed, basked in the moonlight streaming in from the sliding door, a predatory gleam in his gaze. It's so unlike him, so vastly different to the relaxed Kellan the rest of the world sees, and my body heats thinking it's *me* he looks at like that, like he can't get enough, like he'll combust if he doesn't have me.

He leans over me, crawling over my body, a wicked gleam in his eyes, and it's a struggle not to profess my love for him right then and there. Instead, I settle for bunching his white T-shirt in my hands and lifting it over his head, leaving him gloriously shirtless. It lands somewhere on the floor, and my shirt and shorts soon join it. His eyes trace my body, clad in nothing but my bikini, something he's seen hundreds of times over the years and every day of this trip, but still he drinks me in like it's the first time. I shiver when his finger delicately traces the hollow at my throat, down my sternum and between my breasts.

His eyes are on mine when he says, "You are so fucking beautiful."

I can't take it anymore, being so close but so far from him. My fingers tighten in his hair and tug him down to me, drawing his lips to mine. I wrap my legs around his waist, trying to eliminate all that space between us until I can't focus on anything except his skin against mine. My heart is pounding so loud in my ears it's like the sound fills the entire room.

Kellan pulls away from me, his lips hovering a fraction of an inch from mine as we catch our breath. "Is that Lori?" he asks, and I'm too confused to process his words.

"Lori?"

A pounding resounds through the room, and I realize it wasn't my heart earlier, but someone at the door.

"That can't be Lori," I say as Kellan sits up, "she knows we're in here."

There's another knock on the door, and all the blood drains from my body when a voice calls out, "Faye! Open up."

In my haste to get up, I practically shove Kellan off the bed. "Shit!" I hiss, throwing my shorts and shirt on as fast as humanly possible. Kellan's sprawled on his side on the bed, and I toss his shirt at him as he stands.

"Why is Adam here?" Kellan asks, his voice low as he slips on his shirt.

The knocking stops, but I doubt my brother gave up. Does he know Kellan's here? Is he aware of what's going on between us? My heart's pounding just as hard as before but for a totally different reason. Dread creeps up my spine.

"Hide!" I order Kellan as Adam calls out, "I know you're in there, Faye."

Shit shit shit.

Kellan looks around the hotel room dramatically. "Really? Where, Faye? Maybe we should tell hi—"

"The bathroom!" I interrupt him, grabbing his hand and rushing him to the only available hiding place. It's way too close to the front door for comfort, but there's no other option. For some reason Adam's intent on getting into this room, and I'll be damned if he finds me with his best friend with our pants around our ankles. I won't be able to face his anger, his disappointment, his betrayal, his validation for hating me more than he already does. No. This is our only option.

"Faye . . ." Kellan protests, and I pause. He scans my face and must see the sheer desperation there, because he relents and steps into the small bathroom, drawing an imaginary zipper over his lips and giving me a wink. His playfulness calms my nerves somewhat, and I mouth *thank you* at him before I shut him in the bathroom. With Kellan concealed, I take a moment to compose myself and straighten out my hair. I try to calm the wildness of my pulse as I pull open the door, but the sight that meets me freezes the blood in my veins.

There, on my doorstep in the middle of the hallway for all to see, is my brother, his hands gripping Lori's waist, her arms thrown around his shoulders.

And they're kissing.

SIXTEEN

Night Four of Cuba

Lori

Faye disappears as soon as she pushes me into Dean, and I'm too busy being embarrassed to seethe over her antics.

"Sorry about that," I say, my waist still tingling from the memory of his hands when he prevented me from falling over. "That's just . . . Faye."

He sends me a good-natured smile. "Yeah, I'm getting how Faye operates."

I haven't seen him since last night, and my memory hasn't done him justice. He looks devilishly handsome with his sharp jawline and his ruffled wet hair. A memory surfaces of Faye pressed up against him last night, but I push it away just as fast. I trust Faye's explanation of what went down, and that he was oblivious about what she was doing. She even said he might have asked about me!

"So where did you run off to last night?" he asks, and I internally squeal. He *must* have asked about me.

I can't tell him I got jealous of him and Faye and ran out, so instead I school my expression into one of detached innocence. "I was just tired and ready to go home. What were you up to today? We didn't see you guys."

"We were at the beach," he says. "I'm guessing you stayed at the pool?"

"Yeah, with the girls," I say, which I thought was fun, and even Faye didn't hate it as much as she expected she would. It was relaxing too, at least until I checked my phone and saw all the messages from my mom, sending me links to MCAT prep courses and souring my mood.

Dean gestures at my shirt. He's wearing a matching one in his size, but it's wet and clings to him in all the right places. "Have you crossed anything off? I've only done a shot with no hands and a dare, which was to jump in the pool fully clothed. At the time I thought it was a dumb dare because I was in swim shorts anyway, but this wet shirt is getting annoying."

"I just got here, so my shirt's blank." It's an effort not to glance at his shirt and stare at all the places it clings to his sculpted body. "But if it makes you feel better, it's warm out so it'll probably dry fast."

There are tons of people walking around, splashing in the pool, giggling, and yelling with their friends, and I'm painfully aware of how many of the girls eye Dean as they pass us. I suddenly wish I was a better conversationalist because Dean is here, talking to *me* instead of anyone else at this gigantic party, and I'm utterly boring.

"Well, why don't we fix that?" Dean says, and I have to remind myself that he's talking about my blank shirt. "Shot with no hands? It's an easy one. I'll even do it with you."

It does sound easy—much less daunting than any others on the list, especially *kiss someone*. Faye told me to kiss Dean tonight, but now that I'm standing in front of him, the thought of me gathering enough courage to lay one on him is almost laughable. Plus, Faye said the list will help me put myself out there more, and a shot with no hands sounds doable, fun even.

"Okay," I agree, then hastily add, "But no tequila. I don't ever want to see, smell, or taste tequila again."

Over Dean's shoulder, I spot Adam. He catches my eye, his expression giving nothing away before he strides over to us. In front of me, Dean laughs, the sound washing over me. "Deal. I'll surprise you."

Adam's joined us now, and the memory of the words between us last night surfaces in my mind; his statement that *the Lori I know* would never have fun and let loose and dance onstage, and the unspoken words that the Lori he knows is boring. I was *so mad* at that moment, but if I force myself to think about it, he was just trying to look out for me and make sure I was safe, even if it was in his own annoyingly overprotective way.

"Hey, Adam. Want a shot?" Dean offers. "Lori's going to check the first thing off her task list."

Adam's eyes narrow at that. He assesses my shirt, as if he can see the list of tasks on my back and they personally offend him.

"No thanks," he answers Dean.

Something in Dean must know that I want to talk to Adam, at least to address this tension between us and to apologize for taking my anger out on him last night, because even though his smile doesn't falter, he says, "All right. I'll be back with something that's not tequila."

Once Dean disappears, Adam nods at my shirt. "You're doing the tasks?"

Something in his tone sounds doubtful, like he could never imagine me doing a dare, a dance-off, or the more brazen activities like kissing someone or doing a body shot. My defenses rise instantly, but instead of letting him see how bothered I am, I shrug a shoulder in answer. "Maybe. Why?"

He steps closer to me, something akin to concern in his eyes. "Are you being serious? You're not doing any of the tasks, Lor. I know how you are."

His words hit me right in the chest, and I take a step back from him as if they're a physical blow.

"What's that supposed to mean?" I ask, even though I know *exactly* what he means; it's the same thing he's been telling me all trip, the same thing I've never thought about myself until he pointed it out—that I'm sweet, predicable, *boring*.

"Come on, Lori. 'Do a body shot'? 'Kiss someone'? Fuck, even *dance-off* is pushing it for you," he says, oblivious to the effect of his words, the way they stab me, twisting in deep, releasing a wave of anger with every doubt he throws at me.

"You don't think I can do it?"

His eyes scan my face. "Why don't you come over and join me, Dylan, Alessio, and Kellan? You can watch them making asses of themselves trying to do the tasks as quickly as possible."

Heat pricks at my skin. Adam doesn't think I'm capable of having fun. He doubts I can do a *dance-off*. Even last night he practically forbade me from getting up on stage. It's like he wants me to stay *sweet*, *boring*, and *predictable* instead of trying new things and having new experiences, and he's doing it all under the guise of caring. He's never told Faye not to do anything, only me, who he apparently doubts can be *strong* like Faye. Why doesn't he think I can move out of my comfort zone? Why doesn't he think I can decide for myself what I am or am not capable of? Faye believes I could do all the things on the list. Even Dean doesn't doubt me.

Looking away, I see Dean talking and laughing with the bartender on the other side of the pool. *He* didn't ask me if I was going to partake in the fun; he simply asked me if I'd started yet and volunteered to do a task with me. Dean's never insinuated that I was boring. He didn't tell me I'm not doing the tasks because he *knows how I am*, even though he knows I don't enjoy being the center of attention, knows I'm a bit awkward, knows I have a hard time with new experiences, just like Adam knows. But the difference is that Adam doubts me, tells me to sit out and stay in my comfort zone, while Dean has never made me feel like I was incapable of doing something.

"No," I tell Adam, my voice practically shaking with restrained anger. "No, I will not join you guys. I'm going to do a shot with no hands. Then maybe I'll do a dare or participate in a dance-off. And who knows, if I feel like it, I might even do a body shot or kiss someone." My voice grows stronger and louder the more I talk, the more the meaning behind his words sinks in. "But I'm going to make my own decisions, not sit on the side and watch everyone else have fun because I'm too *boring* to join in."

"I never said you were boring," he says, his brows furrowed.

"You didn't have to."

A muscle in his jaw twitches. "Why are you getting mad at me? I'm just looking out for you."

No, he's not. Maybe in some messed-up way he thinks he is, but the way it's coming across is making me seem like a useless little porcelain doll, one that's only meant to sit on a shelf and never be touched or played with, like I'm too delicate and breakable to do anything other than stay safely hidden away in her little box.

Something in me snaps. *No more Little Miss Sweet and Predictable*. "Don't worry about me, *I'm* not your sister, who you've been treating badly not only this vacation, but your entire life."

With that, I shove past him, marching toward where Dean's collecting two shot glasses from the bartender. Was I too mean to Adam? I'm not sure, but I don't really care. I know how much Faye hates that Adam wants nothing to do with her, and maybe it wasn't my place to say any of that, but Adam's shown more concern for *me* this week alone than for Faye the entire four years I've known her. It's not fair to Faye, and it's not fair to me that Adam's always unintentionally putting me down.

By the time I reach Dean, he's found a table near the bar. He places the purple shot glasses on either side of the table and gestures at them with a grin.

"What is it?" I ask, leaning over to sniff it. I'm pleasantly surprised when it smells sweet and nothing like tequila.

His grin widens. "It's called a pornstar. You'll like it."

I almost choke on nothing, which makes his amusement grow. "I swear it tastes way better than tequila. Ready?"

Am I ready? I'm with Dean, who could be with a ton of more interesting people but is here with *me*, trying to get *me* to have fun. I glance around the party and every single person looks like they're having fun. Through the crowd I can even make out Faye across the pool with Dylan, Kellan, Alessio, and now Adam. Last time I hung out with Dean at a pool party, I loved it, and I'm ready to experience that again. I'm going to enjoy myself.

I clasp my hands behind my back, lowering my face toward the shot. "When you are."

I ignore the butterflies in my stomach when my excitement is mirrored in Dean's face, and he copies my position.

"Go!" he exclaims, and before I can doubt myself, I wrap my lips around the shot glass and tilt my head back, feeling the liquid slide down my throat. After I swallow, I set the glass back on the table and wipe my mouth with the back of my hand.

"How was it?" Dean asks, his own shot glass empty in front of him.

I can still taste the sweetness of the drink, and I'm happy that it wasn't strong, or at least, I don't *think* it was strong.

"It was good," I say, and something akin to relief floods Dean's face, which is odd because I hadn't even realized he was nervous.

"Good," he repeats as my phone in my back pocket vibrates, making the blood drain from my face.

Dean's eyes track my movements as I grab my phone and unlock it. I don't even know why I brought it, force of habit, maybe? I wish I hadn't, because it's a text from my mom, and her name plastered on my screen is like a bucket of cold water thrown over me.

"You okay?" Dean asks as I read my mom's text.

Are you having fun? You didn't answer my messages before. Take a look at those links when you have time.

"Fine," I tell Dean, though I'm sure my tone and pout tell him I'm anything *but* fine, but he doesn't say anything as I text a quick *okay* back to my mom.

"You sure you're okay?" Dean asks, and the openness and understanding I've always experienced with him compels me to answer truthfully.

"My mom's on my case about med school again. Every day it's something with her, and I get that she's excited, but can't she even give me a week without shoving it down my throat?" I stuff my phone into my back pocket, trying to keep my throat from getting tight. "Every time I think about my future in school for the next like, fifteen years of my life, pursuing a career I don't even want, I feel like I'm going to break out in hives."

Dean says nothing, and I'm a little self-conscious under his thoughtful gaze. Finally, he says, "Give me your phone."

"What?"

He holds out his hand expectantly. "You heard me. Give me your phone. Tonight is going to be a worry-free, phone-free night. I'll keep it safe for you, and my swim shorts are already dry, so don't worry about it being in my pocket."

Is it that easy? Just hand the phone over to Dean and ignore it and everything it symbolizes for the night? I don't want to think about it, and I don't want it to sour my mood more than it already has.

Hesitantly, I pull out my phone and drop it in his outstretched hand. "Promise you won't jump into the pool with my phone in your pocket?"

He slides the phone into his front pocket. "Fun fact, Dylan's done that about five times in the last year alone. Once he even had *my* phone."

I giggle at the mental image. "That's not reassuring."

"I promise I won't jump into the pool with your phone," he laughs, and the heaviness in my chest eases, as if the weight of my phone in my pocket was actually weighing me down. But just because it's not on me doesn't mean I'm not still thinking about it, still wondering how I'm going to survive those MCAT courses without wanting to pluck my eyeballs out, still contemplating just how miserable I'll be for the rest of my life if I go down this path.

Before I can spiral any more, Dean notices something behind me, then grabs my hand. "Time to cross the next thing off the task list."

I'm frowning, my thoughts consumed with all things med school even as I ask, "Which one?"

He pulls me through the crowd with determination, throwing a "You'll see" over his shoulder.

The music is already pretty loud, since speakers are spread out evenly throughout the area, but it somehow gets even louder when we reach the open space where the DJ is set up. People are dancing there, and it seems like a little outdoor night club, except we have *space* to dance and aren't being jostled around every which way from overpacked bodies.

Still holding my hand in his, Dean walks right into the middle of the dance floor and up to a group of three other couples. To my surprise, Naomi is there with the guy from the club and the pool. Thomas, maybe? She waves at me as we get closer.

"Hey," Dean says, his easy smile putting everyone at ease. "We challenge you to a dance-off."

What?

I'm so shocked I almost rip my hand from Dean's as I turn to stare at him incredulously.

"Hell yeah!" one guy says. Another high-fives Dean's free hand and says, "You're on, Dean."

So I guess they know Dean. He's so charismatic he's probably made friends with everyone at the resort. Naomi catches my eye and exaggeratedly bulges her eyes out at Dean's hand in mine, then winks, like we're sharing some kind of secret, like she knows I feel something more than just our connected hands.

Since I can't exactly tell her how sparks appear everywhere his skin touches me, I settle for turning to Dean just as he's finishing talking to one guy and pulling me some distance away from the group.

"Dance-off? Dean, I don't know if I can do it."

He gives me an amused expression. "What? Of course you can. It'll be fun. Plus, we're in it together."

I'm about to protest that people will be *watching* when the DJ fades the current song into a Maluma one, the one I always sing with Faye.

Dean registers my sharp intake of breath and the way my hips move slightly of their own accord.

"See?" he says. "It was meant to happen."

This is it. The big, bad dance-off Adam thought I was incapable of doing. But here I am. About to do it. In front of all these people. With Dean.

Before I can think too much about it, Dean uses our connected hands to throw me away from him then spin me back toward him, the action taking me by surprise and causing a giggle to escape. He catches me, hugs me close to his chest, which is already dry, and starts moving, while my feet automatically match his steps. He spins me around again and catches both my hands in his, and we move together to the music, falling into an easy partnership where I follow his lead. Everything but the music and Dean falls away. I don't hear the people around us; I don't care if they're all looking at us; all I'm focused on is the music and the way Dean's body moves with mine, the way he grins down at me and the way my chest feels light. All I can do is laugh as Dean spins me again. I don't care how big and cheesy my smile is as all my previous worries and fears melt away. Just a few minutes ago I was panicking about my bleak future, and now the tightness in my stomach is replaced with a pleasant sore feeling from laughing so much. His hands land on my waist and my arms wrap around his neck as we dance, and as he gazes into my eyes, realization hits.

"I know what you're doing," I tell him, biting my lip to hide my smile.

He twirls us around to the song. "I have no idea what you're talking about."

I was in a tailspin about my future, and suddenly Dean's challenging people to a dance-off, which is really just a bunch of us dancing and having fun and me spinning around in a way that makes it impossible for me to fret about med school, impossible for me not to have fun.

"You're trying to distract me," I state, my tone anything but accusing.

"Again, I don't know what you're talking about." He grabs my hand and throws me away from him only to spin me back, catching me so my back is pressed right against his front, my arms wrapped across my body as our hips sway together to the music, which I just realized isn't even Maluma anymore. "But is it working?" he breathes in my ear, and I shiver at his closeness, wishing he would hold me here forever, then immediately hope he didn't notice because that's so embarrassing.

"Maybe," I whisper.

He moves us so I'm facing him again, but it must be the adrenaline or the moment or the realization of what he did for me, because this time *I'm* the one pulling him closer to me. The space between us disappears until I'm plastered against him, my hands linked around his neck. His hands slide around my back and hold me to him, and it takes everything in me not to shiver again, not to acknowledge how good he feels against me, not to show him how much his touch affects me, how much *he* affects me.

My breath hitches when my eyes connect with his, and like the last time I was this close to him, I'm struck by all the different shades of blue in his eyes, by the tiny ring of hazel surrounding each pupil.

Loud cheers go off around us and break me out of my little Dean bubble. I had completely forgotten we were in a dance-off. It was just me and Dean having fun and not caring about everyone else around us. But to be fair, it wasn't like dance-offs in the movies. No one's that serious when we're all just having fun. Either way, I'm glad I did it, and I'm even happier that it was with Dean.

Naomi's arms come around me, pulling me away from Dean.

"Girl, that was *hot*!" she exclaims, thankfully out of Dean's earshot.

As she dances me to the edge of the makeshift dance floor, I catch Dean's eye. He winks at me from where he's chatting with Naomi's friends until I lose sight of him in the crowd. Naomi stops at a table.

"You keep telling me you're not confident, but I saw you pulling the moves on that dance floor." She picks up a marker from the table. "Hell, *I* was getting turned on near the end there, so I can only imagine how that poor boy feels."

My face heats as she puts her hands on my shoulders and spins me around so my back is to her. I hear her uncap the marker and draw on my shirt.

"You haven't done any of these yet?"

"I . . . um . . . I did the shot with no hands," I tell her, still reeling from what she said about Dean and me dancing. Did he like it as much as I did?

She checks something else off on my shirt, then turns me to face her. "You planning on laying one on Dean to cross off the kissing task?"

I almost choke. "What? No!"

She doesn't laugh at me, but I can tell she wants to. Instead, she hands me the marker and turns around, holding her braids out of the way. "You should. I doubt Deany-boy over there would mind. Check off *dance-off* for me."

The only tasks she has left now are *body shot* and *do a dare.*

"Who did you kiss?" I ask as I recap the marker.

"Oh, just one of the guys," she says like it's not a big deal. "Now come on, let's go dance!"

I follow her back onto the dance floor and meet her friends. She introduces me to them, but the music is so loud I can't even make out their names, except for Thomas. It doesn't matter though, because Naomi grabs my hand right after introductions and pulls me to dance. I'm sweaty and laughing in no time, and when I catch Dean's eye, he gestures with his hand like he's holding an imaginary drink and lifts an eyebrow in question. He's asking me if I want a drink, and my stomach squeezes at his thoughtfulness. I nod and smile in thanks before Naomi spins me around and I lose Dean to the crowd.

"He totally wants you." Naomi grins as Thomas and another guy come over.

"Hey, Naomi, want to cross the last two things off your task list?" Thomas asks, balancing shots on a paper plate like a makeshift tray.

Challenge sparks in her eyes. "You know it."

He holds out a shot glass to her. "I dare you to do a body shot off Lori."

Naomi laughs triumphantly, like the dare is too easy, while I stare at him like he's lost his mind.

"You game, Lori?" Naomi asks.

Normally, no, I wouldn't be cool with a practical stranger doing a body shot off me, but I'm supposed to be letting loose and trying new things I never would've done. I *am* on vacation, after all. Worse comes to worst, I don't like it and don't do it again, but at least I can say I tried it. Besides, all I really have to do is lie there.

"I'm game."

Naomi cheers and grabs a shot from Thomas, which has a lime wedge resting on the rim. "What is this?" She sniffs it. "Ugh. It's vodka, isn't it? You're sick, Thomas."

"Better than tequila." He shrugs, then heads over to their other friends, offering the plate out to them, and I'm assuming daring them to do the same thing.

"Thomas wants to make sure everyone has fun," Naomi tells me as we move off the dance floor and to some pool chairs. "He's been especially doting since the whole I-was-drowning-and-he-didn't-notice thing. He hasn't even been drinking."

I'm not sure what to make of that statement, but before I can mull it over, she pushes me down into a pool chair. A girl who's friends with Naomi sits on my other side with a girl she introduced as her girlfriend. She shoots me a smile as she lies back in the chair. On her other side is Naomi's other friend with a guy. The three of us recline, and I ignore my nerves to instead copy the girl beside me, pulling up my shirt and setting the lime in my mouth with the fruit part facing out.

Naomi pours the shot into my navel, and I force myself not to laugh at the sensation. Before I even know what's happening, Naomi takes the shot then grabs the lime from my mouth, her lips not even touching mine.

"Woo-hoo!" she hollers when she removes the lime from her mouth. "All the tasks crossed off!"

It was over so quick I barely even realized it happened at all. That wasn't so bad, and when I sit up and join in the high-fives with the girls beside us, I realize I'm grinning. The girl and guy on the other side of the girls join in the revelry, and we all take turns checking *body shot* off the backs of each other's shirts.

"Hey," Dean says, appearing out of nowhere with a beer in one hand and a glass in another. Naomi sends me a wink and disappears as Dean holds out the glass to me. "I didn't know what you wanted but you're always drinking vodka cran, so I figured that was a safe bet."

My heart pounds because *he remembered my go-to drink*! "You noticed I like vodka cran?"

"Well, it's kind of hard not to notice when you threw one at me yesterday," he jokes, and my face heats instantly.

"I really am sorry," I say, rising from the pool chair and taking the drink. "I promise I won't throw this one at you."

It's clear he doesn't care about the incident last night at the club—he didn't even care in the moment it happened. I probably could've thrown a whole pitcher of cranberry juice on his favorite white shirt, and he still wouldn't have cared or gotten angry with me. Actually, I've never seen Dean mad except when Pervy Gym Guy took a picture of my butt and when Terry threatened to beat me up on the second night here. Both times he was defending me, and both times he made sure I was all right.

I try not to think about it as I sip from my glass. "Thanks for the drink."

"No problem. Did you just check *body shot* off your list?" he asks.

"She sure did!" Naomi interjects, walking back to us with a drink in her hand. She eyes the back of his shirt and I'm not sure I like the mischievous way her eyes light up. My suspicion is confirmed when she says, "I see you haven't checked *body shot* off. Lori, why don't you help Dean out?"

Out of Dean's view, she waggles her eyes at me, and this whole thing is such a Faye move I'm not even surprised. I'm almost scared of what would happen if the two of them became friends.

"I—umm—that's—" I sputter, my mind imagining Dean leaning over me, his lips on my stomach, then hovering a fraction of an inch above my lips when he takes the lime. It's one thing to have Naomi take a body shot off me, but for *Dean* to do it . . . I might spontaneously combust before his lips even touch me.

Naomi must take pity on me because she says, "Oh, Dean! Thomas was looking for you earlier. Something about your opinion on some game or something."

She points to where Thomas is talking with some guys. "We'll meet you here, after."

Before Dean reacts, Naomi grabs my hand and tugs me to a little table where I plop down in a chair. "I *cannot* believe you did that to me!"

She laughs as she sits across from me. "I was trying to help you out. I didn't think you'd freeze like that."

Her laughter is infectious and soon I'm joining in. "You know I'm not confident!"

"Yeah, that's what you *said*, but all I've seen is you being badass and making moves."

I giggle at the thought of *Naomi* thinking *I'm* badass. I didn't think I was making any sort of moves today, but everything seems to come naturally with me and Dean, even if I embarrass myself in front of him. He's never made me feel bad about it—he's never made me feel *boring*—even when I blew on him. If I think about it, Dean's always made me feel special, always made me feel like he enjoys me for *me*, awkwardness and all.

"Having fun?" Faye appears, dropping into the seat beside me.

"Oh my goodness, yes, I've been having so much fun! Where have you been?"

"With Kellan." She turns to Naomi. "Hey, I'm Faye."

"Naomi," she replies, then shakes her empty glass. "I'm going to get a refill. Lori?"

"No thanks." I point to the still full drink that Dean got me, and Naomi disappears to give Faye and me some privacy.

Faye wastes no time telling me what happened with Kellan and how she admitted to him she wants to be more than friends with benefits. I'm proud of her for doing that. I know it's hard for her to open up about *real* feelings and let people in, but she did it with Kellan and it looks like it's paying off. She finishes my drink while telling me her plans for the room, then disappears to meet him.

"Was that Faye?" Dean asks just as Faye vanishes from sight.

"Yes. You know her, running around all over the place."

Just as he's about to drop into Faye's vacated seat, Naomi appears, a new drink in her hand.

"Nuh-uh!" she chides him, causing him to hover over the seat as if frozen. "We're not sitting around. This is my favorite song! Let's go dance."

I don't recognize the song, but Naomi must really love it because she grabs Dean and shoves him toward the dance floor. "Come on, Lori!" she summons me.

She pushes me toward Dean and says, "I'm going to find Thomas. Have fun!" And with a wink at me, she's gone. She doesn't care about this song; this is all about her matchmaking effort. She didn't even try to be discreet.

Though I'm sure he's onto Naomi's antics, Dean just grins and holds out a hand to me. It's not a fast song, not like the others we were dancing to, so instead I wrap my arms around his neck, and he pulls me closer with his hands on my waist. There are no fancy spins like last time, but our steps and the flow of our bodies comes naturally.

"Are you having fun tonight?" he asks as we move together.

"I am," I admit, then because I'm hit by a strange wave of confidence from Naomi telling me I'm a badass, I add, "Mostly because of you, though."

A mix of delight and surprise lights up his face. He looks like he's struggling to fight his smile. "Because of me?"

I nod and bite my lip, and his eyes track the movement. "Yes . . . thank you for today."

"Why are you thanking me? You don't need to."

I shrug a shoulder. "I don't know. For having fun with me, I guess."

He gives his head a sad little shake. "Stop thanking me for

hanging out with you. You make it sound like a chore when it's the complete opposite. I look forward to seeing you. You're amazing, Lori."

He's looking at me like he means every single word, and maybe even more that he's leaving unsaid.

Now I'm all too aware of his hands around my waist, of my chest pressed up against his, of the rapid beating of my heart that he's sure to feel. I don't hear the music anymore—don't notice all the other people around us—it's just me and him and the intense way we're looking at each other, a spark in the air that signals we're on the precipice of something new and exciting, something that could change everything between us. My eyes are drawn to his lips, and I can't look away.

"Lori," he breathes, and the sound practically makes my knees weak.

Oh my gosh! He's going to kiss me! It's really going to happen!

At this point we've stopped dancing altogether, too lost in each other to care. My hands act on their own volition and tangle in his hair, which is so soft, way too soft. He leans in closer to me, and his lips brush mine in a featherlight touch and—

"Lori?"

Dean and I break apart at the sound of my name being called, and I have to blink a few times to rid myself of this hypnotic state. Adam emerges from behind a group of people. Did he see that almost-kiss between me and Dean? Is that why he called out to me? To stop it from happening?

No, that can't be it, because he looks around the crowd as if trying to spot me, and when he does, he heads over.

"I thought I saw you here," Adam says when he stops in front of us.

I can't tell what Dean's thinking because I'm too terrified to look at him, too terrified to show him how disappointed I am that the spell we were under has broken, and that our almost-kiss was interrupted.

"Here I am," I say weakly.

He glances back and forth between Dean and my probably bright-red face before saying, "Did something happen with Faye?"

His question takes me so off guard I completely forget about the kiss-that-would've-been.

"What? No, why?"

His eyebrows draw together like he doesn't quite believe me. "Because it's barely midnight, and she told me she wasn't feeling good and went up to her room . . . and then guilt-tripped me about it."

There's so much to unpack in that sentence, I don't even know where to start.

Faye must have run into Adam and lied about not feeling good, since she can't exactly tell him she's leaving to do naughty things with his best friend. But what does he mean about guilt-tripping? Is he feeling bad about how he's treated Faye? Especially after I also said something to him about it?

"Um, no," I say. "She must've just been tired. Nothing happened."

He seems to struggle with that before he gives a long-suffering sigh. "I'll go check on her."

Wait, what?

And with that, he turns and wades through the crowd and toward the exit, leaving me staring after him.

He's going to check on Faye . . . who's currently in the room with Kellan . . . doing things Adam would kill them both for if he found out . . . and he's going there . . . to the room . . . where he *will* catch them in the act . . . and then kill them both.

My logic circles until I come to one conclusion: I need to stop him.

"You all right?" Dean asks, and I wonder how long I was standing there with wide eyes staring at nothing.

"Yes. I'll—uh—be right back. Sorry!" I take off after Adam before Dean can reply.

I may be naïve sometimes, but even I know how this looks—like I'm fleeing from Dean after our would-be kiss. All I do is run from Dean, so it punches me right in the gut that he's going to believe that's what's happening again. There's nothing I'd like more than to pick up where we left off and feel his strong arms wrapped around me, feel our hearts beating fast in our chests, feel the pressure of his lips against mine, but my best friend needs me right now. I need to make sure Adam doesn't see Kellan leaving our room and connect the dots, so all I can do is chase after Adam and hope Dean knows I wanted that kiss, that I'm not running from him, not this time.

Adam's nowhere in sight, so I jog all the way back to our hotel and sprint up the stairs.

"I know you're in there, Faye," he says as he knocks on the door to our room.

Crap. Crap crap CRAP! He's going to flip and they're going to argue, and Faye's going to act tough, but it's going to kill her to have Adam mad at her, especially since he's not the most affectionate brother to begin with. She's not ready to tell Adam about her and Kellan. Hell, she barely knows what's going on between the two of them, so it's way too soon to throw Adam being pissed at them into the mix.

"Adam?" I call out before I even have a plan. How can I get him away from here? How can I distract him?

He turns to me as I close the distance between us. "Why is she ignoring me?" he asks. "I can hear her moving around in there. Is someone else in there?"

He's about to knock on the door again, and before I know

what I'm doing, I throw myself at him, wrap my arms around his neck, and kiss him.

He's too shocked to move. *I'm* too shocked to move. But after a beat, his hands grip my waist, and he kisses me back, transforming the kiss from a simple press of the lips and deepening it, stirring me into action. We're kissing, *really* kissing, and it hits me that *I'm kissing Adam Murray*, and it feels . . . nice? But where are the sparks? Where are the toe curls?

"*What the fuck?!*" a voice screeches, and I pull away from Adam, too shocked to form words. *I kissed Adam Murray. He kissed me* back.

Faye's standing in the doorway, alone and fully clothed, glaring at me and Adam like she wants to rip our heads off.

"Stay away from Lori!" she shouts, then grabs my forearm and yanks me into the room, slamming the door shut behind her.

I'm still too numb to process anything. Did I really just kiss Adam?

"What the actual fuck?" Faye's jaw is set and her eyes flash. "You and Adam? Seriously, Lori?"

I'm taken so off guard by her anger that I stare at her for a few moments to collect my thoughts. She doesn't seem bothered by my lack of speech as she continues.

"I know you've always had a crush on Adam, but you can't act on it! It's *Adam*! You can't seriously *like him* or *be* with him!"

I've never seen Faye like this. Is the thought of me and Adam together so terrible that it sends her into a blind rage? What if I did want to be with Adam? Would she have a real problem if we got together? If we had feelings for each other that we wanted to act on? From the way she's pacing and her flared nostrils, it's clear that she would.

"I can't believe you kissed him!" She continues her rant but stops pacing to focus on me. "Never do that again. You can't be with Adam. You're my best friend, and he's my brother."

"Do you not realize how selfish you sound right now?" I ask, finally shaking off my shock. It's not even about Adam, not right now. The longer she talks, the more upset I get, and right now I'm more upset that she cares more about her own feelings regarding me being with her brother than caring about if I actually like him or not. "If I wanted to be with Adam, then you should be happy for me."

Faye looks taken aback. "I'm not selfish! Why does everyone keep saying that?"

Now we're staring each other down and there's a sort of electric tension in the air that only riles me up more. "Maybe because it's *true*! I've been locked out of my room two out of four nights, not including today. I've barely seen you all trip because you've been busy concocting this ridiculous plan to make Kellan jealous instead of just telling him how you feel. And you've been really mean to Kiara even though she's really nice, in fact, she spent more time with me last night at the club than you did!"

"Oh, grow up, Lori. Do you seriously want me to hover around you the entire time? You're a big girl, you don't need me to hold your hand twenty-four seven. You were fine. You were having fun. Plus, I only had this room *once* with Kellan, and you came back after. I never kicked you out." She flings her arms out as if making her point is exhausting. "Besides, I told you all about why I've been acting all fucked up lately, and you said you understood. I thought we were over this. I didn't know you were going to keep being dramatic about it."

I don't want to consider if there's any truth behind her words, and instead feel a kernel of anger burning in my chest and hold on to it, flaring it to life.

"I'm not the one being dramatic," I fire back. I've never been this angry before, not at Faye, not that I've ever vocalized. "You're the one who got all huffy about seeing me with Adam!"

She doesn't want me to be with Adam because he's her brother and I'm her best friend? Does she not realize how hypocritical that is?

"Yes! You shouldn't be with Adam! You can literally get any guy you want by blinking in his direction and he'll fall at your feet, and you want my *brother*?"

Her words shock me to the core. She's got our roles mixed up. *She's* the one who can get any guy to fall at her feet. I can't do anything except trip over my feet *and* my words in front of any guy I like.

"That's not true and you know it," I accuse, though it comes out just barely above a whisper.

She laughs. "You're so busy being insecure that you don't realize people fall over themselves to get a moment of your attention. You walk into a room, and everyone stares at you, Lori, and you hide from that because you hate attention. You don't even realize that they're not staring at you because something's wrong, but because you're so fucking pretty and perfect and have all your shit together and they just can't help it." Her breathing is coming out harder now, and apparently, she's not holding anything back. "What I have to work so hard at comes so easily to you, and you don't even realize it. Dean barely knows you and he'd already do anything for you, and now you have Adam wrapped around your pinky finger! Meanwhile, Adam's *my brother* and he can barely stand me, and I can't even get one guy to like me for anything more than a cheap hookup!"

My head swims as her words sink in, and before I can even

process, the door to the bathroom swings open and Kellan steps out.

"I was trying not to interrupt to give you time to sort out . . . whatever's going on here . . . but clearly it's getting out of hand," he says, looking back and forth between the two of us. "Faye, you can't tell Lori who she can and can't kiss."

She looks absolutely appalled that Kellan would take my side over hers. It only adds fuel to her fire. "I can if the person she's kissing is my brother!" she shoots back, and Kellan's face grows grim.

This is going to turn into a very different conversation, and I don't want to be here for that. Plus, that anger burning in my chest is growing the longer I stand here in front of Faye, the longer I absorb her words, the more we shout at each other. I back toward the door, but I can't resist throwing some parting words.

"You have no right to say any of that. And besides, the only reason I kissed him is because he was about to walk into this room and see his best friend fist-deep in his little sister, and nothing else would distract him. So, you're welcome."

With that, I open the door and storm into the hallway. I've never said something so crass before, I don't even *swear*, but I don't have it in me to care. The air out here is lighter now that I'm away from Faye's stormy tension, but it does nothing to ease the burning in my chest or the thoughts spinning around in my head. Adam's not here anymore, so he must've given up when he saw Faye was all right and yelling at him. I guess that means the kissing him strategy worked, even if it wasn't in the way I intended and caused a fight between me and my best friend, the biggest one we've ever had.

Something shiny on the floor catches my eye, and I pick up a key card. The room number on the back is Adam's—he must have dropped it. Do I bring it back to him? Can I face him after I threw myself at him?

But he kissed me back.

I square my shoulders and cross the hall to his room. I'm going to have to talk to him sooner or later, and I guess while I'm in this confrontational mood, it's going to be sooner.

SEVENTEEN

Night Four of Cuba

Faye

The door slams shut behind Lori, and the silence that fills the room in her absence is almost louder than our arguing.

"Can you believe her?" I ask Kellan, pacing to burn off some of this energy. "Lori and Adam? Lori and my *brother*?"

Kellan doesn't say anything, just watches me as I process everything that happened in the last five minutes.

"Does she actually *like* him? How could she? It's *Adam*. She knows he hates me! And did she forget he let his girlfriend torture us for four years? Because I sure didn't!"

"Faye . . ." Kellan starts, but I'm not done with my rant; my brain's moving at a hundred miles a minute.

"And what was that whole thing about her stopping Adam from finding us? We had it under control!" Right? He wouldn't have come in to find Kellan; he didn't know he was in here. Lori didn't have to kiss him unless she wanted to, and apparently, she wanted to.

"Would it really be terrible if Lori and Adam got together?" he asks quietly.

I stop my pacing to stare at him. "Yes! She's my best friend! She can't be with my brother."

"That's a little hypocritical, don't you think?" he asks in a tone more sad than accusing.

Hypocritical? How am I being hypocritical? He says nothing, only looks at me with a grim face as his words sink in, and then I get it.

"No. No, we're different. This is different."

A muscle in his jaw jumps. "How, Faye? Everything you said about Lori and Adam is everything you're afraid that Adam's going to say, and here you are, telling Lori who she can and can't be with because she's your best friend and Adam is your brother. We're in that same position. If you really believe what you told Lori, then that means you consider *us* being together wrong."

My heart leaps into my throat. I didn't think about it like that, and that's not what I meant at all. Of course I don't think being with Kellan is wrong; nothing about the way he makes me feel is wrong. But thinking about *my* Adam with *my* Lori set something off inside me that still angers me to think about.

"I didn't mean it like that," I tell Kellan. "We—we're different," I add pathetically, not knowing what to say, how to get him to stop looking at me like that, like I'm a disappointment.

He's quiet for a moment. "Do you really think I thought of you as a cheap hookup?"

A pang runs through my chest. I don't even remember saying that.

My silence must confirm it for Kellan because he shakes his head. "Is that how you think of me? That I just wanted you as some quick fuck? That I never actually cared about you?"

That's exactly what I've been thinking this whole vacation, but I can't say it out loud, especially not now that he's making it seem like the thought is preposterous. But I can't get off the hook by not answering this time, so I find my voice, even if it comes out small, and say, "You wanted to keep us a secret."

"No, *you* wanted to keep it a secret. I'm not good enough for the great Fayanna Murray." He shakes his head again, and the way he's looking at me is so different from how he was when we first got into my room tonight. I craved that look, needed it to breathe, but now his look makes my skin go cold, makes me feel like shrinking into myself. He continues, "I wanted to be with you. You're worth the fight I'd get into with your brother, you're worth everything. *You're* the one who was only ever interested in sex."

"That—that's not true," I say, my voice shaky. "You didn't want people to know. You didn't want us to be exclusive."

His laugh is humorless. "I've wanted to be with you since I was sixteen. It was obvious you never felt the same way, so I said nothing, but then we slept together, and I thought you finally felt the same way, at least until you demanded that I tell no one what happened. I was *your* dirty little secret, not the other way around, Faye. And the fucked-up part of it all is that I'm so crazy about you I didn't even care. I'd keep being your dirty little secret for as long as you wanted, as long as it made you happy, as long as I could keep being near you."

The room's spinning with the admission as every single interaction I've had with Kellan plays through my mind. Kellan's wanted me this whole time? That can't possibly be true; I would've known it, right? But there's nothing in his face but raw honesty. He really cared about me this whole time. Was I always too blind to see it? I didn't realize my own feelings for him until recently, but I know they've always been there, just pushed down and ignored until we got to Cuba. When it came to me and Kellan, maybe I was always scared to look deeper, to dig beneath the surface and discover the truth.

Still, I say, "But you've always been with other girls, or flirted with them, even if I was around. You even flirted with Kiara in front of me!"

"Nothing happened with me and Kiara. Besides, I was trying to give you space. I know how you are, Faye; you like to be free and go where the wind blows and act on whatever whim you have. The last thing I want to do is crowd you and scare you away. I didn't want to force you to do anything you didn't want, especially when you made it clear you didn't want *me*."

I want to deny it. Deny, deny, deny that he wouldn't have scared me off, that I needed him to make it more obvious, to tell me how he felt; but the fact is he knows me, probably even better than I know myself. He isn't wrong that it would've scared me off. He's known me long enough to see how I run away from a guy once he wants to become serious—saw it happen with his friend Zach too. Knowing all this and that Kellan understood and still wanted to be with me causes my throat to constrict.

"But I do want you," I say thickly. "I thought *you* just wanted it to be a hookup."

"You're the one who made me swear never to tell anyone."

"Because my brother would freak out!"

His anger morphs into something akin to resignation. "Would it really be so bad if he found out we were together? I wanted to tell Adam, tell everyone, but you were so against it." He pauses, collecting his thoughts, and swallows. "You told me tonight that you wanted to be with me, *really* be with me, but what does that mean if you still want to hide us? Hide me?"

My mouth opens to tell him I'm not hiding him or us, but nothing comes out. I'm in love with Kellan and I want to scream it from the rooftops, tell everyone he's *mine* and that we're together. I'm not ashamed of him, and I don't want to hide us, but not telling Adam is the same thing as hiding us. Why do I care so much about Adam knowing? Why am I clinging to this notion that Adam will somehow like me more if he doesn't find out about me and Kellan? I hate that I'm desperately seeking his approval, hate that I'm seventeen fucking years old and still moping around after my big brother, hoping he'll see me as his equal, as his friend, or at least as his *sister*. I want to tell Kellan all of this, that it has nothing to do with him and everything to do with my fear of disappointing Adam and driving that wedge even further between us. But I can't say anything, and the quiet sadness Kellan was displaying before turns into a resolute hardness.

His jaw sets. "You know, Faye, it might kill me, but I can't be with you if you want to keep me a secret."

My heart aches at his words. This is the last thing I thought would happen after we left the pool party tonight. We started off on such a high, finally admitting we wanted to be together, but here he is saying the opposite.

"I don't want to keep you a secret," I blurt, rushing toward him but halting when he holds up a hand, like he can't bear to have me any closer.

My pulse rushes in my ears. I don't like this; I don't like any of this. I don't want to lose Kellan—I just got him. We were happy together for barely an hour before everything came crashing down around us.

"So you don't care if Adam finds out?" he challenges, but there's hurt in his eyes. "You'll go over right now and tell him?"

My hesitation gives Kellan his answer, and his face turns to stone. "That's what I thought."

He opens the door, and everything inside me breaks.

"But—wait!"

He's almost out the door and only turns halfway to face me. "You only care about yourself, Fayanna."

He disappears into the hallway, the door closing behind him punctuating his statement.

I don't chase after him. I can't. I'm rooted to the spot, unable to move, unable to process what happened in a few moments. The events of the night play over and over in my mind. How did it all go to shit so quickly?

I want to scream. I want to cry. I want to talk to Lori about what happened with Kellan. I want to talk to Kellan about what happened with Lori. I want to chase after them and beg them to make up with me, to make everything go back to normal, but I can't do any of those things. Everything's numb after the revelations of tonight; my mind is too overwhelmed to fully process.

In a daze, I wash my face, brush my teeth, change into my pajamas, and slip into bed, staring at a spot on the ceiling without really seeing it. Should I chase after Kellan? Should I go find Lori? Probably. But I've never fought like that with Lori or Kellan before. I lost my two best friends in a matter of seconds, I'm all alone in a different country in a bed that's not mine, and I have no one to turn to. Even if I wanted to go find Dylan to seek comfort, I'm too numb to move.

The worst part about all of this is I'm the reason everything is going to shit. *I'm* the reason Lori and Kellan are pissed. This was supposed to be the best vacation ever, and all I've done is fuck everything up since getting here.

The silence is getting to me. It laughs at me, reminds me how alone I am and how I ruin all the relationships in my life, and soon I can't stand it. I slide out of bed and turn the fan on, then get back into bed. I'm not hot, but the whirling sound of the fan blocks out the deafening silence, and the spinning blades are a welcome distraction from the blandness of the white ceiling. I track the spinning blades as best I can, my mind replaying all my conversations over and over, and soon I think of nothing as I embrace the darkness sleep brings.

EIGHTEEN

Night Four of Cuba

Lori

With Adam's key card in my hand, I march to his door and knock. Normally I'd run after what just happened; I'd run far away and hope we never had to talk about the fact that I threw myself at him, and that *he kissed me back*. But after that fight with Faye, my adrenaline is spiking, and if I'm honest with myself, getting some stuff off my chest felt good. Arguing with Faye was awful, of course, but maybe I don't always have to sit back and wait for the right time to jump in. Maybe sometimes it's best to face things head-on.

Adam doesn't answer, so I knock again. There's music coming from inside the room, so I know someone's in there. I'm pretty sure Adam and Kellan are sharing this room tonight, and since Kellan's currently in my room, it has to be Adam.

"Adam?" I call out, but the door still doesn't open.

Is he ignoring me after what happened? Does he regret kissing me? I fiddle with the key card in my hand.

Up until a few moments ago, we hadn't been on the greatest

terms, and then we kissed, and now I don't know where we stand. The Lori that Adam thinks I am would never force him to talk to me, to try to clear the air between us. No. That Lori is *sweet* and *predictable*.

My hand tightens on the key card.

Maybe I don't want to be *sweet* and *predictable*. That Lori never would've gotten any answers. She would've wallowed in uncertainty all night and gotten anxiety anytime Adam came close, analyzing every single action, agonizing over what happened until it ate at her from the inside out.

Now is not the time to be *that* Lori. I'm too hyped up from the words hurled back and forth between me and Faye to consider walking away now anyway. I'd already be up all night thinking about the fight I had with my best friend—it's too soon for me to fix that—but I can figure out where I stand with Adam. So, instead of backing away from his door, I slide the key card into the reader and turn the handle when it beeps.

The fast-paced bachata music is louder once the door opens, loud enough to drown out my thoughts, and before I lose my resolve, I charge into the dark room. I pass the little hall where the bathroom door is and step into the main part of the room. Once my eyes adjust to the dim glow from the lights streaming in through the sliding door, I freeze.

Oh my goodness!

Faster than I've ever moved, I scramble back to the door, fumbling with the handle until it finally clicks. With my heart pounding in my ears, I throw the door open and run out into the hall, relishing the fresh air, and slam straight into a hard body.

Adam steadies me before I regain my balance and his arms drop to his sides.

"What are you doing?" he asks, his eyes tracking the key card in my hand and landing on the closed door behind me.

Suddenly, all the bravado I was feeling before leaves me in one great whoosh. Everything I wanted to say to him evaporates, and instead all that comes out of my mouth is, "Alessio and Priyasha are having sex in your room!"

His eyebrow lifts a fraction, but other than that he gives no indication that he's surprised, nothing to show this is a revelation to him too.

"I know," he says calmly. "Why do you think I'm out here?"

My jaw drops. "What? You knew?"

"Yes, since day two," he states. He's completely unfazed. Meanwhile, I feel like the hallway is spinning. "Why were you in my room, anyway?"

I force myself to unscramble my thoughts. "I didn't know Alessio was in there, obviously. I found your key card on the floor and went to talk to you."

He takes the card I hold out to him with his brows drawn together. "If you knew this was my card, how could you have thought I was in my room? I wouldn't have been able to get in."

His logic is a shock to my system, making me want to face-palm. He's right. If I was thinking about something other than my anger and my fight with Faye, I would've realized Adam *couldn't* be in his room, because I was holding his key card.

The picture I have of Priyasha and Alessio together is burned into my mind. It wasn't even this bad last time I walked in on Faye and Kellan because I didn't really *see* anything then, just knew they were doing it. But I got a good view of Priyasha and Alessio, good enough to know that neither one noticed me, and good enough to know that it couldn't be mistaken for anything other than sex.

"Did Alessio and Olivia break up?" I ask Adam, and from the set of his jaw alone, I already know the answer.

"No."

"Is he planning on breaking up with her?"

Alessio's obviously not remorseful considering this isn't the first time he's been with Priyasha, and he keeps going back to her. Clearly, he's not thinking about his relationship, or about the girl he's been with for years.

Adam's jaw works as he considers what to tell me before finally relenting. "Alessio decided to pretend nothing happened and not to tell her."

I'm too stunned to figure out if he's joking. But he can't be joking, not about this.

"Are you serious?"

If Alessio plans on *staying* with Olivia, then he can at least be remorseful for cheating on her, not treating this vacation like a free pass to sleep with whoever he wants behind his girlfriend's back! Adam shrugs a shoulder, and his uncaring attitude bothers me. He's acting like this is any other day, like nothing is amiss, like it doesn't matter to him one way or another if Alessio enjoys a week of cheating on his girlfriend, who's also Adam's friend, then returns to her like nothing happened.

"His girlfriend has been your friend since elementary school. You're the one who introduced them. You don't even care?"

"Alessio can do whatever he wants, I'm not going to tell him what to do."

What? Does he really not care about what's going on? Is he seriously as unaffected as he's making it seem?

"So, you're not going to talk to Alessio? To at least convince him to come clean to Olivia? She deserves to know!"

"Lori, it's none of our business," he says patiently, like he's explaining this to a petulant child. "I'm not saying anything to Olivia or Alessio because it's not my relationship."

I can't believe he's saying this right now. I get not wanting to mess with your friend's relationship, but to not say something to him when you know he's doing something wrong is *wrong*. As his friend, and as *Olivia's* friend, Adam should tell Alessio he's being a complete ass! But he's acting like this is no big deal, like this is *normal*, and that it's not his place to tell Alessio to get his act together. If Adam were really his friend, he'd tell Alessio that he's wrong. Faye wouldn't hesitate to rip me a new one if I was acting like that, and that's why she's a real friend. Real friends tell you when you're messing up because they respect you enough to tell you the truth, and Adam's not being a true friend to Alessio or Olivia by turning the other cheek on this situation.

"I can't believe you're cool with him repeatedly cheating on his girlfriend, then looking her in the face when you get back and pretending nothing happened!"

I would never be okay with being her friend and keeping something huge like that from her. If it was me, I'd want to know, and if I found out all my friends knew and never told me, I'd be doubly crushed.

"Just drop it, Lori," Adam says, guiding me away from the door. "You weren't supposed to find out."

I push his arm away from me, not even able to stand his touch right now. Who is this Adam? The guy I've been getting to know over this vacation is nothing like the guy I've had a crush on for four years. Or maybe he is, and I've just been all too happy to ignore the signs, all too happy to mesh his face with the perfect image I had of him in my head, and I can't fault anyone for that except myself.

"I can't believe you," I say, walking across the hall and down the stairs. Adam follows.

"Where are you going?"

"I don't know. Somewhere that's not here." I don't want to be around him right now. The night started off as so much fun, then turned on its head so fast. When I reach the bottom of the stairs, Adam's hand on my forearm stops me, and by now I've lost count of the number of times he's done that to me this week.

"Wait," he demands, and I turn to face him. "What was that back there? The kiss."

The blood drains from my face. The image of Alessio and Priyasha together made me forget all about our kiss and the reason I sought Adam out in the first place.

"The kiss?" I repeat to stall for time. Suddenly the anger that was building in my stomach completely burns out, leaving me in a panic instead.

I can't tell him the real reason—that I froze trying to get him away from discovering Faye and Kellan. I might be upset with Faye, but I can't throw her under the bus.

"Yeah." He steps closer to me, his eyes laser focused on me. "The kiss. Between me and you. About ten minutes ago."

His gaze is so intense I almost shrink into myself, but I force myself to appear unbothered. "Oh. Oh, *that* kiss! That was for the tasks." It comes to me out of nowhere, and I try to channel my anger from before to make it more believable. "I crossed off all the things you said I couldn't. Body shot, dance-off, all I needed was to kiss someone."

I'm almost surprised at how steady my voice comes out, even as Adam's eyes narrow at me.

"It was for the task?"

"Yes." I back away from him. "You said I couldn't do it, and I did."

I didn't do anything for him, and I completed the tasks because they were fun and I wanted to, not because I was trying to prove a point to him. But he doesn't know that, and I'll let him believe the kiss was just to prove a point rather than the truth, or have him think I kissed him for other reasons, like because I *wanted* to.

"You *sure* that's the only reason?" he asks, and the distrust in his voice only makes me more defensive. "Because body shots and kissing people isn't *you*, Lori."

My hands form fists by my side. "How would you know if it is or isn't me?"

I brace myself for him to say it—that I'm *boring*—but then decide I don't have to stand here and let him insult me.

"Actually, forget it. I need some air." I start down the path away from our little hotel, then look back at him. "And *don't* follow me."

He freezes. I shoot him a warning glare for good measure and then continue down the path.

"Lori!" he calls after me.

I don't slow my pace, only yell back, "I mean it!"

He doesn't follow me. I don't have any clear destination in mind; I only know that I don't want to be near either of the Murray siblings right now. I'm not even mad anymore. The anger dissipates the farther I walk from the hotel. Now I'm . . . sad. And a little uncertain. What do I do now? Where do I go from here?

I don't know what time it is, but there are still so many people out and about, walking with friends and family and enjoying the warm night. People wave at me as we cross paths, and I wonder if I look that happy walking around the resort.

Eventually my feet find their way back to the pool party, but I stop once it comes into view. I'm not really in a party mood, but I don't have anywhere to go, so instead I sit on a bench dimly lit by one of the path lights.

"Hey," says a voice, and I look up to find Dean.

"Hey," I reply.

Behind him the party rages on. The music's at full blast and the place is still packed. People are shrieking and laughing and giggling and splashing in the pool, and a pang of sadness hits me as I realize that was me an hour ago.

He gestures to the bench. "Mind if I sit?" he asks almost timidly. I've never seen Dean so unsure of himself, and then I remember how I ran from him right after our almost-kiss.

Dang it.

I spent so much time daydreaming about that exact situation—about his hands on my waist, my hands on the back of his neck, the feel of his body pressed against mine, the butterflies in my stomach, his lips on mine—and then I screwed it all up by running away from him right after we were interrupted. It's probably too much to hope he'll jokingly reprimand me for running from him like he has in the past, not now, not when my actions hold significantly more weight.

"Sure," I reply, and even though he sits beside me, the space he leaves between us is almost mocking.

He hitches his thumb toward the party. "All the guys left. At least, I think so. I'm sharing the room with Kellan tonight and I haven't seen him, but he's got the key, so I hope he's in the room." Dean gives a little laugh.

"He's at the hotel, yeah," I tell him, refusing to specify *where* in the hotel he is. I'm sure by now he's left our room and returned to his own; at least I hope he did before he runs into Adam in the halls.

Dean nods and pulls something out of his pocket. "You told me you'd be back, and I have your phone, so I stayed put, but after a while I figured you weren't planning on coming back, so . . ."

He trails off and guilt punches me in the stomach. I ditched him after he spent all night making sure I had fun, then I forced him to wait around for me.

"I'm really sorry," I say, taking my phone from his

outstretched hand. The weight of it is a reminder of what he did for me tonight, how he took the phone so I wouldn't obsess over my mom and med school, and then distracted me with the dance-off.

"It's okay," he replies, a welcoming smile still on his face.

My gaze drops to the phone in my lap. He's so sweet, so understanding. He's not upset at all with me.

"Is everything okay?" he asks me after a few moments of silence.

This whole trip has made me confused about who I am. Apparently Faye thinks I'm perfect and have all my "shit" together, when I usually feel like I'm anything but. If that was true, wouldn't I know exactly what I want to do with my future? Wouldn't I be happy to get my life sciences degree and then go to med school like my parents have always planned? I wouldn't get sick at the thought of that future if I was perfect and had everything together. Besides, isn't that just another way of saying I'm *boring*, like Adam's been telling me? He thinks I'm *sweet* and *predictable*, and if that's true, that would mean I'll do the predictable thing and follow through with the future planned out for me. If that's true, that means I'm going to wake up every morning hating my life, hating my career, dreading the future. I don't want that, but is that what I'm going to do anyway because that's who I am? Someone who always does what's expected of them?

I remember that day at the beach with Dean our first night here, when he shared how he started standing up for what he wants and about his twin, Dustin. He told me life's too short to let other people make my decisions for me. He told me to go after what I want. Faye basically made my decision for me by saying it doesn't matter if I want Adam because I can't be with him, and Adam has basically been telling me I'm incapable of going after what I want because it's not like me. Maybe because Dean doesn't really know me, he hasn't put me in a box like they have, but deep down I know it's more than that. Dean sees more than I give him credit for, and I trust he'll be honest with me.

"Do you think I'm boring?" I blurt.

Dean's eyebrows draw together. "Boring?"

"Yes. And predictable."

Dean tries to stifle a smile. "You are probably the least predictable person I know."

I'm too serious to blush. "I mean besides the times I've thrown food and drinks of varying viscosity at you." Or blew in his face, or kicked him in the chest, or ran in front of a moving car, or any of the other embarrassing stuff I've done around him that I don't want to remind him about.

"Hmm." He considers it when he sees how serious I am. "I think everyone is predictable in their own way to some extent. But I don't think you're predictable in a bad way. What's going on?"

I fidget in the seat. "I think people think I'm boring."

His eyebrows raise. "Are you joking?" he asks, and when I only avert my gaze and bite my lip, he continues, "Lor, not one thing about you is boring. Hell, even the way you come up to me isn't boring, *or* predictable."

I'm silent as I ponder his words. He places his finger under my chin to gently tilt my head up. When our eyes connect and he's certain I won't look away, he drops his hand.

"I've always thought you were captivating, and I wanted to get to know you better, but the one time I worked up the nerve to talk to you at the gym, you ran from me."

I remember. I thought he wanted the machine. "Old habits, I guess," I reply shyly.

He laughs, his blue eyes as intense as ever. "Yeah. But once you stopped running from me and I got to know you, I found out just how amazing you are. You literally saved a girl's life, Lori. You made snorkeling so much fun, even though you were scared at first."

"Was not," I mumble, but he just chuckles since he knows the truth.

"You helped me carry our drunk friends back to the rooms even as we got puked on. You danced on stage at that club like you owned it, even though I know you have stage fright. Everything we've done together was made ten times better with you there. I always look forward to hanging out with you. So no, I don't think you're boring; I don't know how you got that in your head. I think you're you, and you're amazing."

I never expected him to say that. I never expected him to say any of that. Just last week at the gym I was trying and failing to find the confidence to talk to him—to get him to notice me. And now here he is, saying all these beautiful things about me, telling me I'm amazing and that he enjoys spending time with me.

"You think that even when I run into you and force us both off balance, or when I embarrass myself in front of you?" I breathe, almost not wanting to know the answer.

His smile widens. "Especially then."

We spent the earlier part of the night with our arms around each other, but I feel closer to him now. I've always been myself with Dean—even if that meant being awkward or trying new things or being vulnerable—and he doesn't find me boring.

"For the record," I start, "I didn't run from you because I didn't want to be near you. In fact, it was the opposite." My face heats from the admission.

Dean shifts closer to me on the bench, and I'm all too aware of him, of the space he takes up, the heat his body gives off, the blue of his eyes, the beauty of his smile.

"Does that mean you're not planning on running from me now?" he asks, voice low.

The air thickens, just like it did when we were dancing. Scared to break the moment, I just shake my head.

He leans closer, slowly, so very slowly, as if giving me a chance to change my mind, to run away. But I stay planted where I am, my eyes pinned to his lips. I'm not going anywhere. I want this; I want him to kiss me more than I've ever craved anything. Nothing can make me run away from him this time.

My eyes flutter closed as his lips touch mine, and with that simple brush he sends tingles down my spine, all the way to my toes. He parts his lips to deepen the kiss and my mind empties of everything except the taste of him, the feel of him. What I thought was tingling before is nothing compared to what his touch is doing to me now. His hands land on my hips, and in a fluid, effortless motion, he slides me closer to him, turning me so more of us is touching. I throw my arms around his shoulders, pulling him even closer to me, wishing we were standing so I could feel the strength of him pressed up against all of me. Not once has any kiss felt like this. No one has ever felt this good against my lips, has ever made my heart pound in my chest this hard. I've never felt this good wrapped in someone's arms before, but with Dean I can stay here forever. My fingers bunch in his hair and a low growl sounds from deep in his throat, making my heart flip. All that time I wasted running away from him when we could've been doing *this*.

He pulls away from me and rests his forehead against mine, our lips less than an inch apart as we catch our breath. His fingers tighten on my hips, and I resist the urge to pull his lips back to mine.

"What the fuck?"

Dean and I jump apart at the angry voice. The irony is not lost on me that this is the second time those words broke up a kiss tonight.

Adam is standing a few feet away from us, face hard, his accusing eyes focused on me. "I came to make sure you were okay, and here you are, not only okay, but making out with *him*, not even twenty minutes after you kissed *me*."

My stomach drops out, and I'm too terrified to look at Dean. This sounds really bad, and I can't even deny it because it's true.

"This isn't . . . the task . . . that's not . . ." I trail off because I don't know what to say. This whole situation is terrible. It looks like I ran from Dean at the party as we were about to kiss, so I could go kiss Adam instead, only to kiss Dean right after. I want the ground to swallow me whole. I want to disappear. I want the best moment I've ever had to not have been tainted by my mistakes.

Even though I can't see Dean, I feel him go stiff beside me.

"Did you really kiss Adam tonight?" he asks, but it's not accusing like Adam's tone is. It's sad, and it causes my heart to crack.

The kiss I had with Adam barely qualifies as a kiss, especially compared to what just happened with Dean. I felt nothing with Adam, no fireworks, no stomach flips, no tingles, only lips pressed against mine. But with Dean . . . with Dean I felt *alive*. With Dean I never wanted it to end, and now I'll never know the feeling again.

"I . . . I did," I confess. His face is closed off, none of the earlier emotions shining through, not like when he was telling me how amazing I am. I doubt he still thinks that. "But it wasn't like that."

"Then what was it, Lori?" Adam asks, closing the distance between us.

I'm pinned by his glare. He obviously doesn't buy that it was just me completing the *kiss someone* task. I can't say I kissed him to distract him from finding Faye and Kellan. I can't do that to Faye. And besides, it was my idea to kiss him. No one told me to do that, Faye never asked me to, so even though I don't want to throw Faye under the bus and admit that as my reason for kissing him, it doesn't matter, anyway. My actions were my own, and I kissed him. And then I kissed Dean.

But I don't regret it. Maybe that makes me a terrible person, or maybe it doesn't. I don't really care, and the thought is both terrifying and liberating. Kissing Adam worked for its intended purpose since it kept him from finding Faye and Kellan together, and I refuse to regret that kiss between me and Dean, and everything it made me feel.

But I can't voice any of that out loud. I can't face the rushing of my blood in my ears or the glare Adam's sending us or the way Dean looks like he's just been crushed. So instead of staying and facing both of them, I jump onto my feet and run. The shocked look Adam sends me as I pass him is almost comical. He's the one who's been repeating over and over that I'm predictable, so he should've seen this coming a mile away.

My flip-flops pound on the uneven stone path, and I only take a second to register how dangerous this is before cutting onto the grass and running on that instead. I don't think Dean or Adam follow me, but I don't slow down. This night has been full of highs and lows. I was already unsure where to go or who to turn to, and now the feeling has doubled after that confrontation.

Adam obviously hates my guts, and Dean must think I don't care about him at all. I let them both down, and that's something

I've always hated. Being unable to tell my parents the truth about med school is evidence of that.

I've never been involved in this much conflict before. I've never even been in a fight with anyone. And now I'm stuck in Cuba, at odds with almost everyone, and I have no idea what to do or where to turn.

My steps slow as I near the hotel, and I force air into my lungs, gulping it down in huge breaths. I don't want to go back to the room and face Faye right now, not after the way she spoke to me, even if I really could use her advice. She thinks I'm always perfect? *Ha!* Not even a full hour after she said that, I proved her wrong.

I stand in front of the building contemplating my options. Where do I go? Who can I talk to? Adam's sharing a room with Alessio, and Dean said he's sharing with Kellan. That leaves the spare room . . .

I fly up the steps to the third floor. It's quiet and I don't pass anyone else as I cross the hall and knock on the door, hoping Dylan's still awake and doesn't have any *company*.

The door swings open. Dylan's in nothing but black boxer briefs, his torso and tattoo sleeve on display, his hair wet. "Lori?" He falters when he takes in my tearstained face.

I don't care that he's basically naked. His friendly face cracks through my minimal composure to free the rest of what I've been holding back, so I throw my arms around him, bury my head against his chest, and cry.

"Um . . . it's okay," he says awkwardly, but wraps both arms around my back and holds me close. "Come in."

I release him to follow him into the room, which is thankfully company-free. I sit on the bed that doesn't have rumpled sheets and second-guess my choice to come here. I'm not *friends* with Dylan, not like Faye is, but I was compelled to turn to Dylan anyway. So when he sits a respectable distance away beside me on the bed, wipes my tears with his thumb, and asks me to tell him what's wrong, I do. I tell him everything.

NINETEEN

Day Five of Cuba

Faye

The sound of a door closing jolts me awake. I rub the sleep from my eyes as I sit up in bed. Sunlight from the balcony door bathes the room in light since I hadn't bothered closing the curtains, but even the sunlight seems muted, gray, like my mood.

I slide out of bed and stretch in an empty room. Lori must have just left.

I'm not sure what time she came back in, but when I woke up around three, her bed was still neatly made. My phone had messages from Adam asking if I knew where she was, then angrier texts since I wasn't answering, then nothing. I messaged Dylan right after and he replied immediately saying Lori was crashing with him, and that Adam and Dean had already asked him the same thing. She probably came to get her stuff for the day and left quickly so she didn't have to see me. I don't blame her. I don't really want to see me either.

The night at the club with my head in the toilet was supposed to be my lowest, the night I realized I was acting like a tool and turned it all around. I thought I had. I wasn't supposed to be feeling this low anymore. I should be happy, living my best life and having the best vacation ever with my best friend and my boyfriend, if that's even what Kellan was to me for those few precious moments before it went to shit. Instead, I'm alone in a hotel room, friendless and boyfriendless, with a huge knot in my stomach and a stress-induced headache coming on.

I wash my face and brush my teeth, but I still feel terrible. If I were at home, I could wallow in my room or go out to distract myself, but I'm stuck at the same resort with the same people I want to avoid.

Some people might think *it's not so bad, at least my brother is here, and he'll always have my back*. But not me, and that only makes my stomach knot tighten, my mood darken. I wish I could turn to Adam for support, but he'd rather eat his own arms then wrap them around me in comfort, and the thought stings my eyes. I'm basically alone.

But Dylan is here, and he always cheers me up. I send him a text as I change into my bikini. When I step out onto the balcony to gauge the weather, there's a slight gloominess and chill in the air that's not usual for the mornings, so I put my jean shorts and a loose T-shirt over it. I really hope it doesn't rain. It'll be a lot harder to hide from Kellan and Adam if we're all trapped inside in a common area.

Dylan messages me back saying he'll meet me by the pool closest to our hotel—the one that's not the main party one—in ten minutes.

I'm still fresh out of flip-flops, but I have Kellan's oversized ones. It feels wrong to wear them now after everything last night, but I slip them on anyway, wanting to be closer to him in any pathetic way.

Dylan's at the pool before I am, lounging in a pool chair

away from other people. None of our friends are here, so he must have left them at breakfast. Or maybe they're all somewhere else, enjoying their day, oblivious to my inner turmoil. I refuse to wonder where Kellan is, so I push his sparkling eyes and pouty lips from my mind.

Most of the people here are older couples relaxing in the peace of the morning with a book, or small children splashing around. There's no music blasting at this pool, not like the others, so the atmosphere is calm. The clouds over us are a deep gray, which only adds to my somber mood.

"Hey," I say, plopping down in the lounge chair beside him.

"You look like shit," he greets.

"Has anyone ever told you how charming you are? Because you have a way with words that makes girls feel so special."

He snorts at my sarcasm. "Would you rather I lie?"

My fingers comb through my hair, sorting knots out of the tangled waves. "Maybe some couth next time? Like *Hey, Faye. You're always gorgeous, but something seems off today. You all right?*"

With a heavy sigh and obvious indifference, he repeats, "Hey, Faye, You're always gorgeous, but something seems off today. You all right?"

"Why no, Dylan, I'm not. Thank you for making me feel better while also recognizing that something's wrong. You are so refined and sophisticated."

Dylan rolls his eyes and lies back in the lounge chair, getting comfortable while we fall into our easy routine. "That's me all right. My grasp on the English language and manners knows no bounds. I won *Mr. Delightful, Intelligent, Couth, and Kind* four years in a row."

"The acronym for that is *DICK*."

His lips turn up at the corners. "Is it?"

"Mm-hmm. Maybe the *Delightful, Intelligent, Couth, and Kind* committee is trying to tell you something."

Dylan shrugs, playfulness in his eyes. "Well, it wouldn't be the first time someone's called me a dick, and it certainly won't be the last."

Despite my gloomy mood, I laugh, mirroring his body on my lounge chair so I'm lying back. I'm already comforted by his presence, his familiarity, his easygoing personality. In so many ways Dylan's more of a brother to me than Adam is, but a small part of me wishes it was Adam here beside me; Adam amusing me with pointless banter that doesn't matter but does in the way that counts, Adam who conversation flowed so easily with. But Adam's not here, and our relationship will never be like what I have with Dylan. I wouldn't trade Dylan for anything.

We fall into a comfortable silence, side by side in our loungers, staring out at the mostly empty pool.

"How's Lori?" I ask. Does she miss me like I miss her? Does she hate me?

"She's . . . having a tough time right now."

My breath catches. "Because of me?"

Dylan shifts in his chair. "Partly. But it's not all about you, Faye. She's going through some stuff right now, and she wants to talk to her best friend about it."

What stuff? Wouldn't I know what stuff she was going through? What's happened from the last time I talked to her to this morning?

"What happened?"

"I'm not going to tell you. She'll have to tell you herself when you apologize for freaking out at her about Adam."

"She told you? And you're on her side? Is she *with* Adam?"

My best friend and my brother. Kellan has a point. It's

hypocritical of me to be okay with us but not okay with them. But it's not the same thing, not even in the slightest.

"Again, it's her choice to tell you what happened," Dylan says, though his words aren't harsh. I shouldn't have expected Dylan to tell me anything; he's loyal to a fault. "But what's going on with you?"

I want to talk about what happened with Lori, but that's best left for when I see her. Talking to Dylan about Lori won't help, so instead, without looking at him, I whisper, "Kellan broke up with me."

He's so silent for a moment I think he didn't hear me, but then he shifts, and I feel the full force of his gaze on me.

"He broke up with you?"

I nod, still refusing to look at him in case my eyes water.

"But I thought you weren't together?" he says slowly, like he doesn't want to offend me even though he's stating the truth.

"We weren't . . . but we were? It was so complicated, but whatever was between us is officially over."

Dylan sits up and swings his legs over the side of the lounge chair to face me. "And how does that make you feel?"

"You sound like a shrink."

He says nothing, just waits patiently for me to answer.

I sigh. "Like my heart's breaking in two. I . . ." The words dry up in my mouth. I don't want to tell Dylan I love Kellan before I tell Kellan, especially not now that I'll never get the chance to. "I didn't want it to end like this. I wanted to be with him."

Now that the threat of crying has passed, I sit up to face Dylan, our knees almost bumping.

"You guys seemed all right at the party," Dylan says. "What happened?"

It all spun out of control so quickly. "Lori and Adam were kissing, then I told Lori she shouldn't be with Adam, then Kellan told me I'm a hypocrite and that I only think of myself and that I'm hiding him, and he doesn't want to be with me." The last part pours out of me in one breath.

Dylan blinks at me, processing, and I tell him what happened between me and Kellan last night in more detail. When I'm done, I wait for Dylan to deny it, to say I'm none of the things Kellan said. But the longer we sit in silence now that I've replayed the situation, the more Kellan's words sink in. Lori said the same thing. So did Adam.

"I . . . I *am* a hypocrite. I do only think about myself."

Dylan raises his hands, palms toward me. "Don't look at me like that. You're the one who said it."

"But you're thinking it, right?"

Dylan scrubs the back of his neck, stalling for time, before dropping his hand and saying, "You *are* a bit self-absorbed, Faye. You zero in on what you want and you're on a single-minded mission until you attain it. Normally it's not a bad thing to set goals and do whatever it takes to acheive them, but sometimes you forget about those around you while your eyes are on the prize."

Is that what happens? I'm so obsessed with my target that I neglect my friends? "I don't mean for that to happen."

"I know," Dylan says. "And Lori and Kellan know that too. But after a certain point, enough is enough. Kellan's been letting you do it your way, but he's right when he said you can't tell Lori who to be with, especially since you're in the same situation with Kellan."

"I don't even think it was really about Lori and Adam. I think it was my own issues with Adam I was deflecting onto Lori."

Now that I've said the words out loud, I can see the truth with absolute clarity. If Adam and Lori get together, it's like Adam chose her over me. Not that I want to be with Adam like that—*barf*—but he hates spending any time at all in my presence. What does Lori have that makes her worthy enough to hang out with Adam that I don't have? She's awesome and my best friend and everyone loves her and always chooses her, but Adam is *my* brother. I'm used to people falling over themselves to get to Lori, but not Adam—never Adam. If he hates me, shouldn't he hate my best friend too? Is something inherently wrong with me? Or another thought that's even worse than that, could Adam steal Lori and make her hate me too?

That was what I was thinking about when I went off on Lori, but those are my selfish thoughts, my insecurities, my self-absorbed worries causing me to lash out. Lori's done nothing wrong, and if she really wants to be with Adam, then I'm going to have to get over it and remember not everything's about me.

"What do you mean?" he asks, but only talking to Lori will make me feel better, so I wave him off.

He seems to get it and drops it, instead saying, "Okay. But he's also right in feeling like you're ashamed of him and keeping him a secret."

"I know. I spent all that time wondering if he wanted me, I didn't consider that he *did* and that he wanted to be public about it. I don't want to hide Kellan; I just don't want Adam to hate me even more than he does."

"Adam doesn't hate you."

"He does and you know it."

"Faye, that's not true. And either way, it's not fair to Kellan. You can't be with him and expect him to be happy sneaking around forever. If you really care about him, you'll risk telling Adam and possibly upsetting him in order to be with Kellan."

I let his words sink into the deepest part of me, considering everything with an open mind instead of only thinking about what *I* want. "You're right, especially about me being single-minded and self-absorbed. It's not Kellan's fault I'm scared of disappointing Adam."

As I say it, a weight lifts from my chest. Making Adam's disdain for me even greater scares the shit out of me. But I'm in love with Kellan and have been probably forever, and I want to be with him . . . at least, if he still wants me after all of this.

A humorless laugh escapes me. "Adam told me a couple times this trip that I'm selfish. Who would've thought he was *right*? I hid Kellan because I was worried about Adam's opinion, got so wrapped up in Kellan that I used you, and even Dean, in a stupid plan to make him jealous, hurt Lori, and had a grudge against Kiara. Am I . . . am I a terrible person?"

I never thought I was, but hearing everything listed out like that, from this week alone, it's obvious I really am self-absorbed. How have I never noticed before? Why has no one called me out on it? My eyes sting as I hold back tears.

"What?" Dylan straightens and grabs my hands with both of his. "No, Faye, that's not what I was saying. You're not a terrible person. No one's perfect, and no one expects you to be."

"You literally just told me I'm selfish." My throat burns, but I still refuse to cry.

"No. *You* called yourself selfish."

I rip my hands from his. "Because I am! Will Lori even want to be friends with me after the way I lectured her? Will Kellan want to be with me?"

Dylan's voice is stern, his jaw set. "Everyone makes mistakes. You're *seventeen*, Faye. You're going to make a shit-ton more before you figure it out, and that's okay. It's life. What matters now is how you fix it. Lori and Kellan love you, and right now they're hurt. Stop this pity party you're throwing yourself and go do something about it. Lori had a rough night, and I'm a poor substitute for you. I had absolutely no idea what to say to make her feel better, and even when I channeled my best Fayanna Murray, it was terrible. She needs you. Find Kellan and sort that out as well. It's not the end of the world, and this—mopey—version of yourself isn't you." Dylan stands, his voice growing stern and more confident, like a coach riling up his team before a big game. "Your best—and sometimes worst—quality is going after what you want. But make it work for you. Right now, you want to make up with Lori and Kellan and make them happy. You have a goal in mind, now go get it the way only you can when you lock in on it. Let nothing stand in your way."

He's right. This isn't me. I don't sit around throwing myself pity parties, and the one and only time I allowed myself to do that was when I was puking my brains out at the club. I'm Fayanna Murray, and I always get what I want.

I jump up from the chair. "I want Lori and Kellan back."

A grin slides onto Dylan's face. "Then go do it!"

"Yes!" I exclaim, feeling better and refreshed, tears no longer threatening to spill. Dylan doubts his pep-talking skills with whatever he said to Lori last night, but I'm reenergized. Who knew *Dylan* was so wise? The dude dips pickles in mayonnaise and downs it with a side of milk, yet he's spouting good, usable advice like a well-trained life coach. I'm going to make this better the only way I know how, and nothing is going to stand in my way.

"Thanks Dyl, you're the best!" I throw my arms around him and squeeze him tight, then take off toward the gate, Kellan's too-big flip-flops slapping on the ground with each determined step. I make it to the gate before I pause, then backtrack to Dylan, who's staring at me with amusement.

"Where—"

"Lori's at the small beach. I think Kellan's at the party pool."

"Great!" I hug him again because I just can't help myself. I knew I could count on Dylan. He's always been there to pick me up when I need him. He's the one who wrote me fake notes signed by my dad when I wanted to get out of class. He's the one who always convinced Adam to let me play video games with them when I was a kid. He's known me practically forever, and he's always been there for me.

When I leave Dylan and charge down the path, I don't hesitate at the intersection where left leads to the pool and right leads to the small beach. I veer right and march toward Lori. As much as I want to beg Kellan to forgive me and fill the hole in my heart where he's always been, Dylan said Lori's upset—about more than what happened between us—and she needs me. My need for Kellan is going to have to wait until I sort Lori out and get her back to her cheerful self. Then, and only then, can I find Kellan and beg him to take me back, to be my boyfriend, to convince him I'll set things right.

Even though my mood has lifted with my new resolve, the clouds above me are still gloomy. The breeze is warm but strong, and the temperature isn't cold, but it's cooler compared to the rest of the week. The path runs parallel to the water, where a thin strip of sand separates me from the angry crashing of waves. Wind whips my hair in front of my face as I look for Lori, stumbling a few times on the uneven path in Kellan's flip-flops.

As I shove my hair out of my face, I spot her on a beach chair a few feet away from me. She's alone, none of our friends in sight. In fact, the only other people at this beach are a few families and some older couples sitting on beach chairs scattered on the sand. Most people visit the bigger beach, since that's where the crowds, the space, and the activities are, so Lori's choice to be here is a commentary on her need to be alone. Her knees are pulled up to her chest, her head resting on them.

As I'm about to step off the path and into the sand, a voice calls my name. I freeze, my heart picking up speed. I'd know his voice anywhere.

Lori must hear it too, because her head pops up, and her eyes, red-rimmed and swollen, connect with mine. She perks up a bit and moves her beach bag from the seat beside her onto the ground, silently inviting me to join her. Even from here the brilliance of her blue eyes is a noticeably brighter shade than normal because of the tears.

"Faye," he repeats, closer now. I turn to face him, practically holding my breath.

He looks good—really good—and my heart knows it too, picking up into overdrive. The wind tousles his hair, and my fingers itch to tug the strands. His tank top shows off his toned arms and my body wishes they were wrapped around me. His full lips press together in a frown, and I wish they were pressed against mine.

"Hey," I greet when he stops in front of me, though it sounds like a question. After last night, I didn't think he would be the one coming to me. I was all prepared to seek him out, to tell him everything on my mind, even if it's embarrassing, even if he doesn't love me back, and try to make it work. But he's standing in front of me, everything I've ever wanted, everything I feared I lost, his eyes devouring me like all those words thrown between us last night didn't happen.

"Can we talk? It's important," he asks.

I know it's important. It's about everything hanging over us. About our past and our present and our future together, or at least the possibility of one. I want to talk to him before he changes his mind and decides it's not worth even a conversion with me, before he decides he wants nothing to do with me at all. I want to sort everything out now, to figure out if and how we can move forward, *together*. It's on the tip of my tongue, *Yes, of course*, but the words dry up in my mouth.

"Faye?" he prompts, and I hesitate. My gaze moves back to Lori, and she visibly deflates, like she knows I'm going to change direction and leave with Kellan. She looks away and wraps her arms back around her legs, resting her head on her knees as she watches the tide smash onto the shore.

"I'm sorry, Kell. I can't right now."

He blinks. "What? Are you serious?"

This might mess everything up, but Dylan's right. Lori's obviously going through some things, and I made everything worse by taking out my own insecurities on her. She wasn't mad I was going to her. In fact, she seemed *hopeful*, and I will not fuck that up, not for anyone, not even for myself. Maybe I am selfish and self-absorbed, and even though I want nothing more than to fix this with Kellan right *now*, my eye is on the prize, and that prize is Lori.

"I'm sorry," I tell Kellan, backing away. "I'll find you after, okay? I promise."

Before he says something that I can't unhear or convinces me to stay, I turn from him to head to Lori, but pause. Somehow, Adam's intercepted me, walking up to Lori from the opposite direction. Lori's eyes widen a fraction when she notices me going to her over leaving with Kellan, but then Adam calls out to her, and she stands and turns.

Do I stay and let her have alone time with Adam? Does she want me to wait? Or leave to give her privacy? I'm unsure what to do until Lori looks over her shoulder at me, sending me an *SOS* look, and resolve fills me. I plant the oversized flip-flops on the sand and cross the remaining space to my best friend and brother.

TWENTY

Day Five of Cuba

Lori

Faye was going to come to me. I saw it in the look on her face, in the determined straightness of her spine. But then Kellan called out to her, and I realize she'll choose him over me.

I spent the night with Dylan, and while he cheered me up in his own way, he couldn't tell me what I should do or how to fix things with Dean and Adam. It doesn't help that this morning Mom texted me my daily *don't forget about med school* reminder in the form of links to practice questions.

I wanted to scream.

Instead, I sent her a thumbs-up emoji and contemplated Dean's words from last night. Dean would encourage me to tell my mom I'm not going to med school. I wanted to; I almost did, too, but I couldn't disappoint another person. Dean, Faye, and Adam are enough.

Faye would know what to do, how to explain to Dean that the kiss I shared with him was nothing like the kiss with Adam. She'd make him believe our kiss meant something, that I felt it to my very toes. I needed to talk to Faye, and she was coming here, right until Kellan intercepted, and my hope deflated, knowing he's more important to her.

I rest my head on my knees and watch the ocean without really seeing it. I haven't seen anyone other than Dylan since this morning, and I'm hoping to keep it that way.

"Lori!"

My entire body tenses at the sound of Adam's voice. I didn't think I'd have to see him so soon, or deal with his accusing tone.

I look back at Faye. She's facing me, and Kellan's standing behind her with a hurt expression. She's leaving him to come to me?

Adam calls my name again, and I jump off the chair to meet him. He's closer now, close enough that I can see the hard set of his jaw, the intensity in his hazel eyes.

I don't want to face him alone, not after last night. I meet Faye's eyes over my shoulder, and she gets the hint because she charges toward us.

Adam stops in front of me, and we stare at each other. His jaw works, and I force myself to keep my shoulders back and not cower under his intensity.

Finally, he says, "I don't know what's gotten into you this trip, but you're not acting like yourself."

"Adam!" Faye scolds as she approaches us, but I hold up a hand. She's always been good at reading me, so she stops a few feet away from me, giving me space but ready to intervene, which I appreciate. I thought I wanted her help when Adam walked over, but his words awakened something in me, something that's been lying dormant when it comes to standing up for myself. The pressure sitting in my chest expands as Adam speaks, the same way it's been doing this whole trip.

His eyes briefly flick to Faye, but he doesn't spare her another glance. "You're dancing on tables and running around without telling people where you're going and drinking alcohol and making friends with strangers and doing body shots and kissing him!" He flings out his arm behind me and I follow where he points.

Kellan hasn't moved from his spot, which is within hearing distance, and he's been joined by Dean, Dylan, and Alessio. The four boys are staring at us, like they're in shock at what Adam's saying, and it's clear who Adam's pointing at. He continues, "You don't even know him, and you kissed him! What is going on with you?"

Everything he's listing is everything that I did because I wanted to, everything that I had fun doing. I loved doing every one of those things he mentioned, but somehow it isn't like me to do them?

"Who are you to tell me what to do?" I retort. "If I did those things, then it obviously *is* like me to do them, don't you think?"

"No. You wouldn't be doing any of that stuff if *he* wasn't making you."

Again, I know who he's referring to even without him saying it. His refusal to acknowledge Dean while simultaneously insulting him only makes me more upset. "No one is *making* me do anything. The only person here who's making me do stuff is *you*. You're telling me not to drink, not to talk to people, not to participate in events, not to have *fun*. And right now, you're making me angry."

Adam must not expect my words to sound so harsh because his eyes widen slightly. "I'm not trying to make you angry; I'm just trying to watch out for you," he says, doubling down on the intensity. "It's easy for people to take advantage of you, and I just want to make sure you're not letting him change you."

On the surface, his words make sense. They'd even be sweet

if I didn't know any better. But I'm able to move past them and get to the meaning, to see his words for what they truly are, and they're not flattering.

"No one is taking advantage of me, Adam, especially not *Dean.* In fact, Dean has never expected me to do anything. He's not the one who expects me to act one way or another. He's not telling me what I should or shouldn't be doing. *You are.*"

Adam's defensive walls rise at that statement, his chest puffing up. "*I'm* better for you than him. I get that you're upset about Jenna and the stuff I let her get away with, but you're smarter than this, Lori. You're not going to choose *him* over *me*. I know you. I know who you are, and what you need."

He's right. I'm at his house almost every other day; it's impossible for him not to know me, simply because I've been in his proximity for years. But it's clear he doesn't really *know* me, or doesn't care to watch me grow, to help me figure out who I truly am. I've been floating for a long time, unsure of who I am or what I want—which is why I want to go to Europe so badly. But even though I'm not entirely sure of who I am, I do know I am *sick* of doing what other people expect of me, *sick* of trying to make them happy, *sick* of people telling me what's best for me. Whether it's Faye telling me to stay away from Adam, or my parents telling me to go to med school, or Adam telling me an entire laundry list of things. I just want to be *me*, and what I want right now is to stop being talked to like an incapable toddler.

"I'm not a child, Adam! I don't need you to tell me what's best for me. I don't need you to make decisions for me! You want me to stay in this perfect little box and be the perfect little Lori I've been my entire life, not making any waves, letting other people run her life. Well, sorry to break it to you, but I'm my own person! I can and will make my own decisions, and I'm over you telling me what those decisions should be."

A muscle in his jaw jumps as his eyes bore into mine, his gaze fiery and commanding, mine determined and finally seeing the truth.

"You want to make decisions?" he asks, even though it's rhetorical. "Fine. Right now. It's either him or me, Lori."

I'm taken aback by his statement. "Wait, what?"

He steps closer to me, forcing me to tilt my head up. His lips press in a straight line. "You heard me. It's him or me, and if it's not me, I'm walking away and I won't be there when you fall, which you will."

Besides the fact that he wants me to choose between him and Dean right here, right now, his confident assumption that I'm going to fail and come crawling back to him spikes the anger in my chest more than ever before. I don't know what to do with it, how to deal with the frustration of being treated like I'm incapable of doing anything or knowing what's best, of always taking the easy way out so I don't have to confront or disappoint anyone.

I glance back at Dean, who's still standing with Kellan, Dylan, and Alessio. All four boys are just as wide-eyed as they were the last time I looked in their direction. They heard everything.

I haven't talked to Dean, so I'm not sure where his head's at after last night, but as I meet his eyes, words he said to me our first night here replay in my mind. *Life's too short to let other people make your decisions for you*. It feels like forever ago, and while I agreed with him in theory when he first told me, I get it now.

"Choose, Lori. Right now," Adam commands, and my resolve hardens, his words bolstering my decision and giving me the confidence to announce what I want, what I *really* want.

"You want me to choose, Adam? Fine. I choose neither of you!" I shove him, and he's so thrown off by my words that he stumbles back a step. "I choose myself! I'm done being told what to do and being pushed around. I'm done making decisions for other people. I'm choosing *myself* and doing what *I* want to make myself happy, and I don't need you or anyone else telling me what that is. I only wish I figured that out sooner."

Adam's staring at me like he's never seen me before. He didn't expect me to say that and genuinely thought I would choose him. He probably didn't think I'd grow a backbone and stand up for myself, but everything that's happened this week has been leading up to this moment, *this* decision. It's time I put myself first, and if that means stepping out of the shadows and causing some conflict while doing it, then so be it.

"Yeah! You tell him, Lori!" Faye exclaims, joining my side. "Tell him that—"

I round on Faye, effectively cutting her off. "That means you too, Faye. I get it; you're the outgoing, confident one who's always got a plan, and I'm the quiet one who always follows your lead. It's worked for us, but sometimes you push me around and take my shyness for granted. Not anymore."

Faye pales. "I—I'm sorry, Lori. I didn't mean to. I was actually coming over to apologize for last night. I had no right to say any of that stuff to you. I was projecting my own insecurities on you, and you didn't deserve it."

It's obvious she means every word, and it softens my anger. I can see she wants to add more but hesitates because we have an audience. Other than our friends and the random families that are here, there's also a group of guys around our age, maybe older, who are walking on the shore. They're loud and have beers in their hands, clearly already started with the day-drinking. Suddenly I'm claustrophobic, even though I'm on an open beach and the breeze whips at my hair. I came here to get away, to have time to think, and now Adam is confronting me while all our friends, as well as strangers, are here to witness it.

"It's okay, Faye, we'll talk after," I tell her, bending down to scoop up my bag and flip-flops.

She nods and breathes out a sigh of relief. Right now I don't want to talk to anyone. I just want to *be*, to figure out how this new resolve will fit into my life.

Adam glances at the stuff in my hands. "Where are you going?" He steps closer to me as I take a step back, my toes sinking into the sand. "Let's talk about this, Lori. Stop running away."

I bite back my response that if he knows me as well as he claims, then he'd know that running away is basically my go-to. But this time, I don't feel like I'm running away. I'm done being talked down to, and I said what I had to say. I stood up for myself, and there's nothing else I can say that'll change Adam's mind. The longer I stand here, the angrier I get, and I'm done being angry.

"I'm not running away, Adam. I'm just done with this conversation. I'll talk to you once you get your head out of your ass."

Deciding to stay barefoot, I slip my flip-flops into my beach bag and march away.

"Lori!" Adam calls out, but I keep on my path, my spine straight, my head held high. I'm proud of myself for not caving. The only issue is that I need to walk right past Dean and our other friends, and that makes my confidence waver. They're standing on the stone path, so I decide to continue walking on the sand along the shoreline, so I don't need to come within a few inches of them. But now I have to walk right past the other guys, the loud ones who are drinking, who are now throwing a football back and forth. All three eye me as I approach, and even though I'm only wearing a triangle bikini top and jean shorts, I don't back down when they blatantly check me out.

"Hey beautiful, wanna join us?" asks the one closest to me, who's wearing his baseball hat backwards.

I continue walking without acknowledging him when an arm wraps around my waist and a hand lands on my butt. "Hey, come on, don't be like that," he prods, the heat from his hand burning through my jean shorts.

I suddenly remember Pervy Gym Guy, who Dean had to confront for me, the guy from the club who Naomi had to rescue me from, and the tons of other guys who've put their hands on me, and how I was too timid to do anything.

Without a second thought, I slam my knee up between his legs and shove him away from me. "Don't *fucking* touch me!" I yell as he keels over in the sand with a groan.

His friends take a few tentative steps toward the guy in the backwards baseball hat, but the rage must show on my face because when I meet their eyes they hesitate and glance down at the sand.

With my blood still pumping, I risk a glance at my friends, and every single one of them is now closer to me and frozen where they are, staring at me with wide eyes. The only person who doesn't seem shocked into stillness is Dean, who's now the closest to me, and his lips pull up at the corners as he regards me.

My own lips curl up in answer, and he nods at me once. I shouldn't care as much as I do, and I don't need his approval, but the thought of Dean seeing me standing up for myself, that I proved I *can,* not only to him but to myself, makes me giddy with pride. Adam's frowning at me, and my smile widens thinking that I just did something *sweet, predictable* Lori wouldn't dream of.

Instead of facing them all, I adjust my beach bag on my shoulder and stride toward the hotel, ignoring Adam calling out to me. I need to cool off, and so does he. Until he realizes he can't keep telling me what to do, how to act, and what to think, I have nothing to say to him. And maybe I should go talk to

Dean, to sort out everything that happened, but I don't want to overwhelm myself. It was only last week that any kind of confrontation made me ill, and even though I'm trying to become someone who stands up for herself, I don't want to overdo it.

Barefoot, I step onto the stone path just as the first raindrop hits my shoulder.

TWENTY-ONE

Day Five of Cuba

Faye

We all watch Lori fade into the distance with facial expressions ranging from pure shock to awestruck to admiration. When that guy grabbed her, we all made a beeline toward her, Dean faster than any of us, but she stopped us all in our tracks by kneeing him right in the balls. It was a total badass move, and it serves him right for groping her. I just hope she's okay after that, and especially after what happened with Adam. Hell, she *swore*—dropped a full-on eff bomb—and I've never even heard Lori say *shit* before. If that didn't tell us how pissed she is, I don't know what will.

Until now, I thought she wanted to be with Adam, but after seeing her stand up to him, I feel even stupider than before. She can handle herself, clearly, and doesn't need me to fight all her battles. I realize that now; I realized that before with Dylan too. I just hope Lori knows that, and knows how much I love her, and that I never meant to hurt her, on this trip or before.

Adam rounds on me. "This is all your fault."

"What? Me?"

"Yes, you," he repeats, the disappointed face he reserves just for me on full display. "It's your fault Lori's feeling like she's being pushed around. You do it to her too often without realizing."

His statement takes me aback and fills me with rage. "Were you not listening during that conversation? She was talking about *you*! And yes, while I see what she said applies to me too, her entire spiel was directed at you!"

Water lands on my forehead, and I glance up at the sky. It's darker than it was before, and while it's not full-on raining, it's working up to it. The football guys have left with their gropey friend, and the other beachgoers are packing up their things now that raindrops are falling, albeit slowly and spaced apart. But Adam and I stay where we are, our friends close by as well.

"This wouldn't have happened if you weren't so damn selfish all the time, Faye," Adam accuses, crossing his arms over his chest.

I peer at the guys standing only a few feet away and catch Kellan's gaze. Everything he's told me runs through my mind, and his brown eyes reinforce my confidence. I know what I need to do, and I'm too fed up to be as scared as I should be.

"You're right," I admit, taking him by surprise. "I have been selfish, but not in the way you're thinking. I was trying to protect myself from you, your disappointment, your resentment, your disdain, and in doing so I was being selfish and hurting Kellan."

Kellan rushes to us. "Faye, you don't have to do this. It's okay."

"No, it's not okay," I tell him with resolve.

Kellan's eyes bore into mine as he studies me. "Don't do this for me. Only if it's what you want, if you're ready."

My heart pounds in my chest as I take in his face, the concern written all over it. Concern for *me*, not for Adam freaking out. Even though he feels like I'm hiding him, like I don't want people to find out about us, he's still not forcing me to reveal our relationship to Adam. I'm not sure if we even *have* a relationship, but I still owe it to myself, to Kellan—hell, even to *Adam*—to come clean about my feelings. All this time I thought Kellan didn't want to be with *me*, that he was ashamed of me. Meanwhile, he's been feeling the same way because of me. Well, not anymore. I'm fixing this now.

"What's going on here?" Adam asks, eyes bouncing back and forth between me and Kellan.

"Kellan and I . . . we're . . ." What exactly am I supposed to tell him? We're fucking? We *were* fucking? We were exclusive for about an hour?

Kellan's silent beside me, and Adam huffs out an impatient sigh. "You and Kellan are what, Fayanna?"

I don't know if I'm feeding off the high of Lori's badassness or the heat of Kellan beside me or the annoyance on Adam's face, but I blurt out, "I'm in love with him!"

The second the words are out of my mouth, I freeze, and so do the two guys standing with me. I've never said it out loud, and never to Kellan. Now not only does he know the truth, but so does my brother.

Adam's deathly still as he processes this, glancing at his best friend for only a second before yelling, "You're *what*?" at the same time Kellan asks, "You're in love with me?"

Turning to face Kellan, I ignore my brother's shock and the sporadic fat raindrops that are cold against my burning skin. "Yes. And have been for a long while, I just never realized it until this trip, where I was so stupidly jealous of you and Kiara. I'm sorry for how I've been acting, and I never meant to hide you or hurt you."

Now that the truth's out there, my chest is lighter. The only issue is that Kellan's expression is neutral, so I'm completely in the dark about what he's thinking.

He didn't say he loves me back.

"Wait," Adam says, knocking Kellan aside so he can come between us. "Have you and Kellan . . . have you been *fucking*? How long has this been going on?"

And *there* is the anger and disappointment I was trying to avoid. But my mere existence garners those emotions from Adam, so telling the truth about me and Kellan shouldn't faze me. But it does, and I shrink under the ferocity of his gaze.

Before I can answer, Adam rounds on Kellan. "My *sister*? Seriously, Kellan, what the fuck is wrong with you? And doing it all behind my back? Have I ever been home while it was happening?" He pauses his rant and his face pales, then he lowers his voice and speaks slowly. "Have I ever—and I mean *ever*—heard the details of you and Faye without knowing you were talking about my *sister*?" He looks nauseated, and the fluctuation of his emotions isn't helping me gauge how he's processing the news.

"What? No!" Kellan exclaims. "I've never talked about me and Faye to you. And I'm sorry for keeping it from you, but it was for the best."

Even now, facing Adam's wrath, Kellan's not throwing me under the bus. He *wanted* to tell Adam, wanted to tell *everyone* from the second it happened. *I'm* the one who wanted it to be a secret, and he's not revealing that to Adam. He didn't say he loved me back, but he's protecting me, even now, even though I don't deserve it, and I feel like crying and throwing myself at him and never letting go.

But I won't let Adam take out his anger on Kellan. "No, it's not his fault, stop looking at him like that."

Kellan looks at me in surprise, but I'm so overwhelmed I can't read the other emotions on his face.

"Hey!" someone yells, causing Adam, Kellan, and me to search for the source. Dylan, Dean, and Alessio join us just as a very large, *very* muscular guy comes into view. To say he's angry is an understatement, and he marches toward us with a purpose.

"Is that . . ." Dylan starts, eyes widening. "Is that *Terry*?"

Terry? "He a friend of yours?"

Dean, Dylan, and Adam exchange a dread-filled glance.

"At least there's no beer bottle for him to throw here," Dylan murmurs instead of answering my question.

The guy is *huge*; his biceps alone are like three of mine. Dean works out, and still he's got nothing on Terry.

"Which one of you is the one fucking my girlfriend?" Terry demands as he stomps toward us.

"What?" Kellan asks when Terry reaches us.

His nostrils flare, and his hands form fists. "I know Priyasha has been cheating on me this vacation!"

I gape at him. We all do. Everyone but Adam and Alessio. Did they know Priyasha had a boyfriend? I've only ever seen her with Kiara and Anaya, though they've always said they're here with other people, but we've never seen them because Priyasha was arguing with them. Was this who Priyasha was avoiding? Her *boyfriend*?

"You must be confused," Dylan tells him, causing Terry to focus his furious gaze on him.

"I'm not *confused*. How many Priyashas could you possibly know? I saw her talking to you multiple times this week!" He invades Dylan's space, going almost nose to nose with him. "Was it you, Tattoos? I knew there was a reason I didn't like you."

Dylan backs up with his hands raised at the same time the other guys try to step between them.

"Terry!" Priyasha dashes to us, appearing out of nowhere. She's wearing running shoes and has no trouble traversing over the sand. The rain is picking up, but it isn't heavy. Either way, none of us are moving. "Stop it, Terry!"

He throws an arm out to the guys. "Which one of these punks have you been cheating on me with? Huh?"

Priyasha reaches us, not even out of breath, and Kiara, Anaya, and another guy about half Terry's size are in the distance running toward us. Priyasha stands between my friends and her boyfriend, but that does nothing to calm him down. If anything, it only makes him angrier.

"We've been on-again, off-again for months and have been fighting this entire trip. Right now, we're on a break, so I'm *not* your girlfriend. You have no right to be upset!"

"Yes the fuck I do!" he spits, eyes blazing. "We were going to get back together this trip. Now tell me which of these fuckers I'm beating up or I'll just face all five."

"No, we weren't!" she cries. "Let's just break up and stay broken up! Leave Alessio alone."

Until now, I've been too shocked to do anything other than stand here and watch the drama unfold. But with Priyasha's words, everyone's gaze swings to Alessio. The blood has drained from his face, and he can't seem to move. He doesn't shake his head, doesn't do anything to deny it.

He slept with Priyasha, and the worst part is he won't even get the chance to grovel for forgiveness to his girlfriend of five years, because Terry's about to rip his head from his shoulders and feed his organs to the ocean.

"Terry, security warned you the last time you picked a fight with these guys," his friend says. "Just relax, man. You're going to get kicked off the resort."

It's raining harder now, soaking through my clothes and matting my hair to my face. He picked a fight with us before? What happened then?

He ignores his friend and zeroes in on Alessio, who all of us stupidly gave away because we looked at him when Priyasha said his name. "This prick?" Terry asks, pushing Priyasha out of the way and sauntering over to Alessio, who backs up in the sand. "You just took your last breath."

Everything happens so fast. Priyasha, Anaya, Kiara, and the guy that's with them all try to grab Terry as he lunges for Alessio. My friends try to help as well, and Alessio jumps backward, tripping over his own feet and toppling over in the sand. Terry's a man on a mission and shoves Anaya and Kiara, causing them to fall with a scream. Kellan and Adam check on them, while Dean and Dylan restrain Terry as Priyasha yells at him to stop and his friend tries to reason with him. But Terry's beyond reason; his eyes are narrowed on Alessio, the promise of pain written all over his face.

"No one touches my girlfriend!" he yells, struggling against the people holding him.

Alessio's still on his ass in the sand, but quickly scooting away from Terry. I'm standing there with my jaw on the ground, trying to process everything that's happening in what feels like seconds.

"Faye! Get security!" Adam orders, pointing to the hotel that's barely visible through the onslaught of rain.

For the first time in forever, I don't argue with him. I have no idea how this is going to play out, but the last thing I want is my friends getting hurt, or even having *them* kicked out of the resort for fighting.

I spin around and run through the sand, struggling because not only is it wet, but Kellan's flip-flops are too many sizes too big for me. Without pausing, I kick them off, running full force for the hotel. The second my foot connects with the stone path, I realize I messed up, because my foot flies out from under me. It doesn't happen in slow motion; it's too quick for me to process. One moment my feet are under me as I'm sprinting, the next I'm airborne, and then there's nothing.

—

When my eyes open again, Adam's face comes into focus incredibly close to my own. He's snapping his fingers an inch from my eyes.

"Fayanna? *Faye?*"

"Stop that." I shove his fingers from my face and groan when that makes me dizzy.

He leans back a bit but stays way too close for comfort. I'm lying on the hard ground on my back in the rain, Adam's crouching beside me, and my head is absolutely pounding.

"Faye?" he pushes again.

"What?" I roll my neck and sit up, which does nothing to ease the hammering in my skull. Why does he keep repeating my name like that? And why is he so damn close to me? The rain is cold despite the warm weather and slams loudly onto the ground. I shove my hair from my face since it's soaked and sticks to my skin. When my hand brushes the back of my head, I wince from the pain.

"You slipped and banged your head," Adam tells me. There's something in his eyes that I've never seen before. Is that . . . concern? "You were unconscious for a couple minutes."

That explains the dizziness and the jackhammer going to town in my skull. No one's on the beach anymore, which is weird because last I checked there were like ten people going at it with no intentions of leaving. Kellan's not here, and my stomach plummets. I was unconscious on the ground and he just left me?

Adam follows my gaze and turns back to me. "When you

weren't moving everyone was crowding you, which wasn't helping. I yelled at them to back off. Kellan and Alessio ran to find the hotel doctor and call an ambulance."

"I don't need an ambulance, I'm fine."

Adam's jaw clenches. "Can you get up? Sitting in the rain isn't helping."

I squint at him. Is he concerned or just annoyed that my slip is screwing up his good time? I twist my back to crack it. "Where'd everyone else go?"

Adam swipes his hair off his forehead, but the rain pushes it back. "Terry punched Dylan in the face trying to get to Alessio. I think he broke his nose; I don't know. There was a lot of blood. But then we saw you slip and not get up, and Terry took off. The girls went to get security, and Dean helped get Dylan to the lobby to stop the bleeding."

But why did Adam stay? Because he was forced to? Or because he wanted to?

"Are you going to sit there all day or get up?" he asks.

I just smashed my head and blacked out, and he's *still* barking orders at me. Maybe it's the fact that my head is pounding, that my tailbone aches and my left shoulder is sore. Or maybe it's the fact that I told Kellan I love him, and he didn't comment, and that Adam was yelling at us, and Dylan's somewhere bleeding, and Terry's running around cursing Alessio, and Adam's stuck here taking care of me when he obviously doesn't want to. Maybe it's a combination of all those things that makes me blurt out, "Why do you hate me?"

He blinks at me. "What?"

My throat tightens and tears slip from my eyes, mingling with the rain. "You hate me. You always have. Why? I've only ever wanted you to like me, and here you are, pissed at me for slipping."

"What? Seriously, Faye?"

"Yes, seriously. I'm sorry I'm ruining your vacation, okay? You didn't want me to come in the first place and then the stuff with me and Kellan, and now you're stuck here in the rain instead of having fun with your friends." It all comes out in a rushed breath, and I leave even more unsaid. He doesn't only hate me because of this trip; he's always been cold toward me, has always acted like he didn't have a sister, and it's always hurt me, even when I acted like it didn't.

"I don't hate you, Faye."

I hug my knees to my chest. I've never felt this vulnerable before. Not even when I was telling Kellan I wanted us to be a thing. "Yes you do, don't lie."

He sighs, his entire face softening, "I've been asking you to get up because we're getting soaked, and you probably have a concussion and should get it checked. But you want to do this here in what's probably going to become a storm? Fine." He shifts from his crouch in front of me to sit beside me, uncaring of the rain pelting at us from above. "I don't hate you, you idiot. You're my sister."

I hold my knees tighter and ask the question I've never had the nerve to ask before. "Then why do you act like you do?"

He pauses, pursing his lips as he stares ahead of us at the crashing ocean waves. He says nothing for a while and neither do I. This feels like the longest we've sat together in silence without scowling or verbally sparring, though I'm sure it only feels that way because of my words hanging in the air between us.

"Faye," he starts, his voice lacking its normal hard edge. "I don't hate you. I'm just . . . I don't know. You've always been so bold and confident and headstrong. You never needed me to be the big brother who took up your battles for you. If anything, it pissed you off if I stepped in. Remember when you were in third grade and some boy twice your size pushed you in the mud at recess and splashed more all over you? I saw it and punched him, then you punched *me* and told me I made you look weak, then you tackled him and shoved his face in the mud."

The corner of his lips tilts up the tiniest bit, and so does mine. I remember that. Justin left me alone after that, but he asked me to every school dance after sixth grade when my boobs came in. I always turned him down because I remembered the mud incident.

"It was always like that, Faye," he continues after I nod. "Every time I tried to step in, you got pissed, so I just stopped trying. I never thought you needed any attention from me. You're the kind of person who never cared about what anyone thought. I didn't think you cared about my opinion or needed me to fuss over you. You're strong. You didn't need anything from your big brother, and I guess I just got used to that over the years and it ended up becoming this."

I frown as I consider his words, my heart fluttering because he called me *strong*. I've always been independent, and he's right that I don't care what anyone thinks. But he's not *anyone*; he's my brother, and he's never seemed to care about anything in my life unless it directly affected him. Did my independence make him think I didn't need him at *all*?

"I don't need you to fuss over me. I just needed you to have my back and be, I don't know, somewhat nice to me." I never thought I'd be having a heart-to-heart with Adam, or that he'd even *care*, but he's sitting here, listening to me, talking to me like I'm his *sister*, and it gives me the confidence to continue. "You're my big brother. All I've ever wanted was for you to care about me. Not because you feel forced to out of family obligation, but because you actually care about *me*. You always seem like you can't stand my presence."

Adam runs his hand through his hair, either out of a nervous tic or just to get the wet strands off his forehead. Maybe both. "I've done a shit job of this brother thing, haven't I?"

Has he? He hasn't been the warmest person ever, but he's always been blatantly honest with me. I knock my shoulder with his. "You *were* the first person to point out my selfish tendencies, and that's something that's messed up a lot of my relationships. Maybe it could've been prevented if I'd considered what you were saying. Besides, I haven't been doing any better in the sister department. Especially considering I'm the one . . . you know . . . screwing your best friend."

Adam grimaces, no doubt because his mind is conjuring up images of Kellan and me together against his will. "*Never* say that again."

We fall silent, and the rain lets up a bit. Adam speaks first. "You and Kellan, huh?"

Is he going to blow up again? Tell me I can't be with him? Tell me I already ruined one relationship with his friend and not to do it again with Kellan?

"I love him, Adam." My voice comes out small. Kellan never said it back, though I didn't actually *tell* him, more just blurted it out to Adam and Kellan heard. But it still hurts more than I want it to.

Adam nods, keeping his gaze out to the ocean. His jaw tightens, but his voice is calm. "Does he love you back?"

"I don't know. He wanted to tell you about us, but I made him hide it."

He nods again, still not looking at me. "I guess I should've seen it coming. You two have been flirting in front of me for years. But that's the way you are with all the guys. I didn't think it meant anything with Kellan, and I thought you were done dating my friends after what happened with Zach."

Maybe not at first, but I think even back then I always knew I was in love with Kellan and wanted him to be mine. "It was purely innocent flirting until a few weeks ago, if it makes you feel better."

He's not yelling, not giving me that disappointed look, not doing any of the things I feared. He's hearing me out; we're having an actual conversation and no one's insulting anyone. There's a pang in my heart. I wish we could've done this earlier and more often.

"Are you . . ." I gather my confidence. "Are you going to tell me to stop seeing him?" I wouldn't. I love Kellan too much to stop seeing him, but having Adam accept it would mean a lot to me, more than I think he'd even know.

He contemplates it for a moment. "No. I can't tell you who to date, especially since you hated Jenna and I dated her anyway."

"Good riddance to that total c—" I cut the word off when Adam shoots me a look. Right. He was in love with her "—cankerous bitch." His eyebrow raises. "What? It was better than what I was *going* to say."

He huffs out an amused breath and shakes his head. We fall into a comfortable silence again, both lost in our own thoughts.

"I'll try harder to be a better brother to you. Less inconsiderate."

His words take me by surprise. There's not a drop of sarcasm in his tone. I try not to let him see how excited I am by his promise.

"Thanks, Adam. I'll try to be less selfish and more considerate too."

Even though my head is pounding and I'm slightly dizzy and I'm soaking wet, and I probably bruised my entire back, I've never been better. I'm on top of the world. My brother doesn't hate me; we're going to work on our relationship. If I wasn't sore all over, I'd be jumping up and down.

"So," he starts, "does this mean I'm supposed to be all over Kellan, threatening him pain if he hurts my little sister?"

A laugh escapes me. "I don't think we need to get *that* extreme. Maybe we can hang out sometimes, and you can like . . . not act like you're being held at gunpoint to endure my presence?"

"I do not act like that."

I tilt my head and give him my best *really?* face.

"Okay fine," he relents. "I'll be nicer. But in my defense, that's kind of my default."

I smile, knocking my shoulder against his again. He has a point, but it makes me feel special that he'll try for me.

It's kind of silly that it took me smashing my head and being unconscious for a few moments for us to finally have this conversation—and in the rain at that—but I'm glad it happened. And if we fall into our old ways again, which hopefully we don't, I'm not going to be shy about talking with Adam about it.

"Hey, Faye?" Adam asks.

"Yeah?"

I wonder if he's going to order me to stop staring at him with the creepy little grin that's plastered on my face. But he doesn't. Instead he says, "Can we get out of this fucking rain now?"

A giggle bursts out of me, my happy mood indestructible. *There's* the Adam I know and love.

TWENTY-TWO

Day Five of Cuba

Lori

After I strut away with my head held high, I run into Naomi, and we have lunch together inside as it rains. When we finish and head to the lobby, I see Alessio, who tells me Faye was just looked at by the hotel doctor because she fell and banged her head. She doesn't need stitches or a hospital visit but is resting in our room. I apologize to Naomi for abandoning our plans to hang out and instead rush to my room.

The curtains to the balcony are drawn shut leaving the room mostly dark as I slip in.

"Adam, I told you I'm *fine*. This doting brother thing is getting a bit excessive," Faye says, adding a laugh at the end.

I pass the little hall where the bathroom is, dropping my beach bag on the floor and come into view. She's in bed with the thin covers pulled up to her neck.

"Oh," she says, sitting up and switching on the bedside lamp. "Hey, Lori."

"Hey," I say, stopping at the end of her bed. This hesitancy and awkwardness isn't normal for us, but then again neither is fighting. "I heard you fell. You okay?"

Her damp hair is drying in its normal waves, and she smells like pineapple shampoo.

"Yeah, just a mild concussion according to the hotel doctor. I don't need to go to the hospital, but he told me to rest for my headache. Adam kicked everyone out after."

"Good," I say, not knowing what to do with my arms. I settle for wrapping them around my chest.

"So," she starts, "that was awesome, back there. Standing up to Adam then kneeing that dude in the dick."

I bite my lip to hold back my smile. "Yeah, it really was."

Faye gets comfortable against the headboard. "And get this! After you left, some huge dude named Terry came over!"

I sit on my bed. Terry? The guy from the bar that wanted to fight Dylan for accidentally spilling his beer?

"And he was *pissed*," Faye continues. "He came over saying that *Alessio* was sleeping with his *girlfriend*!"

My jaw drops. "Priyasha is his girlfriend?"

A shocked look replaces her scandalized one. "Wait, you *knew* about it?"

My cheeks heat. "I kind of walked in on Alessio and Priyasha last night."

Faye gasps. "Like while he was midstroke—"

"Ew! Faye!" I cut her off, trying to block the mental image. Despite the grossness of it, I feel like laughing. Everything about this conversation, while weird, is so *me and Faye*. It feels like everything is back to normal between us, like that fight didn't happen.

"But yes, I saw *everything*," I continue, holding back a shudder.

"Wow," she says, leaning back again. "Alessio and Priyasha. Poor Olivia, I hope she kicks his ass."

I try not to think about what Adam said, that Alessio wasn't going to come clean to Olivia. Now that *everyone* knows, I wonder if his plans have changed.

"So, what happened with Terry?" I ask, crossing my legs on my bed and settling in.

A light sparks in Faye's eyes, the same one that goes off when she has interesting gossip to share. She tells me what happened right up until she slipped and fell.

"Are you sure you're okay?" I ask, gesturing to her head.

"Yeah. I just need some rest, and I'm supposed to stay out of the light and avoid loud noises. So, no clubbing for me tonight."

I raise a skeptical eyebrow at her. Faye's never been able to sit still and just *be*. She's probably hating the prospect of having to sit out parties these last two nights of our vacation.

"Enough about me." Faye waves off my concern. "I need to apologize to you. Properly. I never should've gone off on you about Adam. It was stupid of me, and was more about myself than it was about you and him together."

I say nothing, instead letting her sort through her thoughts.

"You're amazing, Lori. You're pretty and smart, and everything comes so easy for you."

I open my mouth to tell her she's just reiterating what she said last night, but she rushes to beat me. "No, wait. It's not a bad thing, and it's not your fault. That's on me and my own issues. Sometimes I'm insecure standing next to you, knowing everyone's comparing us and I'm falling short in every category."

I gape at her. "Faye, that's not true. You're the one everyone's captivated by. You're the one who makes an entrance every time you walk in a room. You're the one who owns who you are and is unapologetic about it. I can never be any of those things, but I'm trying." I realize it as I say it. The person I'm trying to be is someone who makes her own decisions, who speaks her mind, someone like Faye.

Faye continues, "I'm sorry I yelled at you about Adam, and I'm not saying that because you already told him off. I was coming to say that before he interrupted us on the beach. Obviously you can handle yourself, and I realize that sometimes I push you around. I just always think I know best, and I only want what's best for you. But that's wrong. I don't always know what's best and sometimes I'm a complete idiot. But either way, I need to let you make your own decisions. I'm your best friend. I should be there to help you work through things, not tell you what to do."

I can tell she's put a lot of thought into this and really means it. I'd already forgiven her, but it means a lot to me that she's reflected like I have and realized some things need to change, and that change isn't necessarily a bad thing.

"And I'm sorry for not being around as much this week while I was focused on my own stuff."

I haven't spent much time with Faye at the parties, but that's just her personality. She's always done her own thing and made friends easily and can talk to anyone about everything. Looking back, not having her here to lean on has forced me to open up to Dean or Dylan, or Naomi, or Kiara, Priyasha, and Anaya. But deep down, I know Faye wouldn't ditch me if she didn't think I'd have our other friends to hang out with. If it was just me and her here on vacation and I didn't have any other friends, I know she'd stay by my side and force me to have fun, like she's done throughout high school. I've always had Faye, and this vacation she's been busy dealing with her emotions about Kellan, so her presence has become especially scarce. Her absence has forced me not to hide in her shadow at these social events like I would've been content doing, and instead it's given me the space to see who I'd be without Faye to hold my hand.

"It's all right, Faye. You were right before when you said I didn't need you to babysit me all week. Plus, I'm going to try being more vocal, so I'm prepared to call you out on stuff in the future."

She laughs. "You better! I realized I'm a bit selfish and have an eyes-on-the-prize-so-screw-everyone-else kind of attitude, and it'll be good to have both you and Adam check me on it."

"Me and Adam?"

"Yeah. We talked. It was . . . nice." She clears her throat. "But enough about me. Dylan said something was going on with you. What's up?"

If anyone can give me boy advice, it's Faye. "Well, I kissed Adam, which again, I didn't plan, it was just what I did to distract him from finding out about you and Kellan."

"Thanks for that, by the way."

I nod. "Right. Well, after that, I found Dean, and we kissed."

Faye gasps and throws off the covers, leaning forward and giving me her full attention. "Lor! Yes! I'm so proud of you! Wait . . . all that stuff Adam was saying at the beach makes so much sense now."

"Yeah, he saw the whole thing. He said some not nice things, and I ran away. I haven't talked to Dean since then either. I might've ruined it, but I still feel like I owe Dean a conversation, if he'll even talk to me."

Faye frowns. "You're not with either of them and don't owe them anything. Remember that time I made out with three different guys all in one night at that party? I had fun and didn't care what anyone thought. Guys will literally *sleep* with a bunch of girls in one night, or a different girl every day, and no one looks twice at them. Don't let double standards stop you from being who you are, or stop you from having an actual conversation with Dean. Just talk to him. Don't assume you know what he's thinking, that's literally what made everything so complicated with me and Kellan."

She has a point, but every time I'm with Dean I embarrass myself or screw it up.

"Dean is a great guy," Faye continues. "He compliments you in ways that my brother could *never*. He got you to swim with fish! You never would've done that by yourself. And I'm not just Team Dean because I don't want you to be with Adam."

She's right. Dean's never cared when I embarrassed myself in front of him. In fact, he called me *amazing*. He said lots of butterfly-inducing things last night about me.

I jump up from the bed. "I'm going to talk to him!"

A smile fills her face. "Atta girl! Tell me how it goes." She settles back into bed and pulls the covers up before turning off the lamp. "You got this!"

When I reach the door, I turn around and race back to her bedside, throwing myself on top of her in a hug. She's my best friend, and we may not be perfect, but we'll always have each other's backs.

She huffs under my weight but laughs. "Love you, Lori."

"Love you too." I get off her and straighten out my bikini top. "Get some rest!"

Now that we've made up, I can breathe easier. There will be other times when we fight, but we'll always come back to each other.

I fish my key card out of my bag and slip it into my front pocket, opting to leave the bag here. When I open the door, Kellan's standing there with his fist raised, ready to knock.

"Oh, hey Kellan," I greet. From within the room I hear frantic rustling.

"Hey," he says. "How's Faye? Adam kicked me out before I got the chance to talk to her."

A presence appears at my back. "Hey, Kellan."

Behind me, Faye's running her hand over her hair, smoothing the flyaways from lying on the pillow.

"Hey," he greets, eyes boring into hers. They stare at each other, almost longingly, and when Kellan clears his throat, realization sinks in.

"Right! Well, I'll be off, then!"

Kellan steps aside so I can rush out of the room and give them alone time. But once I'm in the hall, I have no idea where to go to find Dean. It's still raining, though it slowed down and looks like it'll clear up any minute now, so that limits the number of places he can be. Maybe the lobby? It's huge and there are tons of couches for guests to hang out on, plus a full bar.

When I get downstairs, I see lots of guests gathered in the lobby to wait out the showers. People are everywhere, talking and laughing and lounging on the couches and drinking at the bar. At the other end, I spot Dean. He's with Dylan and Alessio on a couch. Dylan's holding an ice pack to his face and Alessio's clutching a beer between both hands.

Before I get there, Adam steps into my path.

"Hey," he says.

"Hey, Adam."

He's lacking the usual confident coldness he wears so well. Possibly because I yelled at him a few hours ago.

"Can we talk?" he asks, motioning to a nearby empty couch.

Why? So he can tell me what's best for me? So he can call me boring? I'd rather speak to Dean before my confidence wavers, but I can at least hear him out.

"Sure," I say, following him to the couch and sitting a good two feet away from him. It's weird thinking about how I *want* to leave distance between us, when prevacation I would've done anything to sit beside him and talk.

He rubs the back of his neck, seeming unsure of himself. I've never seen this side of Adam before.

"So I, uh . . . I owe you an apology."

I wasn't expecting that, but I sit in silence, waiting for him to continue.

He takes a deep breath. "I'm sorry for this morning on the beach, for saying all that stuff about how you're acting, for making you choose between me and Dean, and for just being an ass in general."

I raise an eyebrow at him. He seems to mean it. I wonder if Faye said something to him.

"You had no right to say any of that to me."

"I know." He huffs out a humorless laugh. "I've been telling Faye she's been acting selfishly toward you, not even realizing I was worse."

He has been. But looking back, I wouldn't have found the confidence I needed to stand up for myself if it wasn't for Adam pushing me. Would I have preferred him to *not* be a huge jerk to force me to get my act together? Yeah. But it happened and we can't turn back time, plus he's here apologizing now, so it is what it is.

"You're not just saying this so I'll choose you, right?"

Another clipped, humorless laugh. "No. I realize I screwed that up."

"You and I never would've worked," I tell him with a small smile. Sixteen-year-old Lori would hyperventilate if she knew seventeen-year-old Lori would say these words to Adam Murray, but here I am, turning him down, and that's a great indication of how far I've come.

He nods, a solemn look on his face, but he must recognize the truth in my words. Adam wanted me to stay the exact same. He liked that I was *sweet* and *quiet*, didn't rock the boat and did what I was told. Maybe because that's so different from his ex, or maybe because that's what he's used to with me. Either way, Adam wanted to decide for me, while Dean . . . Dean challenges me. He's always been about wanting me to do what *I* want, not what others expect me to do. If I'm going to be with anyone, I'm going to be with someone who encourages me to make my own decisions.

"Hey," a deep voice says, and Adam and I both glance up into Dean's brilliant blue eyes. It's like my thoughts summoned him, and my face heats. "Can we talk, Lori?"

He wants to talk to me? I'm torn between squealing and hiding under this couch. "Um, yeah, sure."

I start to rise but Adam beats me to it. "It's okay. I'll catch you guys later." He gives Dean a nod as he leaves, and Dean returns it before he sits next to me. I wonder if Adam apologized to him too for his comments this morning.

Dean's gotten more and more sunburnt every day he's been here, but it does nothing to detract from his looks. His dark hair has dried wavy after getting caught out in the rain, and it looks good on him. More than good—just like the gray T-shirt that stretches across his chest. I suddenly wish I had thrown a T-shirt over my bikini top before I left the room.

"Oh, no. You have that look on your face," he says, causing me to freeze.

"What look?"

He tries and fails to bite back a smile. "The one you make right before you run away from me."

My eyes widen. "I'm not going to run."

"Good," he says, and I hope I'm not blushing. "I just wanted to see how you were feeling after . . . everything."

"I'm good," I say and mean it. "I'm sorry I ran away last night after our . . . you know . . ." I can't even say the word *kiss* when he's looking at me like that. I guess some things will never change.

"It's all right. Adam and I had a few words, but we sorted it out after the doctor checked Faye."

Outside, the rain is letting up, and it looks like the sun is going to appear from behind the dark clouds soon. Some people venture outside before the rain fully stops.

"Listen," Dean continues, and my gaze focuses on his eyes, blue and serious. "I'm just going to come out and say this, and it's probably not the best time after everything going on, but I need to get it off my chest."

I hold my breath, and the way his eyes bore into mine doesn't help my anticipation.

"I like you, Lori. When we get back, would you go on a date with me? A real one?"

My heart hammering in my chest is so loud he must hear it. *Yes!* I want to yell, then jump up on this couch and do a crazy happy dance. *Yes, yes, yes!* After everything, he actually *likes me.* The memory of his lips against mine sends tingles all the way down my spine. He wants to do that again!

But then reality sinks in and I remember that I'm choosing myself, and the thought doesn't make me sad, really, just level-headed about what's truly feasible.

"I would really like that, but I meant what I said about choosing myself. I'm going to tell my parents I'm not going to med school, and that I'm taking a year off to backpack through Europe. It's what I want to do, what I think will help me truly figure myself out, and I don't think it's fair to either of us to start a relationship when I'm going to leave for an entire year."

It's the first time I've voiced my decision about not pursuing med school and following through with my European experience even if my parents are against it, and it's terrifying but also an immense relief. I'm going to have to face my parents' disbelief and disappointment, for sure, but I'm not going silently into a future I'm going to resent and regret. I *am* taking a year off before university to travel, and either my parents are supportive or they're not, but I'm sure they'll come around eventually. I need to do it for *me*, and I have all summer to plan the trip and for them to get over the initial shock.

Dean nods thoughtfully. He doesn't seem upset, even though a small, sad smile touches his lips. "I understand. I'm proud of you, Lori. You're making the best decision for you, even though it sucks for me." He chuckles, and I know there are no hard feelings. "You should do what makes you happy."

"Thanks, Dean. I owe a lot to you." I fight the blush threatening to emerge. "You've been encouraging me to do what I want instead of what other people expect me to, and I'm finally doing it."

He waves me off. "I did nothing. It's all you."

In the short time I've known him, he's had such a huge impact on my life, and even though I'll be traveling, I don't want to lose him forever. "But we can still talk and be friends, right?"

His smile isn't sad this time. "Of course. And if it's okay with both of us, and if we're both still single, maybe when you get back we can go on that date?"

I nod my head and mirror his smile. I'd really like that. We won't be closing the door on us, on what we could be, just getting to know each other better while I figure out who I am. And when I get back, if it feels right and we're still into it, we can see if we're suited for something more.

"Here," Dean says, handing me his phone. It's open to the contact section. "So we can stay in touch. This way I won't have to chase you down at the gym."

Holding it while trying to forget how he tackled me out of a moving car's path, I enter my name and phone number before handing it back to him.

The Lori who would pine after Dean at Grant's Gym back in Canada would *never* believe that I turned down not only Adam, but also said *not right now* to Dean. But everything settles in my chest with a *rightness* that tells me this is the best choice for *me*, and I wouldn't have it any other way.

TWENTY-THREE

Day Five of Cuba

Faye

After Lori rushes out of our room, Kellan stands in the doorway, shifting from foot to foot.

"Come in," I offer, stepping aside so he can enter, hoping my voice seems calm and composed even though I'm anything but. I wish I had brushed my hair after my shower, or at least put on cuter pajamas than the oversized navy blue T-shirt that completely washes me out and hangs to my midthighs.

Why is he here? What can he say after that clusterfuck on the beach this morning?

Instead of facing him, I busy myself with opening the curtains to the balcony to let in some light. It's still gloomy outside, so it doesn't bathe the room in sunlight, but it's better than sitting in the dark.

I'm all too aware of Kellan behind me, of every breath and movement, every glance my way. It's funny to think that Adam and Lori called me *strong* and *confident*, yet here I am fussing over the curtains rather than facing the guy I love, the guy who knows I love him.

The vulnerability I felt with Adam earlier dulls compared to this moment with Kellan. I've never not been the one holding all the cards, I've always been in control, and lately it seems like Kellan's got me dangling by my little toe, completely at his mercy, with all the power to stomp on my heart. It's terrifying.

The temperature in the room suddenly spikes, so I open the sliding door to let in a refreshing breeze. The rain is slowing down.

Kellan clears his throat, apparently deciding I've stalled enough. "How are you feeling?"

Dizzy. Flushed. Short of breath. But I'm not sure if those are symptoms of the concussion or his proximity.

"All right," I say instead. "Just have a headache."

I turn to face him and my breath hitches. I wonder if I'll ever stop being affected by him—by his deep-brown eyes that stare straight into my soul; by his pouty lips that are too soft for my own good.

"I wanted to make sure you were okay, but Adam—"

"I know," I say. "Adam and I talked, and now he's taking his brother role just a tad too seriously." I chuckle at the end, since those are words I never thought I'd say.

After Adam and I left the beach, we ran into Kellan and Alessio, who were rushing the hotel doctor to us. Since I was up, clearly conscious, and declined to go to the hospital, the doctor looked me over in his office. After that, Adam ordered everyone away, barking at them to let me rest, as per the doctor's advice. I may have grumbled about him going overboard, but I secretly love it. Usually *I'm* on the receiving end of Adam's grumpiness, but this time he was using it *for* me, to look after me, and that's a new feeling I'll never get over.

Kellan sits on the side of Lori's neatly made bed, and I cross the distance between us, sitting on my messy one.

"I'm glad you guys talked," he says. "You didn't have to say anything to him about us, you know."

Looks like he doesn't want to beat around the bush. "Yes, I did. It was time to come clean." I collect my racing thoughts. This is important. This is my future, *our* future, and I don't want to screw that up. This needs to be perfect. "I'm sorry for making you feel like I was hiding you, and for actually hiding you. It wasn't about you, I swear. I'm not embarrassed of you or anything like that. I just . . . didn't want Adam to hate me any more than he already did if he found out about us. Especially after how everything turned out with Zach."

Kellan nods, his face softening. "I know, Faye. I know. And I appreciate that you told him about us."

There's a *but* coming. I feel it. Its imminent arrival deflates any hope I had about Kellan and me pushing past this.

"But," he says, and my heart breaks, "I didn't want you to feel forced into saying something."

That's not a *but we're through*, and my pulse races.

"I was selfish hiding you, and it wasn't fair to anyone involved—you, me, or Adam." I take a breath and bolster all my confidence, all my courage. It's now or never. "I meant what I said on the beach, Kell. I'm in love with you."

Kellan's eyes sharpen, making him look so much more intense. I almost want to look away, but it's a physical impossibility to draw my gaze from his.

He stands, and for a second I fear he's going to leave, but he steps closer to me.

He gives his head a little disbelieving shake. "Do you know how long I've waited to hear you say that?"

The heat in his eyes ignites new life in me, decimating any

lingering nerves and fear. I remember something he said from what feels like years ago.

"Since you were sixteen?"

He chuckles and sits beside me on my bed. Close. So close his leg brushes my bare thigh.

His voice is low. "I meant everything I said last night about my feelings for you. I really have wanted to be with you since I was sixteen. Probably been in love with you since then too."

My heart stops. Kellan's in love with me, *has* been in love with me. My mind races over every interaction we've had since we met. All the late-night drives with the roof down blasting my favorite music. All the times he's made faces through the window of my classroom door to make me laugh before a test he knew I was nervous about. All the times he put aside whatever he was doing if I wanted to talk or hang out or simply not be alone. Every little thoughtful action. Every brief brush of our skin. Every late-night conversation. It all floods my mind, showing me everything that reinforces what Kellan's saying, everything that made me fall in love with him.

He's always *gotten* me—always *seen* me.

I swallow the raw emotion in my throat. "So, you're saying . . ."

"I love you too, Fayanna. Every beautiful, stubborn part of you."

Any last lingering doubt or insecurity completely dissipates, leaving me happy, so incredibly happy I can't stop the giggle from escaping my lips.

He loves me. Kellan Reyes loves *me*.

He grabs my waist and pulls me against him, and I sink into his chest. He kisses me, forcefully, confidently, urgently, as if no other kiss we've shared is as important as this one. It feels different, does incredible things to me, because this time, we're kissing as Faye and Kellan, two people who *love* each other.

Kellan pulls away and I swallow a protest, not wanting this high to end. We're only an inch apart and I can't stop staring at his lips, delicious and as swollen as I'm sure mine are. I try to pull him back to me so we can pick up where we left off, but his hands tighten on my waist, holding me in place. He leans back a bit, his eyes scanning my face in a way that leaves me feeling stripped bare.

"Be my girlfriend."

I'm assuming it's not a question, because he already knows my answer. But he holds his breath anyway, like there's even the slightest possibility in hell I'd decline.

"Yes," I say, and finally he lets me pull his lips back to mine.

I would agree to anything at this point to get Kellan to keep kissing me like this, like the world could be burning around us, but he wouldn't care because all that matters is us and this moment. Agreeing to this is no chore. It's everything I wanted for years but didn't realize. Everything I know now I can't live without. It's *him*.

—

The rest of the vacation goes by relatively fast. Obviously, I'm unable to go to any clubs or parties after my fall. Flashing lights and loud music with this headache? That's a huge *no* from me. Instead, I grab a quick dinner with Kellan and go to sleep, while the rest of my friends apparently have a "chill" night.

In the morning I'm marginally better, and I go to the smaller, calmer beach with everyone to enjoy our last full day here. My headache is persistent, so I sit under an umbrella with my sunglasses and Lori's wide-brim beach hat on the entire time. Even though I can't drink or play beach volleyball or go in the water with everyone else, I still have fun sitting and watching, and have plenty of people to keep me company.

Dylan stays in the beach chair under the umbrella beside me for almost the entire day, sporadically icing his nose with every new cold beer bottle. When I tell him he probably shouldn't be drinking, he says, "My nose isn't broken, there's literally not a better reason *to* drink. I'm celebrating." I let him be after that.

Alessio stays in the chair beside him, seemingly too melancholy to join in any of the fun. Earlier, Lori told me how Alessio was planning on returning to Canada pretending like nothing ever happened after cheating on Olivia all week, and I had some very choice words with him. He's been glum all day, even before our talk, and I can only assume it's because now that *everyone* knows about him and Priyasha, he has to come clean to Olivia. Good. I hope she rips him a new one. Whether she'll stay with him or not, I don't know, but either way, all this worrying he's doing serves him right.

Priyasha, Kiara, and Anaya join us later in the day, as well as Lori's friend Naomi and her friends. Lori doesn't even have to nudge me before I approach Kiara and apologize for my standoffish behavior and attitude toward her. It wasn't really about *her* anyway, and I shouldn't have taken my frustration with Kellan out on her because he was paying attention to her instead of me. That was really uncool of me, even if she maybe did undo my bikini top during the chicken fight in the pool. She tells me we're cool, and I don't think either of us harbor any ill will toward each other. Whether she *actually* undid my bikini top that day, I'll never know, but it doesn't matter anymore.

The girls tell us that Priyasha had a proper conversation with Terry, and he got on an early plane home this morning. Apparently, he was so heartbroken over Priyasha ending their relationship permanently he didn't want to stay any longer. Plus, security kicked him off the resort. She's adamant their breakup is forever this time.

Alessio stays away from Priyasha, stays away from everyone, really, since he's too worried and sad to have any fun, but she asks him to talk. Kellan tells me later that they were on the same page about it not being anything more than a fling, and they didn't want an actual relationship.

At night, our *last* night here, no one's in the clubbing mood. I can't, and Kellan and Adam don't want to go without me. Dylan's nose is swollen, and his eyes are bruised, so he doesn't want to get all dressed up for a party. Alessio's depressed, and Lori and Dean are exhausted from all day in the sun, which included another snorkeling expedition this afternoon. Lori told me she jumped in before Dean this time, and wasn't scared when Mattias threw bread at her, whatever that means.

Instead, we hang out in the chill area of the lobby on the couches, ordering snack food and drinks from the bar, talking and playing cards, and just being together. It's so fun I barely register the pounding in the back of my skull, although I'm sure the Ibuprofen and Kellan's nearness helps. Even Adam's less grouchy and quicker to smile than usual.

Waking up on the last day is bittersweet. We go to the pool instead of the beach today, since it's closer to the hotel for when we need to shower and check out after lunch. We don't go to the big party pool or the small, chill one. Instead, we go to the medium-sized one. It's still a large pool, but there aren't any events going on, just people hanging out and music playing at a tolerable level in the background. Like yesterday, I plant my butt under an umbrella and shade my eyes from the blaring sun, but I keep my legs out, loving the warm feeling and hoping for a last-minute tan. Lori's beside me in her own lounge chair, reading the book she brought but never had the chance to finish.

"Did you have fun?" I ask her as some teenagers jump into the pool.

She lowers her book and lifts an eyebrow. "Calling my parents and telling them I one hundred percent am not going to med school, no exceptions, is not my definition of fun."

I laugh. Lori told me how she didn't want to disappoint her parents by not attending med school like they'd hoped. I supported her decision to take time off to travel, though it'll break my heart when she's so far away for a year. But she called her parents this morning and told them what she wanted, instead of waiting until she got home, saying she wanted to give them time to digest it. There was lots of *We'll talk about this in person, Lori*, but she was resolute, and I seriously doubt anything they say will sway her. She told me she was going to *channel my best Fayanna Murray* and *keep my stubborn eyes on the prize*. I laughed.

"Other than that. Did you have fun this week?"

She tilts her head, considering it. "Yeah. I did. Did you?"

Kellan cannonballs into the pool, splashing Adam and Dylan, who grumble about him getting their shirts wet. It brings a smile to my lips.

"Yeah. I did too. I'm just sorry we fought, and that I was a jerk."

Lori giggles and sets her book down. "I'm sorry we fought too. But we'll always be best friends. Faye and Lori."

"Forever," I agree as she stands. She's developed a tan, and though it's not as deep as mine since she's been more liberal with applying sunscreen, it's still noticeable against the white of her string bikini.

"I'm going to grab water. Want one?"

I shake my head, and she walks across the pool to the bar. She turns heads as she does, but that's nothing new. Some things never change, like our friendship and love for each other.

On her way back, a guy who looks a few years older approaches her. He says something that makes her eyes bulge out of her head. She shakes her head and keeps walking, her face slowly turning red, but the guy follows. As she gets closer, I'm able to pick up some of what he's saying to her.

"All I'm saying," he says, "is that there are worse places to sit than on my face, especially with that ass."

I lean forward as his forthcoming action becomes clear, but Lori grabs his arm as if by reflex right before his hand lands on her butt. Her jaw tightens, and now I'm swinging my feet to the side of the lounge chair, ready to go kick this guy's ass, concussion or not.

But I pause when she asks him, "Can you swim?"

His eyebrows draw together. "Yes? But what does—" He never gets to finish, because Lori, the badass that she is, pushes him right into the pool.

His arms cartwheel almost comically before he lands in the deep end with a heavy splash. Lori continues walking with her head held high. When he finally reaches the surface and sputters out the water he swallowed, she spares him a glance. "You'd have better luck with girls if you weren't a disgusting pig who feels entitled to my body."

She flicks her hair over her shoulder, a whole-ass shampoo commercial–worthy hair flip, and struts away like she owns the place. I resist the urge to cheer, instead settling back into my chair with an amused laugh as she rejoins me.

"What?" she asks, setting the water bottle down. "He deserved that, right? You should've heard what he said to me."

I can't help but laugh again. "I heard the tail end and saw where his hands were wandering. I would've thrown in some swear words, but yeah, he deserved that."

She nods and leans back in her chair, picking up her discarded book and flipping to the proper page. "Good," she says, not even bothering to watch the guy stomp away from the pool, splashing water everywhere, back to his friends with his head down.

I slide my sunglasses into place as contentment fills me. This really was the best vacation ever. I'm leaving not only with Kellan, but with a healing relationship with my brother, with a recognition of how I can be selfish sometimes, and with my best friend.

Lori's different, and so am I. We're best friends, and while that will never change, some things will and already have. We're leaving Cuba happy, as girls who are free to make our own decisions, and now carrying a bit of each other's personalities in us forever.

ACKNOWLEDGMENTS

As always, thank you to you—the reader. This book is a different vibe from what I normally write, so it's so special to me. Thank you for coming on this journey with me.

Also, thank you to all my Wattpad readers who encouraged me to continue with this story. I only posted half the book on the site, and it still got five million reads, which shocked the hell out of me. Thank you so much for all your support and comments. It inspired me to finish this offline and get it out there in book form.

Thank you to my brilliant friend Deb Goelz, who is an absolute genius in more ways than one. Your book coaching and edits got me through my panicked rewrites and to such a good place to start edits.

Thank you to my wonderful editor, Fiona Simpson, for helping me make this book shine with your insightful edits and suggestions. Thank you to my copy editor and proofreaders who made sure this book was perfect for print. Also, thank you to Deanna McFadden and the team at Wattpad Books, from marketing to production to everyone in between. Thank you all for championing my stories and getting them out there into the world. And thank you to my creator manager, Austin, for everything you do.

Thank you to my parents, Bruno and Carmela, for being the best parents ever and taking me on all those vacations across the world over the years. And thank you to the rest of my family and friends for always having my back and cheering me on.

Thank you to Mario for being the best boyfriend there is. And thank you to his entire family for being so genuinely encouraging and supportive.

To my friends SJ, Lauren, Ken, and Jordan—you're awesome. Thanks for being there for me always. And to my friends Rodney, Mason, Van, Andi, and Deb (again!)—thanks for being the absolute best and for sprinting with me to help me get this book done.

And, as always, I'm also going to be that person and thank Leo. You're a good boy.

ABOUT THE AUTHOR

Jessica Cunsolo's young adult series, With Me, has amassed over 140 million reads on Wattpad since she posted her first story, *She's With Me*, on the platform in 2015. It has won a Watty Award, been published in multiple languages, and is in development with Wattpad WEBTOON Studios. Jessica lives just outside of Toronto, where she enjoys the outdoors and transforming her real-life awkward situations into plotlines for her viral stories. You can find her on Instagram @jesscunsolo.